OF
RICE
AND
MEN

OF RICE AND MEN

A Novel of Vietnam

Richard Galli

BALLANTINE BOOKS

NEW YORK

Copyright © 2006 by Richard Galli

Map illustration on p. 334 copyright © 2006 by Richard Galli

Published in the United States by Presidio Press, an imprint of
The Random House Publishing Group, a division of Random House, Inc., New York.

PRESIDIO PRESS and colophon are trademarks of Random House, Inc.

Library of Congress Cataloging-in-Publication Data

Galli, Richard.
Of rice and men: a novel of Vietnam / Richard Galli.
p.cm.
ISBN 0-89141-885-7
1. Vietnamese Conflict, 1961–1975—Fiction   2. Americans—Vietnam—Fiction.   3. Soldiers—
Fiction.   4. Vietnam—Fiction.   I. Title.

PS3607.A4164O35 2006
813'.6—dc22
2005048093

Printed in the United States of America on acid-free paper

www.presidiopress.com

2   4   6   8   9   7   5   3   1

First Edition

Book design by Mary A. Wirth

For Toby (a girl back home)
and her big paper bag full of memories

With gratitude to Sorche Fairbank, Ron Doering,
Nancy Coble Damon, and Sherry Goodman
for carrying me to the finish line

War is not worth fighting without a good liberal arts education.

GUY LOPACA, 5TH PLATOON

Contents

OF
RICE
AND
MEN

Crash Landing

The men thought they were dying in a fiery plane crash, but it was only a perfect landing at Tan Son Nhut.

"Jesus Christ!" Guy Lopaca swore.

"Jesus Christ," Arthur Grissom prayed.

It felt as if their pilot had jettisoned the airliner's wings. The plane suddenly pointed its nose straight down, took on maniacal speed, and headed dartlike toward Asia.

A moment before, as the intercom casually told them to get ready for landing in Vietnam, Guy Lopaca had experienced a moderate chill, and thought:

I might actually die in this war. . . .

Now, as the plane abruptly rotated and the earth down below became the earth directly in front, and rushing closer, Lopaca began thinking:

I might actually die in this seat. . . .

The young men expected an erratic flight path, to minimize the hazard of enemy ground fire. But right now, to the frenzied soldiers hurtling down an insanely perpendicular flight path, a few casualties from ground fire seemed to be a reasonable price to pay if it meant coming in with some survivors. Most of the frantic GIs held their breath, some closed their eyes, and one tried to vomit but, because of the awful speed, nothing came out.

At the last possible instant, the pilot pulled the nose up, and the plane crashed—*Screech! Whomp!*—safely onto its landing gear. The terrified young men had arrived in the war zone. They were not dead yet. As the troops shivered, thanked their gods, and wondered what horrible feeling the war would inflict on them next, their twenty-one-year-old stewardess pixie with hips to die for shimmied down the aisle and told them to keep their seat belts carefully fastened *for just a little bit longer, y'all.*

At that moment, she was everything the young men desperately wanted, and would have to do without. She was the girl some men had sought all their lives; the girl some men had left behind; and the girl some men would die without ever knowing. Arthur Grissom wanted to reach out and touch her. Guy Lopaca wanted to go home, meet her at the door, and tell her once more that he loved her. She left a froth of terrible longing in her wake.

Even before the airplane came to a stop, the young men felt as if they had been in Vietnam, dazed and lonely, for a hundred years.

Guy Takes His Turn
at War

Inside the terminal, the young men were mashed into muttering clumps, then herded outdoors to a corral near their ground transportation, at which they would gaze in frustration for hours before boarding. But Guy Lopaca was culled from the crowd.

As soon as he entered the terminal, Lopaca noticed a slender GI waving a big sign:

**WELCOME GUY LOPACA
NICE TEST SCORES!**

"Are you looking for me?" Guy asked the stranger. The young man smiled back, and kept bobbing his sign up and down.

"Hell no," he said, "I'm looking for one of those *other* Guy Lopacas they got on the plane. You know, one with some common sense."

Guy blushed. "I'm Guy Lopaca," he said. "I don't think there are any others."

"Well, let's take a chance on that," the young man said. "Follow me."

The GI led Guy out of the terminal and walked him to a small prop jet whose engines were idling.

"This here's a Guy Lopaca they had on that plane," the GI said to the prop jet's crewman. "He swears there ain't any others. So I guess you can get along now."

"Nice to see you," the crewman said, helping stow Guy's duffel bag. "Strap yourself in and we'll be on our way."

"Where are we going?" Guy asked.

"Well," the crewman said as the engines lit up, "I'm planning on going to heaven, the pilot's going to hell for sure, and you're going to Hue, eventually."

"Hue's pretty far north, isn't it?" Guy asked.

"Way up north," the crewman said as the plane started to move. "Real far north. They say when Ho Chi Minh takes his dog for a walk, it shits on Hue."

As the plane thrust upward, Guy put his head back and tried to visualize Hue on the map of South Vietnam. But all he could see, when he closed his eyes, was a grainy old newsreel film of the landing at Normandy, on D-Day, 1944. The puffy gray shape of an overloaded GI staggered up the beach a few steps and then, as a German bullet hit him, collapsed into a nameless, faceless lump on the sand. Guy Lopaca had been witnessing that soul-searing sacrifice over and over since he was ten years old.

Guy owed so much to that unlucky young soldier. That young man had given everything he had, just to be there on the beach with other young men who needed to be there with him. Guy hoped he could live up to the standard that brave stranger had set.

It's my turn now, Guy thought sadly. He joined hands over the decades with his brother soldier on the Normandy beach. *It's my turn now, as it was your turn then,* Guy promised him.

Then Guy looked around the cabin of the little jet, in which he was the only passenger. The crewman was smoking a marijuana cigarette, and reading a *Playboy* magazine, while rock music blared from nicely-tuned stereo speakers. There was a can of cold soda on Guy's tray, next to a package of salted peanuts.

It's my turn now, Lopaca called to his long-dead comrade on the Normandy beach. *But, you know, my accommodations seem to be a whole lot better than yours were. . . .*

Full-Boogie Jam

The shuttle chopper angled out of the clouds, settled onto its macadam nest, and dropped a single egg: Guy Lopaca, wide-eyed and fresh from The World. Guy stepped onto the tarmac elated and terrified. Elated because his great adventure had finally begun. Terrified because he sensed that somewhere in the dark hills around him, under the heavy concealing clouds, an Asian sniper was drawing a patient bead on Guy's anxious body.

It was raining lightly. Guy shivered, damp and apprehensive. He didn't know what to do now that he had arrived. He didn't know where to go. The helicopter crew—who had picked him up where the prop jet had set him down—were no help. They didn't talk to new guys. Only short-timers could speak on their ship.

Soon a young man appeared from out of a Quonset hut. Hatless in the drizzle, his red hair matted and bright, he had a wide smile on his face as he jogged toward Guy. The young man carried an enormous duffel bag, overstuffed. He flipped it around casually, as if it were a helium balloon.

"You the guy for the 5th Platoon?" he asked as he loped to the landing zone.

"Yes," Guy said, "I think so."

"Fantastic," the young man said. He pushed his duffel into the helicopter, turned and shook Guy's hand enthusiastically. "You're beautiful, man," the redhead said. "You're beautiful. Everything is beautiful. Aw, hell . . ." He reached out and gave Guy a big hug.

"Here's the deal," the young man said. "Vietnam is beautiful. *Bong bong bong ga bong bong.* It's a great country. *Bong bong ga bong.* Nice scenery. Wonderful people. I love the people. Vietnamese, Vietcong, NVA . . . *Bong ga bong.* Love them all. I especially love you."

Guy blushed as the young man gave him another big hug.

"You're my replacement, you stupid bastard," the young man said. He hugged Guy some more around the shoulders. The young man was amazingly strong and exuberant. He was also, obviously, an "Oh Four Bravo"—an Army interpreter—as was Guy himself. That was Vietnamese he was speaking all right. But what the hell was he *saying*?

"You're going to have a great time here," the young man said. "*Bong bong bong ga bong bong.* The drinks are cheap, the movies are free, and the women are beautiful. If you have to be in Vietnam at all, you can't ask for better than this. *Bong bong bong ga bong bong.* You'll love it here. I guarantee it. *Bong bong ga frigging bong!* Good-bye."

The young man jumped into the helicopter and began to stow his gear. Then, just as the engine was beginning to rev up for takeoff, he leaned out of the doorway and shouted at Guy over the roar.

"There's just one drawback," he yelled, "which is that you could more or less get killed, you know? Otherwise it's fine."

The helicopter picked itself into the air and threw itself laterally across the landing zone, out of Guy's life forever. It took only a minute for it to dissolve in the rain and mist. After a while Guy picked up his duffel bag, shouldered his M-16, and headed for the Quonset hut.

Except for the imaginary sniper with the rifle in the hills, the thought of whom provoked an awful twitching in Guy's crotch, Guy felt suddenly quite alone.

Before he reached the door of the Quonset hut, Guy noticed a muddy truck parked nearby, with two men leaning against its fenders.

They both wore flak jackets and floppy bush hats. They both eyed Lopaca coldly, arms crossed over their chests. One man carried an M-16 rifle. The other soldier wore a .45 caliber pistol and also held a stubby M-79 grenade launcher, with snub-nosed grenades in a bandolier slung over his shoulder.

"You the guy for the 5th Platoon?" the GI with the rifle shouted at Guy.

"I guess so," Guy shouted back, and began walking toward them. "I'm Guy Lopaca," he said.

"Big frigging deal," the GI with the rifle snarled.

"Get in the frigging truck," the man with the grenade launcher growled. He pointed to the cargo bed.

Guy got in the frigging truck. The cargo bed was empty except for one corner, in which four green sandbags had been arranged.

"Sit on those sandbags the whole way," the man with the grenade launcher said to him, "unless you want to have your ass blown off by a mine." Guy squatted on the sandbags with his back to the truck's cab.

"You got any bullets for that rifle?" the grenade launcher barked at him, nodding toward Guy's M-16.

"There's two magazines in my duffel bag," Guy replied. "Should I get them?"

"Of course not," the grenade launcher scoffed. "Why use bullets to shoot people when you can run up and hit them with the stock of your rifle? Let the duffel bag keep the ammunition. You don't want your duffel bag to run out of ammunition on a dangerous trip like the one we're going to be taking."

"You got a flak jacket?" the stranger holding the M-16 asked Guy.

Guy hesitated. "It's in my duffel bag," Guy said.

"That makes me feel a lot better," the M-16 said. "I wouldn't want to go where you're going unless I knew your duffel bag had a flak jacket. I've seen duffel bags that were hit by bullets and shrapnel. It's not pretty."

"I'm not moving from this spot until that man's duffel bag is adequately supplied with ammunition," the man with the grenade launcher insisted as he climbed behind the wheel of the truck. "Are we sure that two magazines is enough ammunition for his duffel bag? Should we loan it some of our ammunition?"

"Don't worry," the man with the rifle said. "It seems like a very responsible duffel bag, that knows the importance of fire discipline."

"If you say so," the grenade launcher said, and started the truck.

The two strangers sat in the cab, leaving Guy in the truck bed alone. A minute after they started moving, Guy began to steal the duffel bag's flak vest and ammunition.

"Are we going to Hue now?" he asked after a while.

"Sure, if we make it," the driver said. "You never know, when you consider the mines and all those assassination squads they have roaming around here."

"Don't talk anymore," the chubby one with the rifle said to Guy a few minutes later. "We're coming to a pretty bad stretch right now. Get down low in the truck and keep your eyes open."

The fellow with the rifle climbed out of the roofless cab and into the truck bed with Guy. The stranger pushed Guy off the protective sandbag mat, and kneeled so he could peer over the side of the truck, revealing no target below his eyes.

I wish I had some sand under me, Guy thought. *I wish they had brought some bags of sand for me.*

He imagined his hometown obituary: local hero dies in Vietnam when sandless part of truck blows up.

The jouncing road angled onto a slightly wider track lined with banana trees. The rain stopped. Guy began to notice that there were people out there. Vietnamese people. Old ladies hunkered by the roadside, chewing and spitting dark juice. Girls with baskets on their heads. Lots of kids. And men.

Teenage men. Old men. Middle-aged men. All kinds of men, all of whom stared hungrily, as if Guy Lopaca were the most important target of opportunity the battlefield offered today. The Vietnamese men were cold. They were lean. It was obvious—*they all wanted to suck his blood dry.*

The road linked up with a wider street. It filled up with clumps, then crowds of people. Jeeps and bicycles and motor scooters coagulated around them. The entire population of Vietnam seemed to be converging on this one little bit of highway. The truck slowed, gears changed, the engine whined, bystanders regarded him crookedly, and Guy Lopaca thought of gun sights. Russian gun sights, Chinese gun sights, captured American gun sights, rusty French and Japanese gun sights. All those gun sights—brought to Vietnam by so many angry foreign armies—were now trained on Guy Lopaca.

Men with guns were hiding and aiming. They were hiding in that wooden hut, on that corrugated roof, behind that bush, up in the leaves of that tree. They were in that truck a few yards up ahead, and on the backseat of that scooter which had just made a suspicious U-turn and was heading his way. All of those hidden gun sights were sniffing out the vital parts of Guy Lopaca's body—which, he suddenly decided, had no parts that *weren't* vital to him. Guy felt the gun sights on his skull, his eye sockets, his belly, and his precious knee and elbow joints. The truck hit a pothole and bounced noisily. Lopaca chewed his lip. The truck's metal skin was not so thick. A bullet could pass through it. No shot was impossible.

The driver pointed the truck into less populated country, and eventually waved at a stretch of open ground.

"This," the driver said, "is where they found some of the mass graves after the Tet Offensive." They rode on in silence for a while, and then the driver pointed at another stretch of ground.

"And *that's* where *your* mass grave will be," he said.

"Hey," said the man in the back of the truck next to Guy, "it's better than being eaten."

Guy began to question the design of his Army-issue flak vest. The shrapnel-resistant rib pads came together in the front, as would a standard vest, leaving an unpadded vertical channel that seemed to offer an unimpeded shot to his heart.

His heart was a necessary, combat-sustaining organ—that you would think the Army would want to protect.

Just when Guy was ready to draw critical conclusions about the design limitations of the Army flak vest, the driver of the little truck stopped at the top of a hill and shut the engine off.

It was a nice hill. They were on the crest of a nice little hill in pretty, rolling open country, something like Vermont, but with even more guns than they have in Vermont, all of them being loaded and cocked—Guy imagined—now that he had become a thoroughly motionless target in plain view on top of an exposed hill in Vietnam.

The driver stood up on the seat of the truck, so that his head and upper body poked through the roofless frame. The driver stretched himself up as high as he could go, making of himself the tallest motionless target on the top of the hill. The driver spread his arms straight out, wide to his sides, like Jesus Christ deciding that an AK-47 bullet was better than nails any day. After a few seconds, during which Guy Lopaca held his breath, the driver began to yell as loudly as he could.

"Hey, all you nice VC out there! Listen to me! I'm Paul Gianelli. This is Tyler DeMudge. You know us. We've been here before. You VC! Listen! Remember us? We're nice guys. We smile a lot. We say please and thank you. So don't shoot us, OK? You hear me, all you VC? We're nice guys. *Don't shoot us!"*

He waved both arms wildly over his head for attention, and then suddenly pointed his finger at Guy Lopaca.

"Shoot him!" the driver screamed.

•   •   •

Paul and Tyler had a fine hearty laugh, as they always did after torturing a new guy; and during the rest of the trip they took care to point out all the lovely scenery, and told Guy that apart from the occasional land mine—like the one that blew up that tank—there was nothing much to worry about and the countryside around Hue City was actually very nice to drive in, very scenic. He would enjoy Hue very much. Oh, look, we're coming to Hue now. Let's take him by The Citadel, and across the bridge. It's pretty busy today. Oh, shit, something's happened up ahead. No telling how long we'll be stuck on the bridge.

And suddenly, just like that, Guy Lopaca really arrived in Vietnam.

The truck lurched to a halt in a full-boogie traffic jam, and Guy was overrun by Vietnamese. Thousands of Vietnamese. Yelling, honking the horns of their trucks and motor scooters. Pedaling bicycles and rickshaws. Walking across traffic or against traffic or climbing over traffic. Running with bundles on their heads. Waving their hands, and frequently hollering. Suddenly Guy was swept up in the frenzy of a maximum-energy Vietnamese crowd; as single-minded as a panicked mob, as sociable as baseball fans near the end of a winning game. At any moment he could have reached out and touched six of them. He was close enough to smell them, to feel the breeze they made when hurrying by him.

And their voices! A cacophony of twanging, bubbling voices. Vietnamese was a tonal language, a musical language, and in Army language school Guy had tried to master the tones. Judging from his test scores, he had succeeded.

Now he was buffeted by a hosanna of real voices, a frantic traffic-jam choir of voices, a thousand chattering people showering him with sound that beat upon his ears, filling him with awe and desperation . . .

Because he understood none of it. Not a single word. He had come all the way from safety to Vietnam, to be an interpreter of Vietnamese. That was his only reason for being here. And now that he was here, he understood not one goddamn thing they were saying! It was, to him, like trying to translate fireworks on the Fourth of July.

Vietnam Has Its
Little Tricks

I t was dark when Arthur Grissom's part of the bored and anxious
crowd finally left the Tan Son Nhut air base. They were loaded onto
beat-up, wheezing, clattering buses. Arthur noticed that his bus had no
window glass. Instead, the window frames were covered with a heavy
metal mesh, like frozen fishnet. It was perfectly logical. Shattering window glass would have added to the hazard of small-arms fire. The mesh
kept the hand grenades out.

The current bus design was probably a consequence of lessons the
Army had learned. The first buses would have been ordered with standard glass windows, *why not?* And then, when enough young men had
been sprayed with glass chips, the word would have gone out: take the
glass away. And then, when enough young men had been sprayed with
shrapnel from hand grenades tossed through the open window frames,
the word would have gone out again: attach some metal mesh. Arthur
hoped he could get through his tour without becoming a bloody lesson
for someone else's retrofit.

Arthur was eventually dumped inside a mammoth military base a few miles from the airport. To get inside the base perimeter, the convoy passed by armed checkpoints and a variety of defensive strongholds. Barbed wire. Claymore mines. Sandbagged gun emplacements. Men wearing flak vests and helmets, bearing rifles and grenade launchers. Everything was designed to repulse any hostile force that might try to attack the base from the dark, desolate, unprotected wasteland beyond the perimeter.

Where Arthur had just been riding in a bus.

Once inside the base, Arthur's contingent of new soldiers began the process of waiting. First, they waited to be unloaded. Then they waited in line for assignment to their transient barracks, where they would wait—indefinitely—for their in-country orders to be cut.

"Don't think of enlisted men, think of inventory," Arthur Grissom had once heard a stateside officer say to another, "and don't think of an enlisted man's career, think of his shelf life."

It was a cheerless memory, becoming even more so as Arthur was shown to his temporary warehouse: a grim wooden box, with a metal roof that clanged like machine guns in the heavy rain, which drenched Arthur as he waited in the mud in front of the barracks door. Once inside, he was permitted to select a shelf according to his particular taste: an upper bunk or a lower bunk; a beer-stained mattress, a bloodstained mattress, or no mattress at all.

Eventually, after lying on his bunk for hours, unable to slap the swarming bugs away or maintain a conversation with them, Arthur decided to take a shower. He sucked in some courage, retrieved his most precious cargo from his duffel bag, and headed for the latrine.

They had hot water, that was good. And he must have come at an unpopular time—imagine four o'clock in the morning being unpopular—because there was only one other man in the shower bay. Arthur stripped and hustled under one of the shower heads, turning the valve until the water was just right. Then he stepped in.

Wow!

Showers at home were wonderful, but nothing like this!

Well, to be fair, he had never felt this filthy before. It was amazing how thoroughly filthy you could get from doing absolutely nothing in Vietnam. He was covered by a layer of slimy Oriental ooze that clogged his pores and smelled awfully bad. How it got there Arthur didn't know. It was as if they had run him through an automobile paint spray booth, and substituted smelly slime for the red pearlescent with clear-coat.

The shower water was marvelous, for a while. There was plenty of volume, and it warmed him to the marrow. Then Arthur heard some banging in the pipes, the water spurted off and on, and then . . .

"Ow!" Arthur screamed, jumping back as a blast of scalding water scorched him.

"It's air in the pipes," a tomato-faced naked grunt said from a safe distance outside his own shower's killing zone. "Somethin' about the way the pipes're put together, traps bubbles or somethin', and when they build up enough pressure they make the damn thing . . . I don't know . . . hiccup or somethin'." He laughed. "Y'all'l get used to it."

"Get used to it!" Arthur whined. "It *burned* me. Look at my arm!" His right arm grabbed his left arm as if it were a foreign object, raising it to show a red swath of skin from the scalding. "It's *dangerous,*" Arthur said. "Someone should do something about it."

"Oh, that's been tried," the stranger said, stepping back into the spray which—for some reason—didn't instantly kill him. "A while ago the Secretary of Defense come through here, and asked the guys was there anythin' he could do to make their life less . . . I don't know . . . screwed up or whatever. And this one guy said, yeah, there was this shower that needed fixin', and couldn't the Secretary get in some plumbers to fix it up so the men could take reg'lar showers without wor-ryin' about no sixth-degree burns on the skin of their asses. He says this with reporters around."

"Did they shoot him?" Arthur asked.

"Hell *no,*" the grunt said. "Secretary just smiled for the cameras and shouted so all the reporters could hear him, and he says 'Well, you boys go out there and kill yourselves enough of them Vietcong, like we taught you back home, and this war'll be over before the plumbers won't have no chance nor need to get their hands wet.' "

"And that was it?" Arthur asked.

"Hell *no,*" the grunt said, "that was not *it.* The next day, the base commander sent some plumbers over to work on the showers, and all's they did was raise the temp'rature of the water ten degrees."

"Damn," Arthur said.

"Welcome to the Nam," the grunt said, chuckling.

"And anyway," the grunt said, "it's only a matter of you listen to the pipes, listen for your *Whumps,* and get yourself a rhythm." He paused. "Listen now," he said, "the water's fine now, but you just wait. Listen for that first *Whump.*"

Arthur waited. After a while, he heard a *Whump.*

"That's the first one," the grunt said. "Water's still fine, now you got to wait for your second *Whump.*"

Arthur waited for the second *Whump,* which came in about thirty seconds.

"OK, now that's your signal to get ready to get out," the grunt said. "That third *Whump*'ll be coming along right . . . about . . . now!"

The pipes *Whump*ed, right on cue, and five seconds later Arthur watched in amazement as the water pressure died briefly, then spurted to life, shooting liquid fire. Flesh-melting steam seemed to be spattering from the shower heads, and the droplets when they hit the floor sizzled like spit on a griddle. It lasted a few seconds, then subsided.

"You just listen for your *Whumps,*" the grunt told him. "After your second *Whump* you begin to get the soap from your eyes, and when you hear that third *Whump,* get out of the way. You'll do fine."

Arthur watched as the cycle repeated a few times.

Whump, Whump, Whump. Hiss, sizzle.

Whump, Whump, Whump. Hiss, sizzle.

Whump, Whump, Whump. Hiss, sizzle.

I can do this, Arthur thought. *I could never do the twist or the jitter-bug, but I can do this.*

He stepped into the shower and lathered a little.

Whump. Lather, lather.

Whump. Rinse, rinse.

Whump. He stepped out of the spray.

Hiss, sizzle. The water became lethally hot for a few seconds, then returned to normal. When it did, Arthur stepped back in.

This isn't so bad, Arthur thought. *Vietnam has its little tricks, and I can learn them.*

Whump.

Arthur began lathering his hair and face. Lather, lather.

Whump.

Arthur rinsed his hair and face off. Rinse, rinse.

Whump.

Arthur stepped out of the spray zone.

Hiss, sizzle.

Wham.

Wham? Arthur thought. *What the hell is a 'wham'?*

"Incoming!" the red-faced grunt screamed. "Incoming! Rockets!"

Arthur turned to ask what the grunt was talking about, and saw the man lying along the back wall, face to the floor and arms over his head. Oh, I get it, Arthur thought sluggishly, rockets . . .

Rockets?

His recently civilian brain finally processed the information:

$$rockets = death$$

Arthur dropped to the floor, waving his arms madly and reaching for the floor as he fell.

He landed in a trough in which the shower runoff water collected and—before Arthur blockaded it—would usually sluice in a greasy river down a gradual slope to the drain. Just like the red-faced grunt, Arthur had his face to the floor, and his hands over his head. Unlike the red-faced grunt, Arthur had become a kind of dam that caused the runoff water to eddy around him.

Whump.

Arthur opened his eyes. Oh! Look at the pretty rainbow on the surface of the shower runoff water. The shimmering colors swirled in bright, immiscible patterns, like the liquid light show at a San Francisco rock concert. Arthur had seen Country Joe McDonald sing with that kind of light show swirling on a screen behind him. Or was it Grace Slick? Now here was the same wonderful rainbow of color, working its way toward him atop a river of Vietnam latrine-shower wastewater slime.

Whump.

In addition to the sweaty body oils, motor-pool grease, urine, and mud constituents that had brought so much vivid color to the runoff slop he was lying in, Arthur could see small floating objects: a piece of toenail; a pubic hair; a puffy sliver of soap.

A bug came paddling down the foul-smelling drainage river and tried to dock in Arthur's nose. Arthur snorted, and the bug withdrew a couple of inches. It was about the size of a really fat black ant, and was suspended by long, slender legs that lay along the surface of the waste-water without breaking it. The bug's twitching antenna seemed to be employing some sort of sign language to contact Arthur:

Hi! I'm an Asian mutilation beetle. What are you?

Whump.

Arthur had never felt so filthy in his life.

"Hey! That's it, attack's over," the red-faced grunt called to him. "You can get up now." Arthur started slowly to raise his body, the front of which was now covered with Vietnam latrine slime. *It can't get any worse than this,* Arthur thought, just before the steam blast hit him.

Hiss, sizzle.

"OOOWWWW!" he screamed. He frantically crawled out of the shower's zone of annihilation, a strawberry blotch already forming on his lower back and buttocks.

Damn, Arthur thought, *I lost track of my Whumps!*

Now he was cowering on his hands and knees, half covered with runoff slime, with a patch of burned skin on his back, feeling greasy grimy on one side and prickly hot on the other. *It can't get any worse than this,* Arthur thought, just before the water shut off.

The silence was unbearable. There was no water coming out of the shower heads. Not a single *Whump*'s worth. He had no cold water to soothe his flaming backside. He had no hot water to help scour the runoff slime from his frontside. The Asian mutilation beetle was climbing up his arm.

"One rocket's not so bad," the red-faced grunt said. "Dependin' on where it comes down."

Arthur looked up at the grunt, hoping the stranger could say or do something, *anything,* to make the situation . . . *what?* Less painful? Less slimy?

The grunt looked down at Arthur. The grunt bent a little, almost offering to help Arthur up. When the grunt saw the colorful slime that was dripping off Arthur, the grunt pulled his hand back.

"Like I say, *welcome to the Nam,*" the grunt said, as he rubber-tire-sandal-flopped his way out of the building, taking Arthur's only towel with him.

• HUE •

Why Are We Here?

Captain Haven was a big, easygoing, sandy-haired youngster who might have been a football player, and probably was, until the last season ended in his senior year and he stopped exercising for the rest of his life. Now instead of big and brawny he was big and merely beefy, and would probably stay that way until he was forty, when all hell would break loose. But it wouldn't matter because he already had the perky blonde, and the kids would come soon, and the vice presidency of something or other was just a matter of time. At least, that's how he appeared to Guy Lopaca.

"Nice test scores!" Captain Haven said as he waved off Guy's salute. "Did it never occur to you that scoring well on Army tests might get you into trouble?"

"No, sir," Guy replied, "I just answered the questions they put in front of me."

"Well, you did a good job," Captain Haven grinned. "Those are the best test scores I have ever seen or heard of. They're even better than

Tyler DeMudge's test scores, and those were pretty good. Do you know how Tyler DeMudge got his Army test scores?"

"No, sir," Lopaca said. "I just met Tyler DeMudge."

"You'll get to know him better soon enough. Here's how DeMudge got his scores. On every test, he answered all the questions. However, on each test DeMudge selected the *wrong* answer to the question whose number most closely matched the square root of the total number of questions on that test, and *also* the question whose number matched the square root of the square root of one hundred times the total number of questions."

"Is the square root of the square root the same as the cube root?" Guy asked.

"Who the hell knows?" Captain Haven shrugged. "And Tyler also chose the wrong answer to every question number thirty-six, because that was his girlfriend's—you know—chest size."

Captain Haven sat down, and invited Lopaca to do the same.

"But you might have beat him anyway," Captain Haven said, "straight up."

"Thanks," Guy said.

"We've been waiting for you," Captain Haven said. "We've always had linguists here, but no one real good. No one with your test scores. How long did it take you to learn Vietnamese?"

Guy swallowed hard, thinking, *it begins right now.* The charade was over. His utter incompetence was about to be revealed.

"I don't really speak Vietnamese," he said.

Captain Haven smiled.

"Say that again in Vietnamese," Captain Haven said.

"Tôi không nói dược tiếng Việt," Guy said haltingly.

"Sounds good to me!" Captain Haven said. "What's the first words you ever learned in Vietnamese?"

"The first words?" Guy asked. "I learned the first words out of a dictionary, before classes started. . . ."

"So what were they?" Captain Haven asked.

Guy sighed.

"Xin ông tha thứ cho tôi," Guy said. "It means either 'please

have mercy on me' or 'please forgive me.' It's OK with me either way."

Captain Haven laughed.

"Listen, that's the last we're gonna hear about you not speaking Vietnamese," Captain Haven said. "You're the only American translator I ever met who could say 'I can't speak Vietnamese' in Vietnamese."

"But I really *can't* speak Vietnamese," Guy said. "I mean *really*. I can remember a phrase or two, a few words, but . . ."

"Let me tell you about how things work around here," Captain Haven broke in. "I am a captain and I run the 5th Platoon. You can call me Captain, or Captain Haven, or sir. I will call you Lopaca or Specialist Lopaca or Specialist. You will not enter my office until you knock and I tell you to come in. I will not enter your hootch until I show you the same courtesy, unless it's a surprise inspection or I'm in a hurry. I'm rarely in a hurry and I've never conducted an inspection, surprise or otherwise. When outsiders are around, you will salute me. When it's just us guys in the unit, don't do it. Saluting is for storm troopers."

He put his feet up on the desk. Apparently, the discussion of Guy's translating capabilities was over.

"This is a Civil Affairs unit," he continued. "Our platoon reports to company headquarters in Da Nang. They leave us alone and that's the way we like it. Our mission is to help the Vietnamese civilian population in a number of areas. You're going to be working mostly in agriculture. Over the next few months you're going to have more contact with the people than practically anybody else in the Army. You'll be spending more time in the boondocks and the villages than the grunts who blow up the boondocks and burn down the villages. How does that sound?"

That's what "please have mercy on me" is for, Guy thought. *For when I meet those Vietnamese in their boondocks and villages!*

"I don't know anything about agriculture," Guy said lamely.

"You don't have to know anything about agriculture," Captain Haven said. "You're just the translator. Let the lieutenants worry about not knowing anything about agriculture."

Captain Haven chuckled.

"One of them just got here yesterday," he said. "You'll meet him later. Nice guy. Name is Rossi, though you'd never take him for Italian. You know what he said when I told him what his job was?"

"No," Guy said.

"I tell him he's going to be teaching agriculture," Captain Haven said with a sparkle in his eye, "and he said—and I quote—'*I don't know anything about agriculture.*' Sound familiar? You two ought to get along just fine. He got his college degree in forestry, so naturally the Army sent him here to teach people how to grow lettuce and peanuts. What a joke."

Guy sat in silence for a while, imagining how it would be for a forester who knew nothing about peanut farming to teach the subject through an interpreter who didn't know the Vietnamese word for *peanut.* Or *farm* or *grow* or, for that matter, *dirt.*

"When we go out in the villages and boondocks, will we be armed?" Guy asked. "Will we have some kind of escort?"

Captain Haven laughed.

● ● ●

"It's Paul Gianelli's turn to run the orientation today," Captain Haven said to all the men in the 5th Platoon, assembled on the shady veranda outside his office. "We call it the 'Why Are We Here?' lecture. We give this lecture every time some new guys arrive. It helps everyone get acquainted, and it gives all of us in the platoon a chance to rededicate ourselves to our single most important mission, the absolutely primary mission of our platoon, which is—all together now . . ."

"Going home alive!" the veterans shouted.

Guy Lopaca and Lieutenant Rossi looked at each other and squirmed.

"For the two of you who don't know Paul Gianelli," Captain Haven continued, "I should explain that he has been in Vietnam for a really, really long time. He says this is his third tour, but it's hard to tell exactly how long he's been here because almost every time a tour is about to expire he extends it. I've read his file, and still can't figure it out. He claims he's spent more time in the war than Ho Chi Minh . . ."

"It's true," Gianelli mumbled from his seat, "if you don't count Ho's years of exile in Paris. Or my semester of exile in college."

"Anyway," Captain Haven continued, "he has had way more time in the war than I have, and his qualifications are far superior to mine. And what's his most important qualification? More important than knowing every bush and tree in the province? More important than knowing every village chief and all their daughters? Get ready, guys. The most important thing about Gianelli is this. Every time he comes to Vietnam—all together now . . ."

"He goes home alive!" the veterans shouted.

Gianelli unslouched from his seat and took Captain Haven's place at the front.

"First," he said, "I would like to welcome to the 5th Platoon our newest members, Lt. Gunnar Rossi and Specialist Guy Lopaca, whose lockers are being looted even as we speak. Second, I want to register a formal objection to the 'Why Are We Here?' lecture that Tyler De-Mudge gave last month, when Lieutenant Frickleman arrived. Although Lieutenant Frickleman is short and doesn't have a lot of hair, he is an officer and he deserved to hear more from Tyler than the lecture Tyler gave him which was, in its entirety, 'Why Not?' "

The veterans chuckled.

"Tyler should be ashamed," Gianelli continued. "The Army's fighting men deserve an inspirational, esprit-building rationale for their participation in the war. I know I do. 'Why Not?' doesn't deal with any of the geopolitical or moral implications of the war, nor does it help our newly arriving comrades resolve their personal concerns about what they are doing here, and why they ought to risk their lives to do it.

"So," Gianelli said, "the topic is 'Why Are We Here?' and I have spent a lot of time thinking about it. I believe I have the answer. I think I know why I am here, why Tyler himself is here, and why all of you are here. I want to take this opportunity to look the two newest members of the platoon squarely in the eyes and tell them, from the bottom of my heart, that the reason Why We Are Here is this: *shit luck.*"

The men—with the exception of Lopaca and Rossi—applauded and hooted and stamped their feet.

"I'm serious," Gianelli said, smiling broadly, "a Civil Affairs unit like ours could not have come into existence except by chance, shit luck. We don't fit in with anything else the Army is doing. We are as accidental as a colony of mutants. Even if the paychecks do come regular every month."

Gianelli held up his hand, with three fingers extended.

"We have three main missions," he said. "Not one of our missions is warlike. Listen up, new guys, this is the part of the lecture where I sneak in your education. Our most important mission is agriculture. We help civilians grow crops and raise animals. Think about that."

Gianelli pulled into view a tripod with a presentation pad. He flipped the first few pages to reveal a hand-drawn map of Vietnam. Guy squinted. It was just a blob of messy green. Gianelli tapped his finger on the blob.

"If I told you that American soldiers staged a *military action* here in the A Shau Valley yesterday," Gianelli said, "what would you think of? Would you think of a large-scale Allied ground assault, involving the massive deployment of infantry and armor, preceded by a heavy artillery bombardment, and supported by the bombing and strafing of rotary and fixed wing aircraft? Is that what you would think of?" He paused. "Or would you think of planting watermelon seeds?"

"Seeds!" the men shouted. *"Seeds!"*

Gianelli walked over to Rossi and Lopaca and dropped a few hard brown ovals in their hands. "There you go, guys," Gianelli said. "Plant 'em deep and make us proud."

"What we do is too bizarre to be anything other than a mistake that the Army hasn't yet corrected," Gianelli said. "So from *our* point of view *it's just shit luck.* That's Why We Are Here."

He returned to the front of the room to a smatter of applause, and a loud "Boooo" from Tyler DeMudge, who was lurking at the back of the room.

"You two new guys will be helping the farmers," Gianelli said, "along with Lieutenant Prout and Lieutenant Frickleman. While the Air Force drops bombs and makes lots of big holes on one side of a mountain, you may be on the other side digging one little hole that people can draw their water from. It's exactly that absurd." He sighed theatrically. "I know you think I'm kidding, but I'm not. You'll find out. It's nuts. But it's a nice nuts.

"Tyler DeMudge's job," Gianelli continued, "is so insignificant that even a lieutenant wouldn't be allowed to do it. Tyler is our liaison with something the locals call Youth Services. Educational stuff, village schools, some clubs that are kind of like scouting, some sports stuff, camping, that sort of thing. Tyler organizes volleyball teams on the theory that young people ought to be kept occupied in clean, character-building sporting activities until they're old enough for the shooting and the whoring.

"Buddy Brier is the unit clerk and scrounger. We pay for a part-time secretary so he has more time for the scrounging. Buddy learned Army Vietnamese, too, but swears he forgot it all. I have heard him try to speak it, and I believe him.

"And then there's my area of responsibility, which is . . ." He paused. "I forget. Captain Haven, can you help me out?"

"You almost took over for the guy who was liaison with the civilian police," Captain Haven said, "but as I recall you said the cops are all crooks and refused to meet with them. So Sergeant Nesbitt over in the corner there became our police liaison."

Sergeant Nesbitt nodded and smiled.

"So what do I do now?" Gianelli asked.

"Anything you want to do," Captain Haven said.

"Oh, right," Gianelli said. "They classify me now as a medical advisor. I mostly help build medical dispensaries out in the boondocks. It's a cooperative relationship. The Army provides all the building materials and the Vietnamese provide all the sickness.

"This compound we're in, including the buildings and the parking lot, we call it The Villa," Gianelli said. "We have some trucks and jeeps. A short drive that way"—he pointed—"is the main bridge over the Perfume River to the town. Take a right at the end of the bridge and you'll go to the commercial area and the open market. Take a left and you'll go to the main gate of the big fortress they call The Citadel. It's the ancient imperial capital. Inside the walls are some ARVN and police detachments, some civilian government offices, some small farms and animal pens, and some good places for taking photographs of statues and gardens."

Suddenly Guy realized that the Why Are We Here show had turned into a real lecture of sorts. No one was laughing or joking. Guy thought: they've heard it before, they know where it's headed, and they're bored.

"You're going to see a lot of the bridge, and The Citadel," Gianelli continued. "You're going to see a lot of Hue, and the villages around it. You're going to see a lot of the open country. You're going to see a lot of the people. And they're going to see a lot of you."

He sat down. Captain Haven stood up and took his place.

"Unlike other American soldiers," Captain Haven said, "we have no travel restrictions. We go where we want, when we want. We go where the job takes us. When you leave this compound in the morning, no one but me will be checking you for orders. Unfortunately, no one at all will be watching your back. I don't say that to scare you more than you need to be scared. This platoon has never taken a casualty. Not one. But don't ever get the idea that you're safe out there.

"Don't let a stranger get on your vehicle," he continued. "Be careful where you park it. Don't stop at street corners to buy things. In fact, just don't buy things. Anything you smoke or eat or shoot up your arm can poison you, and everything else can blow you up. Don't provoke anyone or let anyone provoke you. Some cadre that we work with might make you drive thirty miles over country roads that scare the shit out of you; but don't make it worse by taking a shortcut he doesn't want to take.

"The Vietnamese are the friendliest people in the world," Captain Haven said. "And some of them are the most dedicated killers the world has ever produced. The Army has thrown everything we can at them, and they keep coming. They have been at war since before you were born. Every family has had a tragedy, and every person bears a grudge. Every square inch of this country is contested every day. Not a single road is completely safe. Not a single Vietnamese can be completely trusted. Even our best friends can find a reason to hate us.

"Compared to other American soldiers," Captain Haven said, "we in Civil Affairs enjoy a special kind of freedom, and along with that goes a special kind of vulnerability. When you enter the parking lot for this compound, you pass by a guard. He is about seventy-five years old, and I think his gun is older than that. There are at least two ways that a small armed force could attack us and kill us all, right now, before suppertime. The first way would be to walk quietly past the guard so as not to wake him up or bother him, and shoot us as we sit here. The second way they could get us would be to wait until we try to walk or drive back to The Hotel, and pick us off. We are all dead whenever they want us to be dead."

He paused.

"Oh, shit," Captain Haven said, "I just thought of *another* way they could get us. They could plant a command-detonation mine at night, here on the veranda, and they could set it off anytime they want to. They could just watch from across the road, and when the time is right, and enough of us are sitting here having a nice chat, all they have to do is just press the button and . . ."

WHAM!

At this point Tyler DeMudge fired a single round from his pistol down into a big metal tub of sand, which had been set against the back wall out of sight of the new guys.

WHAM!

The explosion was so loud that even the veterans who planned the setup jumped a little; but the new guys Rossi and Lopaca were absolutely *catapulted* from their chairs. Their feet actually left the floor.

Tyler giggled. His timing had been even better than Gianelli's had been last month, when Lieutenant Frickleman was the new-guy sucker, and ended up on his knees beneath a table.

Gianelli approached Rossi and Lopaca and surveyed their crotches.

"No one pissed his pants," he reported. The men all laughed and clapped and stamped their feet. Guy looked dazed and disoriented. But not Lieutenant Rossi.

He walked slowly toward Captain Haven and didn't stop until there was practically no space at all between them. Haven was taller and heavier and had more rank, but Rossi was hard as burled walnut, a natural athlete, and if there was any fear in him you couldn't see it behind the anger.

"I've been hazed before," Lieutenant Rossi said, looking straight into Captain Haven's eyes. "Do we get our asses paddled next? Why don't you tell me what else we have to do before you let us into the club?"

Captain Haven smiled. "That's all there is, Gunnar," he said.

He's going to be a good one, Captain Haven thought. *He'll have to run the "Why Are We Here?" show the next time we have one. If he learns how to laugh in time.*

Tetrawhatchamacallit

When he arrived at the big military base at Nha Trang, in the southern coastal region, Arthur Grissom was assigned to work as an office clerk at Headquarters Company of the 23rd Radio Research Battalion. The HQ office was located in a Quonset hut outside a restricted, high-tech inner core: a rectangular compound, heavily bordered by multiple loops of sinister concertina wire, with MPs at its only gate.

Inside the high-security compound, a dozen trailers—the size of double-wide motor homes—were arranged side by side in two neat rows. Some of the trailers sprouted dish antennae, fan antennae, and antenna towers. There was a constant roar from electricity generators.

"You can't go in there," Arthur's first sergeant told him, pointing to the restricted compound. "You don't have a security clearance high enough." The first sergeant paused. "Neither do I," he said, "and I been in the Army since before you were born."

They assigned Arthur to menial work as an office clerk. They sat him at a typewriter, gave him a stack of carbon-paper forms whose drafts had been filled in by hand, and walked away. A few minutes later the first sergeant and the captain who commanded Headquarters Company stood side by side and looked across the orderly room toward Arthur's desk.

"Jesus, would you look at that," the first sergeant whispered.

"He can type like a civilian!" the captain giggled.

Within a week, the captain assembled the office staff and told the men that Arthur had become the company's chief clerk, a position which until then none of them had ever heard of. Immediately, Arthur became envied and despised by the other clerks.

While he was new at it, Arthur's job was interesting. Almost the instant he arrived, Arthur was given all of the most important paperwork of every kind. It seemed that the life's blood of the whole command flowed through his own nimble fingers on the typewriter.

Eventually, however, the work became pretty boring. Every duty roster was like all the others. Every requisition was the same, a mass of double-speak and jargon to procure, for example, a ten-foot sidewalk extension. It took the captain at least half a day to get one of those requisitions right. The captain would order Arthur to retype the form six times until its prose was just precisely *perfect* for sending up a chain of discriminating literary critics to the officer in charge of extending sidewalks.

Arthur soon found himself to be the single most essential person in the company.

"I had to stay in the office an hour later than the other clerks again," Arthur wrote to his parents one day. "That's what I get for having a fancy title I don't want."

Whenever one of the clerks was in a bad mood, he would call Arthur "Chief," and laugh.

"Hey, Chief," he would say, "how about typing me up my transfer to Germany?"

"Hey, Chief, why don't you type me an encyclopedia before lunch?"

"Hey, Chief, what else do you use those fingers for besides typing?"

It went on for about three weeks. Finally, the first sergeant called the jokester into Top's office and told him: "We don't need any Indians here. We do need a chief. You can be jealous of him at the motor pool starting tomorrow morning." Within an hour, Arthur had become the most hated soldier in the company.

I'm really not an Army stooge, Arthur thought as misery descended on his lonely barracks life. *I'm not a brown-noser or an ass-kisser. I just type well. It's not my fault if the others are incompetent and lazy.*

To salvage some sense of the integrity he had maintained as a politically astute young citizen before he got drafted, Arthur began to engage in secret, pleasurable acts of rebellion.

One of Arthur's jobs was keeping a big set of Army regulations up-to-date. Every few days a packet of new pages would arrive from the States, with holes punched for insertion into ring binders kept in the first sergeant's office. All the new pages would be put into their proper places in the binders, and the obsolete pages they replaced would be thrown away. That was the idea, at least.

"I decide whether the new regulation is essential or nonessential," Arthur wrote his parents. "If the subject is nonessential, like the length of GI haircuts, I decide whether the new regulation is better than the old regulation. If I don't like the new regulation, I throw it away and the old one stays in effect. No one checks me."

One day, the captain taped an antidrug poster on the orderly-room wall. In enormous block letters, it asked:

WHY DO YOU THINK THEY CALL IT *DOPE*?

When he was alone, Arthur sat at another clerk's typewriter and banged out an addendum, which he attached at night when the fellow assigned to charge of quarters duty was out back having an unauthorized beer. The next morning, the poster read:

WHY DO YOU THINK THEY CALL IT *DOPE*?
because if they called it "tetrahydrocannabinol"
stupid shits like me couldn't pronounce it

The first sergeant guessed right away that it was Arthur who had messed up the poster. The two of them shared in the prank, because the first sergeant actually chuckled when he saw the disfigured poster, whereas the captain just frowned in a way that a stupid shit would frown if he couldn't pronounce tetrahydrocannabinol.

The captain was so angry that he offered a twenty-five-dollar reward for exposing the troublemaker who had defaced the poster. Arthur blissfully stapled the notice to the bulletin board, knowing that every GI in the company would gladly turn him in for free, if only they knew.

"If I knew who messed up that drug poster," the first sergeant said after reading about the reward, "I might offer to keep my mouth shut for only fifteen dollars."

"Do you think a glass of chocolate milk from the mess hall would be enough?" Arthur asked him.

"It might," the first sergeant replied. "Which reminds me, do they have any chocolate milk at the mess hall today?"

"Let me go check on that for you," Arthur said.

"That's awful nice of you," the first sergeant said. "Get one for yourself while you're there. If they don't have chocolate milk, see if they have any of that tetrawhatchamacallit."

"Sure thing, Top," Arthur agreed. "Anything you say, or nearly say, is OK by me."

- HUE -

A Nice Place
to Be Massacred

Doezema Compound was paradise on a postage stamp. Or, if you were less optimistic, it was a very nice place to be massacred among friends.

"It used to be the best hotel in Hue," Tyler DeMudge told Guy Lopaca. "That's why we call it The Hotel."

The main building was three stories high. The Army had simply added to it a system of walls, chain-link fence, barbed wire, towers, and bunkers to complete a compact rectangle about 200 yards wide and 300 yards long. Within the compound, the Army had thrown together a disorganized jumble of supply buildings, offices, hootches for the men, latrines, a medical clinic, a chapel, and—as DeMudge put it—"the amenities."

"Ten yards that way is the Post Exchange," DeMudge said, pointing from The Enlisted Men's Hootch that was exclusive to the 5th Platoon.

"Stereo equipment comes in once a month and gets sold out before noon. Buy cheap stuff for using while you're here and send the good stuff home. Let your family send you photographs of the good stuff, to keep your hopes up.

"Next to the PX is the tennis court. It's not very good. There's not enough room behind the baseline. You'll keep banging your racquet against the ammunition bunker. We sometimes play volleyball on the tennis court, but most nights the athletes take it over for basketball."

DeMudge walked Guy out the back door of The Hootch and pointed down a concrete ribbon.

"If you're inclined, the Steam and Cream is that way. The women are dogs." He pointed in the opposite direction. "The Enlisted Men's Club is small, but they always have ice." They went back into The EM Hootch. "They show movies at The Hotel three or four nights a week. They have free popcorn. An old woman comes in every day to clean up and do your laundry. We call her Mama-San even though we are not in Japan. Don't ask why. This is the Army, and that's what we have to call her. You pay her in funny money and give her a carton of cigarettes every week. What else is there?" He looked around. "Oh, yeah."

DeMudge stepped onto a chair and lifted one of the plywood ceiling panels. His arm disappeared up to the shoulder. When his hand came out, it was holding a plastic bag stuffed with dark green marijuana.

"We call it S-4, or Supply," DeMudge said. "Looks like there's about a pound left. Take a smell."

Guy took a smell. It was moist and aromatic, like a forest in springtime after a week of rain that contained lots and lots of hallucinogens.

"Pretty good stuff," DeMudge said. "S-4 belongs to everyone in The Hootch, or at least trustworthy people like yourself who have passed our rigorous membership exam. You can ask for any other kind of drug you want in Vietnam," he said, "and what they actually sell you will be pretty close. But I'd stay away from that other stuff if I were you. If you need it, have it somewhere else. Don't bring it here." Tyler put the dope back in the ceiling.

"This place is unreal," Lopaca said. "It's perfect."

"Not quite," DeMudge said. He picked up a tennis ball. "Follow me," he said.

They left the main gate and walked down the street, to the intersection at a corner of the compound. Now they were on a wide, teeming avenue on which traffic passed in a steady stream. Trucks, jeeps, cars of every American, Japanese, and European variety. Dozens of buzzing motorbikes, carrying one rider or six riders grasping one another in a knot of arms and hands. Pedestrians by the hundreds, some of them balancing bundles or crates on their heads. Bicycle rickshaws pedaled by drivers with sinewy arms and legs.

"This is Highway One," DeMudge said, bouncing the tennis ball a couple of times. "It's the busiest highway in the country."

The two men stood at the corner of Guy's new Army base in Vietnam, and watched as thousands of Asian strangers passed them by, close enough to touch.

"Let me show you one of the ways in which The Hotel is not nearly as perfect as you might like," DeMudge said. He spun Guy around and pointed his nose at the perimeter fence. "Watch," DeMudge said.

He tossed the tennis ball over the wall, into the invisible innards of the compound.

"An athlete could throw a hand grenade even farther," DeMudge said, "do you think?"

Lopaca got the point. The base was vulnerable to the simplest kind of ground attack, and the opposing force could be assembling on the street behind him right now, or anytime else.

"Does it happen often?" Guy asked at last.

"With one improbable exception, it has never happened," DeMudge replied. "Do you remember the Tet Offensive? It was in all the papers."

"I remember it," Guy said. He could still see the images of American and ARVN troops besieging The Citadel, the great fortress that the enemy had taken over and—by attracting the attention of the world's press photographers—converted into a fabulous symbol of South Vietnam's persistent vulnerability.

"Believe it or not," Tyler said, "during the Tet Offensive this little pipsqueak Army camp was the only piece of American dirt in Hue that didn't go under. Or so they say. That's the legend at least. Personally, I think it's a lie to help us sleep at night." He picked up a rock, made a show as if to throw it into the base, and then flipped it onto the ground.

"I don't need Army lies to help me sleep at night," he said as they walked inside the compound. "A couple of martinis will do very nicely. With a couple of nice martinis, I can sleep soundly anywhere, even in a tiny fortress that's built next to an unrestricted public highway. Although," he said, "I'll tell you one thing that bothers me." He pointed to the concrete sports slab next to the ammunition bunker.

"If Ho Chi Minh tells his men they have to take up tennis, we're all goners."

Tap Tap Tap

When Paul Gianelli and Guy Lopaca walked into The Villa on Guy's first full day at work, Captain Haven was leaning over a map of Vietnam that he had spread on a table so everyone present could point to it and tap on it at once. One of the Vietnamese—there were three of them competing for attention—was grabbing Haven's sleeve and tapping the map with a finger, tap tap tap. Each time the man tapped, his finger came down on map coordinates that were separated by ten or twenty miles. The man's two friends tapped the map as well.

Captain Haven rose up straight and started puffing madly on his pipe, as if stoking a small locomotive for a long, hard uphill pull.

"I've had it," Captain Haven said. "I don't know what the hell they want. I think they're trying to sell me a house. Why the hell did Denehy have to leave?"

Gianelli gave Lopaca a shove from the rear. "We all miss Denehy," Paul said, "but here is his replacement, sir. Don't forget Specialist Lopaca's Army test scores."

Captain Haven brightened. "Right," he said. "Lopaca, step over here and try to figure this out for me."

"I've never done this before," Guy said.

"Now's your chance, Tiger." Captain Haven smiled. "Show me what you got. Ask these jokers what they want."

Guy approached the three men and uttered an uncertain Vietnamese "hello" with a smile. One of the men smiled back, one frowned . . . and the other put a hand on his pistol.

"Bong bong bong ga bong bong," the smiling Vietnamese said, *"bong bong bong ga bong bong."* The man spoke Vietnamese with an orangutan accent.

"This is going to take a while," Guy told the captain.

"That's OK," Captain Haven replied. "I have several months to use up. Take all of it that you need."

The process of communicating with these Vietnamese took *much* longer than it had taken for Guy to communicate in Army language school with American college graduates. Compared to the American college graduates, these native Vietnamese seemed to be speaking a really horrible brand of Vietnamese. For one thing, it was too fast. One word just ran right into the next. And for another thing, these native Vietnamese tended not to use those familiar words that Guy's instructors had most frequently employed, such as "blackboard" and "eraser."

"We need some mechanically sound four-wheel-drive vehicles so we can get to the villages in our service area," the lead man said. *"Bong bong bong ga bong bong . . ."*

"They like our American cars," Guy eventually reported to Captain Haven.

"We learned by telephone this morning that two vehicles, International Scouts, are available in Saigon"—the lead Vietnamese tapped the map, and the other two tapped as well—"but we must have the vehicles driven up here to us in Hue . . ." He slid his finger up the map and tapped on Hue, and the other two did the same.

"There are two cars full of telephones in Saigon," Guy told Captain Haven. "They're trying to call us in Hue."

The head Vietnamese slid his fingers back and forth between Hue and Saigon. The other two tried to do the same, but he swept their hands away and shouted at them. Then he smiled and nodded at Guy, and began again to slide his finger back and forth along the slippery map track between Hue and Saigon.

"You Americans must drive the International Scouts to us here in Hue," the lead man said. "You ought to use Highway One."

"There is some kind of road between Saigon and Hue," Guy told Captain Haven.

"Yeah, so?" Captain Haven said. "What about it? That's Highway One. So what?"

"Say again?" Guy asked the head Vietnamese for the fourth time.

"We need you to drive the two International Scouts from Saigon to Hue," the head man said. *"Bong bong bong ga bong bong . . ."*

"Yes?"

"Bong bong bong ga bong bong . . ."

"Drive what?"

"Bong bong bong ga bong bong . . ."

"What about the *telephones*?"

"Bong bong bong ga bong bong . . ."

"Cars . . . drive . . . drive cars . . . down here . . . up here . . . from here to here . . . drive cars from here to here . . . your cars . . . International Scouts . . . drive International Scouts."

"Bong bong bong ga bong bong," the head man said happily, with exquisite, grandfatherly patience, smiling and nodding. *"What jerks these Americans are,"* he whispered to his friends, *"sending us German interpreters."*

"They need to have two International Scouts driven from Saigon to Hue," Guy proudly—and confidently—translated to Captain Haven.

"So what do they need us for?" Captain Haven asked. "They know the way, don't they? It's north, tell them, if they don't know."

"Bong bong bong ga bong bong?" Guy asked. He pointed to the head man's chest, spoke the Vietnamese word for *"you"*—or *"beehive"* if you pronounced the word the way Guy did—and made a pumping-circling motion with both hands, thereby pantomiming the unique mammalian behavior of using hands with opposable thumbs gripped to

an automobile steering wheel to navigate Highway One from Saigon to Hue.

"Hah, hah!" the head man laughed. "So funny. Number one funny!" He shook his head. *"Bong bong bong ga bong bong,"* he said. He bent over the map again, and put his finger on Saigon. His two friends bent over with him, fingers at the ready. He shot them each a look of doom, and they put their hands behind their backs.

"NVA here," the head man said, tapping. "Mines, ambushes, all here," he said, moving his finger and tapping every quarter inch. "VC here," he said. Tap tap. "Very bad here." He tapped firmly. "Worse here, much worse," he said. "More mines, more infantry. Very bad." Tap tap. Guy expected the man's finger to trip a mine any second, and get blown off the map. "All in all, a terrible journey," the man said, tapping Hue smartly with his closed fist.

"He says it's a dangerous trip," Guy told Captain Haven.

"Wish them luck," Captain Haven replied.

"Bong bong bong ga bong bong . . ." Guy tried to explain to the head man.

"Oh, no," the head man laughed, and so did his two friends. "We can't drive that road," he said. *"Bong bong bong ga bong bong,"* he explained. "We would never make it. You Americans put the International Scouts in Saigon. If we are to use them, you must drive them to us." He tapped Guy's heart-shaped 24 Corps shoulder patch. "You are military," the head man said, "you do."

"He says we could do the job better than they could," Guy told Captain Haven.

"Bullshit," Captain Haven said.

"You are American!" the head man—who understood the American word for bullshit—said angrily, and decisively, in Vietnamese. *They were American! It was no trouble for them to bring the International Scouts to Hue. Think how far they had brought them already!*

"I don't understand this, sir," Guy said dejectedly to his captain. "I don't understand this at all."

"You know," Gianelli interjected, "that's what Denehy used to say at this point in a conversation."

"Tell them to wait outside for a few minutes while we discuss the matter," Captain Haven said.

"Bong bong bong ga bong bong," Guy said, pointing to the door (meaning "outside"), then pointing to the head man (meaning "you"), then circling and pinching his right thumb and forefinger not quite together, intending to convey the concept of a small interval, a very minuscule delay, a little itty-bitty piece of time that the head man would have to wait.

Unfortunately—in the local hand-language dialect—Guy's pinching of fingers had just accused the stunned head man of being a poorly endowed, impotent sissy.

When the three Vietnamese had left—the struck-dumb, humiliated, and enraged head man having to be shoved out by his sympathetic friends—Haven and Gianelli applauded Lopaca on his fine job, told him that Denehy had never done any better, and offered him another cup of coffee, which was handed to him even though he refused the offer.

"When you finish drinking that, in ten or fifteen minutes, and not before," Captain Haven said, "go out there and tell those guys that we have already called our headquarters in Da Nang about their request. Tell them to check back with us in about a week and we'll let them know what arrangements are being made about those cars. You tell them that. Don't tell them a goddam thing more than that."

Guy slowly drank his coffee, and went into the hallway with the disappointing message. Despite Captain Haven's orders, Guy thought it was his duty to soften the message.

"Bong bong bong ga bong bong," Guy said. "Anything for our Vietnamese allies."

"I am strong as a bull elephant!" the furious head man replied bitterly.

"Bong bong bong ga bong bong," Guy said. "We will all work together," he assured them.

"Bong bong bong ga bong bong!" the insulted head man growled as he turned to leave. "Bend over and I will show you what makes the cow elephant bleat so loudly in the night!"

"Did you have any trouble?" Captain Haven asked as Guy reentered the office.

"No, it was great," Guy replied, "it should go like this all the time."

"And it probably will," Gianelli said. "By the way, Lopaca, do you know the Vietnamese words for fairy, homosexual, pansy, poof, fag, or queer?"

"No, I don't," Guy said.

"Well, you should learn them," Gianelli said. "Fast."

What Would We Do
without You?

The villagers of An Duong hamlet wanted a medical dispensary. The 5th Platoon was glad to help them build one and had just the sort of fine young Americans who could do the job. Gianelli drove the jeep, Lieutenant Frickleman rode next to him, and Guy Lopaca sat in the rear, checking each tree for snipers and wishing the machine-gun mount behind him had a machine gun on it, with a ruthless teenage Marine to shoot it.

After leaving The Villa they got on a road that shadowed the river for a mile or two, then veered off into a busy village, then onto a ragged pathlike road on which only a few people walked or rode bicycles. After a while the road became rather like a mere *notion* of a road as it passed through flat open spaces, some of it paddy land, some of it unimproved or abandoned. Guy noted the occasional round pit, where a bomb had fallen.

They passed a pair of slovenly men who seemed to be ARVN soldiers. The two men shouldered their rifles stock-to-rear, gripping the barrels, a disrespectful way to carry a weapon. Fifty yards down the road Guy began to wonder if they were targeting him. He squirmed anxiously but held fast to his courage and didn't look back. . . . Yes he did, he did look back. But, to his credit, he didn't look back twice.

After a few miles, Gianelli turned onto an even lesser wisp of a road and the land began to roll beneath them. The land first became wavy, like swells on a heavy ocean, and then became nearly mountainous. It was the perfect place for a hike, a picnic, or an ambush. It was also lovely, and as the jeep navigated the sinuous sandy stripe of road, Guy began to have fun. They were young men on a sunny jaunt in the open air, in a frisky topless automobile. Gianelli must have sensed it, too, because he crushed the accelerator and the jeep began to slide through bends and prance up hills. Lieutenant Frickleman laughed, and Guy Lopaca held on, wondering if this was the kind of fun he would be having every day, and whether shrapnel might someday sour the experience.

As they broke over the crest of a hill, Guy saw below him a narrow river serviced by a ferry. Guy's road and others equally rudimentary met at the ferry landings. The jeep drove down the hill, passed an ARVN guard sitting on a box, crossed over in the ferry, passed another guard sleeping in a hammock, and then headed into a dense, not-quite-jungle forest.

An Duong hamlet eventually appeared in front of them. They practically collided with it. One moment the jeep was whining through the forest, then suddenly they were skidding to a stop on the trampled margin of the village, and three skinny men who had been squatting nearby rose to wave and say hello.

They said hello in Vietnamese.

Frickleman turned to Guy Lopaca as the men approached. "What did they say?" Frickleman asked Guy.

"They said hello," Guy replied. Guy knew the men had said hello by their smiles, their nodding heads, their body language, and because of Guy's familiarity, as a fellow human being, with the universal practice of delivering a greeting to expected guests. But Guy had not recognized a single word they spoke, hello or otherwise. They could have said "go away or be killed" for all he knew.

"Find out who the head man is," Frickleman said as the Americans disembarked their jeep.

Guy mumbled at the men, who smiled and chattered back. Guy pointed to the Vietnamese elder who stood in front of the other two, and—guessing—Guy told Frickleman, "The head man is the one in front."

"Good, let's talk," Frickleman said.

"I'm going to look around for a while," Gianelli said.

"I wonder if anyone here speaks English or French," Lopaca said.

"I do," Gianelli said as he walked away.

They were at An Duong hamlet for only an hour. The head man and the rest of his committee showed Guy and the lieutenant every single hut and hovel in the village. *Damn* it would have been nice if Guy could remember a Vietnamese word for "house" or "building" or *anything* but "this thing here" or "that thing there" with all the pointing to this and the touching of that. Oh, wait, doesn't "hootch" mean "house"? Let's hope so.

Part of Guy's time was spent trying to adapt his ear to the native lingo. It was not simply tonal; it was a smorgasbord of twangs and clangs and clucks and *sproings,* as if they had broken Jews' harps for vocal cords.

It took several minutes just to introduce themselves.

"This is Lieutenant Frickleman," Guy said in Vietnamese, tugging the lieutenant's sleeve. "*Bong bong bong ga bong bong.* And my name is Guy Lopaca. *Bong bong bong ga bong bong.*"

"Ah, Ferick-El-Mon," the head fellow said with a nod to the lieutenant. "Ah, Low-Par-Car," he said to Guy.

Then touching his own breast the head man said to Guy proudly, *"Bong bong bong ga bong bong."* Turning to the assistants on his left and right, the head man explained to Guy that *"bong bong bong ga bong bong,"* and *"bong bong bong ga bong bong."*

The man might as well have been speaking Laotian, or Sperm Whale. Just when Guy had given up all hope of communicating with the men in Vietnamese, they patiently taught him how to do it. The process required that they frequently grab hold of him, usually at the wrist or elbow, and tug him sharply up or down. It also required laborious repetition:

"Bong ga bong bong."

"Bong ga bong *bong."*

"Ga booong *bong."*

"Ga booooooooong *bong!"*

After about a half hour, Guy finally realized that the head man was disappointed because the Americans had not brought his new pigs. A few minutes later the head man finally realized that today the Americans had come not to supply livestock but to *plan the medical clinic*—the "sick hootch," or "not-dead-house."

The head man—who was a pig specialist—smiled, bowed, and walked away, to be replaced exactly where he had stood by his second-in-command—a not-dead-house designer—who smiled, nodded, and brought them to a patch of bare ground, into which he drove four stakes, and said *"bong bong bong ga bong bong"* as he pointed to what might someday become a medical-clinic floor, or perhaps a lettuce garden.

Captain Haven had sent the Americans to An Duong to get some idea of the material requirements for the dispensary project. Guy kept the two Vietnamese busy conjuring walls and doors and windows—simple Vietnamese words that Guy had actually learned once and might remember some day—while the lieutenant kept prodding Guy to translate ornate, philosophical questions salted with obscure, unimaginable concepts, like "cement" and "nails."

Just when Frickleman was beginning to get impatient, Gianelli walked around the corner of a hootch whistling, accompanied by a weathered young peasant woman in dirty pajamas whose hair fell in two ragged pigtails to her waist.

"It's getting late," Gianelli said. He walked up to the lieutenant and gave him a few sheets of paper.

"Here's a rough floor plan of the layout," Gianelli said, "and a list of the materials they need to get started. The most important things are cement, concrete blocks, washed sand, and corrugated steel for the roof. The size of the clinic they build will depend on how much we can give them." He headed for the jeep.

"In other words," Gianelli said, "it's just like every other medical clinic I've ever built." He got in the jeep and started it. The girl got in back.

"She needs a ride to Hue," Gianelli explained.

Frickleman shook hands with the two village elders, and stepped into the jeep. His uncomfortable American interpreter got in back with the Vietnamese girl. Guy felt that he was sitting much too close to the dark-skinned young woman with the ugly teeth and perky breasts, and a scar above her left eye.

"Chào Cô," Guy Lopaca said, delivering a well-crafted greeting with elegant situational propriety, hoping that it meant "hello or good-bye, young probably unmarried sister-girl with no children."

The Vietnamese village girl squinted at his name tag and then at the insignia on his sleeve.

"Hello, Specialist Lopaca," she said in lilting English. "Are you feeling well today? Did you enjoy your visit?"

Before putting the jeep in gear, Gianelli turned to Guy and patted him on the head.

"Don't know what we'd do without you," Gianelli said.

Paul and Tyler

Paul Gianelli had come to the 5th Platoon in Hue by way of Tan Son Nhut, Da Nang, and a broken heart. He had been a young business student at a small New York college when his girlfriend began upwardly dating a boy whose family had more money in the bank and fewer vowels in their name. Crushed and despondent, Gianelli left school and signed up for what became an indeterminate hitch in the Army.

While his Army career was still fresh, his mother sent Paul a letter in which she related the sad story of his former love. The girl had "somehow" gotten pregnant by her popular blond quarterback, whose dad threw together a lavish wedding that was over in time for the football season. In the first game, the groom—distracted by the thought of being married forever to someone who did *not* look like one of those cheerleaders over there—turned the wrong way, and got thrown to the ground by a lineman who never would have touched the quarterback when he was single, light-footed, and never got enough sleep at night.

"It's so tragic," Paul's mother wrote. "There she is with a baby on the way, and her husband paralyzed in a hospital bed, staring at the ceiling, neck broken, can't feel or move anything below his chin. Poor girl, things have gone so bad for her so quickly."

Having read this, Gianelli's careworn face began to sport a twinkly smile, and he credited the reorientation of the universe—in his direction—to his unexpected decision to join the Army. He decided he would stay in the Army as long as interesting things continued to happen in his life.

Because at that time the most interesting thing happening in the Army's life was Vietnam, Paul volunteered to go there; then he volunteered to stay there; and when he came back home, he volunteered to go there again. And so on.

Meanwhile, on his former girlfriend's wedding anniversary, Gianelli anonymously sent her a box of starch. "She's too stupid to get it right away," he told his old friends. "She'll have to think a long time before she gets it. That's how lucky I am that she jilted me."

None of his friends got it either.

• • •

It became Paul's great goal in life to be untouched by the fear of adversity. The trick, he decided, was not to evade the possible hazards of life, but to be more mockingly perverse than fate itself. "Don't take me seriously," he would caution new guys. "God is my straight man. He sets you up, and I knock you over."

Whenever anyone left Vietnam, for a temporary holiday or permanent rotation home, Gianelli shook the man's hand, slapped him on the back, and called to him as he walked away: "I hope you're killed instantly when your plane goes down, before those sharks have a chance to eat you. You're a nice guy and if anyone deserves a painless death, it's you."

His smile was so bright and his humor so transcendent that people who knew him superficially thought there was nothing in him but the evil elf, the jokester with the big nose and the comical handlebar mustache. It took some time for you to notice how often he drove into the bushes alone, risking his life when no one was around to join the fun. When you asked him why he did it, he was shy. He didn't want to explain that part about himself, and he didn't want to joke about it either.

"I'm a Civil Affairs advisor," he once confided to Guy Lopaca, "and an audience sometimes gets in the way. Every once in a while I do the job they ask me to do. Someday I'll leave Vietnam and never come back. When I do, I want to remember that some of the time I wasn't an asshole."

• • •

Gianelli's closest friend in Hue was Tyler DeMudge.

There were many things in DeMudge's life that he didn't like. Given the chance, he would list them for you: "Republicans, low-calorie diets, claymore mines, insubordinate waiters . . ." His list of unsatisfactory phenomena was endless: "cats, the *New York Review of Books* until I am featured there, Democrats, the blue balls I get at the end of my standard date with a nice girl . . ."

While many things offended Tyler, nothing ever really seemed to defeat him. Tyler acted as if the good things in life would come soon and last forever, and the bad things were merely preliminary to something else. *"It's good training,"* he would say in the face of any misfortune. It was an old Army saying that suited him well.

Ordered one day to go on a waste-disposal detail, Tyler reminded the ill-tempered man working with him that it was "good training for you, in case your civilian career involves burning tons of shit with gasoline."

When a fellow in basic training grumbled angrily about having to wade in a stagnant lake to retrieve a careless officer's binoculars, Tyler assured the wet, smelly draftee that the experience "was good training for you, in case you ever have to jump in a swamp full of leeches and typhus bugs *again*. Which, you know, could happen, and now you are prepared for it."

No matter how bad things got, DeMudge could make the awful experience you had already been through seem bearable—while at the same time inciting fear that it could possibly get worse.

When two shaken men at a nearby base described hiding under their bunks as the compound took hits from three enemy rockets, Tyler bought them drinks and told them it was all "good training, very good training" for them, which would really help some day, "when the VC get their *supply problems* straightened out and have enough rockets to lay down a nice tight *pattern*."

He absorbed his own heartbreak the same way. Tyler got a letter one day from his fiancée in Portland, Oregon. "I'm having second thoughts," she wrote. "I'm not sure anymore that getting married is the right thing to do. I'm not sure you and I are the right fit." DeMudge's response was immediate:

"Being married to me will be very good training for you," DeMudge wrote. "When the *right* man finally comes along, you'll be ready to give him everything he needs. . . ."

Perhaps the fact that both men had been jilted by their hometown sweeties explained in part why Paul Gianelli and Tyler DeMudge had become so attached to each other. "I know *Paul* isn't going to leave me for some second-year law student," Tyler confided once, "as long as I own the enlisted men's refrigerator."

DeMudge was the most intellectual of the 5th Platoon's unusually cerebral group of enlisted men. His mail was composed largely of boxes full of paperback books, some of which he ordered himself, others of which were sent to him by college friends and professors. An art history graduate, DeMudge nearly always found time in his job to make pilgrimages to local temples and assorted public ruins.

"No one works in stone around here," he would grouse. "They use cement, and bad cement at that. I think all the cement work was jobbed out to Mafia contractors. Look at this mess," he would say, using his fingers to tear away part of a crumbling house of worship only forty or fifty years old. "This is the worst concrete work I've ever seen in a public place. Christ! At least the Romans *tried* to make things last. We should let the Army Corps of Engineers rebuild all the temples, and the Joint Chiefs should hire the Mafia to assassinate the Vietcong. I think that makes financial sense, by the way."

It shocked DeMudge's sensibility as a historian that many of the people in Vietnam were older than its relics. At a musty hillside temple, DeMudge was being shown around by a young man who acted as tour guide for the price of a pack of cigarettes, and could fix Tyler up with a younger sister for the price of a carton. Tyler was inspecting a pockmarked fresco, apparently ancient, and asked the young man "how old?" in Vietnamese.

"Oh, very old," the boy replied. "Nineteen-oh-seven."

"What? My *mother's* older than that!" Tyler shouted, and stalked back to the truck. "She's in better *shape,* too," he yelled as he drove away.

It was the French, Tyler decided. They were to blame for screwing up the country in every way possible. In an agrarian society where the average person slept under a roof made of indigenous plants, on a floor made of indigenous dirt, the French had somehow convinced the population in dozens, perhaps hundreds of backward villages to build a cathedral-like concrete church, with a spire that reached in crumbly gray majesty to the sky, until the Vietminh or the Vietcong or a seasonal storm tumbled the spire down onto the main body of the church, turning it into another ruined recent relic for DeMudge to spew and sputter over.

"I swear if you open the cornerstone on that falling-down temple up near the Montagnard village," Tyler told Gianelli one day, "you'll find some Château Musilly and a pack of Gauloises. There are Hollywood *movie sets* that have lasted longer than the public buildings the French left in Vietnam."

If DeMudge was disgusted with the oh-so-recent ancient architecture of Vietnam, it was nothing compared to his opinion of Vietnamese wartime art.

"The best black velvet painting I've seen since Mexico," he would say.

His collection of black velvet was amazing. He kept a dozen portraits in The Hootch. He would flip through his gallery any time a stranger expressed the slightest interest. "I have them organized by breast size," he would explain, "from the simply enormous on one end all the way up to this one here . . ." And the stranger would agree that he had never seen anything like *those* on any Vietnamese woman.

Every few weeks DeMudge would work up a good martini high and show off his collection at the Enlisted Men's Club.

"I know you guys don't see ladies like this on the street," he would lecture the men as he pointed out the lecherous artistic choices that made the paintings so fascinating, "but that's because ladies like this exist only in mythology. Look at the eyebrows, look at the lips. . . . All right, look at the breasts, too, they're hard to miss.

"The important thing is not that you can't date real women like this *yet* . . ." As he said the word "yet" there was a hush in the room. "The important thing is that some of the downtown girls are actually trying to look like this already. Right now it's only a matter of lots of mascara and plenty of stuffing, but you wait. If the war lasts long enough for evolution to kick in, I predict their gene pool will catch up with their black velvet paintings, and you will have the kind of top-heavy, google-eyed women you seem to *want* . . .

"Personally, I prefer Natalie Wood," he would say, flipping to a black velvet painting of Natalie Wood, which Tyler had paid a local artist to make from magazine clippings. "You will notice that Natalie's breasts appear no larger in this black velvet painting than they do in real life," he would point out proudly.

All the men assured Tyler that Natalie's breasts were big enough. It was the least the men could do. It made Tyler happy, and he was buying the drinks until the lecture was over.

Methods of
Peanut Farming

For Guy Lopaca and Lieutenant Rossi, the closest thing to a "regular beat" would be the Montagnard village in Nam Hoa district.

"When the Vietnamese get kicked off their land," Captain Haven explained, "the first thing they do is look for some Montagnards and do some kicking of their own. What you will see at Nam Hoa is what happens when an entire Montagnard village is suddenly uprooted, loaded on trucks, and dumped on an open hillside. They had no homes, no raw materials to build homes, and no money. Until we came along, they had nothing. Believe it or not, people still tried to kill them. They had their first attack before they had their first hootch."

"What are we going to do out there?" Lieutenant Rossi asked.

"It's already been started," Captain Haven said. "We've sort of adopted the village. Our excuse is that we're running a demonstration farm, and that's true. We're helping them plant corn, peanuts, watermelon, and beans. We provide them with seed, some hand tools, fertilizer and insecticide, spray cans, and advice. Whatever they need, but really simple stuff, nothing that runs on gas or electricity. Cheap and simple. Eventually you'll help them dig a well or two and improve the irrigation."

Captain Haven let them soak it in. He knew what they were thinking: Help them dig a well? Jeepers, how hard can that be? Look, there, it's called The Earth. . . . *Put a frigging hole in it!*

"We get involved in some nonfarming things as well," Captain Haven said. "Most of the hootches out there were built with scrap lumber we provided. We've gotten them some ammunition for their old guns, so they can protect themselves. They'll need protection even more if the farm starts to produce any food. Maybe just going out there two or three days a week is the most important thing we do, because it makes it less likely that the Vietnamese will send the trucks again and haul them out. The Montagnards need a rest."

"Is there any kind of organization out there?" Lieutenant Rossi asked. "How do we deal with them?"

"You talk to Mr. Hoa," Captain Haven said. "You'll meet him when you get there. Shaggy green hat and a World War II officer's carbine. He's on our payroll. He may be the only man in the village on any kind of payroll. He speaks Vietnamese and a little English, which made him the only candidate for the job. We brought him down to Da Nang for some training. When he went back, we let him go in with a load of supplies, and that did the trick. Water buckets, clothing, sprayers that you pump up, lots of little stuff. We let him control it all, to establish his authority. The big deal was the tractor. He came up the road standing on a tractor, waving his hat. The whole village came out in a crowd. The tractor cut out the land for the demonstration plots. Mr. Hoa has been the boss ever since. Whatever he says the tribe does."

• • •

Lieutenant Gunnar Rossi looked like a California surfer. He was trained to be a woodsman.

"I grow *trees,*" he complained during his first visit to Nam Hoa with Guy. "I'm supposed to be growing a mountain full of *trees* in some forest in Oregon or Washington. Do you know how many years I spent learning about *trees*? I've been studying trees since my first science fair." He sighed. "Now look at me." He waved at a demonstration plot of barren rusty earth. "Peanuts," Rossi said, "I can't believe it."

Guy Lopaca tried to help. "At least you're growing something," he said. "You're just scaled down a little."

"Have you ever seen a tree?" Lieutenant Rossi asked. "Do you think of peanut plants as scaled-down trees?" With the toe of a boot he touched a dry clod of soil, which crumbled into a tiny cloud of dust.

Rossi pulled a small pamphlet out of a pocket and thumbed it disconsolately. Guy caught the title: *Methods of Peanut Farming,* by Professor Ông Ba Tên.

"What's that?" Guy asked.

"Officer crap," Lieutenant Rossi replied.

"Oh," Guy said, happy to know that officers had crap of their own.

"Did you know that Vietnam has a lumber industry?" Rossi asked. "They do. It's in trouble now, not just because of the usual wartime disruption, but also because"—he stomped on half a dozen desiccated clumps of earth—"the bombs and artillery shells fill the trees with shrapnel, and when the tree trunks get run through a lumber mill's band saw the blades get ripped to pieces."

Lieutenant Rossi jumped up and down on the arid earth, ferociously stomping it with both feet.

"I could be helping out with their forestry problem," he grunted as he angrily smashed the ground, "but the Army probably brought over a *peanut* farmer to do *that.*"

•   •   •

While Rossi was having his soil-thrashing tantrum, Mr. Hoa stood off at the margin of the demonstration farm and tried to calm the fears of his village brain trust. "It's a ritual," he assured the other four Montagnards who helped him administer the farming program. "The new officer is marking his territory, as a dog does by urinating," Mr. Hoa said authoritatively. "The new officer is striking at the earth with his feet to prove his mastery over the plants and insects that grow in it. Later, in privacy, he will show some humility before his god."

The men did not seem convinced.

"We are *lucky* to have an officer with so much spirit," Mr. Hoa argued. "Look at how vigorously he is stomping on those weeds."

A couple of them nodded. That was enough for Mr. Hoa. He had a clear majority. Screw the other two.

He invited his friends to leave him alone to bond with the new Americans, and suggested that a little tea be prepared for a general caucus later. They would have to find some women to attend to the tea. It was a woman's job to prepare tea for men. Ordinarily, when there are tea leaves, the job is not very difficult. They asked Mr. Hoa to give them . . . oh, half an hour to see if they could find some tea leaves.

"If we can't find any tea leaves," one man asked Mr. Hoa, "do you think the Americans would chew some betel with us?"

"I doubt that," Mr. Hoa said. "If you can't find tea leaves, boil any leafy thing there is. They won't know the difference."

Mr. Hoa walked over to the Americans and renewed the acquaintance they had made just a few minutes before.

"So are you satisfied with our demonstration farm?" Mr. Hoa asked in Montagnard-tainted Vietnamese. "*Bock bock bock ga bock bock?* We have done everything the other soldiers have told us to do. *Bock bock bock ga bock bock.*"

"*Bong bong bong ga bong bong,*" Guy Lopaca said. "Please speak Vietnamese."

Mr. Hoa shook his head. *How did these ignorant men ever beat their Indians? If the Bru Tribe had horses, there would be no stopping us. Horses and, oh, seven or eight helicopters.*

Over the next half hour, Mr. Hoa and Guy Lopaca worked out the complicated protocols that would govern all their subsequent communications. Gradually, Guy learned that it was possible to communicate with a Montagnard, as long as both men said everything four times, including sign language.

"Hello, Mr. Hoa, how are you feeling?" Guy said, as a test of the method. "*Chào ông Hoa, ông mạnh giỏi khong? Bonjour, Monsieur Hoa, comment allez-vouz?*" Wave hand, pat stomach, pat heart, look concerned about health.

Mr. Hoa smiled and responded in kind: "Hello, Lowparker, I number one. *Bock bock bock ga bock bock. Bum jur, Miss Lowparker, jur see bum.*" Wave hand, pat stomach, pat heart, hold up one finger.

In this way, with some patience, Guy managed to ask Mr. Hoa how he was feeling, and Mr. Hoa succeeded in replying that he felt fine.

"I think it's going to work," Guy finally reported to Lieutenant Rossi, having taken thirty minutes to translate the two most popular sentences human beings have ever spoken to each other.

"Good, great," Rossi said. "Now ask him how many pounds of Amophosko fertilizer he needs. And when was the last time they sampled the soil's acidity?"

It was a long first day in Nam Hoa.

Virgin Mary

They called her "Virgin Mary" because her price was so damn high. She had a code of professional conduct that she followed religiously. She never slept with more than one man at a time, and never more than one per night. She never permitted her men to use any mechanical device except a condom, which she supplied to every one of them. She never slept with the same man twice in any calendar month. She never slept with any paying customer more than three times ever.

She never bargained her price, which everyone knew and no one contested. She charged each man, regardless of rank, one half of his month's base pay, and she knew what it was because she was a soldier herself.

She never slept with a drunk, nor with any man who was unsociably high on drugs. She preferred but never demanded payment in advance. The men knew that she would wait until the next monthly payday—but no longer—and no man was made to feel small if he were short on cash when he spent his time with her.

Mary was no knockout, but she knew the law of supply and demand. The demand for round-eyed girls was high, for American girls even higher and for American blondes there was almost no limit. She qualified on two counts by nature and on the third by rinse. She had no local competition in the American Blond Girl category. Her body was topographically interesting, with a more or less uniform viscosity.

"Look, I'm no fool," she once told one of her pals. "I know who I am and I know where I fit. No one who spent the night with me ever stopped dreaming of the girl back home."

Guy had known about Virgin Mary for a month before they said their first words to each other. Like every other American male, he had watched her in the mess hall, in the PX, or in passing within The Hotel grounds. Most often he had seen her in the evening, at the Enlisted Men's Club. She was the only woman allowed in The Club after the 7:00 o'clock males-only curfew. And she was an officer, too, so she could have been excluded on both counts. But she was welcome everywhere. She was an Army nurse by day, a working girl by night, and a good one to have at a table full of beers anytime at all.

She visited the EM Club at least a couple of times a week, and Mary's table was always full. In addition to regular troopers who were her friends, there were always hustlers around her. Guy noticed that some of the men laughed harder than she did, or laughed at jokes that had no punch lines. Those men thought they could catch her with their charm instead of their money.

It was interesting the way men were drawn to her. She was kind of pudgy, and although she had a nice, pleasant face and there was heft in the right places where her uniform bulged, she was not a great beauty by any means. She was the girl next door, ten thousand miles from the old neighborhood, and that made her special. She might not have been the one perfect girl a young man was longing for, but she could have been the one perfect girl's older sister.

One night as Guy watched Mary from across the room she looked up suddenly and stared at him, her eyes narrow and dark. She stood up and walked toward Guy without changing her grim expression. Grabbing the back of the chair across from his, she leaned over the table at Guy and said, "Mind if I sit down?" in the same voice any strange woman would use when asking to stick a knife in his heart six or seven times.

"Sure, sit down," Guy said, startled. He had not tried to attract her attention. The four men whose table she had left were silently watching Guy, and they did not seem very pleased.

Mary sat down and put her chin in her hand. Her dark eyes stared at him. No, wait, they were blue eyes. They just appeared to be dark because there was some anger in them.

"What are you writing?" she asked.

"A letter," Guy said.

"How do I figure in it?" she asked.

When Lopaca couldn't think of anything to say, she went on.

"I've been watching you. You've been watching me. Why do you think I'm so fascinating?"

Her eyes moved away from his eyes, down to his pad lying on the table.

Without thinking, Guy pushed the pad toward her. That caught her by surprise; he could tell by the way her face softened, then set again but not so hard as before.

She didn't touch the pad, but read the half-filled page where it lay. Then coolly, and without reluctance, she picked up the pad and read the letter Guy had been writing. She read it from the first page straight through to the end. When she had finished reading it, she took a sip of Guy's beer, and read the letter again entirely.

"That's a pretty good letter," Mary said. "I wouldn't mind getting a letter like that. Who's it going to?"

"The girl back home," Guy said.

"I thought you were writing about me," Mary said.

"I wasn't," Guy said.

"I can see that," she said. "I thought you were. It was a feeling I got from the way you were watching me. As if you were taking notes. Not just tonight. Other nights."

"Well, I wasn't trying to bother you," Guy said. "It's a small room. There's not a lot of interesting things in it."

"You think I'm an interesting thing?" Mary asked.

"No, I think you're interesting."

"Not a thing?"

"No, not a thing. I think you seem to be an interesting person."

"Not like I was some kind of bug under a microscope, a specimen, that kind of thing?"

"No," Guy said. "Is there some way we can get past this *thing* thing?"

"Sure," Mary said. "We're past it already."

"Well . . ." Guy paused. Then he stuck out his hand. "I'm Guy Lopaca."

"My name is Mary after my shift ends," she said, taking the hand and giving it a single shake. "On duty they call me Lieutenant Crocker. If we're lucky, you may never use the name Crocker again."

"I haven't used it yet," Guy said.

"You're sharp," Mary said. "Are you the kind that doesn't like it when a girl gets sharp back at you?"

"I can tolerate it," Guy said.

"We'll see," Mary said. She spun the pad in a circle.

"So that's a nice letter you're writing to the girl back home," Mary said. "Does she write nice letters back?"

"So far she does. It's still early in my tour, though."

"They always write back for the first few weeks," Mary said. "By now the guys she said no to the first time are asking her again. Do you mind if I say that?"

"I don't mind if you say that," Guy replied. "I guess I'm more concerned about how I'll react . . . oh . . . two or three hours from now, when it sinks in."

One of the men from Mary's table came over and reminded her that she had a beer waiting, and it was getting warm.

"I'll be right there," Mary said. "This Lopaca hasn't even offered me a beer, so there's no use staying here."

"Do you want a beer?" Guy asked. The GI shot him a look.

"Nah," Mary said. "You go ahead and finish your letter to the girl back home. I've already kept you from her long enough. We don't want to make her jealous."

Mary stood up.

"Not yet, anyway," she said.

Guy watched her walk back to the table. When she got there, she shooed a GI out of his chair and sat down with her back to Guy, so he couldn't use his microscope to its full advantage for the rest of the night. There wasn't much to watch but the tilt of her head, and the faces of the men around her. After about half an hour, she got up and left with one of the men. She left without glancing in Guy's direction.

After she left, Guy went back to writing his letter. Before she left, he had run out of things to say.

Historical Parallels

Dear Professor Aranow:

Here I am in Vietnam, doing my part to safeguard an important parallel—I think there is one—which divides North Vietnam from South Vietnam. And I am remembering that old saying about people who forget history being doomed to repeat it.

It's hard not to think about history right now. In fact it's impossible to avoid thinking about important historical things like Asian parallels.

As I sit here drinking my cold soda and eating my greasy hamburger that may or may not be made of meat, all I can think about is that Vietnam-splitting parallel up there to the north, looming over me like some kind of heavy girder, which if we let it fall will come swooping down and straightedge me, like a squeegee on a window—pardon my confusion of imagery—until I get swept in pieces into the Pacific Ocean.

That's quite some important parallel they have up there, and I hope it stays stuck right where it is, and never moves or gets compromised in any way.

Did I mention that this club I am in is run by South Koreans? I forgot to mention that? Well, now you can understand why all I can think about is frigging parallels and doomed histories repeating themselves.

Yes, we have a club on the base that is run by South Koreans. The Koreans have a pretty big presence in the war, people say. All I know is that their soldiers look mean and their club is a mess. They sell us American soda and South Korean ice. The soda is served in the original American cans, and the ice is brown. They charge ten cents more for a can of soda than we pay if we buy it in our own club—but our club is temporarily shut down again, so we have to cope with South Korean profit margins, which we probably taught them.

If Notre Dame had a football team in Asia, Koreans would get all the scholarships. They're that big. The Korean troops seem to live in a world apart, aloof from Vietnamese and Americans alike. The Vietnamese chatter and flutter about and seem constantly in haste to do something other than what they are already doing. The Koreans move without haste or bother, as if they are always going somewhere pleasant, and are ahead of schedule. They have the eyes of predators who have just fed well; and they have a reputation for being tenacious in battle. I used to worry about night assaults and rocket attacks. I think I should spend more time worrying about these Koreans. They look like they could stab you in the eye without changing their expression, or, in fact, even their mood.

So now you can understand, with all these lethal Koreans around here, why it's impossible for me to avoid thinking about historical things like Asian parallels.

We kept that Korean parallel stuck tight for the South Koreans, and now they're helping us keep the Vietnamese parallel up there where it belongs, way to the north of me, while the Koreans make a very nice profit selling us our own soda.

Oh, I just started thinking that we might not have a "parallel" situation here in Vietnam at all. We might have only a demilitarized "zone." That doesn't sound nearly so good. A "parallel" seems way more certain and reliable than a "zone." Everyone on the planet recognizes parallels. Parallels are on all the globes and in all the atlases. Just try to move a parallel a few miles north or south. You can't do it. They won't let you touch a parallel. No one cares about a crummy "zone." You don't see transitory things like "zones" being chiseled onto all the globes. If there has to be something between me and all those North Vietnamese, I would rather have a "parallel" than a "zone" any day.

I'm thinking it's time that America got its own parallel. Maybe that's why the Civil War turned out so poorly. All they had was the stupid Mason-Dixon "line." They should have had a real parallel. That's the trouble with history. You can never find a parallel when you need one.

Best regards,
ARTHUR GRISSOM, B.A., M.A. (*someday*)

Many Sand at Phu Bai

Captain Haven had a theory—universally praised by the enlisted men because *it made sense, can you believe it?*—that each linguist ought to be "attached" to particular Civil Affairs efforts, rather than used indiscriminately. Captain Haven realized the interpreters would adapt to their jobs more rapidly if each was immersed in his own specific field. Whereas Guy Lopaca might have to recognize Duroc and Yorkshire hogs, know their names in Vietnamese, and translate their illnesses and medicines, Tyler DeMudge could occupy his estimable brain learning the Vietnamese term for volleyball ("va-li-bal") and, of course, looking for imaginary volleyballs.

Captain Haven let Tyler run Youth Services his own way because there had never been any complaints. As the only American assigned to Youth Services, Tyler was responsible for transmitting complaints. According to Tyler, no one had ever complained about his failure to transmit complaints.

Tyler was an easygoing, brilliant, bookish kind of guy who had found within the Army a position whose duties never required him to be late for supper.

. . .

Tyler DeMudge's current assignment was to deliver washed sand to a local school-construction project. Tyler needed help, and—because Paul Gianelli was passing Captain Haven's office at the wrong time— Paul was asked to drive one of the two-and-a-half-ton trucks that Tyler's civilian workforce would load and unload.

No one in the 5th Platoon ever questioned why American soldiers should drive Vietnamese sand or rice or other bulk cargo from one place in Vietnam to another. No Vietnamese civilian chief with a load of rice seed or lime to deliver would think twice about having six or seven of his idle men call Captain Haven to get a Whiffenpoof from Yale to drive the truck all by himself.

To the men in the 5th Platoon, it was just assumed that the job of hauling Vietnamese bags or blocks or buckets was important enough for American soldiers to be doing, "Because if it's not," DeMudge once pointed out, "they'll find something *more* important for us to do, and who the hell knows what *that* will be? I'm sure they don't."

. . .

"We just have to pick up our workers at The Citadel," Tyler said, as he climbed into the lead truck, "and then we'll go to Phu Bai to get the sand." Paul fired up the second truck and stayed close on Tyler's tail as the two big monsters grumbled and wailed over the bridge and through the busy part of town. They parked on the lot at the Youth Services office, and Tyler went to look for their crew. After a few minutes he came back with six young men, an older man, and a frown.

"I thought we were going to Phu Bai to pick up the sand," Tyler said. "For a week they've been telling me our sand was at Phu Bai. Now this guy says it's somewhere else."

Tyler shook his head and started chattering with the older man, who smiled and nodded to show that everything was absolutely all right, couldn't be better, while he disagreed with everything Tyler said.

"Not Phu Bai," he told Tyler. "Sand not at Phu Bai."

The more frustration Tyler exhibited, the more the crew chief added brightness to his smile, and energy to his nodding, until he seemed to be the happiest person in the world.

"I take you to sand," the crew chief said, smiling, "I show you." He smiled wonderfully.

Tyler frowned some more and ran his hands through the sweaty hair that he wore much too long under his bush hat.

"I don't like this," Tyler said. "There are mountains of washed sand at Phu Bai. Now this guy tells me we have to go somewhere else. This is screwy. You've seen the sand at Phu Bai. The piles are huge. British Lords fly in on expeditions to climb those Phu Bai sand piles and plant flags at the top of them. Am I wrong?"

"You know," Gianelli said to Tyler, "the sand in this parking lot is looking pretty good to me right now. Why don't we scrape it all down about a foot and get this over with."

"Personally," Tyler said, "I'm thinking that maybe this is a good time for us to go look for more volleyballs. I have found some good places to look for volleyballs, you know."

Tyler chatted brusquely with the leader of the work crew, and the two of them went walking off together to the Youth Services office. The six young workers found some shade and squatted in a group, talking and smoking hand-rolled cigarettes.

When Tyler came back, he wasn't happy.

"Captain Haven says we have to go," he told Paul. That was all he said.

The work crew climbed into the back of Tyler's truck, and the crew leader rode in the cab beside Tyler. Paul followed, alone and lonely.

They drove out of The Citadel, back across the river, out into the wilderness, for more than an hour. The six young men in the back of Tyler's truck talked and smoked and glowered back at Paul, who noticed for the first time that none of the work crew had smiled since the moment he saw them. Maybe they were Cambodian.

After traveling for a long time on the crudest of roads, the crew chief waved them down something that wasn't a road at all. Tyler shouted and ran his hands through his hair, while the crew chief smiled and nodded happily to show that everything was fine, absolutely fine, and would be even better once Tyler had propelled his vehicle down that narrow, dark, tree-and-shrub-enveloped pathway to hell.

Tyler looked back at Paul and shrugged. Before Paul had a chance to register his refusal, Tyler let out the clutch and heaved his truck into the woods. Gianelli followed.

There was no road. There was only a sandy rut which, like a carpenter's chalk mark, they used as a guide as they bulldozed a tunnel through the forest. For fifteen or twenty minutes, the coughs and growls of the truck engines competed for dominance with the sound of leaves ripping, branches breaking, and shattered tree trunks being knocked down or uprooted. The racket ended suddenly when Tyler's truck broke through the edge of the forest onto a wide, dusty plane on which was situated something that appeared to be an abandoned factory.

The crew chief directed them around the big building to where the front door would have hung, had the building still contained doors and windows. The chief and the two Americans got out of their trucks while the work crew stayed where they were, in the shade under the canvas canopy.

Gianelli was impressed with the flatness of the broad plane upon which the abandoned factory was situated. The flatness of the plane was accentuated by the fact that it was so flat. *And by that I mean,* Gianelli told himself sadly, *there are no big piles of sand on it.*

The crew chief stood next to the truck with his hands on his hips and chattered loudly into the air. He walked around the truck and surveyed the flat, dry land on which no sand piles bloomed. He smiled and nodded joyfully at Tyler and Paul, assuring them that everything was fine, absolutely grand, no doubt about it. Then he went to the back of Tyler's truck and started yelling at the work crew, who looked back at him with the deadpan disregard of men whose station in life was so low that nothing was ever their fault.

The crew chief walked off a few meters, and stood by himself, chattering angrily and slapping his floppy hat against his knee. Eventually, he turned around and started back toward Tyler, an expression of meaningful joy on his face, assuring the world that everything was indeed fine, couldn't possibly be better. . . . Then he stopped dead still, the smile vanished, and he stared with an open mouth beyond the trucks, toward the factory.

A Vietnamese who looked about thirty years old was standing in the doorless doorway. He was smoking a cigarette. The stranger's black hair was long, tied straight up but allowed to spray wildly at the top, like a sheaf of straw that had been hit by a mallet. He was wearing a uniform of loose black shirt and loose black pants. He took a few casual steps, sliding his sandals in the dirt. He shouted two words to the crew chief.

The crew chief hurried to him. The crew chief said a few words, after bowing deeply. The stranger said nothing, just jerked his head to the side in the direction of the trucks and the two Americans. The crew chief quickly returned and spoke to Tyler.

"Pop-lar foss," the crew chief said, pointing to the stranger. Then he whispered loudly to Paul, *"Pop-lar foss."*

Turning back to Tyler, the crew chief said, "You stay. I take care." He had reserved his merriest smile for moments just like this one. A smile like that could cause brownouts in regional power systems.

In Vietnam, they used to say, the dead sometimes smile so that the living doubt the wisdom of survival. Or maybe they used to say that somewhere else. It applied to the Vietnamese in any case, whether they said it there or not. . . . *That doesn't make any sense,* Paul Gianelli thought, but he thought it anyway.

The maniacally smiling crew chief walked quickly back to the stranger, put his shaggy hat on, then took it off again, and squatted down for a conversation. The stranger didn't move at first, but then reluctantly squatted down himself, and the two men began to talk. Soon after they started talking, two more Vietnamese, much younger than the stranger, came out of the building and squatted on each side of the doorway, diffidently watching the scene play out. Although all three of the men in black wore ammunition pouches, none of them carried a weapon.

Tyler DeMudge moved slowly close to Gianelli and put his hand on Paul's shoulder.

"Our crew chief says these guys are Popular Force," Tyler whispered, squeezing Paul's collar bone. "I'm willing to believe that if you are."

"Don't let me stop you," Paul whispered. "By the way, Popular Force soldiers do wear black uniforms, don't they?"

"Absolutely," Tyler whispered, "they do wear black uniforms. Although I think they also wear brown uniforms," he continued. "In fact I wonder if they don't wear *only* brown uniforms."

"No, as usual you're wrong," Gianelli whispered. "They sometimes wear black uniforms. Just like those." He nodded slightly. "And they don't wear any insignia. Just like those guys."

"I'm willing to believe that if you are," Tyler whispered forlornly.

"That fellow is either the most impressive Popular Force soldier I have ever seen," Paul replied, "or he is a VC field marshal."

"What are we going to do?" Tyler asked.

"I don't know," Paul replied, "but I think picking up a load of sand here is now completely out of the question. Anyway, if the crew chief says they're Popular Force, and you're willing to believe that, it's okay by me."

"They're on our side, Paul," Tyler whispered. "Just keep believing that. Our side."

"Our side," Paul whispered, "definitely our side."

The crew chief and the mysterious soldier spoke quietly together for about five minutes. Finally, the meeting broke up. The crew chief and the soldier stood up. Holding his hat with both hands, the crew chief bowed twice quickly. The enigmatic soldier just waved his hand with a look of disgust and went back into the old factory, followed by his two aides-de-camp.

Wearing a friendly and totally insufficient smile on his sweat-drenched face, the crew chief approached Tyler and Paul and told them that there was no sand at this facility.

"Many sand at Phu Bai," he said, smiling warmly and nodding to show that everything was fine, the day was turning out so well, nothing could be better. "We go to Phu Bai now?" he asked.

"Yes, we go to Phu Bai now!" Tyler exclaimed to the crew chief, smiling and slapping him heartily on the back. "Let's all go to Phu Bai now!" Tyler laughed.

Everyone got into the trucks, and Tyler led the way, hurtling back down the ragged tube they had made through the woods just a few minutes before.

"We go to Phu Bai now!" Tyler shouted occasionally as they lumbered through the forest. *"We go to Phu Bai now!"* he yelled as they broke onto open ground again. *"We go to Phu Bai now!"* he periodically shouted as he led the little convoy back to Hue, over the bridge, and right back to the Youth Services office inside The Citadel, where he screamed at the crew chief to get the hell out of his truck or suffer an Army-boot transplant.

It was still only lunchtime, but neither Paul nor Tyler were hungry, so they found a shady grove in a remote corner of The Citadel where they could look for imaginary volleyballs for a couple of hours in solitude before returning to The Villa.

"You realize that nothing happened today," Paul said before closing his eyes for a nap.

"Of course nothing happened today," Tyler replied.

"We still have to get that sand," Tyler said a couple of minutes later.

"We still have to get that sand from Phu Bai," Paul said.

"Absolutely," Tyler said. "From nowhere else but Phu Bai."

Tyler was silent for a minute.

"He was one of ours, wasn't he?" Tyler asked after a while, his voice finally cracking as the adrenaline ebbed and the tension released. He felt lucky to be with someone like Gianelli. Tyler turned to Paul, offering a full, unashamed view of the humorless, acid fear that was just now abating. "Do you think he was really one of ours?" Tyler asked Paul.

"He was today," Paul said.

Sergeant Dong Knows French

Sergeant Dong was the kind of chap who would have been kicked out of a Rotary Club. He would have gotten in—he had that hale fellow, business-generating charm—but he was too overtly the hedonist to last long among prideful men uncomfortable with their desires.

Gianelli brought Dong and Guy Lopaca together for the first time. Lopaca found them in The Villa's parking lot. "Hey, Guy, come over here," Gianelli called. Guy turned and saw Paul and an amiable Asian standing at the front of an ARVN jeep. Paul was looking at some photos in an open billfold. The stranger's arms were crossed, and he wore a magnificent smile.

As Guy approached, Gianelli said: "Specialist Guy Lopaca, let me introduce you to Sergeant Dong. He works with the civilian police, or the ARVN military police, or the GVN city administration, depending on which big lie he is telling us today. Just call him Dong, because even you can't pronounce his other names."

As they shook hands, Dong said to Guy, surprisingly, words that

Guy could understand. "It's pleasure to meet you, Specialist Lopaca," Dong said in English. "Would you, also, like to see my pictures?"

"He's got pictures of his wife and his mistress," Gianelli said, holding one of them close to his eyes, from which he had removed his aviator sunglasses.

"He has a mistress?" Lopaca asked.

"Oh, yes," Dong said proudly, "all important Vietnamese men have mistresses."

"Take a look and tell us what you think," Gianelli said, handing over two small, poorly developed photos. In one, Sergeant Dong was displayed in a formal garden wearing an impeccably tailored, fastidiously pressed uniform, while next to him stood a young, utilitarian, pregnant, peasant female. Her right arm was linked with Sergeant Dong's left arm, and in her left hand she held a small red box tied with red ribbon. She smiled with gusto; but her upper lip smiled more exuberantly than her lower lip did, giving the impression of a sneer.

"The picture is too old," Sergeant Dong said, tapping her big belly with a finger. "The child is born already. My first son."

In the second photo, Sergeant Dong was resplendent in yet another impeccable and fastidious uniform, while arrayed beside him were two adorable females. A young girl, about six or seven years old, had her arms around her mother's waist, and had nearly buried her face in her mother's hip. The mother, half a head taller than Sergeant Dong, stood a few uncomfortable inches apart from him. She wore a blood-red *ao dai,* embroidered with golden dragons. She seemed older than Dong, more commanding, evidently bored, but still the center of the camera's eye; and she was heartbreakingly lovely.

Guy looked back and forth between the lumpy pregnant peasant in white and the majestic woman in red, and wondered how Dong could keep such a magnificent woman on a sergeant's pay, whatever it was.

"Your mistress has a daughter?" Lopaca asked.

Dong smiled brilliantly. "Oh no," he replied, "I cannot afford to have a mistress as beautiful as my wife." He tapped one of the photos. "The ugly woman is my mistress."

Guy reddened with embarrassment. As Guy handed Dong the bill-fold and pictures, Dong patted Gianelli on the shoulder. "You are correct as always," Dong said. "Good lesson."

"What's going on?" Lopaca asked.

"Well," said Gianelli, "Sergeant Dong and I were discussing some of the differences between his culture and ours. Today the subject was mistresses, which are very popular here. I told him most Americans think a mistress is same-same as a whore. Dong insisted that Americans were too open-minded and tolerant to think that way. I said we were really arrogant bastards. We don't tolerate the traditions of others; we *ignore them,* because we are reckless. Is that what I said, Sergeant Dong? That Americans are reckless?"

"Yes, very much," Dong replied, nodding.

"Lopaca, you just proved my point," Gianelli said "You just called his wife a mistress, which to an American is the same as calling her a whore. I don't think you can get more clumsy than that."

"It was very surprising," Sergeant Dong agreed. "I am awakened for sure."

Lopaca choked. He had been worried about his skills—hell, he could barely translate tape recordings of *himself* speaking Vietnamese—and now he had mangled intercultural relations while speaking entirely in English. And not so many words at that.

"I am very sorry," Lopaca said to Dong. "I hope you can forgive me."

"Oh, I can do that for sure," Dong replied. "And anyway, I must tell you that my beautiful wife was indeed a whore before I married her."

Guy Lopaca tried to remember what part of his military training had prepared him for this conversation.

"Do you wonder why I have a mistress?" Dong asked him, and then quickly added, "No, even though my wife is so beautiful, you do not wonder why I also have this mistress. Because I have already told you: *that is our way here.* When you tell me all important American men wear ties around their necks, I do not wonder why they do that. I understand. The French showed us how to wear ties around our necks, as did important men from other countries that have visited us. I understand you need to have your neckties, and you now understand that I should have a mistress. We are both civilized people." He smiled warmly.

"My friend Gianelli tells me that you speak my language," Dong said.

"Not very well," Lopaca replied. "Very badly in fact."

"No, I am sure you are very good," Dong said. "We will try now to speak together."

And he spoke. *"Bong bong bong ga bong bong,"* he said slowly and clearly.

It sounded like someone quickly plunking out-of-tune piano strings, under water.

"I'm sorry," Guy replied in Vietnamese. *"Bong bong bong ga bong bong.* I did not understand you. *Bong bong bong ga bong bong.* Please speak more slowly."

"What?" said Sergeant Dong. "What did you say?"

"Bong bong bong ga bong bong. I did not understand you," Guy repeated in Vietnamese. *"Bong bong bong ga bong bong.* Please speak more slowly."

"Bong bong bong ga bong bong," Sergeant Dong said. "I did not understand you. *Bong bong bong ga bong bong.* Please say again more slowly."

"Uh," said Guy in English, "were you *repeating* what I said or telling me you didn't *understand* what I said? Which is correct?"

"I would not deceive you," Sergeant Dong replied, frowning.

"No, no," Lopaca said, "I need to know if you *understood* what I said and you were just *repeating* it in English, or . . . if you were telling me that you didn't *understand* . . ."

"Lopaca," Gianelli finally cut in, "remind me not to let you spot rounds for the Vietnamese artillery."

"It's impossible," Lopaca moaned, "I'm never going to be able to do this job. I can't speak this language. It's hopeless."

"C'est dommage," Sergeant Dong said in French. "It's too bad."

"Parlez-vous français? Do you speak French?" Lopaca asked Dong in nearly perfect French. Lopaca had excelled in five years of French during high school and college, something which the Army had paid absolutely no attention to when they sent him to a former French colony.

"But of course I speak French," Sergeant Dong replied in absolutely perfect French. "Every important Vietnamese speaks French. The French were our guests for many years. First, they taught us the language, and the neckties, and then they taught us about the mistresses."

The Kids They Send Me

Arthur Grissom was there when Specialist Bowen told the Army to go to hell.

Bowen was not the kind of fellow who made you think "revolution" when you saw him. Short, thin, squeaky . . . he was everything you would never see in recruiting posters at an enlistment center. But Specialist Bowen seemed to have a line, and the Army appeared to have crossed it.

It started off quietly enough. Bowen's job as an electronics technician required him to go "behind the fence" into the Radio Research Battalion's high-security compound. Bowen would love it there. It was a geek's fantasy playground. Getting inside the compound required a higher security rating than the one Bowen brought to Vietnam.

So, the first sergeant asked Arthur to prepare a Form 398, which Bowen would countersign, and which would go back to the States, directing military investigators to do their background checks. It was just a formality, of course, a brief delay before Bowen would be unleashed upon those tubes and dials and staticy delights.

The Form 398 Arthur had typed was laid in front of Specialist Bowen, who squinted.

"I won't sign that," Bowen said. The first sergeant blinked. No one had ever said that to the Army, to his knowledge.

"Why the hell not?" he said, not as loudly as he should have, he realized too late.

"Look, Top," Bowen squeaked, "I was drafted. I didn't ask to come here. You guys do what you have to do, but I'm not going to volunteer for a bunch of shit-brained feds to go messing around with my family, my friends, or my privacy."

"You don't have a choice here, Bowen," the first sergeant explained. "This is a necessary part of your military assignment."

"Well," Bowen peeped, "you might be right. All I know is that I'm not going to sign that form. That may or may not be a choice. I don't care what you call it. I just know I'm not going to sign."

"You need this clearance to do your job," the first sergeant growled. "You could be cleaning the grease trap at the mess hall every day until it comes through. You understand that? You understand that?"

Bowen looked at the floor and shrugged.

"Son," the first sergeant said less brusquely, "you're making a big mistake. You're having an easy tour now, over in supply, not doing your assigned duty. But this is a *radio research* unit. That's like the Army's CIA. You don't sign that form, you're going to be declared a security risk. We'll ship you out. We won't just send you to the mess hall or the motor pool. This is a war zone. You could end up walking point on a recon mission to Hanoi. Do you understand? The Army will ship your young ass anywhere the Army wants it to go."

"I know, Top," Specialist Bowen said softly. "That's how I got here in the first place. The Army shipped my ass, and I went with it. I have to go where you want me to go. I just don't have to be who you want me to be."

The first sergeant waited awhile, until the awful red in his face had subsided. Then he told Specialist Bowen to get the hell out of his orderly room.

"Do you believe that?" he said to Arthur—or maybe not to Arthur. "Do you believe that bug-dicked little runt? Does he have any idea the

crushing and pounding this kind of bullshit can bring down on him?"
Top shook his head and looked for a smoke.

"'I won't sign,' he says. 'No, Top, I won't follow orders. I won't
fight. I won't pull that trigger. I won't . . . I won't . . .'"

The first sergeant picked up the Form 398 and went to his private office, slamming the door behind him. Over the sound of ripping paper,
Arthur could hear the first sergeant muttering: "The kids they send
me. . . ."

After two weeks cleaning the grease trap at the mess hall, Specialist Bowen was shuffled back to his old job in supply. The first sergeant
typed up the orders himself, and Arthur did not ask him why.

What Are the Odds?

After a recent trip to the Montagnard village in Nam Hoa, Guy and Lieutenant Rossi discussed their impressions and their current plans with Captain Haven, who nodded and smoked his pipe contentedly, with his feet on his desk and a smile on his face. He was happy that Rossi had taken things in hand so quickly, and what a help that Lopaca must be, with those glorious Army test scores.

When Lieutenant Rossi finished talking, Captain Haven took a puff and repositioned his feet to attain a deeper level of repose, and said: "You know, a civilian vehicle got blown up by a land mine in Nam Hoa yesterday. . . ."

Puff.

Puff.

Puff.

"And another one got blown up last week."

Puff.

Puff.

"In Quan Loc, the captain who has my job was blown up a month ago."

Puff.

Puff.

Puff.

"With two of his men."

Puff.

Puff.

Guy's mind focused on geography. People were getting blown up on the roads in Nam Hoa? He, Guy Lopaca, the body inside which his life and consciousness are carried, had just driven a truck on the roads in Nam Hoa. Well, just how *big* is Nam Hoa? What's the frigging *risk,* for chrissake? *Tell me the odds!*

Is this like "jeep blown up in Texas"? Or is this like "jeep blown up between your house and the grocery store"? I need some goddam *context* and I need it now! Show me Nam Hoa on a map! Screw Quan Loc! No one ever sent me to Quan Loc. I don't care if Quan Loc is in *Europe.*

Puff.

Puff.

"The Vietnamese keep their Montagnards on the dusty edge of starvation," Captain Haven said, "but will never push them completely over the edge, because they like to see them dangle."

Puff.

Puff.

There's a map up on the wall behind me, Guy thought. Maybe I can sneak a quick look for Nam Hoa. . . . I hope Nam Hoa is enormous, like Canada. A land mine could get lost forever in Canada.

Puff.

Puff.

"Next time you go out to the Montagnard village, let me know," Captain Haven said. "I'd like to tag along. The more of us they see, the better. It will help them understand how important we think they are."

Puff.

Puff.

And if you come along, Guy thought, it will make Rossi and me understand how important you think we are.

Screw the map, Guy decided. *I'll live with the odds.* Nam Hoa is as big as it is. The odds are what they are. The odds are the same for me as they are for everyone else.

"So," Captain Haven puffed in Lopaca's direction, "Gianelli tells me you're having some dreams. Some pretty interesting dreams, from what I hear."

Oh shit, Lopaca grimaced. Here we go.

"That was supposed to be sort of confidential," he replied.

"And it would have been"—Captain Haven smiled—"if you hadn't told Gianelli." He puffed.

"Now you can tell me."

He puffed again.

"If you don't mind."

Puff.

"And I know you don't."

Lopaca sighed. The fact that he carried a loaded gun to work every day was not enough to keep his manly self-esteem afloat, now that he was about to appear ridiculous to his superior officers.

"I have these dreams . . ." Lopaca began reluctantly.

"That much we know," Rossi said.

"Gianelli has a big mouth," Lopaca muttered.

"We know that, too," Haven said. "But what about those dreams? Are we going to get to those anytime soon?"

"Well . . ." Lopaca paused. How to describe those dreams? How could he explain those terrible, irrational dreams?

"Well," he began at last. "One night I had a dream that all the Montagnards were trying to get drunk on the insecticide we brought out there for the peanuts. It was awful."

Haven's eyebrows raised, and Rossi sat up straight in his chair.

"And last night I dreamed that the Montagnards misunderstood Rossi's instructions—that I translated for them—and they ended up planting live baby pigs nose down in what was supposed to be their watermelon farm. All the little pig snouts were squealing underground and their little rear legs were flapping in the air."

"Were those Duroc hogs or Yorkshire hogs?" Captain Haven asked.

"Duroc," Guy said.

"I still can't tell them apart," Captain Haven said.

"Listen," he purred at last, "you don't want to lose those crazy dreams you're having. They just reflect the fact that you take your job seriously. That's good. Keep having those dreams. The loonier the better. When you're back home waking up your wife and kids with the screaming ambush willies, you'll miss the easy dreams you're having now. I remember when I first got here, I used to dream about screwing Jane Fonda in a rice paddy. It was fun while it lasted. Now when I undress her, she's wearing satchel charges that go off before I can. Believe me, you're in good shape. In a month, the stuff you're dreaming now will seem like healthy."

That night, Guy had a dream about Jane Fonda. He woke up screaming.

•   •   •

On their next trip to Nam Hoa, Lieutenant Rossi drove with Captain Haven sitting in the jeep beside him, and Guy sat in back, his knees tucked up high and his feet resting on the carefully arranged quilt of sandbags lining the floor.

When Captain Haven got in, he kicked one of the bags with his toe—as Guy might do—assuring himself that it was sand all right, blessed sand, nice sand still heavy-wet from the washings and the rain storms, instead of shrapnel-porous marshmallow or goose down. As they passed the burned-out tank hulk, Captain Haven's knuckles turned white just as Guy's tended to do; and occasionally, when the jeep passed over a rock or into a depression, Captain Haven flinched in a familiar way.

It's not just me, Guy thought, *it's everybody. We all have the screaming ambush willies.*

After a few miles of clutching and flinching, Captain Haven turned to Guy. "I never get accustomed to the feeling that my balls are going to go up like wet confetti," Captain Haven said, "but it's better than sitting at my desk thinking *your* balls are going to get blown up without me. And anyway, if I don't come out here every once in a while, I don't get to see the water buffalo."

He told Lieutenant Rossi to stop the jeep, and the three of them sat there as a herd lumbered by. A small boy circled the herd, patting them gently with a stick. They were like elephants with horns and Manhattan nose jobs. The boy approached the jeep, and Captain Haven dug some money out of his pocket. The boy smiled. The lead buffalo regarded Guy with enormous, stupid, sleepy eyes.

"Is it true that water buffalo are getting blown up in the fields of Nam Hoa?" the lead buffalo asked Guy. "Is it safe for us to walk here? How big is Nam Hoa? What are the odds against us?"

"I don't know," Guy said. "Nam Hoa is as big as it is. The odds are what they are. We just do our job and hope for the best."

"I suppose you're right," the water buffalo said. "The boy tells us where to go. We have to trust him. And yet . . ."

"Yes?" Guy asked.

"Well . . ." The buffalo slowly blinked. "Since you seem to be going our way, do you mind if we walk in the road *behind* you?"

An Unfair Advantage

During the day Virgin Mary appeared to be a standard-issue uni-formed officer in the medical service, but at night she worked hard to perform a transformation. She wore tight shirts or sweaters and psy-chotically short skirts. She wore unignorable makeup, and let her blond hair down. It was long and lustrous, and the ends lashed against her nip-ples as they bobbled up and down, side to side, in and out, like two frisky twins playing hide-and-seek under a blanket.

Guy tried not to antagonize her again, but to tell the truth he still found it fascinating to watch her in action when she came to The Club. Along with the obvious sexual excitement, she evoked in her war-rattled men a kind of innocent immaturity that was fun to watch. Sometimes it was hard to tell whether she was a whore with a bunch of hormone-stoked admirers, or a den mother whose cub scouts were waiting for their milk and cookies.

"Or," Guy told Paul Gianelli one day, "she's a den mother that all the cub scouts want to put in a tub of milk and rub with mushy cookies and have sex with."

"She has an unfair advantage over here," Gianelli said.

"I agree," Guy said.

"At home," Gianelli said, "I wouldn't give her a second look. OK, maybe I'd give her a second look. Maybe I'd even give her a whiney down-on-my-knees *begging* kind of look. But that's just me. I didn't get much at home, and I was never too proud to beg. . . ."

He seemed to lose track of the conversation, then found it again. "But here she has a chance to be a different person. Here she makes out pretty well . . ." He paused for effect. "Here she's got a captive audience." Gianelli sighed. "But, you know, in a uniform she still looks to me like some chicken-shit officer. I wouldn't screw her with Ho Chi Minh's dick."

Methods of
Swine Breeding

Lieutenant Prout had finished reading the Platoon's only copy of Professor Ông Ba Tên's *Methods of Swine Breeding* and was getting ready for his first trip to the new hog brothel inside The Citadel.

"They call it a brothel because of the mating aspects of what goes on inside the building," Guy explained to Lieutenant Prout. "I mean the aspects of mating among the *hogs*," Guy hurried to make clear. "No *people* are involved in mating at the hog brothel," he clarified even more. "That I know of," he concluded.

Lieutenant Prout had spread out on his desk the state-of-the-art swine-breeding tools he would demonstrate tomorrow for the Vietnamese, assuming he was able to teach himself how to use them today. The most brilliant tool by far was a large, heavy, seemingly indestructible Swedish syringe that was made in Germany.

"It's stainless steel except for the needle," Lieutenant Prout explained to Guy Lopaca, "and the needle is made from the finest, hardest surgical steel. And that barrel is made out of unbreakable tempered glass."

It was a fine example of the surgical toolmaker's art, and Lieutenant Prout didn't blame the Swedish syringe a bit when it unexpectedly stabbed him in the thigh and pumped him full of swine hormones.

The accident began to happen when Lieutenant Prout practiced injecting hog hormones into an orange in his office the day before the trip. It wasn't an appropriate way to practice the technique.

In the first place, an orange is functionally dead and doesn't move. In the second place, the skin of an orange is easier to puncture accurately than is the leathery skin of a Yorkshire hog in a poorly lit Vietnamese hog brothel. In the third place, an orange doesn't weigh more than 250 pounds, whereas a Yorkshire hog does weigh more than 250 pounds, and a lot of those pounds are muscle. And, finally, an orange doesn't get wildly angry when Lieutenant Prout strikes bone.

Unlike the orange, which accepted the test injection without complaint, the Yorkshire hog threw a tremendous squealing fit when Lieutenant Prout thrust the surgical steel needle into some hog bone that wasn't pictured anywhere in the copy of *Methods of Swine Breeding,* which Lieutenant Prout held in his left hand while stabbing with his right.

All the Vietnamese animal husbanders were standing behind the new metal fencing when Lieutenant Prout showed them how to stab the Yorkshire hog, so they got an excellent panoramic view of the hog pretending to be a bucking bronco, or one of those Brahma bulls, that jump into the air and simultaneously twist energetically, with enough force to throw Swedish syringes out of their bones if they have any stuck in them.

In the case of this particular panic-stricken Yorkshire, his screeching twisting gyration was easily energetic enough to toss the syringe out of his bone and flip it point first into Lieutenant Prout's own thigh, which accepted the needle as fusslessly as the orange had. When Lieutenant Prout fell down from the shock and surprise, to say nothing of the pain, he grabbed the syringe in just the right way to inject himself with what was left of the swine hormones and, of course, whatever other hog fluids the needle had picked up on its journey between the species.

All the Vietnamese animal husbanders were delighted with the performance and wanted to know when the hog would need stabbing again.

Lieutenant Prout was unable to say, being too busy deciding whether to pull the needle out before he went to the hospital, go to the hospital before he pulled the needle out, or shoot himself before any swine characteristics began to appear.

It took Lieutenant Prout a month to get up enough courage to return to the hog brothel with his syringe, another vial of hormones, his copy of *Methods of Swine Breeding* by Professor Ông Ba Tên, and five cartons of American cigarettes, which he was sure was all it would take to convince some Vietnamese farmer to stab his own damn pig.

A Concrete Clinic
Nobody Needs

Guy Lopaca was not in the mood for another trip to An Duong.

Perhaps Gianelli wouldn't show up. Perhaps he wouldn't be able to find the key to unchain his truck. Perhaps a great fault in the earth's crust would open directly under An Duong, and the whole village, dispensary site, garbage heaps, and raucous population would be sucked into a gaping dark hole, never to bother Lopaca again.

Perhaps the commander of the 101st Airborne Division would declare An Duong a "free sickness zone," in which anything that *moved* deserved to get *sick*. Then it would be stupid for Civil Affairs troopers like Guy Lopaca to build a medical dispensary in An Duong.

Gianelli arrived, eventually, with an unimpeachable excuse for being late again. "I'm busier than you are," Gianelli said with a contemptuous smile.

He found Guy on the veranda at The Villa, doing sit-ups. All the skinny Asians made Guy's belly feel enormous.

"You know," Gianelli said, "I'll bet you could get a Vietnamese to do that for you if you paid him a thousand piastres."

"Why don't we just pay him to go to An Duong for us?" Guy asked. "Let him drive the truck and I'll do my own push-ups."

"It would take too long," Gianelli said. "First, he would have to go to the United States, become a citizen, and get drafted into the Army so he could rightfully wear our uniform, which seems to be a requirement for hauling sand around here. There isn't enough time."

"There's plenty of time," Guy said. "I'm willing to wait."

"Let's talk about it on the way," Gianelli said, as usual being completely willing to listen to opposing opinions at any time when he was getting what he wanted.

They loaded the truck with sand at Phu Bai and negotiated their familiar route through the familiar boondocks. At the river they sat in the sun for a while, waiting for the ferry to come and take them across.

"Have you noticed how many other buildings in An Duong are made out of concrete blocks and cement?" Guy asked.

"Do you mean have I noticed that there are *no* other concrete buildings in An Duong?" Gianelli responded.

"Yeah," Guy said. "Have you noticed that?"

"Of course I have," Gianelli said. "It's hard to miss. I wouldn't miss something like that. I've been doing this a very long time."

"Why is it," Guy asked, "that you and I have to help build concrete buildings in Vietnamese villages that have never had concrete buildings before, and have gotten along pretty well for hundreds of years without them?"

"The people at An Duong don't need a concrete clinic," Gianelli said. "They don't need any kind of concrete building. They just *want* one, and they could use our help to get one. It's a reasonable request. If you had a broken leg, and you had a choice where you went for treatment, would you go to a thatch-hut clinic or a cement-block clinic?"

"Cement-block," Guy said. "But if you were planning a military campaign in a third-world country, would you put your troops in harm's way to build concrete shacks in villages that had nothing but thatched huts? What's the sense in that?"

"I don't plan military campaigns," Gianelli said. "I look at it purely from my own point of view. The sense to me—to me *personally*—is that the people want a concrete building, and that's good enough for me.

That's all I need. I don't look for any military or political advantage. I don't care if there is none. Actually, I hope there is none. All I care about is that they want the building, and I can help deliver it. When the building is done it will be the best thing they ever got from an American."

"They'll remember you for it," Guy said.

"Not me," Gianelli said. "Us. The village will forget me soon enough. But everyone who lives in the village will remember how the building got there. Along with all the other shit that happens, some of us Americans did that, too. They'll remember at least that much."

He grabbed Guy's sleeve and jerked it. "Hey, I've got the best job in the Army. Today I'm going to give them a little piece of something that will last for a while and will actually be worth having. That's the absolute best assignment anyone can possibly get in the Army, the maximum good thing they let us do, and I'm the lucky one who gets to do it. You, too."

As they were talking the approaching ferry nosed onto the landing zone and dropped its broad front gate. The heavy steel slapped down *whump!* sending arcs of spray to the front and sides. A horde of ARVN troops began to debark, slowly, some of them shuffling and lurching unsteadily. They brought with them a low-hanging cloud of dust that persisted even as their boots churned the thick, restraining mud of the landing zone.

"They've been to Laos, to Cambodia, or to hell," Gianelli said. "Some of them survived, so it must have been only hell."

They wore loaded weapons and evil looks. They were the meanest, bitterest ARVN troops Guy had ever seen. The mangy, dispirited group parted, passing by on both sides of the hulking American truck with its two immaculate occupants, who looked down nervously on the troops with the least expression possible.

None of the Vietnamese soldiers nodded hello, or spoke a word. They shuffled slowly up the sloped riverbank, gloomy, silently furious. Four Americans were with them, looking like miners who had just come out of a massive cave-in.

"What are you looking at, asshole?" one of the Americans said to Guy.

"Frigging remfs," another GI said, "frigging tourists."

"Rear . . . echelon . . . mother . . . fuckers . . ." the first GI hissed, choosing Guy to glare at while he said it.

The desolate mob, lucky men every one of them, lucky to be back alive from wherever they had been, moved up the bank, out of the way, eventually out of sight. Gianelli took a deep breath and started the engine.

"I'm going to An Duong to build a concrete clinic nobody needs very much," Gianelli said. "Who wants to come with me?"

The Center
of the Universe

I brought my own beer this time," Virgin Mary said as she took a seat at Guy's table. Her eyes latched onto his notepad for a second or two, then turned back up with a show of rigorous indifference behind which her percolating curiosity could not be hidden.

"That's only half a beer," Guy corrected her. "I would be happy to buy you a whole beer when you finish that one."

"You might not be worth talking to that long," Mary said. "Maybe you should buy me a beer right now. I can always take it with me when you start to bore me."

Guy bought two beers. Before taking a sip from his own beer, he put aside the orange soda he had already been drinking. In fact, he put a napkin on his pad, and placed the nearly empty glass of soda on the napkin. Mary's eyes followed every detail of the operation. Neither Guy nor Mary spoke for a moment.

"You're already starting to bore me," Mary said finally.

"Sorry," Guy said, "I didn't know I had to talk first. I thought you might have brought the conversation with you when you sat down. Are we supposed to continue talking about beer?"

"No, we've already talked long enough about beer," Mary said, "but that means it's your turn to pick something to talk about." She looked at the pad.

"We could talk about that," she said.

"Go ahead," Guy said.

Mary picked up the glass of soda and the napkin, set them out of the way, and began to flip the pages of the pad until she reached the first page. She began reading. As she had done the first time they met, she read the letter twice before putting the pad down. Then she took a long suck of beer from her bottle.

"That's another nice letter," she said.

"Thanks," Guy said, "I'm glad you enjoyed it."

"It's not as nice as the first one I read," Mary said, "but it's a really nice letter."

"I'm sorry the quality is slipping," Guy replied. "I'll try to do better next time. Perhaps you could give me some constructive criticism."

"Jesus." Virgin Mary sighed. "You just don't even know."

"Know what?"

"I got a letter from a guy a few days ago. You know what was in it?"

"What?"

"None of your business," Mary said, "but let's just say there were no words in that letter."

"Words are useful things to have in a letter," Guy suggested. "I'm sorry he didn't give you any."

"He probably thought what he did send me was more spectacular. I'll bet all his friends thought so, too." She poked Guy's pad again.

"How long have you known the girl back home?" she asked.

"Not long. I met her when I was at the Army language school in El Paso. She goes to the university there. I met her at a GIs for Peace rally. We just started getting really close a couple of months before I had to come here." He paused. "When I started that answer, I didn't expect to tell you so much," he said.

"Men have a tendency to open themselves up to me," Mary said. "Sometimes they lose control. GIs for Peace. Is that like Nuns for Fornication? Or maybe Whores for Chastity?"

"It does involve a certain amount of schizophrenia."

"I don't suppose you could use carbon paper when you write those letters . . ." Mary suggested, tapping the pad.

"Why would I need to do that, when you're just going to edit the first drafts for me anyway?"

"I won't ask to read them anymore," Mary declared. "Especially with the quality slipping as it seems to be."

"I suppose I should want to keep them private anyway," Guy said.

"I would think so," Mary agreed. "That's what I would want if I was the girl back home that you were writing them to."

"So now what's left to talk about?" Guy said. "Is it your turn to pick the topic or mine?"

"It's your turn," Mary said, "but I'll help. What does a member of GIs for Peace think about the war?"

"It sucks, but it will make a good movie someday. What does an officer who outranks a GI for Peace think about the war?"

"I cry a lot," Mary said. "Sometimes I cry because the war sucks, as you so *eloquently* put it. And sometimes I cry because I seem to be taking advantage of it so much."

"Then why don't you stop taking advantage of it?" Guy asked.

"Not taking advantage would be such a waste," Mary said. "If the opportunity is there and I don't take advantage of it, that just makes the war even more of a waste, don't you agree?"

"You seem to have it all thought out," Guy said. "Let's go with your theory until something better comes along."

"You're easy to talk to," she said.

"So are you," Guy replied.

She emptied her beer and wiggled the bottle at him. "One more?" she asked.

"Anything you say," he replied, standing up.

"Anything?"

"Almost."

When he came back, Mary was reading the letter again.

"You know what's funny?" she asked.

"Is this the next topic?"

"Sure."

"OK, what's funny?"

"It's funny how your letters don't sound exactly like you." She put the pad down. "They sound like they were written by someone else who didn't really like you all that much."

"Really?" Guy asked, his interest amplified now that Mary had revealed this new capacity for observation.

"It's like someone who didn't like you very much was editing these letters to your girl back home, changing them just enough to show her what a great guy you almost were, but not quite."

Guy smiled.

"Well, see, I know that already," he said. "That's me being self-deprecating because of my tremendous burden of guilt. Now you know what it's like to be a GI for Peace who volunteers to go to Vietnam and packs a gun. Schizophrenia is too nice a word for it. Totally mind-blown and conflicted is more like it. Constant doubts and second-guessing. That's what you see in those letters. That's me being disappointed in myself every second that I spend here."

"I know that feeling," Mary said. "You sound a lot like a nice girl who hates herself because she does tricks for money with dozens of homesick vulnerable men who need her."

"What am I doing here?"

"What am I doing under him?"

"Sounds familiar."

"Sure does."

"We're both pretty screwed up."

"And down."

"Now you have me worrying about my letters," Guy said.

"I love your letters," Mary said. "Those letters are probably the closest you'll ever get to revealing the real you. They're interesting to read, and the girl back home will love them as much as she loves you."

"That much?"

"Exactly that much."

"Whose turn is it to pick a topic now?"

"I think it's my turn again," Mary said. "It seems it has not been your turn at all tonight."

"Well let me try," Guy said. "Are you hustling me? Do you expect that some day I'm going to be one of those homesick paying clients you just mentioned?"

"Sure I'm hustling you," Mary said, "but not for that. I'm losing money tonight because I said no to one of those homesick guys so I could sit here and hustle you."

"But, you know, it's not going to work," Guy said.

"You mean you aren't going to let me read your letter to the girl back home a *fourth* time tonight?" She chuckled. "That would be a really big disappointment."

"Is that all you want?" Guy asked. "Just to read the letters?"

"No, that's not all," Mary said. "I'll bet you know that's not all. I think we both want the same thing, and to a certain extent we're both getting it right now."

"So tell me what that is," Guy said.

"It's the conversation," Mary said.

They sipped their beers at each other.

"I think you're right," Guy said.

"We both want something we can't get, at least not now," Mary said. "We both enjoy talking around that with someone else in the same predicament."

"That must be it," Guy agreed.

"Conversations we have in Vietnam don't follow us home," Mary said. "What we say here doesn't linger, doesn't follow us around, so we can afford to be reckless. We can say everything we really mean to each other."

"It sounds like you've heard your share of confessions," Guy said.

"No, when men say it to a priest it's a confession." Mary laughed. "With me when they say it they think it's bragging."

"That sounds like the introduction to another topic," Guy said.

"You know," Mary said, "we could pretend that we've discovered this little table here, at the center of the universe, where talking to each other in an interesting way is all we need to do to keep the rest of the crap out there where it doesn't touch us and doesn't scare us or hurt us so much."

"Now who's being eloquent?" Guy said.

"Now who's being hustled?" Mary replied.

A Boy and His Gun

Guy decided to trade his M-16 rifle for a pistol. The rifle was bulky and conspicuous, and it put something unpleasant between himself and the native people he had to talk with.

So he asked for a standard-issue .45 caliber pistol. "All I want is for the cowboys downtown to think twice about taking the fillings from my teeth," he told the sergeant at the arms room. The lifer nodded, took Guy's rifle, and returned with a frayed and faded canvas holster, from which he removed and handed to Guy an old weapon that was chipped, scratched, and thoroughly de-blued.

"It's a keeper," the sergeant said. There was some disappointment in Guy's eyes. "Look, son," the lifer said, "I could find you a newer piece. But this one will shoot just as good. And this one has some character." He took the pistol back from Guy, held the pistol in his hand, hefted it, shook his head sadly. "Your father could have carried this pistol," he said. "Your grandfather could have carried it." He holstered the weapon, snapped the flap closed, and pushed it across the counter. He also gave

Guy a fabric belt, with an ammunition pouch containing two extra magazines.

"Try it on," the sergeant said. He watched as Guy fed the belt through the loops of the holster, and then fit the belt to his waist.

"There was a time when that hunk of metal had meaning in the lives of men like you," the lifer said. "You and me can only guess where it's been and what it's been through."

"It's fine," Guy said halfheartedly.

"Now I'm going to tell you something," the lifer said, "and maybe you won't believe me, but I want you to listen anyway." He knocked on the counter with the knuckles of his right hand, gently. "Boys like you think you don't belong in the Army. You think you don't belong in this war. Maybe you're right. But let me tell you . . ." Something about the lifer had changed. Guy found himself listening unusually hard.

"Thirty years from now," the lifer said, "when you look back and try to remember what it was like being over here, you're going to find that almost everything has faded and disappeared, and you can't remember nearly none of it. But one thing you're always gonna remember, one thing you're never gonna forget, is the feeling of that pistol on your hip and that belt around your middle."

Guy stared at the lifer, and the lifer stared back. The lifer was a supply sergeant. He had never been in battle, and wasn't pretending otherwise.

"You see, son," the lifer said, "it doesn't matter whether you belong here or not. You're going to walk out of here with a gun on your hip. To-morrow when you get up in the morning, you're going to work with a loaded gun on your hip. For the rest of your life you're going to remember what it was like to be that kind of man."

Guy didn't know what to say. When he walked through the door, he expected to trade a modern, fully-automatic assault rifle—that he already carried every day—for something *less* intimidating. He had not expected to receive a life lesson about passages to manhood. But there was something about the look in the fat lifer's eyes, and the feel of the heavy pistol on his own hip, that made Guy wonder if something important had happened after all.

His hand drifted down to the frayed holster, opened the flap, and withdrew the old gun again. He hefted it, as the sergeant had done. As others had done. And he realized that what the lifer had said was true, every bit of it. The hands of all those fathers and grandfathers had reached out and ripped him from his world, to make him part of theirs.

A few months ago he had been a college student reading books and writing term papers. Tomorrow morning, despite every conception of his former self, he would face the day with a loaded gun on his hip, constantly reminding him, with every bump and jostle—the echoes of tradition—that he was willing to use it.

The secret that the lifer sergeant had tried to impress was vivid now: Guy would remember the gun on his hip because . . . because . . . *it felt so goddamn good.* Nothing felt this good. Nothing felt this real. God help him, Guy Lopaca had been sucked into history.

•   •   •

Guy thought it would be a nice idea to give his antique pistol a workout, in much the same way he might give a beloved old dog a brisk walk around the park.

Gianelli parked the jeep along the side of the road, near a convenient pile of trash that offered some swell practice targets. Guy picked out a large can that had contained vegetable oil, and used his boot to dig out a small shelf on which he set the can. He paced off about fifty feet, turned, unholstered the pistol, chambered a round, took aim, and carefully placed seven shots into the continent of Asia.

"I think I hit Vietnam," Guy said. "At least I think so."

"It depends on where that last shot comes down," Gianelli said.

"I never was very good with a pistol," Guy said. "With a rifle I can't miss. I'm just naturally good with a rifle. But with a pistol, I'm hopeless."

"Well then," Gianelli said, "I can understand why you traded your rifle in for a pistol. Who would want to carry a weapon he already knows how to use? Where's the challenge in that?"

The two men got in the jeep and started back to town.

"Didn't you want to hit the can at least once?" Gianelli asked. "You gave up pretty quick."

"What's the point?" Guy asked. "If I hit the can on my next shot, then I'll be one for eight. That will give me the comfort of knowing that I can defend myself against anyone who doesn't move an inch while I take seven shots at him and then reload and shoot one more."

"Trust me," Gianelli said, "the Vietcong and the NVA are not that patient."

"Why don't you ever bring a weapon?" Guy asked.

"I do sometimes. I have an old World War II burp gun. I shoot worse than you do," Gianelli said.

"You've spent more time in Vietnam than Ho Chi Minh," Guy said. "You usually don't carry a gun, and you've never been in a fight. Is there a trick to being lucky that long?"

Gianelli drove without speaking for a while.

"Are we having one of those talks now?" Gianelli asked.

"I'm willing if you are," Guy said.

"I'm not going to die in a firefight," Gianelli said, "and neither are you."

He looked at Guy, and shook his head. Then he put his eyes back on the road.

"Maybe we will turn the next corner," he said, "and there will be a group of gentlemen waving at us to stop, and we will stop, and they will shoot us. Or maybe they will let their little sister hit us with a seven iron as we drive by. Either way, we're going to end up dead."

Gianelli fishtailed the jeep a couple of times, for fun.

"I'm not a shooter," Gianelli said, "and neither are you. You and I are not even targets."

"How did we get to be so invisible?" Guy asked.

"Remember that tin can you threw back onto the garbage pile a few minutes ago?" Gianelli asked. "The one you missed seven times? The one you actually spent time *trying* to hit with a bullet? Didn't you hate that tin can? Didn't you want to walk up closer, put your pistol in its face, and blow it away?"

"Not really," Guy said.

"That's how it is with us," Gianelli said. "We aren't important enough to care about. If we ever get important enough to care about, someone will spend a couple of minutes killing us, and that will be that. Look around you. This place is crawling with bad guys every night. Where do you think they are right now?"

Gianelli pulled the jeep off the road and shut off the engine.

"Listen," he said, "you and me, we don't get one of those Hollywood deaths. Killing us takes about as much effort as picking your nose.

"By the time we get back to The Hotel tonight," Gianelli said, "we will pass within twenty-five feet of at least one thousand, maybe two thousand people. You're going to tell me they're all on our side? Any one of them could pick up a rock and kill you."

"Thanks." Guy sighed. "And I was just starting to feel good about the rocks."

"Before you rotate home," Gianelli said, "you're going to take two hundred trips in the boondocks with assholes like me and nothing else to protect you. You're going to log hundreds of miles on crappy roads like this, the next best thing to nowhere."

He leaned over and grabbed Guy's shoulder. "If they want us, they got us," Gianelli said. "The only thing we have going in our favor is that we're not worth the effort. They don't care. That tin can back there: you really didn't care whether you hit it or not." He pointed up into the hills. "That's how they feel about you."

"Thanks for cheering me up," Guy said. "I'll try real hard to stay inconsequential."

"You try anything you want," Gianelli said, "it won't make any difference either way."

"Do you really believe that?" Guy asked. "Do you really believe we're not worth killing and that's our only defense?"

"It isn't important what I really believe," Gianelli declared. "It's only important that I say it with enough conviction that you are not capable of doubting me."

"That will never happen," Guy said.

"You should be so lucky," Gianelli replied.

•   •   •

Lieutenant Rossi's marvelous new insecticide had a bouquet that reminded you of landfills stuffed with rotting quarter-horse carcasses and battery acid. Even if the stuff were actually nutritious, the smell would have made most living organisms die, or want to.

While Mr. Hoa and his Montagnard associate Mr. Thon watched Rossi fill one of the spray cans, Guy Lopaca tried to describe for them the formidable protective qualities of this mighty new "not-water."

"This into this," Guy said eloquently, pointing first to the insecticide and then to the spray can. "Then these," he said, running his fingers bug-like across the dirt, "these be dead." He turned his bug-hand belly-up.

Just when Guy thought that his job was finished—the two men were smiling and nodding like profoundly satisfied agricultural chemists— Lieutenant Rossi handed the dripping spray can to Guy.

"Give them a demonstration," Rossi said. "I've already pumped it up for you. Cover the whole plant, get all the leaves, but go easy on the overspray." Rossi smiled in a way that reminded Guy that, between the two of them, Guy was still the only enlisted man.

Guy strained to get the damn strap up onto his left shoulder while bearing the weight of the big supply barrel with his left arm on his left hip.

Rossi had sloppily spilled lethal doses of insecticide all over the spray can. The hot sun on the hot can boiled the oily, smelly volatile stuff, vaporized it, creating a visibly noxious cloud at the center of which Guy calculated how many peanut plants he could cover with an acrid fog *before taking another breath.*

Not enough to matter. There were thousands of peanut plants arranged in dozens of furrows at the demonstration peanut farm. Each of the plants was so tiny and puny it took up hardly any space at all. Guy couldn't complete even a single furrow while holding his breath. He would just have to breathe the poison fog and take his chances.

Guy walked slowly alongside a furrow, directing his spray wand at the peanut plants. The wand tip hissed as it emitted the spray. Rossi had done a fine job pumping compressed air into the can. *This isn't so hard,* Guy thought. *The hard part will come ten years from now, when my lungs start turning to jelly and the doctors tell me they're stumped.*

"He should be wearing a rag over his nose when he sprays that stuff," Mr. Thon pointed out to Mr. Hoa.

"How can he support the additional weight of a nose rag?" Mr. Hoa replied. "Did you notice the size of his pistol? How can one who has to carry such a heavy hand-cannon be burdened with the weight of a nose rag as well?"

"I see your point," Mr. Thon said. "Any minute a platoon of northerners will attack, and he will need that pistol much more than he will need a nose rag."

"Yes, there is always the possibility of attack," Mr. Hoa agreed. "But will he have a fair chance to defend himself with that pistol? After all, look how he is burdened already by the heavy spray can. He is in a vulnerable position, don't you think?"

"I agree entirely," Mr. Thon said. "But, you know, he could use the spray can against the northerners! He could spray them with the poison!"

"He could give them a rash!" Mr. Hoa laughed.

"That would teach them!" Mr. Thon chuckled.

Mr. Hoa shrugged and Mr. Thon sighed.

"Should we tell them that the peanut plants are already dead?" Mr. Thon asked. "If we told them now they might forgive us."

Mr. Hoa shook his head.

"Best not to confuse them," he said. "We'll tell them later and blame the new poison. We need to keep their hopes up for the watermelon."

• NHA TRANG •

On the Same Team

The Inspector General's goon was in the next room scolding Arthur Grissom's first sergeant for not having a blank form on hand.

The top sergeant was defenseless against the inspector's criticism. Top had never heard of the form before, had never submitted one during his long career. He was stuck. Not having the missing form would cost the company a gig—a point off, an insult.

Arthur heard the inspector lecturing the first sergeant about the missing form: "You can never tell . . . you can't assume . . . readiness is more than guns and physical fitness . . . you knew we were coming . . ."

What a bore, Arthur thought. He pulled a requisition form from his drawer and inserted it into his typewriter. He quickly manufactured a fraudulent requisition for office supplies—*including the missing form*—and backdated it by thirty-eight days. Arthur carried a faint carbon copy of the bogus requisition into Top's office.

"Sorry for interrupting," Arthur said, "but I think I heard you talking about this." He handed the carbon sheet to the first sergeant, and showed him where a request for the missing form appeared on the phony document.

"I guess we did order the form," Top said to the inspector, who looked the requisition over and nodded. "You're right," the inspector said, "it's not your fault if they don't send you the forms you ask for." He genuinely smiled. There was not a hint of animosity in him. He was just doing his job, and by gosh it now appeared that this company was doing a damn fine job as well.

Top handed the requisition back to Arthur. This is the point where I can expect a wink, Arthur thought. But there was not a trace of complicity in Top's faint smile. "Thanks for digging that out," he said.

Digging that out? *Digging that out?* It was an act of brazen genius, Arthur thought, and I get credit only for pulling it out of a drawer? He went back to his desk and wondered why he had stuck his vulnerable nose in the Army's private business. He stewed about it for another hour, as the inspector and the first sergeant strip-searched every shelf and cabinet in the building, looking for cracks in the paper foundation without which—according to the inspector—the war would collapse.

When the inspector had finally left, the first sergeant sat in his office for a while smoking a cigarette alone. Then he called Arthur in. And sat him down. And stared at him for a while . . . And waited until Arthur finally fidgeted.

"That was quite a chance you took," Top said.

"It seemed like a good idea at the time," Arthur replied, surprised that Top had known about the deception all along. Top certainly hadn't shown it.

"Anyway, I didn't think about the risk," Arthur said. "That inspector seemed to be dumping on you pretty bad over something I didn't think was very important. And he didn't seem all that bright. So I gave it a shot."

"Well, you're right that he isn't a very smart man," Top said. "None of those inspectors are very smart. They're just thorough. They just do the same boring thing over and over, everywhere they go. They're just checking off a list. This, this, this, that, and the other. Same damn thing day after day. Boring as hell." He puffed. He puffed again.

"But you know what he said before he left?" Top didn't wait for an answer. "He said I must run a good ship, because not only is the office in really good shape but I have a draftee who will put his ass on the line big-time just to save my ass from a no-account paperwork gig. He was smart enough to see that, you understand?"

"Yes, Top," Arthur said, embarrassed.

"You're a good kid, and I appreciate what you did," the first sergeant said. "But you know, that was *my* reputation that you were putting at risk. And that lie you expected me to cover: that was *your* lie. You put both of our asses on the line because you thought the inspector was too dumb to catch you in your little game of peekaboo. You ought to give us more credit. You shouldn't look down on us so much. We win our share of wars, you know? We aren't stupid just because we didn't go to college."

"Sorry, Top," Arthur said quietly.

"It's all right," the first sergeant said. "Actually, I like the way it turned out. I like to think of us all on the same team. All of us old Regular Army buzzards, and all of you hippies in for the two-and-outs, on the same team. And right now, that's exactly how I feel. You lied for me, I covered for you, and the other guy looked away. It's you and me and him against the world, see? Welcome aboard. Now you know how it works." He puffed. "You joined my Army today, son. Now you can't never say you didn't."

• DA NANG •

Waste Not, Want Not

Because Lieutenant Rossi stopped off at the toilet—all the buildings the brass used in Da Nang had indoor plumbing—it turned out that Guy Lopaca was the first one into the conference room. As the others arrived, all of them officers, each fixed himself a cup of coffee from a setup in a corner. As they took their seats, the attention of each officer was drawn to an immaculate blackboard, on which someone had neatly printed:

WASTE NOT, WANT NOT

A couple of the officers read the note in a second or two, then turned away brusquely. One of the officers took a seat with his back to the blackboard, but turned around three times to look at it in silence. One officer put down his coffee, approached the blackboard, took off his glasses, and inspected the letters so closely he almost got chalk on his nose.

Eventually the colonel who commanded CORDS in I Corps came

in, along with Lieutenant Rossi, who had been chatting with him in the hall. The colonel accepted a cup of coffee that a junior officer made for him, and was about to take a seat at the head of the table when he noticed the inscription on the blackboard.

WASTE NOT, WANT NOT

"Someone fancies himself a goddamn comedian," the colonel said. "Some goddamn hippie thinks he's Abbie frigging Hoffstein and this is the University of Southern goddamn California." He grabbed the eraser from the tray below the blackboard, and smudged the message almost completely out. But not entirely.

"Goddamn enlisted men," the colonel said as he sat down. As he took his seat, every other man in the room could see that the message was still visible behind the cloudlike smudge that the colonel had hastily made. The colonel pulled a bunch of papers from his briefcase, slapped them down in a pile, arranged them into two smaller piles, pulled a single sheet from the top of one of the piles, and then looked up to begin his goddamn meeting. As he passed his withering gaze over the men around the table, his eyes settled on the goddamn blackboard, where some incompetent goddamn sloppy fool had made a mess trying—*but not succeeding*—to blot out some mutinous goddamn propaganda put there by some insolent goddamn enlisted man . . .

And then he saw that not all of the men around the table were officers. That young man over there next to Lieutenant Rossi—that sloucher pretending to be counting the fascinating coffee grounds at the bottom of his coffee cup—he was a goddamn *enlisted man. I'll bet he put that slogan up there on the blackboard. I've got a mind to make him lick it off with his goddamn tongue. Who the hell let him into this meeting anyway?* The colonel was about to show everyone in the room who was the goddamn boss of CORDS in I Corps when Lieutenant Rossi spoke up.

"I agree with you," Lieutenant Rossi said to the colonel. "If some lunkhead is going to quote from the Bible, he ought to at least get the words right."

The curse the colonel was about to sputter at the goddamn mutineer enlisted man caught in the colonel's throat. *Quote from the Bible?* That's where the slogan came from? No wonder it sounded so familiar. "Yeah," he said, "they ought to get the words right." He glared at Guy Lopaca. It was still possible he did it. The punk had the look of a goddamn Holy Roller. Look at the way he cowers in the company of men.

"How'd it go, originally?" the colonel challenged Rossi.

" 'Waste not, lest ye want,' I think," Lieutenant Rossi said, "or something like that."

"Nah, that's not it," the colonel grumbled. "It was better than that."

" 'All ye who waste, so shall ye want,' " a captain said confidently, " 'and all ye who waste not, so ye shall not want.' "

"Yah, something like that." The colonel nodded. "Not like that crap on the board."

It wasn't much use taking after that groveling goddamn enlisted man now. If it turned out it wasn't him who shorthanded the Bible, there would be a goddamn sideshow; and if it was him, he was already proved to be a goddamn fool. Better just take back control of the goddamn meeting.

"We're here to talk about that disfoliation," the colonel began. "I mean that *de*-foliation whatchamacallit." He stared at the single sheet of paper in his hand, and then at the two piles of paper on the table, then at the slogan still lurking behind its smudgy curtain.

Waste not, want not? Hmmh! He wasn't sure about the wanting part, but he could tell when his goddamn time was about to be wasted.

"Ah, shit," the colonel said, "ah'm gonna let Major Riegert fill you in on all the details. You got to excuse me while I attend to a few other things."

The colonel departed the room quickly, leaving the two piles of paper at the head of the table, in front of the empty chair that Major Riegert now had to fill in order to lead the meeting, during which he would have to tell the men all about next week's survey mission, the details of which no one had ever told him.

•   •   •

"Officers are not *allowed* to beat the shit out of enlisted men!" Lieutenant Rossi shouted, as he threw Lopaca against the bathroom wall.

"So I may not let you live to testify against me! *Jesus,* what were you thinking?"

"I wasn't thinking about anything!" Guy protested. "I was just doodling."

"Doodling?" Lieutenant Rossi spluttered. *"Doodling?* Are you nuts? This is the Army! They don't *doodle* in the Army!"

"Look," Guy said, "I have spent one year in kindergarten, twelve years in grammar school, junior high, and high school, four years in college, and thirty-six weeks in an Army language school." He paused to pick the right words, but there weren't any. "In all that time," Guy said lamely, "I have never seen a blackboard so clean. I couldn't help myself. I just wrote the first thing that came to mind."

"Waste not, want not?" Rossi bellowed. "That was the first thing that came to mind? In a world where there are slogans like *make love not war,* the best you can come up with is *waste not, want not?"*

"Yeah," Guy admitted. "It was just words. The kind of thing you find in *The Old Farmer's Almanac.* It just came to me, and it was short, so I wrote it. I didn't expect the colonel to blow up that way. I wasn't trying to be political."

"Lopaca, you idiot," Lieutenant Rossi moaned, "that meeting was called to plan a survey on the progress of chemical defoliation. Those guys have been dropping poison from airplanes for years. With the exception of you and me, every other person at that meeting wants to kill everything in Vietnam that's alive and green and fit for a Vietcong soldier to hide in. Do you really think lecturing them about the virtues of *conservation* is a *nonpolitical act?"*

"It was just a nice blackboard," Guy mumbled. "That's all it was. Really."

Lieutenant Rossi took a leak and washed his face and combed his movie-star golden hair, and tried not to show how quickly he recovered his capacity to forgive this unpredictable dunderhead with the legendary Army test scores. "Let's get out of here before they finish looking in the Bible for that stupid quote," he said.

"Was it Benjamin Franklin?" Guy asked.

"Do you want to go ask Major Riegert?" Lieutenant Rossi replied.

"I'm sure he'll be happy to put aside the new assignment you just got for him, to look that up for you."

Lieutenant Rossi finished unlocking the door as he spoke, and walked through it too quickly, almost knocking into the colonel, who was hurrying down the hallway at flank speed, with a bag of golf clubs slung over his shoulder.

"I can take a hint, I can see a goddamn sign from heaven when there's one to see," the colonel said happily, pausing for a few seconds to pat Lieutenant Rossi on the shoulder. "I don't know who wrote that goddamn whatchamacallit on the blackboard, but goddamn it he was right. I been spending too much time in the saddle. I'm taking three days in Japan, starting ten minutes ago. They got the best goddamn fairways and greens I ever played on. Let Riegert count the goddamn leaves and twigs." He set off down the hall again.

"Waste not, want not," the colonel called over his shoulder. "Waste not, want not. If it's not in the goddamn Bible, it ought to be."

Spores, Yolks, and Communists

Danny Maniac was the first person at the Enlisted Men's Hootch to get a genuine nickname. Guy Lopaca was always Guy or Lopaca; Paul Gianelli was always Paul or Gianelli; Tyler DeMudge was always Tyler or DeMudge; and so on.

But Danny was a different thing altogether. He wasn't like the others.

In the first place, he came to their Civil Affairs unit so much better armed than anyone else. When Paul and Tyler picked him up at the airport to put him through the new-guy wringer, he carried an M-16 rifle, a grenade launcher, and a bandolier of ammunition for each. Around his waist he wore a pistol belt with four ammunition pouches. Unusual for anyone, but Danny was supposed to be a *medical* advisor.

The first words out of his mouth as he unpacked at The Hootch were, "You guys have gotta see this."

He dumped everything he was carrying on his bunk, and approached the table where DeMudge and Gianelli had sat down to play high-low-jack.

"You guys ain't going to see too many of these around here," the new man said.

He unclipped the flap of his holster, and laid a pistol on the table.

"So what do you think of the piece?" he asked.

DeMudge sipped slowly from his thermos of martini. "I think it's a pistol," DeMudge said, "although it could be a really extravagant cigarette lighter. I am hardly the best one to ask in either case."

"That's a very *nice* pistol, Danny," Gianelli said. "You didn't get that from the Army, did you?"

"Hell no," Danny Schubert said, "that's a Luger. That pistol is a genuine German Luger, nine millimeter, World War II. My father took it off a dead German. My dad gave it to me when I joined the Army. I'm carrying on the family tradition."

He smiled brightly, picked up the pistol, and twirled it around his finger.

"Tradition is nice," Gianelli said. "Was your father in Civil Affairs, too? What did he do? Volleyballs? Pigs?"

Danny's smile faded quickly. "Screw that," he said, "he was in infantry. He was in the real war."

"We don't get much of that around here," DeMudge said.

"We don't actually want much of that around here," Gianelli said.

"Too much noise and mess," DeMudge said.

"I like to sleep late in the morning," Gianelli said.

"Are those guns on the bed for the rest of your brigade," DeMudge asked, "or do you use them all yourself?"

"Hey, screw you," Danny said. "That's the trouble with the Army. Too many guys who don't take it seriously."

In a huff, he clumped back to his bunk and began to settle in. The artillery went into his metal locker, except for the holstered Luger pistol, which he didn't take off. He divided his clothes and personal effects between the locker and his wooden dresser. Then, using a roll of tape, he stuck half a dozen photographs on the wall above his bed. They were all dead Vietnamese, bearing catastrophic wounds, most of them to the head.

DeMudge and Gianelli watched as the gruesome photos began to populate their home. They didn't say anything to Danny, but looked at each other in horror. Eventually, Gianelli leaned over and whispered to DeMudge: "How did this guy get assigned to our platoon?"

DeMudge lifted his eyes to the heavens, and then whispered back: "Somebody dumped him on us. He's a maniac."

"He certainly is," Gianelli said softly. "Danny Maniac." He held out his hand. DeMudge shook it. "Danny Maniac," DeMudge agreed.

• • •

Danny Maniac was one of the few people in the world about whom it could truly be said, "He didn't know any better." The other enlisted men in The Hootch couldn't get angry at him, not *really* angry, because it was so obvious that all of his many faults were based on a foundation of mush. Nothing about him was well grounded, and even his hatred seemed innocent.

Danny complained bitterly about integration in the South, demonstrations for civil rights, the ghetto riots, and welfare. Yet he played basketball with black men almost daily, and he displayed no hint of malice or distaste in their frequent, sweaty collisions.

For days after his arrival he could not be shut up about communism. To Danny Maniac, the threat was real, the conspiracy demonic, the need for vigilance acute. He spoke of the containment of communism as if it were a religious quest, as for the Grail. He hated communists—the Vietcong, the Russians, and the Yippies in Central Park—all pagan aliens. Yet Danny had no idea that communism was connected in any way with economics, and it was clear that his hate for communism, in general, was not attached to any person or people, in particular. In fact, he professed great admiration and sympathy for all the blameless people in the world who suffered under the yoke of communism. He claimed to respect the Vietnamese people, at the same time he cursed the awful Vietcong, without ever knowing where the Vietcong came from.

"The people of South Vietnam are born of poverty and strife," Tyler DeMudge said one night, trying to imagine a logical core for Danny Maniac's philosophy, "whereas the Vietcong are born of *spores* that are carried by the wind from Hanoi. They appear to be human, but the Vietcong have no souls. They are, in fact, plants similar to the Venus flytrap."

"Now it's all clear to me," Gianelli said, nodding. "Now I under-stand why Danny says the things he says. And I thought he was irra-tional."

When Danny Maniac returned to The Hootch, Gianelli tested Tyler's theory.

"Hey, Danny, what's a yoke," Gianelli asked, "as in 'yoke of com-munism'?"

"The middle of an egg," Danny Maniac replied.

"So when we say the Polish people are suffering under the yoke of communism," DeMudge suggested, "we mean that they are covered by the middle of an egg?"

"Yeah," Danny said, "that sticky shit in the middle. I would hate to be under that stuff."

"Do you know what a spore is?" Gianelli asked.

"How the hell do I know," Danny Maniac replied, "that pointy thing on a sailboat?"

"I think that might be a spar," DeMudge interjected helpfully. "Spores are invisible particles that float in the air and cause plants, like Venus flytraps, to grow."

"I hate that invisible shit that floats in stuff," Danny Maniac said, "like chloride in our water. You know who puts that chloride in there? Communists, the sick bastards."

Danny was a devout enthusiast for the commie-hating John Birch Society. Danny was always telling people, over and over again, how proud he was to be "a Bircher."

"When did you join?" DeMudge asked him a couple of weeks after his arrival.

"Join?" Danny said.

"Yes," Tyler gently continued, "when did you join the John Birch Society?"

"You have to join?" Danny replied.

Tyler got up and retrieved a pamphlet from the small stack on Danny's dresser. "See here?" he said, flipping to the back page. "See the application, and the instructions, and the address? You have to *join* to be a member of the John Birch Society. Like the Boy Scouts. You have to pay dues. You have to put your application in, and be accepted."

"I didn't know that," Danny said. "I missed that part."

"So," DeMudge said sympathetically, "you are a *strong supporter* of the John Birch Society, which is almost as good as being a real member. And you can *become* an official member," he said compassionately, "as soon as you send them your application and your check."

"A check?" Danny Maniac asked.

"From your checking account," Tyler replied gently.

"A checking account?" Danny Maniac whispered, the death of all hope apparent in his eyes.

Making Love

Every weekday Hue City erupted with young women. Hue was a college town, and the ebb and flow of the bubbly young coeds was a sight to behold. They had trim, meticulous bodies with long tasty hair that shone in the sunlight as if every strand were a filament of crystal. They laughed and babbled like songbirds with little cupcake breasts.

Almost all of the girls wore the classic white *ao dai*. It was a long-sleeved affair that fit every feminine curve snugly from a high collar to the hips, where the seam split so the sides were open to the ankle-length hem. As the young women moved, the split seams revealed their satiny black pajama bottoms, that shone and shimmered in sync with their shining and shimmering hair.

They were a vision of grace and innocence, incredibly shy, giggling. Each girl was so slender, you would have to wrap your arms around her twice to hug her close.

• • •

One day each of the men reporting to The Villa found the same piece of mail in his box. It was a memo from a local tailor who was taking orders for *ao dais,* which the men could purchase at the tailor's "very special price" and ship back to their wives and girlfriends. Attached to the memo was a list of the measurements that the tailor would need to make the *ao dai* fit a woman properly:

———— Neck
———— Shoulder width
———— Shoulder seam to waist (sleeve length)
———— Biceps circumference
———— Bust size
———— Waist
———— Neck to waist (back)
———— Neck to ankle (back)
———— Hips
———— Waist to ankle

Sergeant Nesbitt shook his head and laughed.

"Shit," he said, "her neck, bust, waist, hips . . . *They're all the same size!*" He threw his copy of the memo in the trash.

Lieutenant Frickleman read the memo, then the list, then read the list again.

———— Neck
———— Shoulder width
———— Shoulder seam to waist (sleeve length)
———— Biceps circumference
———— Bust size
———— Waist
———— Neck to waist (back)
———— Neck to ankle (back)
———— Hips
———— Waist to ankle

In his mind, he positioned his wife Catherine directly in front of him, as still as a mannequin, and imagined taking an inventory of her beautiful body with his hands and a flexible cloth tape.

He lifted up her hair to measure her neck. He put his hands under the waterfall of blond hair, which tickled the skin on the back of his hands.

To measure her biceps, he stood close before her and draped her forearms across his shoulders. Her eyes looked up into his, and her fingernails scratched his shoulders lightly as he encircled the fleshy part of each upper arm with the cloth tape.

Her *bust:* she held her arms outstretched to the side like slender wings as he positioned the tape around her back and ribs, bringing the tape and his fingertips together at the tender nub of a nipple, which he gave a familiar pinch.

As he measured her waist, he could see the muscles of her tummy tense a little.

He ran the tape slowly from her waist to her ankle, pressing the tape with his fingertips against her hip and thigh and calf, as her toes wiggled and clenched with delight.

Lieutenant Frickleman folded the memorandum and put it in his pocket. He left the office, trying to hide a raging erection that he intended to get rid of quickly. He knew that he would have to give an *ao dai* to Catherine for her birthday. She would look spectacular in it. But the gift would not be a complete surprise because he would first have to ask for her measurements.

●   ●   ●

At home, Catherine was having trouble achieving an orgasm. Her toes wiggled and clenched as she pressed against an unfamiliar body whose rhythms were out of sync with her own. The sensations she had sought were there—more or less. They were enhanced by a feeling of danger, and dulled by a feeling of dread. The man was larger than her husband, filled her more completely, but as the mating process neared his climax she retreated from her own.

Her youth—her body—had made demands on her, had become impatient, had inflamed her with a physical longing that she could not quench in solitude. Without much passion, but with plenty of compulsion, she had given in. One moment she was having coffee with a colleague, and the next moment they were together in his room, her clothes neatly folded on a chair. She had let herself be stroked and suckled, felt her body transformed by its need and its expectation of release. But then some switch of recognition was flicked, and some part of her mind began to peer into the future for repercussions.

Now, at the worst possible moment, she had become pensive, cerebral. Now that her submission was nearly complete, something in her character awakened to fight it. This unfamiliar man with his sharp, uncompromising virility. He was so intensely purposeful. It had never been this way with her husband. It had never been so one-dimensional.

She loved her husband and knew that he was the right man for her; and this persistent substitute was providing no satisfaction at all. She wanted it to be over, she wanted him to go and leave her alone with her loneliness and shame, and to hasten his finish she locked her legs to his and strained against him.

As she comforted herself with the knowledge that she loved her husband dearly after all, and would never do something like this ever again, her eyes rolled back and her jaw opened, a moan escaped her heart, and a ripple of ecstasy overwhelmed her. The unfamiliar man smiled down on her proudly, and kissed her hair, and smiled down at her again, as if waiting for her to say "thank you." She wrapped her arms around his neck and pulled his cheek to hers, so that he could not look at her that way again, at least for a little while.

• • •

Lieutenant Frickleman efficiently dispatched his erection sitting on his cot in his room alone. A magazine full of naked women was propped on a chair, open to his favorite. But when it counted, he closed his eyes and thought of Catherine. She was dressed in a magnificent, pure white *ao dai* over shiny black pajama pants, that followed closely the fullness of her thighs, the gentle curve of her calves, which tapered to her lovely feet, whose toes wiggled and clenched with desire.

Never the Girl Back Home

What I want most of all is a house," Virgin Mary told Guy a few minutes after she sat down at his table. "To me a house represents the freedom to do everything else I want to do."

"Everything else after paying the mortgage," Guy added.

"There might not be any mortgage," Mary insisted. "Here's the math. I go with enlisted men and officers. Let's be conservative and say I average out at a second lieutenant."

"Do you know why Frickleman's a second lieutenant?" Guy asked.

"Why?"

"Because there are no thirds."

"Very funny," Mary said, "but you pulled me off the topic."

"Consider yourself pushed back on."

"Well, now, let's say my average is second lieutenant. Let's say I average ten a month. I actually do better, but let's be conservative."

"With a topic like this one," Guy said, "how can we not be conservative?"

"Shut up," she chided. "Ten times a month, average is second lieutenant, price is half a month's base pay. That means in one calendar year here, I will send back home the cash equivalent of the entire annual base pay of five second lieutenants. Cash, no taxes. Plus accumulated interest from the bank. In addition to my own full pay, overseas pay, hazardous duty pay, all that."

She smiled.

"That's a lot of money for a girl like me. That's a lifetime full of money. I'm giving myself the kind of chance no girl like me could ever have if she stayed home and went the usual route."

"And what do you consider the usual route?"

"The usual route for a girl like me," Mary said, "is ending up with a guy who knows what he really, really wants but is ready to marry someone else."

"The usual route doesn't sound so great," Guy said.

"All my life it seems men have been talking to me out of a script," Mary said. "It seems like there's some 'How to Talk Like a Man' manual that they study really hard before they talk to me."

"I think I know that manual," Guy said. "I think a professor named Ông Ba Tên wrote it. He's from Louisiana State University."

"Thanks for slapping me with a private joke when I'm trying to get some sympathy."

"I'm sorry. I apologize. But look at it this way. Maybe it isn't so bad if the men you know are talking from a script. Maybe they're just nervous and they're looking for help. Is that so bad?" Guy asked. "It sounds like they're trying to get it right."

"With me," Mary sulked, "it sounds like they're just practicing. Once they get it right with me, they'll use it with someone who counts."

"Did you ever talk to them this way?" Guy asked. "Did you ever try to get something better out of them?"

She laughed. "You know what a middle manager is?" Mary asked. "Girls like me get middle husbands. No one else pays attention to us."

"You have a harsh view of relations between men and women," Guy said.

"I have a harsh view of the kind of relations a girl like me can expect," Mary said.

"Are you fishing for compliments?"

"Screw you."

"Not tonight."

"Why is that?" Mary asked. "I keep forgetting."

"Because I promised the girl back home," Guy said. "And she promised me."

"I've been around lots of men who have broken a promise or two," Mary said.

"I suppose that's true."

"How do you know the girl back home is keeping her promise?"

"I don't know," Guy said, "but it's not her promise I'm keeping. It's mine."

"What about the reasons all the other guys use?" Mary said, "Like you might get killed over here, the pressure's greater on you than it is on her, the loneliness is more lonely—that kind of thing? Those are pretty good reasons."

"There are lots of good reasons for breaking a promise," Guy said, "and only one good reason for keeping it."

"See now," Mary said, "you're proving my point. Girls like the girl back home end up with weird guys like you, who say such stupid things, the kind a girl can make fun of and can build an interesting conversation around."

"Yes, but remember that I am the kind of guy who someday soon will have to beg some middle manager to throw me a job," Guy said. "And that conversation won't be so much fun."

"Don't try so hard to miss the point," Mary said. "You know what I mean. Girls like your girl back home have one kind of life, and girls like me end up with the other kind. I don't want to end up having to settle for the other kind. That's what the money I make here means to me. I will have a house and a car and whatever I need to have a decent life on my own . . . if that's the way things go for me."

She was quiet for a few seconds, her lower lip trembling a little. Guy patiently waited.

"I won't have to settle," Mary said at last. "I won't have to settle for the usual kind of life when it turns out the kind I want is already taken by girls like the girl back home."

"But you'll be a girl back home," Guy whispered, "when you go home."

"I will be at home, and I will be a girl," Mary whispered back, "but will I ever be like your girl back home? Tell me the truth. Take a good look at me before you say anything." She tilted her head and smiled in an artificial, Barbie-doll kind of way.

"Don't think of me the way I am here, where I'm special because there's no one else to compete with. Think of me back in the States, where there are ten thousand other girls shopping in the same market, going to the same movies, hopping the same bars."

Guy didn't say anything.

"See," Mary said, "you don't even have the guts to say it. I'm an ordinary person. I'm an ordinary girl, one you wouldn't have even noticed six months ago if I passed you in the street. Am I right, or am I wrong?"

"You're right," Guy said.

Mary looked sad for a while, had a sip of beer, and looked sad some more.

"You know how many men in this room would have lied to me?" she said. "Girls like me don't end up with men who don't lie to us. The girl back home does, and I've never been one of those."

A Complicated Christmas
in Vietnam

It was Christmas in the mess hall. There were strings of colored lights—too few to make things gaudy, but enough to remind them it was holiday time back home. On a table near the main doors to the kitchen a huge turkey sat: dark brown, aromatic, looking crunchy, impossibly plump, impossibly crispy. Every GI had to look at it, as he chewed sullenly on his limp canned turkey, like gelatin, skinless, and wondered who got the real turkey on the table when the show was over.

In the Army, Christmas was the season when pangs of separation felt the worst. No general being pressured for success on the battlefield ever swore that "the boys will be home by Labor Day." Bing Crosby never made a buck crooning "I'll be home for the summer solstice." No, when anyone wanted to make the gloom of being in an overseas war zone seem *unbearable,* they brought out frigging Christmas.

Which had the effect, sadly, of making Christmas the single most miserable period for any overseas grunt or remf to soldier through.

> *Jingle Bells, mortar shells*
> *VC in the grass*
> *Take your merry Christmas*
> *And shove it up your ass*

That made it extra tough on the chaplains.

• • •

The chapel at The Hotel was well off the beaten path, and it was so small and airless that it could have been a shed for the storage of cement or transmission oil. The men called it the God Bunker. On weekends it briefly warehoused a few faithful, who blocked out the strained sermons of embarrassed chaplains (*"Let's put the soul back in soldier . . ."*) by thinking of home. More particularly, while at the chapel men thought about their hometown women, whom they envisioned sitting demurely in a pew beside them, primly dressed and sweetly praying for a change, instead of spread out moaning on a bed or pinned against a tree.

No one laughed at the men who went to services at the God Bunker. In truth, most of the men who had no religious life secretly admired those who had kept their faith alive and their rituals unbroken.

"The really impressive thing is not that they retain their ethical standards in the middle of a war zone," Paul Gianelli told Guy Lopaca one day. "The really impressive thing is that these guys retain their morals in *any place* where no one from home is watching them."

Nor did anyone laugh at the chaplains who roamed The Hotel compound every once in a while, cheerfully waving off salutes as if the chaplains were *not,* despite appearances, detestable chicken-shit officers.

Of all the jobs in the Army, the position of chaplain was the most ambiguous. When wounded soldiers were about to die, there was no one more essential than the chaplain. When vigorous soldiers were about to kill, there was no one who could have gotten more thoroughly in the way. Chaplains helped sustain men in the face of gunfire, and provided the moral authority to shoot at other men. But no one ever asked a chaplain to walk point or interrogate a prisoner.

• • •

During the last week of November a Catholic chaplain, new to the base and different from the others who passed through, supervised the installation of some loudspeakers outside the God Bunker. The loudspeakers were olive-drab green, very large and heavy, and looked to be designed by the same crew that got up the Main Battle Tank. One of the God Bunker believers reported that a fearsome public-address system had been installed, and that the new Catholic chaplain was promising "something of home" to carry them through the holidays this year.

Finally, one December Sunday afternoon, just as Gianelli had puffed his last toke, eaten his roach, and lay his head on his pillow to conjure up his favorite hallucination, the new loudspeakers began to salvo:

"Oh, holy night, the stars are brightly shiii-ning . . . *"*

"That's enough of *that!*" Gianelli cursed, rising quickly and rushing from The Hootch. A few minutes later, a carol abruptly stopped. Gianelli returned bearing wire clippers and some lengths of electrical conduit, with severed wires hanging from the ends of each. He waved the bundle at Lopaca and said, "This is how you do it. Cut out some sections of wire at least three feet long, so they have to spend a lot of time splicing patches, or they have to rewire the whole circuit." He tossed the clippers to Guy. "It's your turn next time," he said, then left The Hootch to dispose of the evidence.

• • •

Although Chaplain Hall had a fine mind and his religious education had been both wide and deep, he had learned early in his tour that in places like Vietnam, simple things worked best.

It wasn't that the Army was no place for heavy religious thinkers. To the contrary, his frequent chats with the better chaplains of other faiths were stimulating, absolutely marvelous. There was a richness to their religious traditions that infused debate with a complexity, a substance and—why not say it?—a *majesty* that politics or baseball could not inspire. Because each chaplain could be called upon as minister to any soldier's faith, it took a special, respectful quality of belief to seek the job, and do it well. For many of these chaplains, faith was more than habit, more than tradition even. It was as real and immediate as a bullet to the heart. In a military service that was all about death and killing, these men volunteered to carry the weight of ultimate consequence.

"When dying men are laid out in a row," a respected senior officer once told Chaplain Hall, "God won't be choosing any favorites. You take them as you find them. When they're laid out in a row like that, you move from one man to the next hoping to reach them all, and it's hard to remember sometimes whose God you're calling on. This one a Jew, that one a Christian, the next one blown to bits with no dog tag to guide you. At the end of the day, the bloodstains on your uniform will all look exactly alike."

Stateside, Chaplain Hall had the reputation of a scholar, well published in history and theological journals. But in Vietnam, he learned quickly that what his men needed sometimes was not a religious tradition to sustain them in the war, but an escape route from it.

Chaplain Hall kneeled beside a stretcher once, to give solace to a wounded soldier. The boy's lower body had been shattered—much of it was simply gone—and it was hard to hear him. Learning from the dog tag that the boy was a Catholic, Chaplain Hall bent close to the boy's ear and asked him gently if he wanted to make his confession. The boy's reply was so faint, his lips moved so slowly. Chaplain Hall put his ear near the lips to hear what the boy was saying.

"Kiss it make it better," the boy whimpered weakly. *"Kiss it make it better."*

In that moment Chaplain Hall was transformed. God himself was a father; nothing could be more important than fatherhood. Chaplain Hall *had* a father but would never *be* one. He would never have to deal with his own little boy's scraped knee. He would never possess the healing daddy-magic this grown-up, scared little boy was begging for.

Suddenly Chaplain Hall felt like an empty vessel, an impostor. He stroked the boy's hair and gave the boy his last rites, speedily but with dignity. It wasn't nearly enough, not for the boy and not for the minister. The boy's wide eyes reached out to Chaplain Hall, desperately, yearning for a miracle. The boy's eyes spoke to Chaplain Hall: *Dad, please, Dad. Please, Dad.* The boy's weak voice implored him with simple words of faith and trust that Chaplain Hall would never be permitted to hear from a son of his own.

Finally, submitting to a power that he had never known, Chaplain Hall put both his hands on the ground, bent low over the hideous wounds below the boy's waist, and tenderly kissed the blood-soaked dressing that packed the place where a leg had been.

Chaplain Hall set his face to heaven and said out loud, with some bitterness: "I hope you're watching. I don't know who you are anymore." He wiped his bloody lips with a sleeve and bent again close to the boy's ear, and whispered to him what he had done: "I kissed it," he said. "I made it better."

The boy smiled faintly, nodded weakly, and closed his eyes. He was still alive as Chaplain Hall wiped his own tears and moved to the next stretcher, laid out with the others in a ragged line upon the ground.

Since then Chaplain Hall had been an impassioned believer in the simple things, like Christmas carols at Christmas. Anything to take the boys away from here, to set their hearts free for a moment or two. To Chaplain Hall a moment spent on memories of home was like a moment in heaven. The night after the wires to his new sound system were cut, he went to bed early, but was too despondent to sleep.

•   •   •

The base commander at The Hotel declined to authorize repair of the God Bunker's sound system. "On reflection," said the base commander, who remembered that his Catholic whore had become distracted from her duties as the first notes began to blare, "it seems to me that every man on this base already has access to personal music systems and is able to choose music suitable to his own taste and religion. It would be unfair to prefer—for example—Gregorian chants over that klezmer crap. And I don't want to have people arguing over how to divide up the loudspeaker airtime."

Chaplain Hall salvaged from his disappointment only a melancholy topic for the next week's sermon. At its conclusion, he beseeched the men to join him in an a cappella Christmas hymn. "God will accompany us with His own music," he prompted them. "The melody of memory," he said, "the harmony of love."

And the men sang quietly along with him. Their memories and the longings that the memories inspired were lifted by their voices and soared to heaven's outposts in Michigan, Oregon, California, Louisiana, Virginia, New York, and Massachusetts. . . .

In the back row, singing louder than most, sat Paul Gianelli, thinking of his own home, and of Mary Frances O'Reilly, whose voice was so sweet, and whose full, glistening, slippery lips made such a lovely round donut on the most delicious notes.

Rebel at Play

The marijuana in Vietnam was what hometown weed aspired to be: mellow, potent, and predictable. You could decide how stoned to get, and get there exactly. You could suck smoke until your lungs nearly melted, and get paralytically wasted, or you could take three puffs and read some fiction, awash in its textures and rhythms.

Vietnamese marijuana—at least the variety of which Guy's friends maintained an inexhaustible supply—was a civilized hallucinogen that adapted to your mood, bringing you a sweet nap or a soaring euphoria, or first one and then the other if you changed your mind. There was nothing you could not do under the influence of this wonder-dope, except (of course) blot out the expectation that one second from right now the enemy would cross the wire, blow open the door, and ram a bayonet into your nose.

. . .

One early evening, just after suppertime, Guy had to choose between a game of basketball and a book. He decided that his body needed the game more than his brain needed the book, and he was lacing up his sneakers when through one of the open doors rushed a large German shepherd with two mismatched officers hanging on his leash.

"Attention! Stand in place!" the taller officer shouted, as the dog came to Guy's bunk and started sniffing at Guy's crotch.

"Off! Rebel! Off!" the shorter officer yelled, pulling frantically on the leash, which had absolutely no effect on the attention Rebel was paying to Guy's crotch. The taller officer grabbed Rebel's collar and jerked hard. Rebel turned toward the man, intending to teach him some manners, but then got distracted by the bag of potato chips in Gianelli's hands.

"I take it this is a search for drugs," Gianelli said cheerfully, as his bag of chips exploded in Rebel's jowls.

"That's right," the taller officer shouted. "Just stay where you are and don't move until we're finished."

Gianelli looked at his mangled bag of potato chips, which the dog had thrown to the floor, and was devouring.

"You might think about feeding him occasionally," Gianelli said.

The shorter officer began to jerk Rebel's leash again, but the dog barely moved until he finished off the chips. Then he yawned, stretched, and curled up in a ball, nose to tail, planning to take a nap.

Both officers took holds on his leash and heaved the dog to his feet.

"Find it!" the taller officer snapped at Rebel. "Find it! Find it all!" Rebel shook his snout, coughed, his tail started wagging violently, and he headed arrowlike to the middle drawer in Guy Lopaca's dresser. Rebel started pawing at it, violently, and whining. The shorter officer pulled the drawer open and Rebel stuck his snout inside, returning with a mouth full of OD green boxer shorts.

"Jeez-uz, Rebel!" the taller officer yelled. "Find it, you frigging poodle!"

Rebel spat the shorts at Guy's feet, sat and waited to be patted, and then lunged for a wastebasket, in which could be found (once the dog had tipped the contents onto the floor) empty fruit cans and a stale pea-nut butter cookie.

For the next few minutes Rebel hauled the two officers around The Hootch, deconstructing beds and bureaus, swallowing a morsel here or there, paying two visits to Gianelli's crotch and one more to Guy's. During the rampage, Guy looked squarely at Gianelli, whose eyebrows twitched toward the ceiling, where more than a pound of lush marijuana was stored. Guy nodded discreetly, and motioned with his own eyes to the top of Tyler DeMudge's dresser, where a glass ashtray—containing several roaches and one virgin joint—twinkled in plain view. The officers passed it several times as Rebel tossed and shucked them around the room, searching for drugs exactly like those.

Finally, when he was sure the officers were paying him no attention, Gianelli slid sideways toward his dresser, and grabbed a small package of beef jerky, which he stripped with his hands behind his back. Then he silently underhanded the jerky through the nearest open door. The oily scent of the smoked meat made it to Rebel's nostrils at about the same time Rebel's ears picked up the subtle *flump!* as the jerky hit the ground. Rebel bounded across The Hootch and out the door, while both officers held on, and one of them shouted, "At ease! All clear!" before he was hauled outside as well.

"I hate beef jerky," Gianelli said, "but I always keep it around just in case."

"Do they sniff for drugs often?" Guy asked.

"Hardly ever," Gianelli said, "but it's unpredictable."

"I was kind of worried," Guy confessed. "Have you ever been caught?"

"Me, personally, no," Gianelli replied. "But The Hootch got caught once. They came through with a good dog and found the ceiling stash in about twelve seconds."

"What did you do?" Guy asked.

"There was nothing we could do," Gianelli said. "We had to pay them a hundred bucks each, and let them take the whole stash."

Guy just stared at him.

"And of course the dog got some jerky," Gianelli said. "That was only fair."

Not If You're Back in Tulsa

The Chinook helicopter is to things that fly what the hippopotamus is to things that walk. Blunt, ponderous, and powerful, the Chinook has a fat tubular fuselage and huge rotors on each end. The Chinook's cavernous body is used to carry equipment and supplies in bulk. The Chinook's sky-sucking rotors also enable it to lift massive objects and carry them long distances, suspended below its belly by steel cables.

One day a Chinook was moving from one place to another a pack of steel sheets, used to make temporary landing fields. Place A was inside The Citadel, and Place B was somewhere on the other side of the river. As the Chinook floated like a blimp over the central market region of downtown Hue, one of the sheets separated from the rest of the pack and tumbled silently downward.

Guy saw the sheet peel off and begin to tumble. He didn't guess what it was until it had nearly reached the jumble of crowded stalls and alleyways of the market. Unlike a playing card, that might float and flutter as it fell from a deck, the heavy sheet of steel bore straight down, gaining speed.

Though he was too far away to hear it, Guy Lopaca could feel the impact through his boots. He pictured the busy market, the narrow lanes, the crowds. He imagined the mass of flat steel falling, the sudden crushing splatter, like a flyswatter.

The Chinook twitched slightly as the heavy plate disengaged. After a couple of seconds, another plate left the pack and fell, then another, and then they all fell together. There was no sound from the distant impacts; just a few gentle tremors through Guy's boots. His feet tingled.

The unweighted Chinook rose a little higher into the air, and began circling the place where its cargo had fallen. The Chinook moved higher still. Guy knew that vengeful small-arms fire would soon become a risk for the young men in the helicopter. They should leave, and leave quickly, before the first insane survivor of the carnage began firing. But they stayed where they were for a while, hovering. They were ashamed to leave this place, Guy thought, and ashamed to land anywhere else.

The cargo cables dangled from the Chinook's belly. A cloud of dust rose from the place where the steel plates had come to ground. The wind from the hovering Chinook pressed down and flattened the dust cloud, spreading it over the market like a shroud.

Eventually the Chinook had to return to its base. As soon as the Chinook landed, the members of its flight crew were sequestered and interviewed. Grim officers asked questions, and sad young men gave answers. The pilot had a long talk about his choice of routes. On a map, he traced with a shaking finger the route he might have taken: over The Citadel wall directly to the river; then following the course of the river with only a boat or two at any point below. "It's my fault," he said. "If it's anybody's fault, it's mine."

When the pilot's interview was over and the statement he gave was signed, an officer who was senior but not much older told the pilot that he was going to be in some deep shit for a while. "We hurt some of our friends today," the officer said. "It's going to cause problems. It will probably be picked up by some newspapers. Your hometown paper will carry the story. They'll call up your mommy and your high-school football coach. You will never forget what happened today." He paused, waiting for the pilot to catch up with him.

"If the load had dropped earlier, you would have killed the guys who loaded it, our own guys. If it had dropped later, just before you landed at the base, you would have killed some of our own supply guys waiting to unload it, or maybe some of us sitting at desks or changing oil on a deuce-and-a-half."

The pilot nodded.

"This doesn't happen if you're back in Tulsa buying power tools at Sears," the officer said. "This doesn't happen if you're living your own life. Do you understand that?"

The pilot nodded.

"If anyone suggests an early discharge, or that you rotate back to The World, you decline," the officer said, "am I right?"

The pilot thought for a few seconds, then nodded.

"You came here to do your job, and you do it," the officer said. "You keep doing your job, just like you were doing it today. And when you're finished doing it, then you go home," the officer said. "Don't let them take that away from you."

The pilot didn't nod.

"Drunken kids in Fords and Chevies are going to kill more people today than you did," the officer said. "You didn't let us down today. The Army let you down today."

The pilot nodded. He thanked the investigating officer, this professional soldier who was not much older than he was. The pilot raised himself up and saluted before the investigator left the room. The pilot thought about getting drunk, but thought better of it. He thought about talking to the chaplain, but thought better of that as well.

The accident was only barely his fault, the pilot knew, but after thinking about it all afternoon and evening he decided to shoot himself anyway, without even trying to reach his mom or his football coach. Alone in his room, he placed the muzzle of his Army sidearm against his head, took a deep breath, and committed a vivid, messy suicide in his imagination, only to give up, the rankest form of coward, or the most worthwhile of pragmatists, in what was passing for real life that day.

The Chinook was examined, but there was nothing wrong with it or its cable or its gear. The ground crew that had packed the steel plates swore they had done nothing wrong.

The day after the accident, an Army team arrived at the market to investigate. The metal plates were already gone, scavenged during the night. Vietnamese laborers were filling in the craters. On the second day after the accident the market's puncture wounds had closed. A scab of reconstructed stalls and alleys had completely closed the gaps.

A week after the accident, Guy Lopaca went to the market to buy a replacement for his floppy camouflage hat, which a young boy had snatched from his head as Guy drove a jeep to The Citadel. He thought: if I had taken a different route, the kid would have stolen someone else's hat.

Too Brainlessly Proud

Guy Lopaca learned Vietnamese at the Defense Language Institute (DLI) in El Paso, Texas. His group was of a higher octane than the usual Army draftee blend.

They were all college graduates, they had all excelled at the Army's test for language aptitude, they had all been put into an "accelerated" course: thirty-six weeks rather than the normal forty-seven. They had all volunteered to take the course. More education? Sure, why not? Some of the men had been in graduate school when plucked by the draft. There was one fellow from Harvard and one from Yale. One of them had already published a book. And none of them had a clue about this screwy, musical language.

A teacher once passed them in the hall, and said, "*Hom nay* something-something," after which a fierce debate broke out among the geniuses. One fellow said it meant "How tall are you?" Another said no, it meant "How hot is today?" Nuts, said another, it meant "Will you meet me at five?" Also in the running were "Are you five years old?"

and "Where are the five blackboards?" They competed to make the most magnificent show of getting it completely wrong.

They spent their first days, hour after hour, telling jokes in English. The sophisticated Vietnamese women who taught them would plod through the textbooks, enunciating, repeating, prodding them to concentrate. But instead the men would carry on their private conversations, loudly ignoring the ladies. The young men were brainy, sarcastic scholastic veterans with many hours to spend. They were three dozen Oscar Wildes plying their sharp-witted trade in three different rooms, congregating in the hallway during breaks to play Frisbee soccer and ridicule each other in iambic pentameter.

Language school was chaos, and they didn't care. They were no longer competing for admission to good schools, or for scholarships, or jobs or tenure or even sack time with some brain-infatuated girl. When the teachers handed out grades, they all got the same thing: "Excellent." None of them could say the word "excellent" in Vietnamese and didn't bother to look it up.

They didn't care. Didn't the Army understand that? *They didn't care.* They would fake it. Hell, if smart guys like them couldn't fake it in the Army, where could they fake it? They knew they could fake it. There was never a time or place they couldn't fake it. Besides, if they flunked, what was the Army going to do? Send them to Vietnam? Hah! So what? They had *volunteered* to go to Vietnam.

That's where the Army had them.

Their defiance couldn't last. Each of them was in Vietnamese training as a volunteer. They had the ability to evade every responsibility the Army might try to impose on them, but not one of them knew how to fall short of a goal he had set for himself.

Within a few weeks, their nature took over, and without abating their contempt for all things Army, they started to learn. They began to tell jokes in Vietnamese instead of English. Awful, ear-gnashing Vietnamese, to be sure, but it was the best they could do, and eventually they were unashamed to be trying to do their best.

"I'm from Harvard," one of them thought. "I should be doing this better than any of the others."

"I'm from Michigan State," another thought, "and that asshole from Harvard is starting to piss me off."

During their hallway Frisbee games they began to shout the score in Vietnamese. When they threw crumpled paper balls in class, they would call out their targets in Vietnamese. For the political goons who were running the American war, the DLI students thought up insulting Vietnamese nicknames, and inspirational Vietnamese tortures.

Along with a vocabulary and some syntax, Guy and his classmates were taught something about the Vietnamese caste system, and history, and politics, and religion. Where does wealth come from? Whose children are educated in Europe? Why do Catholics attain public office and military command, while Buddhists burn themselves with gasoline on city streets?

Their Vietnamese refugee instructors gave the men the kind of far-ranging, enlightened training one might have given ambassadors, and the men wondered what jobs awaited their newfound skills. For months they had no idea what they would be doing once they arrived in Vietnam. Not once did they imagine that the Army had no idea either.

By the time the course ended, none of them could well understand their Vietnamese teachers, but they could all understand one another in a language they had never spoken thirty-six weeks before—and hated, to tell the truth—but there it was on their lips: El-Paso-Texas-Army-Vietnamese, a polyglot porridge of twangs and mucousy coughs in which they were all fluent with one another although none of them sounded the same.

At the end of the course, they all said good-bye to their teachers, who said good-bye back, followed by a few affectionate words that none of the men could understand, but it was too late to bother. They poured into the hall and had a last Frisbee soccer game, yelling out the score and some terrific insults in their personal dialect, native only to a group of brainy college guys, who were too arrogant to learn the language any way other than the way they wanted . . . and too brainlessly proud to let the high-school dropouts take a turn in the war without them.

Warm and Soft

At some point Arthur Grissom became obsessed with flannel. It started in a dream. There was a young blond girl whose shape was well defined but whose face was not. The plot of the dream developed quickly. Somehow he was on a couch with her, then she left the room, and then she returned wearing flannel pajamas. As she walked across the room, her long blond hair fell loosely upon her breasts, which bobbled as young women's breasts sometimes do in life and always did in Arthur's favorite dreams. She stopped, looked down at him, and gently pulled his face against her flannel belly. Arthur was from that moment, asleep and awake, a lost soul.

He thought about flannel all the time. At night he dreamed compulsively about flannel-clad girls, and during the day he thought about them with a premeditated zeal that left him, by day's end, exhausted and excited and ready to jerk off and dream again.

He made a list of the few girls he had dated and the many he had admired in recent years, and spent time imagining each in flannel pajamas, sighing and yielding as he caressed their downy bumps and lumps, and flicked their buttons one by one.

He had a Sears Roebuck catalog, and often looked at the ads for flannel nightwear. He would fix on a pose, and imagine it to a more erotic level. Longer hair, slimmer waist, a turn of the shoulders, and the back arched . . . just . . . there.

• • •

One day an emaciated peasant girl walked by the door carrying the bucket she used to clean latrines. Arthur closed his eyes and imagined her lying beside him in the dark. He ran his fingers through her imaginary hair, so straight and slippery, all the way down her narrow neck and shoulders, the hair ending in the hollow place where began the delicate swelling of her buttocks. If only she were an American girl, and he knew her name . . .

• • •

It was as if he had reduced all of his most primal desires to warmth and softness—just those two. To be warm and to be soft. To be warm and soft. Think of the female breast. Yes, well . . . Now think of the female breast in a flannel nightshirt.

He remembered what it was like when he was a boy in coldest wintertime, when even people of moderate means could afford to keep their bedroom windows open as a sleeping tonic. The heat from the baseboard radiator would rise to meet the crisp air from the open window. At their interface ten-year-old Arthur would squiggle into bed, into clean sheets and heavy blankets, his nose and cheeks tickled by the cold. Wearing flannel pajamas.

Oh, he knew how sick it was, this obsession with flannel. But he rode it like a wave through day after energized day. In a faraway place, surrounded by strange men with whom he had no connection, surrounded by an even greater circle of enemies who terrified him, Arthur had no upstairs bedroom to escape to, no familiar bed to snuggle into. And—let's face it—he had developed beyond the stage when crawling into bed alone would be enough.

He had a little boy's memory but a young man's need. And so, for weeks, he imagined mute, compliant girls, who would present to him in flannel, wrap their arms and legs around him, and smile adoringly as he unbuttoned their furry plaid package and exploded into them a geyser of loneliness and longing.

In the barracks and hootches all around him, every night there were the sounds of men grunting, hired women chattering, and bunks slamming rhythmically against plywood walls. After all that was over, later each night, Arthur would lie in his bed and rub his cheek on imaginary flannel, release imaginary buttons, and wrap himself around the nameless, faceless treasures he uncovered. Sometimes he would fall asleep immediately; sometimes he would run the whole scripted scene— caress, uncover, enfold—three or four times before ejaculating.

● ● ●

For weeks he was enthralled. And then, one night, he went to bed but kept the light on longer than usual as he read from a novel. He read slowly, and it took a very long time for him to get tired and give in to the dark. He closed his eyes finally, and slowly a young girl appeared on the edge of his imagination. The pink and white squares of her pale flannel shirt swelled to eager points at each nipple. Her hips swayed as she stepped toward him.

And then, suddenly, she dissolved into a dim gray mist and was gone. She dissolved into the moist mist of Arthur's tears. He wept.

The only person in flannel I have ever touched is myself, Arthur thought. *I would be this lonely, this alone, anywhere in the world. Vietnam has nothing to do with it. The problem is me.*

A GI passing by stuck his head into the room. "You OK?" he asked.

"Sure," Arthur replied. "I'm OK."

"Being homesick's a bitch," the GI said.

"Sure," Arthur replied, "that's all it is."

Who's the Nurse Here?

If a girl deserves it, maybe a guy should be faithful to her," Virgin
Mary said. "Although, of course, I need to find a certain number of
exceptions every month."

"You keep asking me if I think the girl back home might
be cheating on me," Guy said. "Haven't you asked me that a
lot?"

"Four times," Mary replied.

"Why is it so important to you what I think about her?" Guy asked.
"Sounds to me like you're worried that someone might cheat on you,
someday."

"I'm an Army nurse," Mary said. "If I want bad psychiatric coun-
seling, I know where to find it. And anyway, just because I'm curious
doesn't mean it's important."

"Why is it that you're so curious?" Guy asked. "What are you afraid
of?"

"Rocket attacks, for one thing," Mary said. "And now *you* are beginning to scare me. I guess that's it. I'm afraid of rocket attacks and you, not necessarily in that order. And tax audits. They scare me, too. Not as much as you, though."

"I think you're afraid that you'll go home, find some guy, settle down," he said, "and then the guy will start playing around, and you won't have the right to complain. Maybe you think you don't deserve a man you can trust."

"See, this is exactly the kind of thing a woman wants to hear from a man," Mary said. "We don't need to know that our hair looks nice. No. We need the guy to talk about the psychological baggage we'll carry all our lives because we're such sluts." Mary smiled grimly while she sucked some beer from her bottle.

"Neither of us," Guy said, "knows anything, really, about what makes a relationship between a man and a woman."

"Speak for yourself. I know about relationships two or three times a week."

"We talk a lot about all the sexual encounters you have," Guy said, "but we never talk about mine."

Her eyes widened with interest.

"I thought you didn't fool around," Mary said. "You told me you didn't. You do? Who with?"

"See, that's the thing about me that you don't appreciate," Guy said. He stood up. "Let's take a walk," he said.

They went outside, and Guy took her by the arm and walked her across The Hotel compound. *This is the second time I've touched her,* he thought. *I shook her hand once.*

• • •

He brought her to the latrine nearest to his hootch. He stuck his head inside, yelled "Medical inspection! Nurse coming through!" and led her in. There was no one else there.

"See those three toilet stalls?" he asked, as they walked toward them. "See the one on the far end?" he asked, as they stopped just short of the stalls.

"The stall on the far end is the one I jerk off in," Guy said.

Mary laughed and put her hands over her face and laughed some more.

"Yeah, my gonads would be big as basketballs if I didn't jerk off once in a while." Guy sighed. "You know that. Hell, it's the foundation of a whole industry that I think you're familiar with."

She grabbed his arm with both her hands and shook with uncontrollable laughter.

"I always use the same stall," Guy said. "I didn't have any particular reason for using that stall first, but once I started using it I wouldn't use any other stall to jerk off in. It seems more natural and comfortable for me to use that same stall every time."

"This is just absolutely insane." Mary laughed. "And believe me, whatever you're thinking, I am *not* going into that stall with you."

"I wouldn't let you, and you're missing the point," Guy said. "Men who are really monogamous are monogamous before they're even *ogamous*. We suffer from a single-minded need to share intimacy with one object at a time, a woman if we can get her, and a toilet stall if that's all we can find. It isn't the girl who makes us faithful. It's fidelity itself. It's in our nature to be faithful. Maybe that makes it less special, but that's not for me to say."

"Oh, don't be *silly,*" Mary said. "I think this is *very* special. And I approve of your choice of stalls. If I were a guy, I'd probably want the same stall. Look at the knob."

"That's a latch," Guy said.

"Who's the nurse here?" Mary said. "I know a knob when I see one."

"You know," Guy said, "some of my best friends use any damn toilet stall they stumble into. Imagine my anxiety when I find some other guy in my toilet stall. Do you think I'm nuts?"

"This is quite a learning experience for me," Mary said. "It seems I have been looking in all the wrong places for men of strong character, that I could trust. I just hadn't ever thought of looking in Army toilet stalls."

For a while they just stood there, Guy's arm in Mary's hands, admiring his excellent choice of the absolutely most alluring toilet stall in the whole latrine.

"Of course, in the case of a toilet stall, as in the case of a woman," Guy said, "real beauty is not just skin-deep, and it's definitely what's inside that counts."

"You wouldn't want to choose a long-term toilet relationship based only on a door and a knob," Mary said.

"Or a latch," Guy said.

"Do you think we could pack a lunch the next time you take me on a field trip?" Mary asked.

"No, I think that would constitute a date," he said, "and it's not in my nature to have one of those right now."

Methods of Rice Farming

What the Vietnamese needed from the American Army was not so much an education as a nudge.

"Of course they already know how to grow rice," Captain Haven explained one day to a down-in-the-dumps Guy Lopaca. "But they don't plant the kind of miracle rice we want them to grow. The miracle rice grows like wildfire. The rice they want to plant grows like only 40 percent of wildfire."

"But don't they hate the taste of our rice?" Guy asked. "Isn't taste the only reason why they won't plant it? Don't they already know everything else?"

"Yes, of course they know everything," Captain Haven said, "but the theory is that we should start the reeducation process right from the beginning, and teach them everything there is to know about growing rice, *every goddamn thing they already know about growing rice,* until they are sick and tired of our meddling and will do anything to get rid of us.

"The theory is that they'll give in and grow the damn miracle rice just to stop us from teaching them how to do it. I *think* that's what the

Army has in mind. I can't think of anything else to explain why we teach them what they already know how to do better than we do."

"That theory is all right as far as it goes," Guy said forlornly, "but it doesn't go to the places I go to. No one teaches anything about growing rice in the places I go to. No one but me is there. All I do is deliver rice seed and fertilizer and stuff to places so far away they should have their own embassy, and no one ever asks me how to do a goddamn thing with it."

"And it's a good thing they don't ask you, isn't it?" Captain Haven suggested, "since you don't know anything at all about growing rice."

"You're right, I don't," Guy said.

"That's what the lieutenants are for," Captain Haven said. "It's their job to teach the rice farmers how to grow rice."

"But none of the lieutenants ever grew rice before they got here," Guy protested. "None of them really knows how to grow rice now."

"That's what I am here for," Captain Haven said. "It's *my* job to worry about whether the lieutenants don't know how to grow rice. You just have to worry about correctly translating what they say."

"But half the time I'm out there alone delivering the rice seed and chemicals without them," Guy protested. "They don't say anything for me to translate."

"Well, that should make it easy for you," Captain Haven said. "You're not going to start worrying about what the lieutenants *don't* say, are you?"

"No, sir," Guy said, giving up. After all, driving a truck full of rice to the end of the earth and not translating anything was better duty than driving a truck full of rice to the end of the earth and *also* suffering the shame of a bad translation.

"If it will make you feel better," Captain Haven said, "you can read this pamphlet that all the officers have to read before going out in the field to educate the rice farmers."

He tossed over a pocket-sized brochure entitled *Methods of Rice Farming.* Guy flipped through it and read a few lines and looked at the pictures, and began to realize how simple it might be to grow rice. It was just a linear, step-by-step process that was actually simple to perform, assuming one could arise every morning three hours before going to bed the night before, and spend every part of those twenty-seven-hour-days growing rice.

The book was written by Professor Ông Ba Tên.

"I think his name means 'Man with Three Names' in Vietnamese," Guy pointed out.

"How about that," Captain Haven replied, never happy to have learned something new about the language he refused to learn a single word of because it kept him from sleeping with his wife.

"Isn't this the same Ông Ba Tên who wrote the pamphlets the lieutenants use for the peanut farming and swine breeding?" Guy asked delicately.

"Yes," Captain Haven replied, "he seems to be a prolific writer."

"It says here that Ông Ba Tên is a professor at the Louisiana State University agriculture school," Guy pointed out. "In America," he subtly pointed out.

"Yes, he is," Captain Haven replied. "In fact, I hear it was in Louisiana that he learned how to grow rice."

"And did you notice that this pamphlet is really *two* pamphlets in one?" Guy asked deftly. "Have you noticed that the second half of the pamphlet is the same as the first half, except it's printed in Vietnamese? Have you noticed that?"

"The lieutenants are supposed to read the pamphlets," Captain Haven said decisively. "Not the platoon commander and not enlisted men."

"I was just thinking . . ." Guy said with extraordinary delicacy. "If we had enough of these pamphlets . . . since they're already written in Vietnamese and they contain all the information the lieutenants use . . . then we could just pass them out to the farmers . . ."

"That pamphlet's out of print," Captain Haven said.

"Well then, we could just make some new copies and . . ."

"That pamphlet's copyrighted," Captain Haven said.

"Besides," Guy said, giving in to the obvious, "the farmers already know this stuff anyway."

"Exactly," Captain Haven said.

"But we'll keep teaching it to them regardless . . ." Guy said.

"Exactly," Captain Haven said.

"Until they start using the miracle rice we want them to use," Guy concluded.

"Exactly," Captain Haven said.

"Because they're sick of us butting in," Guy said.

"Exactly," Captain Haven said.

"But sometimes the lieutenants won't be there to teach them or butt in and I'll have to deliver the rice seed alone."

"That's true," Captain Haven said.

"Without any educational component at all."

"It would seem so," Captain Haven said.

"Well," Guy said, "if I can somehow get them to use the rice seed we deliver to them for free, *without* the education that they hate so much . . . can I go home?"

"I don't know," Captain Haven said. "Let's try it and see if it works."

Not in His Nature

uy Lopaca sat behind the wheel of a slowly moving truck, shook his head, and sweated. "Where the hell am I?" he asked himself. "And why the hell am I here?"

Beside him sat a neatly dressed woman of about thirty years. The woman wore big plastic sunglasses with thick black frames. Her lips were slick and red. Her Western makeup was flawless. Her hat, although shaped to the native flat-cone style, could have been done up in Paris by an artist with very fine hands. She was an exquisitely put-together lady who paid no attention to Guy Lopaca unless she had to.

"Where the hell are we going?" Lopaca sighed, not quite out loud, utterly lost and terribly lonely.

The woman said nothing at all. When she wanted Guy to turn left or right, she simply waved her hand left or right. "How much farther?" he asked her once. She kept looking straight ahead, and simply waved in that direction.

Except for the occasional roadside village, most of the trip lay through open rice country. There was little movement on the land: some tilling, some grazing of water buffalo.

In back of Guy, in the bed of the truck, were sacks of miracle rice seed. Last week it was TN-8 rice seed to who knows where. Now it was TN-20 rice seed to somewhere else. Here he was on another tedious supply run, driving a truck, wasting his time and education.

•   •   •

"Agriculture research stations in Burma and the Philippines develop it," Captain Haven had beamed as Vietnamese workers loaded the rice seed in Hue. "The yield is much better than the local Vietnamese variety. If everyone used this seed, we could triple the yield in a year. Maybe better."

"They have to increase the yield," Gianelli told Guy. "Every time there's fighting in rice country, some of the people leave and the land isn't cultivated anymore. Even if the brave ones stayed the season, when the harvest came they would die fighting off the VC, the NVA, and sometimes even the ARVN. Everybody with a gun would try to take the rice from them, so they leave without bothering to grow it."

"This region used to *export* rice ten years ago," Captain Haven said. "Now we have to import thousands of tons of rice from Japan. The new miracle rice varieties we distribute could produce a lot more food on the land that's still in cultivation, to make up for the land they've lost to the war."

When the Vietnamese laborers were finished loading, they bowed. Captain Haven thanked them clumsily, while tapping a bag of seed.

"Good rice. Feed whole country someday," he said. The laborers just bowed again and smiled, confused.

"Good rice!" Captain Haven shouted. He pointed to the rice seed, brought his hand to his mouth, pretended to chew, and rubbed his belly.

"Mmmmm!" he yelled.

"Oi!" one of the laborers replied, holding his nose. Another grimaced and stuck out his tongue. The third pretended to pee on a bag of miracle rice seed.

"They don't like the flavor of the new rice," Gianelli said. "It could save them from starvation, but it's almost as hard to make them eat it as it is to make them grow it."

One of the men blew his nose in a greasy rag, then pretended to wipe his rear end with it. Then he threw the rag onto the miracle seed sacks, fiercely pointed at them several times, and shouted, "Number Ten!" Then he kicked the truck.

"That's why we open demonstration farms," Captain Haven said. "When these guys see farmers pulling out three or four times as much food per acre, they'll get the point."

•   •   •

Guy's assignment was to drive the truck wherever the silently sophisticated woman next to him wanted it to go which, it appeared to Guy right now, was somewhere very near the end of the earth. The earth seemed to have many ragged ends, most of which he expected to visit before his tour in Vietnam was over.

Because no one offered to send a battalion of troops with him as escort, Guy had nothing to rely on but his helmet, his flak vest, his weapons, and his game face. The truck had sandbags on the floor to muffle a mine blast, but that was it for armor. The cab didn't even have a canvas top. He resigned himself to driving in the open sun the whole way, his steel helmet baking like a bread oven. Guy felt nakedly American: a ten-point buck that had wandered onto a gun club's target range.

Guy had taken a long time to arrange his weaponry. In addition to the pistol he carried now, a borrowed M-16 rifle was cleverly hung by its fabric strap from a windscreen knob. Before starting the trip, Guy sat in the truck alone, and practiced reaching for the gun, eventually (with some tuning of the strap) becoming confident that even while tumbling for cover he could grab the rifle and hit the ground without a wasted millisecond. He got himself ready to go, but not happy to go.

It wasn't fair. He shouldn't be given all these solo assignments. Maybe it would be OK if there were another American in the vehicle, to watch his back and share his worry. But to send him out here in the deepest boondocks with . . . He looked at her again. She weighed maybe eighty pounds. She kept her hands folded in her lap, when she wasn't waving him one way or another. Cool. Icy. Imperious. He had tried to say hello when she climbed into the truck, but all she did was face front and wave. "Go," she said, "you go now." "Where?" he asked her in her own language. "Go," she replied, "you go now," and waved with a flat hand, as if shooing away a mosquito, or some bigger pest.

"Don't worry," Captain Haven had told him, "all you have to do is drive. The Vietnamese will show you where. Just drop off the seed and come back. No sweat."

"The Vietnamese." That's what Haven had called the person in whose company Guy would venture into the bush. Guy had imagined a fellow about twenty-five, with muscles, multiple firearms, and a machete on his belt. Not . . . He looked at her again . . .

The lady coughed and waved to the right. Guy pulled off the highway onto a dirt road. They drove the next two miles through paddy fields, on a narrow dikeway pocked with muddy pits. Once the truck began to slide off a muddy shoulder, nearly tipping into a paddy. The woman waved her hand, as if she could slap the truck back into position, while Guy struggled to catch the slide and recovered by furiously playing the clutch and gas pedals.

If we end up stuck in a paddy when darkness comes, he thought, *am I her protection, or is she mine?*

The path through the rice fields seemed to end abruptly at a wall of shrubbery and trees. This was not the jungle Guy had imagined before he came to Vietnam. It was a gnarled and tangled confusion of bushes and branches; an impenetrable hedgerow with a hostile attitude.

If you stuck your arm in that mess, Guy thought, *you'd lose sight of your elbow and you might never see your hand again.*

Guy stopped the truck because he thought there was nowhere he could go. The woman punched him on the shoulder, and when he turned to look at her she scowled and waved her open hand forward.

He looked again and . . . Well, there *was* sort of a road through there after all. It was open at ground level, where he could see a sandy track. The foliage collapsed in above the road, as if to make an arbor or tunnel. This is going to be no fun at all, Guy thought. He put the truck in first gear and nosed into the bush.

The branches pressed against the truck from both sides, making noise like lots of fingers scratching on lots of blackboards. Branches caught on the frame of the windscreen, slapping at his face repeatedly. No matter how slowly he drove, Guy couldn't see turns in the road until he was already in them. Sometimes he would miss a turn, plow into the roadside greenery, and have to back out a yard or two to make the angle. The canopy that closed over the road was so dense that the sunlight was cut in half, made foglike and murky.

Once the road opened suddenly on a group of abandoned huts, two of them incinerated. At another point the road ended altogether, cut off by a barricade of green and brown. The silent woman waved him backward fifty yards until they found a fork in the road that even she had missed. A few minutes later the road widened into a swath of empty ground, that led to a brook and a wooden bridge. As the truck crossed the bridge, a dirty young Vietnamese in shorts and a tattered shirt jumped onto the running board. He sneered at Guy and chattered at the woman, who turned her face away from him and answered curtly.

The young man laughed and hopped to the ground. As they drove on, Guy monitored him in the truck's rearview mirrors. From a lean-to next to the bridge, the young man drew a heavy rifle. He sat in a chair with the gun across his lap, watching as Guy's truck vanished once more into the woods.

"What did he want?" Guy asked the woman. She waved her hand to the front impatiently.

Although the forest canopy had cut off the harsh afternoon sun, Guy became aware of his sweat. "Don't worry," Captain Haven had told him, "all you have to do is drive . . . No sweat."

No sweat? Did Haven think these trucks had air conditioners? Guy's sweat filled his armpits with soapy foam, and sweat ran down his neck to soak his undershirt and fatigues. Dust from the road mixed with leaf chips and shreds of broken branches, spattering scratchy bits on his face, neck, and arms. His crotch and derriere were clammy. All of his sweat was not from the heat. Some of his sweat was from the fear. In the shadows in these woods there could no longer be found any part of the world Guy Lopaca once lived in. He was lost.

He was afraid to look at his watch, afraid to think of what this road would be like if he were still on it at dusk. He had no radio. Not even a signal flare. He was exposed, vulnerable, and scared. The truck clawed at the ragged road, straining to make progress, hauling Guy Lopaca inch by anguished inch away from home. He was in first gear almost all the time now. The road had become erratic and cruel. It jerked the truck left and right. The merciless road was playing nasty games with him now. He was a mouse. Vietnam was the cat.

The road hooked to the left. He braked hard, pulled hard at the wheel, made a hard corner, and cursed as the road skewed to the right again, into another heartless turn that he thoroughly missed. The truck strained, whined, pushed into a mess of bushes, and stalled.

As the truck sat motionless in the scrub, and Guy sat motionless in the truck, an invisible stranger pulled a trigger, and Guy Lopaca's universe came to a sudden, inconceivable end.

BAMBAMBAMBAMBAMBAMBAMBAMBAM . . .

Guy sucked in his breath. He had never heard a sound so loud and brittle. In an instant he realized what was happening, and waited to die.

BAMBAMBAMBAMBAMBAMBAMBAM . . .

As the bullets sped toward him he had time to do nothing but think . . . think about . . . what? . . . think about . . .

Wooooosh.

I think, therefore I continue to be, Guy thought. *I think. I'm still thinking. Keep thinking. I'm thinking. I'm thinking.*

"Easy," God said to him. "Take it easy. Take it easy. Take it easy."

I'm still thinking, Guy thought. *I'm still here. How long will it be? When will it happen and how will it feel?* The steering wheel was in focus. Those were his hands and fingers. *I'm still thinking. Will I feel the bullets hit me? Will they hit me in the head first, will they hit my brain? Will I feel them . . . before I stop feeling them . . . and stop . . . thinking . . . I'm still thinking still thinking I think therefore I continue to think I'm thinking I'm still thinking . . .*

"Easy," God said gently. "Just take it easy. Take it easy. Take it easy."

All right, Guy conceded, *I'm ready now. I can't think about it anymore. It's my time. I'm ready.*

He closed his eyes and waited to receive the first bullet.

Wooooosh.

The bullets streaking through the universe evaporated. The sound waves of humid air, that had started at the muzzle of a gun, finished breaking over him and dissipated somewhere else.

Guy blinked. He let out the breath that he had been holding tight.

His hands released the steering wheel and fell to his sides. For a second or two he looked straight ahead, focusing on nothing past the windshield. He saw grains of dust on the glass, and the corpses of several bugs that had unluckily crossed his path today.

Ponderously, he began to reach for the strap of the M-16 rifle that hung on the windshield knob. A thin hand with polished fingernails slapped his hand away from the gun. He looked to the right. Beside him he saw a striking woman with slick red lips, waving her flat hand at him. "Go," she said, "you go now."

He started the truck, backed it up, and turned it along the path again. He traveled only a few yards before the heavy foliage parted, revealing another thin brook with yet another wooden bridge, and beyond that a large clearing, and a village compound of thatched huts and wooden sheds, one of which bore a wooden pole with a yellow national flag.

On the small wooden bridge, there stood a soldier of the Popular Force militia, who had just cleaned the barrel of her American assault rifle by shooting eighteen bullets into the brook. The PF soldier was a young girl in an American bush hat, like the one Guy sometimes wore. She waved and smiled, her twin pigtails flopping gaily. In the shade under the brim of her hat, between the heavy pigtails, Guy saw . . . could it be? . . . *freckles.*

She was adorable. Look at her. She looked just like Becky Thatcher, whose pigtails Tom Sawyer loved to plunk in the inkwell. She was Becky Thatcher all right, Mark Twain's Becky, and here came Huckleberry Finn to fish with her off the bridge. *Hello, Huck!* She waved and smiled shyly as the shell-shocked American slowly passed her by.

If I get married and have fifteen children, Guy Lopaca thought, *no woman will ever change me the way you just did, little girl.*

It had never been an ambush, and instead of Vietcong he found a cute kid playing with a plastic-stocked toy that went boom. *What did you do in the war, Grandpa? I thought I died in an ambush once, but it* was just a girl in pigtails on a bridge. And, to tell you the truth, *I didn't do anything.*

That was the part that really surprised him. That was the part of the ambush that he couldn't understand. The little girl had taught him what it felt like to be shot at. And he had taught himself what kind of warrior lived inside his skin. *I didn't even take my hands off the steering wheel,* he thought. *I didn't grab my gun or jump for cover or even duck. I let it happen. I gave up my life without a struggle, and a little girl threw it back, like a fish too small to bother with.*

The truck approached the village and was met by half a dozen farmers, and as many militiamen in green and black. They waved at the truck and smiled. Back at the bridge, Becky Thatcher was joined by a young male friend who fired another clip of expensive American bullets into the stream.

The Dragon Lady sitting beside him waved Guy to stop in front of a small shed with plywood sides and a corrugated metal roof. The farmers began to unload the rice seed and put it inside the shed. After that, the door was closed and padlocked. The woman carried the key inside the largest building on the compound. Through the open front door, Guy could see a Vietnamese army officer rise to meet her, take the key, and pocket it. Then the officer came outside, shook Guy's hand, and invited him to come inside and have some tea. Guy and the officer and the woman sat on chairs. It was cool inside. The officer barked, and a man came in carrying a metal tray with a metal teapot and small porcelain cups without handles.

Tea was poured and Guy drank some. It was like no tea Guy had ever tasted or imagined. Apparently they didn't use tea bags or even sieves or strainers here. It was a tea stew, with lots of stuff floating in it, stuff big enough that it could be chewed. The tea was very bitter. It did not taste like tea at all. It seemed rather like boiled forest mulch.

He was surprised that the hot tea did not bother him in the hot Vietnam afternoon. The tea was full of particles. The leaves must have been boiled without a strainer . . . Oh, wait . . . He had already thought about not using a strainer. . . . He had already noticed that. There was no need to think about the strainer again. . . . *If I don't shake the cup,* Guy thought, *the boiled tea leaves will settle to the bottom of the cup, and the tea that I drink will be clear. If I can just stop the cup from shaking, the leaves will settle and the tea will be clear . . . If I can just stop my hand from shaking the cup . . .* He tried holding the cup with both hands, but both hands were shaking and the tea leaves would not settle to the bottom. One of the tea leaves had wings . . . It was an insect . . . Guy plucked it out with his shaking fingertips, while the officer and the cool woman watched him do it.

Before starting the return trip to Hue, Guy stepped off into the woods to compose himself. He closed his eyes, crossed his arms, and took some deep, measured breaths. He was tired and very sad. He tried to come to terms with his disappointment.

The gunfire still chattered in his ears. He still felt the shock waves of sound on his cheeks and in the sensitive hair at his temples. But it was too late to react. The defining moment had passed. All he could do was shiver in the Vietnam heat, while the cool woman in white waited impatiently to wave him home.

If the faux ambush had been a test, he had failed it. In the face of apparently hostile fire, he had done nothing at all. He had become a bullet sponge. He didn't have the instincts of a combat soldier, or even a rabbit.

Perhaps—he hated to think this way—perhaps it was not in his nature to be brave.

It might be even sadder than that.

Perhaps it was not in his nature to survive.

Civilian Warriors

The 5th Platoon shared The Villa with a group of civilian contractor-advisors in the public health and government administration fields. The contractor-advisors were in Vietnam to prove once again that resourceful American middle-managers could make several times more money overseas than they could have made by staying in the States and—*can you believe it?*—wearing suits and ties.

"I'm never going back to *that* shit again," the civilian advisors could be heard drunkenly shouting through the walls two hours before lunchtime. "Send me to *Africa*"—they yelled before knocking off for the day at 2:00 P.M.—"or South frigging *America,* where skills like ours are *needed* and we can make a decent *buck.*"

After having nailed the connecting doors shut, the men of the 5th Platoon tried to ignore the civilian contractor-advisors. "Don't ever go into their part of the building," Gianelli once cautioned Guy Lopaca. "They carry guns," Gianelli said, with a look of alarm. "Middle-aged drunken office workers waving guns at each other. You don't want to go in there."

"You should see their pistols," Tyler whispered as he joined them. "They don't just carry any old pistol. They have to carry special contractor-advisor pistols, that you can see from two miles away. Nickel plated, chrome plated, ivory handles, bright yellow plastic handles. No one has the same gun."

"One guy carries twin .45 caliber pistols with glass grips that he can light up at night," Gianelli said. "They run on batteries. You can see him coming at midnight in a heavy fog."

"One of them broke in here a while ago," Tyler told Guy while the three men sat and had some coffee. "He said he needed ammunition for his new pistol. Started yelling at me when I told him I didn't have any. *'You're the frigging Army and you got to have ammunition!'* he yelled at me. *'I'm an American and you got to help me out,'* he shouted. So I gave him a dictionary. 'Here,' I said, 'try using the ammunition I use.' Boy was he pissed."

"What did he do?" Guy asked.

"He shot the dictionary." Tyler laughed. "Really. I'm not kidding. He and his friends went out back and nailed up the dictionary and shot it all to hell."

"What are they actually here for?" Guy asked. "What do they actually do?"

"Other than pretending to spy for the CIA, the only thing they actually do, that I know of," Gianelli said, "is write progress reports."

"They keep asking us for paper," DeMudge said. "They need that almost as much as they need ammunition."

"And batteries," Gianelli said. "Don't forget the batteries."

"Who's forgetting the batteries?" Tyler shot back. "Where would a public health advisor be without batteries for his illuminated pistol grips?"

Pig Report

Captain Haven called the men together for a strategy session.

"We don't promote ourselves enough," he said. "We're hiding our candle under a basket."

The men looked at one another and blinked.

"My grandmother used to say that," Captain Haven explained. "It means we don't promote ourselves enough."

"Candle alert," Gianelli whispered, "candles under baskets . . . pass it on."

"I had dinner with a friend yesterday," Captain Haven—who had excellent hearing—continued, making a note to take revenge on Gianelli real soon, "and my friend's been spending a lot of time at the Pentagon the last few months. He told me we aren't making the most of our reporting function."

The men blinked at Captain Haven, as vacantly and nonvolunteeringly as they possibly could.

"Every week we call down our usual report to Da Nang, and we don't include anything that could really help us," Captain Haven said.

"My buddy says it's not enough to send them the roster and readiness report and all that crap. We have to tell them the really good stuff we're doing, and tell it in a way they can understand, and can actually use the information. You men can appreciate that."

Blinks all around.

"The Pentagon these days is full of number crunchers," Captain Haven continued, wondering which insubordinate eye he should put his thumb into first. "Because of them, now the whole Army is full of number crunchers. They're like businessmen running a factory. They want to know how many screws it takes to build a car. And how much each screw costs. They want all the numbers they gather to be helpful."

"Like the body counts?" DeMudge ventured, just to keep the conversation going on its workless path toward lunchtime.

"Yes, like the body counts," Captain Haven said. "Body counts are numbers that are easy to collect and easy to crunch. Body counts provide quantifiable data. They carry a message about performance that's easy for people to understand."

"Is that why everyone tells lies about the body counts?" Buddy Brier asked.

"Exactly," Captain Haven replied, "that's exactly why everyone lies about the body counts. They lie about the body counts precisely because the body counts are easy to report and so damn simple to understand. Who really understands big fuzzy things like pacification or defoliation? Nobody. If you want anybody even to think about them, you have to use simple numbers. So many villages. So many acres."

"So many trees," Lieutenant Rossi said. He was a forester. They should let him count the trees someday.

"My friend says we have to do more quantitative reporting," Captain Haven told the men. "We in the Civil Affairs effort are competing with the combat arms for resources. We won't get our fair share unless we start playing their game, which is a quantitative numbers game."

"Do we have to turn in body counts now?" Gianelli asked.

"Yes, Gianelli, and we'll start with counting *your* body," Captain Haven growled. "No, we do *not* have to turn in body counts. We have to turn in counts of the things we actually do, the projects we complete, the accomplishments we achieve. Helpful facts, reduced to numbers."

More frigging *blinking*. He should make them all close their eyes when he talks to them.

"Look," Captain Haven said, exasperated, "here's what I want you to do. It's simple. Keep track of everything you do, and use numbers. Don't say you worked on demonstration plots on Tuesday. Record how many plots, how many villages, how many acres. Every Friday, when we call in the report to Da Nang, I want to include a special report that describes, in numbers, quantitatively, some of the good things we have done."

"Everything?" DeMudge asked.

"No, it doesn't have to be everything," Captain Haven replied. "We'll pick out just one or two things to report each week, but it should be the best things we've been doing. So, for example, if we start five demonstration plots in three villages, we say that. If opening two new fish farms is the best thing we did recently, that will be in the report. Every week should be something good, something with numbers, that can get noticed by someone in Da Nang, and reported easily even higher."

"If we open two fish farms," Gianelli said, "should we say we opened six? Should we say we found dead VC bodies in them?"

Captain Haven blinked.

"Did some judge make you join the Army," he finally asked, "instead of sending you to jail?"

"Sorry, sir," Gianelli said. "I take it we should tell the truth then?"

"Absolutely," Captain Haven said. "No one in this room plans to make a career in the Army. There's no need to lie about anything. I just want people to know we're doing well."

"No bodies then," DeMudge said, brightening, "just rice and volley-balls."

"Rice would be better, I think," Captain Haven said. "Rice would be much better."

• • •

The following Friday afternoon, DeMudge placed the usual call to Sergeant Trotfender at Company Headquarters in Da Nang. When it seemed the usual report was finished, and Sergeant Trotfender was about to sign off, DeMudge asked him to hold on for the pig report.

"The *what* report?" Sergeant Trotfender asked, pressing the telephone harder against his ear. "What kind of report was that?"

"The pig report," DeMudge said emphatically, "a report on Lieutenant Prout's success in the breeding of pigs."

"What the hell are you talking about?" Sergeant Trotfender screamed.

"Lieutenant Prout went to SMDLSC to inspect two sows and eight new piglets," DeMudge bellowed into the high-tech military communications link.

"What? Sows? Whatlets?" Sergeant Trotfender screamed back.

"Piglets! Piglets!" DeMudge shouted at him. "Little bitty piggies! Lieutenant Prout went to SMDLSC to check on the pigs! This is his pig report!"

"Is this serious?" Sergeant Trotfender yelled. "Is this report critical? I'm not going to take this report if it isn't critical!"

DeMudge had his orders. Any time DeMudge's life was interrupted by a military order, it was critical as far as he was concerned.

"Yes, it's critical!" he shouted back. "It's a critical report!"

"Screw it then, what's the report?" Sergeant Trotfender screamed.

"All the pigs are healthy!" DeMudge shouted, reading from Lieutenant Prout's hand-scrawled notes. "The locals never saw such large, healthy piglets. One of the sows is getting on in years, so she looks sick, but she isn't, really."

Pause.

"I'm not going to write that down!" Sergeant Trotfender screamed. "That's not going into your weekly report. The colonel isn't interested in any pigs!"

• • •

DeMudge delivered the bad news to Captain Haven.

"Sir," he said, standing almost at attention, "Company HQ would not accept our pig report."

"Our what?" Captain Haven asked. "Our *what* report?"

"Our pig report, sir," DeMudge said. "The report you asked us to add to the regular weekly report. It was Lieutenant Prout's turn this week. The officers picked numbers out of a hat, and he went first. So he wrote a report on the pig breeding. Big things this week. Eight piglets."

"You sent the colonel a report about baby pigs?" Capt. Haven asked.

"Almost," DeMudge replied. "Sergeant Trotfender wouldn't accept the report. He said the colonel wouldn't be interested in our pigs."

"Our pigs, DeMudge?" Captain Haven said. "You call them *our pigs?*"

"They're beauties, sir," DeMudge beamed. "Do you want to see some pictures?"

"DeMudge," Captain Haven sighed, "if I call your bluff right now, would you be able to pull any photographs of little baby pigs out of your pocket? Are you that messed up?"

"Sorry, sir, I couldn't help it," DeMudge confessed. "I guess I'm overwrought because Sergeant Trotfender wouldn't accept Lieutenant Prout's pig report. After all, they did pull Lieutenant Prout out of graduate school to make him breed pigs in Vietnam. It ought to interest someone that he's doing a good job."

Captain Haven couldn't think of a thing to say.

"With Prout it's piglets," DeMudge said. "With me it's volleyballs. With Gianelli it's medicine, sand, and cement. With Rossi and Lopaca it's rice and watermelons." He paused. "With you it's all of us. I guess we don't reduce to numbers all that well. At least not the kind of numbers that other people in the Army wouldn't laugh at."

Captain Haven thought for a while how lucky he was to have a person like DeMudge in his life. Tomorrow he would find some graceful way of rescinding that ridiculous order for a special weekly report. He would let the unit function as it always had, whether or not Sergeant Trotfender and the colonel knew or cared. He would keep hiding the platoon's candle under a basket, and maybe throw a blanket over the basket if it would help keep them ignored and operating as long as possible just the way they were.

"About the photographs of those piglets," Captain Haven said, after a while.

"Yes, sir?" DeMudge asked.

"Track down Lieutenant Prout and a jeep. Do it right now," Captain Haven said. "We're going to drive out there and take some photographs of those piglets. While they're still cute and we're still proud."

One Less in the Army

"Time to eat!" Danny Schubert aka Danny Maniac said two or three times a day. He never failed to announce his intention to have a meal. Just having the damn meal was never enough; he had to tell you he was about to have it.

"Suppertime!" he would say, dropping his girlie magazine or shutting off the radio.

"Time to eat!" he would cry, in the same voice someone else might use to sound an alert: "Incoming! Time to duck! Bogies in the wire! Time to shoot! Lunchtime! Time to eat!"

After a few weeks, Guy stopped Schubert at The Hootch door and asked him why he got so excited about Army food.

"I don't care shit for the food," Danny replied. "I just like the idea that it's one less meal I'll have to eat in the Army."

Guy thought about this for a while, then mentioned it to Gianelli. "Really?" Gianelli said. "That's really the reason why he does it?" Gianelli squinted his eyes and pondered the news. "That's interesting," he said finally.

The following morning, as Danny Maniac lay asleep in his bunk, Gianelli tiptoed next to his pillow, leaned down, and shouted in his ear:

"Time to shit! Time to take a dump!" and then left for the latrine.

Schubert sat up, blinking, then fell back to sleep.

The next morning, Gianelli repeated the performance. "Time to shit!" he shouted in Danny Maniac's ear. This time Gianelli waited. Schubert woke up, hoisted himself up on his elbows.

"What the hell?" he asked, as eloquently as he was able at the time.

"One less shit in the Army," Gianelli said, smiling. "I thought you would want to know."

Danny Maniac stopped announcing his meals after that, and Gianelli let him sleep in the morning. But they stopped talking to each other as well.

"Was it worth it?" Guy asked Gianelli after a few days.

"Yes and no," Gianelli said. "I never liked him much, but . . ." Gianelli paused, and his voice dropped. "I humiliated him. I'm good at that. And I took away something that was helping him get by." Gianelli shook his head. "You have some brains inside your skull," he said, "so you know what it's like when people like us beat up on people like him. He's not so bad. He didn't deserve it."

Guy nodded.

A couple of days later, Guy was alone in The Hootch when Gianelli walked in with a white cardboard box, which he deposited on Danny Maniac's bunk. Danny came in later, hung some gear in his locker, took out a girlie magazine, and started to lie down. He saw the box, paused, then sat down to open it. He held the lid up for a while, staring inside, and then began to sniffle. Gianelli got up, grabbed Guy's collar, and pulled him out the door.

"Let's leave him alone for a few minutes," Gianelli said.

"What was in the box?" Guy asked.

"Something nice and a note," Gianelli said. " 'One less blueberry pie you'll have to eat in Vietnam.' "

"Does he like blueberry pie?" Guy asked.

"He does now," Gianelli said.

Muddy Boots

As he lay in bed, postponing getting up as long as he could, Guy Lopaca thought about the truest friend he had, at this moment, in all the world: his bleeding asshole.

He had recently discovered that men with certain bleeding rectal conditions were not eligible for induction into the Armed Forces. Guy had been the victim of recurrent bloody hemorrhoids for as long as he could remember, and it was possible that his seizure by the Army was a terrible mistake and a travesty, which a simple medical examination could—to use an optimistic term—rectify.

Today was the day the medical exam would take place, aboard the Hospital Ship Sanctuary, which was now at anchor in the harbor at Da Nang. It was the first step in a review process that might lead to an early out.

• • •

"Well," he thought, "there's nothing for it now but to suck it up and get on that chopper and get to that hospital ship and get this done."

"The devil you say!" his bleeding asshole replied, sounding very British. "A chopper is it? Egad! That's a nasty thought!"

"A chopper it is," Guy assured his pal. "It's just you and me against the Army Medical Corps. Or maybe it's the Navy Medical Corps. What difference. A messy business, whichever."

"A nasty lot of inquisitors," the bleeding asshole muttered.

"Well put," Guy agreed. "I don't suppose you could work up a little something to help out today, could you?"

"I'm afraid you've lost me," the bleeding asshole replied. "What have you in mind?"

"Oh, nothing much," Guy said. "A spasm perhaps. A very little one might do, at the right time. Or a blood vessel rupturing. Or even a cramp? Do you suppose you could manage something like that?"

"Frightfully sorry, old boy," the bleeding asshole balked. "I'd like to oblige, really, but it's quite impossible. You've taken a terrible lot of vitamins lately. Salad. That sort of thing. Not very cooperative, what?"

"I wasn't thinking." Guy sighed. He pulled himself to a sitting position, feet on the floor.

"Well," Guy said, "this is it. I guess it will be just the two of us and our wits. We'll have to be persuasive."

"Oh"—his bleeding asshole sniffed—"I hardly think they will listen to *me.*"

•   •   •

Later that morning Guy found himself in a group with five other men outside the 85th Evacuation Hospital, waiting for the chopper that would take them to The Sanctuary. The other men were grunts from the 101st Airborne Division, the Screaming Eagles. Their conversations were low and incoherent. None of them bothered to talk to Guy. He was clearly a rear-echelon motherfucker, a remf, not of their breed, so he had nothing worthwhile to say to them.

When a helicopter finally arrived, it wasn't the shuttle Guy was expecting. It was a medevac chopper, carrying a load. It came snarling in real quick, and dropped abruptly onto a concrete landing zone. Two enlisted men, orderlies, came out of the 85th pushing a gurney, and with the help of the chopper crew they unloaded something.

The sausage-shaped object was wrapped in an OD green poncho, and as the two orderlies unfurled it Guy began to look upon the body of a young American soldier. Guy could see a dull crust of muddy blood around the young man's neck and chest. At first, shocked numb, Guy began to comprehend the image with the innocent ignorance of a child.

"Oh boy . . . oh, wow . . ." he thought, "this guy has really been hurt in the real war . . ."

As soon as he thought about it that way, he realized just how child-like his reaction had been, and tried to reorient his shock in a more mature, traditional direction. *The kid's a casualty,* Guy thought correctively. *His number was up. A bullet had his name on it. He was in the wrong place at the wrong time. He had shit for luck today.* The jargon helped a little.

The two attendants wheeled the body to a concrete staging area, with a rusting corrugated roof, held up by metal posts but not by walls. It was completely open to the wind and drizzle that cut in slantwise and made the orderlies hunch their shoulders as they tended to the dead boy on the gurney.

The orderlies opened the poncho all the way, so—like a tablecloth—it draped completely over the metal tray. The dead boy's hands were folded primly over his crotch. His uniform was very muddy and his boots were even muddier. His hands, cupping his forgone manhood, were a dusty, bluish gray.

The boy was a dead American, dead at the age of twenty-one or so. The two men from the hospital poked around the dead boy's uniform for a while, then rewrapped the poncho and went back inside. Guy and the other five young men waited. In its poncho casing, the body looked indeed just like a green sausage on a silver skillet. Every once in a while someone from the hospital would come out and open the poncho and do something with the body or the uniform and close the poncho and wrap it very tight, tamping out all the air.

The six waiting men—five real soldiers and Guy Lopaca—watched in silence. When one of the hospital attendants finished inspecting the body, he rinsed his hands off in a mud puddle before reentering the hospital. The iron-rich mud in Phu Bai was red, so the puddle was red. The muddy red water rinsed off the bloody red hands, which came out clean.

A grunt standing next to Guy said "damn" once. A black kid leaned against a wall and shrugged at Guy, who shrugged back. Guy felt good to be noticed.

The attendants kept coming out to look inside the dirty poncho, opening it and rummaging around, pulling on the uniform, tugging the collar, searching the pockets. Twice an attendant visited the chopper, said a few words, received in turn only shaking heads.

"Someone messed with the dog tags," one of the grunts said between cigarettes. "Ain't got no name tag either."

A half hour went by. The rain fell, the grunts smoked, and Guy absorbed the experience. The dead boy was his age. The boy had brown hair like Guy's, though dirtier. He had a pale mustache like Guy's. He was about the same height, about the same weight. As specimens of the same species, Guy and the dead boy were essentially indistinguishable.

But they were not the same species. Not counting the helicopter crew and the occasional hospital staff, there were seven young Americans waiting in the rain that day. Six of them had dirty hair, muddy boots, filthy clothes caked with red Phu Bai mud. Six of them had been sucked into the mud of this place; so that it encased them like a second skin, like the carapace of a bug. They wore the same crust of mud that Guy had seen all his life in photographs: the mud from the trenches of World War I; the mud from Sicily and Bataan; the frozen mud from Korea.

Of the seven Americans in their group—six living, one dead—Guy was the only one without this mantle of red mud. His boots had been cleaned the day before, as they were nearly every day. From the moment he left his bed this morning, his boots had touched nothing but wooden floors and boardwalks, concrete paths, and macadam.

Yes, there was gunfire in the air that he breathed, the sound of occasional battle all around him. But the men beside him lived in places where the echoes of war originated. Yes, Guy got grimy when he went out in the field. But not like this. And not today. The red dirt of Phu Bai covered him not with a crust but with a delicate patina, as if he had been dusted with rouge.

He was so lucky. He thought about how lucky he was. It didn't mat-

ter that there were hundreds of thousands of young men at home, unconcerned with the risks of war, while he was here in the middle of
it. Those men back home didn't matter to Guy. They didn't exist for him.
What mattered to Guy, now, was simply this: among their small group
of seven young men in this war, at this place, at this time, he was the
only one without the mud on his boots.

He felt a rush of remorse: *I have come all this way, from home to
Vietnam, but it wasn't far enough.* He had fallen short. He could reach
out and touch these men; but he wasn't one of them and never would be.
It wasn't that he envied their bravery. It wasn't that he would never wear
the medals that some of them might earn. It was less than that, and
more. *Guy would never wear their mud.*

An officer came out of the main building and said, "Saddle up" as
he passed on his way to the helicopter. The grunts began to shuffle after
him. Guy hung back. He cast a last, long look at the boy on the gurney.
Tired of rewrapping the package so often, the attendants had left it
open. The silence that passed between Guy and the dead soldier was the
only communication they would ever have. It was more than Guy could
endure.

• • •

As the helicopter flew over the paddies and forests that lay between Phu
Bai and the hospital ship, Guy had the melancholy feeling that he
had fallen into debt again. It was like the debt he had originally felt before he volunteered to serve in Vietnam; but this new debt was deeper.
He had paid off the first debt when he landed at Tan Son Nhut on
the first day of his tour. This new debt was . . . hopeless. It was like a
debt you owe to the Mob, that seems to get heavier the more you pay
against it.

Guy looked around at the men in the helicopter. They were occasionally muttering, passing around cigarettes, tired eyes closed or cast
at the floor. None of them spoke to Guy. No one offered him a cigarette,
or asked his name, or his job. Because these men were conquerors, warriors from the Nation of Grunts, and Guy was an outsider, a peasant, a
mudless remf.

• • •

The Hospital Ship Sanctuary was pure white with bright red crosses painted on the sides. The men saw the ship before their chopper had passed the shoreline. The grunts stirred slightly, just enough to check their gear, close their flaps, leave nothing behind and everything secured. The chopper settled down, and the men disembarked. The ship looked huge to Guy as they came upon it; but once on deck he was surprised by how much it pitched in the moderate swells.

The men were directed through a door, down some stairs, down a hall, and into—what else?—a line for processing. Guy took the last place, fished his orders out of a pocket, and waited his turn. He was despondent. He felt like a man who was about to confess to a hanging crime that no one had yet discovered.

A medical officer sat behind a folding table, chatting with each man, checking each man's orders, and directing him to the front or rear alleyway. Guy shuffled his way slowly forward.

Finally, the doctor smiled at Guy. "What's up with you?" he asked brightly.

Guy held in his right hand, at his side, the packet of papers that could—with just a little luck—put him on a plane back home. He felt his heart beating, and he knew his fingers were shaking. The officer smiled, then reached for the papers.

Guy pulled them back. The officer smiled a little less, and cocked his head.

"There's been a mistake," Guy said, then paused, then began again.

"Actually, I changed my mind," he said. The officer waited.

"I have this condition, bleeding from the rectum. The regulations say things like that can keep you out of the Army. But my situation isn't so bad. I've had it for years. It comes and goes." The officer just kept looking at him, as if something unusual but not especially interesting had interrupted his day.

"We started this review thing after I had kind of an eruption a few days ago," Guy said, "but things are back to normal now. I just want to withdraw everything and get back to my unit."

"Let me see those," the officer said, holding out his hand.

Guy turned over the papers and stood with his hands clasped behind him as the officer read each page, much more slowly than he had read any of the papers the other men had given him. Then the officer folded his own hands over the neat stack he had made, and looked at Guy without smiling.

"This is not a request for a medical evaluation," he said. "This is a request for a discharge." He said it very formally, as if he had just remembered that he was an officer and Guy was a shit-heeled enlisted man.

"Yes, sir," Guy replied.

"And you want to withdraw that request?" the officer asked.

"Yes, sir," Guy replied.

"Are you saying you don't have this condition," the officer asked, "or are you telling me you don't care whether you have it or not?"

"Either way, sir," Guy replied. "Whichever works. I just don't want to push it anymore."

The officer paused. After a few seconds he stood up and took two steps toward the hallway to his left. Then he stopped, shook his head, turned around, and took his seat again.

"Go up the same stairs you came down," he said curtly. "Tell the guys on the chopper they should take you back to the same place where they picked you up."

The officer began to write on one of the papers in Guy's stack. Guy waited for him to finish. After a few seconds, the officer looked up.

"You still here?" he said.

Guy walked down the hall, up the stairs, across to the chopper, and climbed in. He noticed again that the ship was rocking on the waves, and tried to imagine that it pitched in rhythm with his heart. Eventually the engine started and they took off.

Except for Guy and the flight crew, the chopper was empty for the return trip. Guy watched the hospital ship grow smaller as they left it behind. Up close, on board, you could see the rust, the gouges, the grease. But from a distance it was an object of straight lines, smooth curves, and pure white. As it receded from view, Guy turned his attention to the front, landward. It was a land of clean sheets and polished boots for some; and for others a land of fire and mud.

• • •

Guy Lopaca was going home. The dead boy at Phu Bai would be going home soon, Guy thought. But Guy was going home right now. He had emigrated from America on that white ship in the bay. *Home,* Guy thought, *is the place where you want to be.* And right now, Guy wanted to be near the men with mud on their boots. He might never be one of them, but he couldn't abandon them either.

He was being irrational and foolish, he knew that. Nothing would be gained from staying in this place. The grunts didn't know him, didn't care for him, wouldn't miss him. But Guy was helpless. He was trapped in a forlorn no-man's-land, a quagmire of self-imposed obligation that lay between clean sheets and muddy boots. He began to cry.

When Guy came to Vietnam he thought that someday he could return to the world a better, more honorable, deserving man. But now he thought that he would never measure up to the standards other men had set. The dead boy on the Normandy beach had set a standard. The dead boy at Phu Bai had set a standard. The muddy boots had set a standard. The constant pang of privilege— *"how lucky I am"*—reminded him that the standard they had set was too high, beyond his reach. He was in the middle of the war zone, and already he was a victim of survivor's guilt.

Guy crossed his arms over his knees, dropped his head, and let tears soak his recently laundered, faintly dusty uniform. He sobbed in helpless despair. He was a rational man in a silly war and he should know better. It had taken courage to come here once, and courage again to decline a way out. But not enough. Remaining a remf in Vietnam—that's all he had done—would never require enough courage to wipe out the awful feeling of privilege, of guilt, that he was afraid would haunt him for the rest of his life.

Why couldn't that be enough? What was it about this war, war in general, all wars, that makes rational men who should know better stake their honor, their opinion of themselves, on a reckless desire to share the misery of other men? He didn't know.

As the chopper moved deeper inland, Guy fell into a deep, gloomy despair. He had set too high the standards by which he judged himself. He would never measure up.

* * *

A few dozen meters below, at the border of a rice paddy, where the flat irrigation land met the sudden stubble of a forest, a young Vietnamese pointed his rifle skyward and took a few shots at an ignorant helicopter that was flying too low. The bullets missed hitting anything American by a comfortable meter or two. Inside the oblivious helicopter Guy Lopaca, who would never know the sanctifying thrill of combat, wiped his tears and tried to act like a man.

Been Here Too Long to Be Naïve

"They might not have sent you home even if you took the damn exam," Virgin Mary told Guy.

"That's true," Guy said. "We'll never know."

"It would have been worse if you took the exam, and they kept you here anyway," she said.

"That's also true," he replied.

"You came back on your own," she said. "I think that's good for you. I think it's better for you that you complete your tour, and that it was your decision."

"You're probably right," Guy said.

"I would have missed you, though," she said. "Did I tell you that? Before?"

"Several times."

"But you would have gone anyway."

"That was the plan."

"Now I'll be leaving Vietnam before you will."

"That's the plan," he said. "One of us leaves before the other."

"Do you want me to carry the whole conversation tonight," she asked, "while you sit there feeling sorry for yourself?"

"Could you do that?" Guy asked. "That would be really helpful. I could just sit here and cry in my beer."

"That's my beer," Mary said. "You're drinking that orange crap again. I almost never see you drinking beer."

Guy poured some of her beer into his orange soda and drank a big gulp.

"How will the girl back home take it?" Mary asked.

"I'd rather not talk about that," Guy said.

"OK, then I quit carrying the conversation. Lug it yourself." She pouted.

"I'm not good company today," Guy said. "I've been thinking too much. I'm getting worn down by the thought of what happens when we leave."

"I buy my house, and you shack up with the girl back home," Mary said. "What's to get worn down about?"

"I was thinking about what happens when America leaves Vietnam," Guy said. "I'm getting worn down from thinking about what happens to the people here, the ones I work with, after we pull out. We'll pull out eventually. And then . . ."

He drank some more of the terrible orange beer.

"You know," he said, "we make friends with these people. Hi, I'm Guy Lopaca. Bend over and let me put this American brand on your ass, and we'll give you some watermelon seeds and fertilizer. If your whole village bends over and gets branded, we'll give you a well and some buckets . . . I keep wondering what happens when we're not their friends anymore."

He rubbed his eyes as he often did when thinking hard.

"We make them pick sides," Guy said.

"I know," Mary said.

"People get shot for picking sides here," Guy said.

"I know," Mary said.

"Vietnam is the great event of our generation," Guy said. "It's not our fault, it's just the way it is. Our parents had World War II to remember and be proud of all their lives. And then they gave us this. All we get is a British rock band and Vietnam. But it's the only great event we're going to get. How could I run away from the great event of my generation? How could I let it happen without me?"

"You couldn't," Mary said. "We couldn't."

"When I volunteered to learn Vietnamese," Guy said, "I don't know what I was thinking. To me learning Vietnamese meant I could participate in my generation's great event, but on my own terms, you know?"

"I know," Mary said.

"I convinced myself that talking to these people was more noble than killing them, that it would put me on an ethical plane above the war," Guy said. "I figured I could participate in the great event of my generation without doing damage, without being responsible for any part of this mess."

"I know," Mary said.

"But I've been here too long to be naïve," Guy said. "Now I realize that talking to them is all it takes to kill them. I've probably already killed them."

"It was more fun when I was carrying the conversation," Mary said. She patted his hand. He left it there to be patted.

Reciprocation

Buddy Brier's skill at speaking Vietnamese was a secret so deep that no one in the 5th Platoon figured he would amount to anything as a linguist. Buddy became the platoon's primary hunter-gatherer, the fellow who would get stuff and deliver stuff, no matter what or where. As a fetcher his gifts were remarkable. After Buddy's first week, Captain Haven practically banished the concept of "requisition" from his thoughts. When he wanted something, he asked Buddy. If Buddy ever submitted a request in writing for anything, to anyone, no one in the 5th Platoon knew about it.

He got fatigues, typewriter ribbons, stereo amplifiers, and cases of rum without asking for a piece of paper with anyone's signature on it. He spent his mornings at The Villa drinking coffee and waiting for an assignment. Whether or not he got one, he was out of the office by ten o'clock. At day's end he returned with a satisfied smile, an adventurer who had blazed another trail through uncharted regions at the edge of the world.

Unbeknownst to everyone at The Villa, he turned out to be a pretty good linguist after all. He made sure that he was horrible in his official platoon capacities, and reserved the bulk of his excellent vocabulary for purely personal use.

Sometimes Buddy would need help hefting the day's cargo, and someone—frequently Guy Lopaca—would be off with him to some place like the unmarked supply shed on the dark side of Phu Bai, where the sun never shone. Or it might be a concrete bunker in the lee of the mossiest wall of The Citadel, where a perpetual breeze swept through perpetual shade, and men of divergent nationalities reclined on canvas deck chairs while Buddy went inside to trade one unmarked box for another.

The only part of his job Buddy Brier did not love was his uncertain transportation. He loved jeeps, but he hated trucks, and he hated having to take any old transport that was available. So, eventually, Specialist Fourth Class Buddy Brier decided to make himself a jeep.

In a corner of one of the platoon's storage sheds one day, Buddy set down what appeared to be a carburetor.

"It's a carburetor," Buddy confirmed to Guy and Paul that afternoon. "I'm building a jeep. I'm going to visit all the motor pools and junkyards, and scrounge the best parts."

"You could just steal a whole jeep," Gianelli pointed out.

"Oh sure, I could do that," Brier replied. "I don't even have to steal one. I could get a jeep that runs just by swapping something for it. But I don't want to. I'd rather build one from parts. It's more fun. And that way, it will really be mine."

Over the next few weeks, the pile of parts in the storage shed grew steadily. Not a bit of it was junk. Every component that made it to the pile was either new or imperceptibly used, freshly scrubbed and polished. And the pile itself was transformed, gradually, into a set of makeshift shelves, wooden slats spanning concrete blocks. Buddy began to organize the shelves by automotive system: suspension parts here, brake bits there, over here ignition coil and battery, over there fuel pump and filter.

"I need help getting a transmission," Buddy told Captain Haven one day. "Can you spare someone?"

"Sure," Captain Haven said, and (as usual) made his choice when the next trooper walked by his door. "Hey, Lopaca," he said, "Buddy needs you to drive shotgun again."

So Guy found himself beside Buddy Brier as they jounced down one of the district's infinite supply of Roads to Nowhere.

"This is a great transmission I'm getting," Buddy said. "The jeep is practically brand-new. Most of the other parts have already been stripped off, but I put a lock on the transmission."

"What did you use?" Guy asked. "A chain?"

Buddy looked at Guy and winced. "What good would that do?" he asked. And then: "I used a telephone number. I knew a good one, and this guy needed it."

Guy wondered how many Duroc pigs it would take to get a good used jeep transmission.

•   •   •

When they arrived at a small junkyard near an American outpost that Guy had never seen before, Buddy drove the truck right next to the twisted hulk of a jeep, up in the air on blocks. It had been picked over pretty well already. No wheels or tires or even axles. The engine compartment was nearly empty. There were no lights. No windshield. Practically nothing remained, except for the transmission.

Buddy hopped out, grabbed a bucket of tools, and went to work. He didn't ask Guy to turn a bolt or grip a nut. Buddy did it all by himself, whistling while he worked, like the eighth dwarf: Scroungy. Having finished what he had to do in the engine compartment, he set to work on the fittings at the aft end of the transmission housing, where it joined the mangled drive shaft. It was unusually easy to get at these parts, since the floor of the jeep had been blown away by some terrific explosion.

"Gas tank exploded," Buddy told Guy between whistles.

"Land mine?" Guy asked.

"Nope," Buddy said, "hand grenade. God, this nut is on tight." He puffed and heaved. Finally, the socket wrench released and Buddy smiled. He held up the transmission nut proudly, as if it were the blue ribbon they award at that contest they hold every year for people who unscrew frozen transmission nuts. "That wasn't so bad," he said.

They drove back to The Villa and put the transmission into the storage shack. Buddy was elated. "It's the last good part you can get from that wreck," Buddy said.

"I guess the driver is finally dead then," Guy said. "He has nothing more to give."

Buddy Brier delivered a sharp and disappointed scowl.

"What driver?" Buddy said, exasperated. "There wasn't any driver. You think I'd buy a dead man's transmission?" He looked as if that were the next worse thing to eating human flesh. "The guy who had that jeep ain't dead, and that's that."

"How do you know?"

"The same way I found out about the transmission. The guy who blew it up told me."

"Why in hell would he blow up an empty jeep?" Guy asked.

"The officer who had that jeep ain't dead, see?" Buddy explained. "But he's a lot better educated than he was before."

*   *   *

Buddy Brier enjoyed speaking Vietnamese. He never spoke fluently in front of the other men in the platoon, though, because if they knew how skilled he had become he would be grabbed for regular translator duty, and lose his freedom.

While he was in Da Nang with Captain Haven, Buddy met a lovely young Vietnamese girl, a government office worker, with whom he struck up an enjoyable if elementary conversation on the subjects of the heat, American film stars, and soccer. After about ten minutes, the young typist or receptionist or file clerk blinked her eyelashes at him and said, in English, "We go play now."

Well, Buddy was more than disappointed that his conversation with the girl had been—to her—nothing more than commercial foreplay.

He could understand the girl's position. Buddy wasn't stupid. It was easy for him to appreciate that people who had practically nothing in the world might try to get something from people like Buddy, who had seemingly limitless resources.

Buddy was a have; the girl was a have-not. That imbalance would always get in the way. Being a have-not, she would always perceive the imbalance, and the opportunity that someone like Buddy presented to her. Being a have, Buddy would always be surprised and hurt when someone tried to exploit him.

Understanding the situation didn't make it any easier though. When the girl offered herself to him, Buddy Brier felt shocked and disoriented, as if he had been rudely propositioned by his favorite little niece.

A week later he still felt dolefully down about the incident. He never figured her for a whore. She was just a nice girl with no mark of the professional about her. He had wanted only to engage in a simple conversation, culture to culture, person to person, brain to brain. Why should that be so hard? Who could be better equipped to cross the cultural divide than he was? He was a modern American with no known prejudice; he had a good education; he had studied and practiced the native Vietnamese language with a missionary zeal but without the missionary's tunnel vision.

All he wanted was to make contact, using those faculties that dwell in people in their minds and hearts, way north of their pelvis, and that don't require any lubrication or latex at the interface.

He was gnawing on his deep discomfort a week later, as he picked at the fragments of his lunch. The mess hall was nearly empty. Two middle-aged Vietnamese women, mess employees, were cleaning the tables in concentric circles around him, coming ever closer, trying to complete their task without disturbing him more than they had to. They were thoughtful that way, he noted. They were small, stooped, scruffy, and—until now—invisible.

Never once, Buddy realized, had he ever struck up a conversation with either of these women. In Da Nang, a pretty girl had caught his eye for just a second, and he had been overcome with desire to communicate with the natives. But here in Hue, two thoroughly native women had shared many hours of his life over a period of weeks, and he had never thought to say hello to them.

He decided that would have to change. First, to be overtly polite, he bussed his own tray and wiped the table with a paper napkin. Next, taking a deep breath and wearing his brightest smile, he approached the two women, made a gracious bow, and said hello in Vietnamese. Then, before the shock of his approach had left their faces, he launched into a conversation.

"Bong bong bong ga bong bong," he said. "My name is Buddy Brier. How is the health today of you two apparently married women of child-bearing age?"

"Bong bong bong ga bong bong," the taller woman replied fearfully, clutching the hand of the smaller woman next to her.

"Bong bong bong ga bong bong?" Buddy asked the smaller woman.

"Bong bong bong ga bong bong," the smaller woman said anxiously, grabbing the arm of the taller woman whose hand was clutching hers.

"Bong bong bong ga bong bong," Buddy said.

"Bong bong bong ga bong bong," the taller woman said.

"Bong bong bong ga bong bong," the smaller woman added.

"Bong bong bong ga bong bong?" Buddy asked.

"Bong bong bong ga bong bong," the smaller woman replied.

"Bong bong bong ga bong bong," the taller woman laughed.

"Bong bong bong ga bong bong," Buddy said, pretending to eat invisible Army food with an invisible bowl and spoon.

"Bong bong bong ga bong bong." The smaller woman laughed, shaking her head and making a contorted grimace with her already complicated face.

"Bong bong bong ga bong bong," Buddy suggested, pinching his nose and shaking his own head.

"You buy me watch?" the taller woman asked.

Buddy startled and flinched, as if she had poked him in the eye. He smiled feebly and bowed, and told her he was sorry, and said good-bye politely, and slunk back to his hootch where he could lick his reopened intercultural wounds alone.

It was hopeless, he decided. He would always be a have, a target of opportunity for every Vietnamese have-not who came close to him. He had neither the skill nor the power to change the way things were.

• • •

After a while he returned to The Villa, where his new, shining, brilliant, but certainly lonesome handmade jeep was parked and could use a nice, reassuring wash. Before hosing it down he checked the air in the tires and the oil in the engine. While he was at it, he lubricated the combination lock on the steering-wheel chain and the gas cap.

Like a thoroughbred horse, Buddy's jeep required a taxing investment of his time, effort, and concern. Without his constant attention, the jeep would surely fall apart, would never run just exactly right, and might get stolen. Because Buddy doted on it, the jeep responded with a peppy ride whenever Buddy wanted one. Like a beloved Labrador retriever, the jeep would consume everything that Buddy Brier was willing to give but would never actually ask him for anything at all.

A Vietnam Soda Thirst

A Vietnam Soda Thirst doesn't happen quickly or spontaneously. It must be nurtured slowly, over the course of a long hot day. The Vietnam Soda Thirst, that Guy was planning to drown at The Club, was born first thing in the morning, when Captain Haven told him he had to deliver miracle rice seed to Phong Dien.

"Who's going with me?" Guy asked.

"Don't you know the way to Phong Dien?" Captain Haven replied, which was not the answer Guy was hoping for.

"I think so," Guy said. "I'm going alone again?"

"Yup," Captain Haven said. "You'll pick up the seed inside The Citadel, as soon as you lube the truck. Grease gun's in the shed. Better hurry, because you'll be making two trips."

. . .

As he fit the key to the lock on the shed, Guy noticed that his uniform was already starting to soak through at the armpits. He filled the grimy lubricating gun from a big tub of grease, then proceeded to the parking lot and stood there, staring at the truck that his life would depend on that day.

It looked like the runt of a dinosaur litter: bulky, ungraceful, stupid. Every part was too big and seemed to have only one engineering objective: *don't break.* And none of them ever would. The big parts might grind to a halt because of rust or friction or boredom, but they would never actually break. Some of the deadest trucks in the Army appeared to be entirely intact. In fact, he once had to paint a dead Army truck, which had not been started or moved in three years, to make it look good for an inspection, which it passed.

The sun was already hot enough and bright enough to sting the back of Guy's neck. The oiled gravel of the parking lot was getting hot and sticky. He sighed. In fifteen minutes, it would be worse. He spread an old tarpaulin on the ground, and wiggled on his back far enough to reach some grease fittings. It took nearly thirty minutes to get them all, because twice he had to rest under the shade of a nearby tree, where he first began to think about how thirsty he could be by suppertime *if he really, really tried.*

What I need is a really nice Vietnam Soda Thirst, Guy decided. I'll stay as thirsty as I can all day, and then tonight when I can't stand it anymore, I'll have some soda on ice. Mmmmmmmmm. It will be wonderful.

When he arrived at the Government of Vietnam agriculture office, Guy had to decide whether to take a sip of water from his canteen before loading the rice seed. He decided to wait. They took him to the warehouse and showed him the seed. Each bag weighed 165 pounds. The boy they assigned to help him weighed 95 pounds. The three men who gave the boy his assignment smiled and nodded, and rushed away before a single bag was hoisted.

Guy bent, squatted, grasped, and hefted, trying to figure the best way to handle his half of the first bag. When he looked for his partner, the kid had already loaded two bags and had his arms around a third.

Now Guy was really thirsty but was ashamed to take a drink. He strained to lift his first bag, got it in the air, started negotiating a gradual collapse toward the tailgate of the truck, and was grateful to feel the boy's shoulder push against his lower back, maneuvering both Guy and Guy's bag to a crash landing on the truck bed. *"Bong bong bong ga bong bong,"* the boy said sympathetically, pointing first to himself, then to Guy, then to the next bag, then to the truck.

"Sure," said Guy, "together."

They had loaded about twenty bags when Guy realized he didn't know how many they were supposed to load. If each bag weighed 165 pounds, then the twenty bags already on the truck would be 3,300 pounds, which would exceed the truck's rated capacity by—let's see— 1,800 pounds, or 120 percent. *I'm going to die today of a ruptured truck,* Guy thought. He decided to take a small sip of water. He offered some to the boy, who gratefully drained half the canteen.

Guy walked to the GVN office. There were now six idle men standing or seated around the lone desk and phone. None of them, apparently, had been assigned to seed-hoisting duty. The senior cadre was happy to tell Guy how many bags he would be carting to Phong Dien, all alone, with none of the six men to accompany him. He would be carting thirty-two bags. Guy smiled, nodded, and silently wished them a greased rail to hell. Then he went back to the warehouse and helped the boy *unload* four bags before setting out with sixteen bags on the road to Phong Dien.

The sun was near its noontime high when he shut down the truck in the village. He had not sipped from his canteen since leaving The Citadel. His fatigues were sticky, heavy with sweat, and his tongue was dry. He was starting to feel proud of his big dry tongue. He began to visualize what it would be like later that day, when he would engulf his sandpaper tongue with an avalanche of icy soda. *Mmmmmmm.*

Five men appeared from a nearby hut to welcome Guy to Phong Dien again, and to unload the truck, completely without his help. It was so nice of them to do it. They hauled the bags into a small, windowless hut with one door, which was padlocked before they opened it to receive Guy's load. When they were finished—it took no time at all—they asked Guy if he would like to have some nice hot tea to take his mind off the bright sun and the oppressive humidity.

Guy politely declined, told them he would be back soon with the second load, and headed to Hue again. He waited until he was out of sight before taking a small, life-sustaining sip from his canteen.

He was developing a blue-ribbon Vietnam Soda Thirst. Coke or orange? Orange or Coke? Which one first? Would he chew the ice cubes? *Mmmmmmmm.*

*   *   *

Back at the GVN warehouse, the boy was asleep on a stack of seed bags. He roused long enough to help with the second load, and then made a running flop to the top of another stack, done for the day.

The second trip to Phong Dien was easier than the first, because Guy was past the midday mark and heading for an iced-soda rendezvous. The thought of frigid fizz on his nose carried him along, and time passed quickly. He took another small sip from his canteen just before pulling into the village. The same five men came to meet him, just as happily as they had that morning. They unlocked the door to the shed, and began to unload the sixteen bags of rice seed, which they stacked alongside the twelve bags that remained from this morning's run . . .

Yes, yes, they nodded and smiled, we know Vietnamese for twelve and sixteen. Those are very good numbers. You speak so well! Sixteen bags? Of course. Twelve bags? Certainly. *Bong bong bong ga bong bong.* Good rice seed, thank you very much. Say again please. Yes, thank you. *Bong bong ga bong.* What? Sixteen bags? Yes, of course. *Ga bong bong.* Rice. The best rice. Twelve bags? *Bong bong ga bong.* There? Yes. Those? Yes, yes. Where? Yes, good seed. What?

Guy was having trouble conversing, not only because the men did not *want* to understand him—that was beyond dispute—but also because most of his mouth was filled with a big dry tongue that stuck to his adhesive palate. He had to take a drink or he would never find out what happened to the four bags of rice seed that were now missing from the first load. He unscrewed the top of his canteen, and as he put it to his lips the five men bowed in unison, then scattered, the elder calling over his shoulder as he ran that it was time again to scald some tea leaves.

*   *   *

When Guy got back to The Villa he sipped only enough water to make a short, furious report to Captain Haven:

"That rice seed didn't just evaporate, and you know they aren't planting it today," Guy said.

"So do you think they're eating it," Captain Haven suggested, "or something else?"

"I bet they're selling it," Guy suggested back.

"But with four bags gone they kept twenty-eight bags," Captain Haven suggested again.

"I don't know how many bags they kept," Guy retorted. "I only know how many they took from the first load. Can I get a drink of water?"

"Sure," Captain Haven said. "You look like a man whose camel died a hundred miles ago."

After Guy took a moderate, voice-restoring sip, he calmly explained his frustration. If they're going to rip off the system, could they at least make the deliveries on their own? Did they have to make an American soldier haul around the stuff they looted? Did they have to rub our stupidity in our stupid faces?

"Am I correct," Captain Haven said, "that the miracle rice seed you delivered today is about three times more productive than the rice seed they normally use?"

"That's what we're told," Guy replied with a moister, more flexible tongue.

"And am I correct," Captain Haven continued, "that the Phong Dien farmers will grow three times more rice on every acre where they plant that seed?"

"I guess so," Guy said.

"And am I more or less correct," Captain Haven continued maddeningly, "that the purpose of your mission this morning was to help the Phong Dien farmers learn about the new rice and improve the rice yield on their land?"

"Yes," Guy said.

"So," Captain Haven said, "if that rice triples the yield, and the men who run the show out there steal one bag out of three, and sell it on the black market, doesn't the village still come out ahead? Isn't that right? The farmers still double their yield, don't they? And they still see how good the seed is. Am I right so far?"

"So far," Guy said reluctantly, fully knowing it was more than far enough.

"And the fellows who make the profit stealing the seed and selling it," Captain Haven said, "won't they make sure that the people actually *plant* some of the new rice seed? Won't they? To prove to us that they're *using* the seed? So that we'll continue to supply them with the stuff they want to steal?"

"I guess," Guy said.

"Well," said Captain Haven, "let's just hope that over time they learn to steal less than two bags out of three. That's the trick."

• • •

Guy took his rage and frustration to the basketball court at The Hotel, where sweaty men were rotating in and out of a nearly perpetual four-on-four game. His world-class Vietnam Soda Thirst—that he had partially squandered because of having to report the stolen bags of rice seed—recovered during the second fierce game he was in, when someone flipped him a pass and he realized that his reflexes were failing.

Coke or orange? Orange or Coke? That's what Guy was thinking as the basketball whizzed by him. *I should have caught that,* he thought, three seconds later.

Soon Guy was so tipsy with dehydration that he no longer even saw the ball or any of the players. Before the game was over, Guy staggered off the court and headed to the EM Club, still undecided: Coke or orange? Orange or Coke? *Mmmmmmmmm.*

• • •

It isn't practical to write with hard-lead pencils on plain paper in a country as humid as Vietnam. The paper gets soggy and the hard lead doesn't leave much of a mark. But the lifer sergeant who ran the EM Club used a pencil anyway, because that's all he could find.

It was enough to break Guy Lopaca's heart.

When Guy reached the EM Club, he bent down close to read the nearly invisible note the lifer sergeant had taped to the door.

"Compressor broke," the note said. "Closed for repairs."

Guy was too battered even to think of a terrible oath. "Oh no," was all he said.

"Oh no!"

His hand stayed on the doorknob as he stared through the note, through the door, into his dreary future. He could get a drink of soda back at The Hootch, if he could drag his heavy feet that far. He was a privileged fellow. Although the enlisted men's refrigerator did not make ice, it kept soda cans refreshingly cold. How could he complain about not having ice cubes, in a world where other men his age were dying?

Still, he pulled at the doorknob—tug, tug—as if the doorknob were a nipple and he were actually trying to milk The Club.

He had been planning his Vietnam Soda Thirst since first thing this morning. He had tortured himthelf to make it happen. He had borne the opprethive heat and had rithked hith life for people who thtole the rithe theed that he wath giving them for nothing. All he wanted wath thome Coke—or orange?—in a glath with ithe. Wath that too much to athk? Wath he wrong to athk that much?

My tongue ith tho dry, Guy thought, *that I can't even pronounth my thoughth!*

He was roused by the feel of a big hand covering his hand on the doorknob, and a big shoulder against his shoulder pushing him aside.

" 'Scuse me," said the lifer sergeant who tended bar most evenings, "got to open up."

The sergeant unhitched the padlock, stepped inside, and flipped on the lights. He was halfway to the bar when he stopped, turned around, and came outside again, so he could rip the penciled sign from off the door.

"Fixed it this afternoon," he told Guy.

"That was for saying 'Oh no!' instead of something worse," an appreciative God whispered to Guy, who staggered inside The Club and straight to the bar.

"A Coke, pleathe," Guy said to the sergeant, "and an orange thoda. And two glatheth with ithe."

The lifer sergeant shook his head and opened the treasure chest in which the ice was kept.

"You think this is gonna taste good now," the lifer sergeant said, "but have you considered holding out till you collapse from heat stroke? They'll bury your whole body in ice if you do. I had one of those in Korea. It's the best."

Whores and Mothers

Danny Maniac's first whore in Vietnam cost him only five dollars, and he was not sure whether he got a good deal or took a hosing. That was a big thing in Danny's life—getting good deals or getting hosed—and it bothered him that he had not learned more about the local market rates before actually closing the transaction.

The whore yelled to him through the front gate, and from fifteen yards away she looked pretty good, so he walked over and listened to her pitch. Back home he could never have got his hands around anything that looked so tasty. He wanted to make the deal, it would be like buying your first car, but you don't want to leave too much on the table and drive away a patsy; it will stick in your gullet later if you got sucked in and hosed.

"One time," she said, "five dollar one time." She would not go lower. Not even four-fifty. He started at three and worked his way up by halves. It seemed like she should come down something, 20 percent at least, who in hell starts at a number and never comes down? Four-fifty was 90 percent of her opening ask; why wouldn't she move?

He tried shaking his head and walking away, but she didn't call him back, and she started yelling at some other guy, so he figured, for fifty cents more he'll close the deal and get his Vietnam cherry popped and he would worry about the good deal and hosing aspects next time. It was only five dollars, a tank of gas and some smokes back home. She had to be worth that much at least.

What he had heard about the Vietnamese girls lying as still as canned sardines so as not to get pregnant turned out to be true. She didn't move or twitch at all. She did moan a little and talked him through it—*too big too big*—which was fun even though he knew it was phony. Hell, movies on the movie screen are phony, too, but you have your fun anyway.

After it was over she let him know that she needed water so she could clean up before dressing. That presented a problem.

He wasn't going to take her to the latrine. That was a man's place. Did she think he was going to leave her alone in The Hootch while he fetched some water?

No, he sure wasn't going to leave that girl alone in The Hootch. He thought of his music tapes, his socks and underwear, his cigarettes, his spare change. And what about everybody else's stuff, that they would blame on Danny if she took some? The place was a treasure trove to someone like her. No, she would have to clean herself with something that was already there in The Hootch. Schubert looked around. The Hootch had no plumbing, of course. He found an empty Planters Peanut can, and then, finding no water anywhere, half filled the can—*why the hell not?*—with ginger ale from the refrigerator.

The woman cursed and spat as she washed herself with the frigid ginger ale, but Schubert didn't care. In fact, he began to laugh about it when he told the story later at the EM Club, where—*this was strange*—the men began to laugh along with him. They seemed to like the story so much that he told it again, longer this time, with more detail, some of which he made up as he went along.

Gianelli jumped in—as usual, grabbing all the attention—and told everyone that ginger ale was a fine idea, but that next time Danny should have the girl with a twist of lime as well.

A twist of lime! Danny pictured the girl squirting lime juice in her crotch, and he fell down in his chair and laughed so hard. So hard. While he was laughing, he looked around and saw the other men laughing, bellowing with laughter, and felt good about himself for the first time since he came to Vietnam.

Suddenly, Danny Maniac took the biggest chance of his life.

"Lime's all right," he said loudly, so everyone would be sure to hear. "But I think what she really needs is . . . is . . . *a cherry!*"

It might not have been the best joke ever uttered in the EM Club. Hell, it wasn't even the best joke of the night. But it was the first time Danny Maniac had ever matched wits with someone like Paul Gianelli.

The men were really laughing now. The poor ginger-ale whore was becoming a comic legend. Delight over her predicament had suddenly achieved critical mass, and the laughter had gone nuclear, out of control. *Ginger ale! Lime! A cherry!* Hey, Danny, did you use your can opener? Can you make that a double? Can I have her on the rocks next time? Was there a lot of fizz?

As Danny looked from face to face, everyone laughing at the joy he had brought them, he came to Gianelli, who winked at him and nodded. What pleasure that wink gave to Danny. It was better than screwing the whore.

●　●　●

A few weeks later Danny Schubert, the 5th Platoon's most warlike medical advisor, found himself confronting his first real medical crisis. She was sitting beside him in the cab of an Army truck, as Guy Lopaca drove them all to the Hue Hospital from the Thu Ang Clinic.

She was a little woman in her early thirties, swollen by more pregnancy than she probably deserved, at full term or very nearly, considering the way her belly stuck out. Something was wrong in that big tummy. Back at the clinic, the Vietnamese officer who had dumped this problem on the Americans had pointed to the woman's crotch, and put his two flat hands together making a small circle between them. He had tugged his hands apart jerkily several times, pointing twice more to her crotch. Something was wrong down there. Danny Maniac imagined a cervix. He formed an image of mysterious female tissue under stress.

Guy was driving as fast as he could, trying to avoid the deepest ruts and the stupidest pedestrians. The woman was literally hanging on to the truck. She had found a large wing nut on the windshield frame, and she held on to it with both hands, squeezing it white-knuckle hard for a long time. She was plainly in agony. Her face was contorted and tears soaked her cheeks and ran down her neck, but she never made a sound. No, that's a myth. She quietly, considerately moaned.

Danny Maniac was much too close to her, uncomfortable, like an adolescent at his first school dance, trying not to notice that his partner had breasts. Schubert fixed his head hard to the right, and concentrated on the passing trees and bushes, paying no attention to the woman reluctantly whimpering beside him.

Hey, there's a nice tree. Oh, look at that cloud.

After a half hour, the woman lost her grip on the wing nut and sagged into Danny Maniac's lap. Schubert held his arms and hands up in the air, not knowing what to do with them or with the wrinkled head drizzling salty tears onto his private parts. Schubert had mated with half a dozen Vietnamese women by now, and had never become intimate with any of them to this degree.

"Shit," Schubert said after a few seconds. He looked down at the woman, then at Guy.

"Got that right," Guy said.

Slowly, Danny Maniac lowered his hands, putting one hand on the woman's shoulder and the other hand on her head. He was grateful that he had only two hands, because finding a place to put any more would have been quite a strain for him. His hands stayed nearly immobile on her head and shoulder for the rest of the trip. Danny Schubert and the woman never spoke to each other and made no eye contact. Her own hands covered her face and eyes. Danny continued to be fascinated by the trees and the bushes, the clouds, the stars he couldn't see behind the sky, anything upon which his rigid eyes could fasten and thereby avoid confronting this shuddering pregnant woman in such awful pain in his sensitive and now quite soggy lap.

There was no hotshot cowboy bluster in Danny Schubert now. This woman was no compliant too-big-GI-too-big happy-time girl that he could poke and pump and brag about at The Club. This woman's tears were soaking his crotch, and the thought made him clench his buttocks and squirm. But he kept his hands on her shoulder and head. Once in a while—not often—his hands would give her a small pat or a squeeze. A spontaneous, involuntary pat or squeeze. Danny Maniac was sure it was involuntary, each time completely spontaneous.

When they arrived at the hospital, Guy and Danny Maniac carried the woman inside, where they were met by several perky Vietnamese cheerleaders in nursing uniforms. As they elaborately welcomed Guy and Danny and the desperate woman, the nurses all laughed gaily, so happy to see them.

Guy tried to get them to fetch a doctor, using Vietnamese words he believed to be useful, and spastic sign language, mostly a lot of pointing to the obviously distressed, twisted little woman and to the fold below her dirigible belly. The happy cheerleader nurses just laughed, so nice to see you, everything so maddeningly fine and gay, while the pregnant woman grabbed the sill of an open window with both arms, using all her strength just to keep from falling to the floor. She didn't say a word to the nurses. Guy thought she was barely conscious.

"Doctor at where?" Guy kept saying in Vietnamese, over and over, louder and louder, "Doctor at where?" And the nurses laughed, so happy to see you, until finally Danny Maniac, finding nothing to throw at them or smash them with, opened a door and then slammed it as hard as he could, making a sound so loud that it summoned from an office down the hall a middle-aged American nurse from CORDS. She hustled to them, took four seconds to evaluate what she saw, barked something to the nurses that made them shut up, and put her arms around the pregnant woman who had almost lost her grip on the windowsill.

Then the American nurse explained the situation to Danny and Guy. It was 5:30 P.M. The bad news the nurses were trying to deliver, which they were trying to soften by their considerate laughter, was that there were no doctors in the hospital, and would be none until tomorrow morning. The men should leave now. The pregnant woman could stay. The nurses would take care of her. Everything would be fine.

Guy and Danny Maniac returned to their big Army truck and started back to the base. Schubert looked like a combat trooper who had just survived his first firefight.

"Shit," Danny said to Guy.

"Got that right," Guy replied.

Danny Schubert examined the palms of his hands for a while, then folded them in his lap, from which the moisture of the woman's tears had started to evaporate. On the way back to The Villa they passed ten thousand Asian whores and mothers, none of whom Danny Schubert saw, such was his weepy fascination with the treetops, rooftops, clouds, and sky.

An Absolutely
Good Thing

According to Lieutenant Rossi's calculations, their Civil Affairs company had distributed enough of the TN-20 and TN-8 miracle rice seed to cover 1,026 hectares of newly constructed demonstration plots. According to Lieutenant Rossi's calculations, only 338 hectares had actually been planted with the seed.

"It's a miracle that the miracle rice seed has vanished," Gianelli said over cards one night.

"There are no miracles in Vietnam," DeMudge said. "There are only mysteries that no one will ever try to solve."

"Sometimes the mysteries do get solved," Gianelli said, "even in Vietnam."

• • •

Guy Lopaca had reached the limit of his patience. He had hoisted, hauled, pitched, rolled, fetched, carried, stacked, and driven hundreds of miracle seed sacks weighing thousands of pounds, at no small risk to his personal safety, and he was ready to exact some satisfaction for their disappearance.

"Did you see this?" he confronted Captain Haven, putting down an open copy of *Time* magazine with such force that Captain Haven could have interpreted it as an impudent slap.

"Yes I have," Captain Haven replied calmly. "It's a pretty interesting article."

"It's a lot more than interesting," Lopaca insisted. "It's all about us. It says we're being sucker punched by the people we work for."

"I don't agree," Captain Haven said. "But you go ahead and make the case you want to make. Get it off your chest."

Lopaca was ready. In fact, he had been primed. For hours last night the men at the EM Hootch had debated how to react to the *Time* magazine article. Finally, they chose the only solution that would guarantee them any sleep because it would cut off discussion: they decided to draw straws and make the loser confront their commander. Gianelli ran the lottery, cheated, and forced the short straw to Guy Lopaca, who now had the pride of the platoon weighing on his shoulders.

"First," Lopaca said, "we send American citizens to Vietnam to help the farmers improve their agriculture. Second," he continued, "we help develop this amazing new rice, that will increase the yield maybe three hundred percent. Then we pay to ship the rice seed here, and we risk our lives to distribute it. We even teach them how to grow it. And then . . ."

With an insubordinate aggressiveness, his forefinger tapped the magazine on Captain Haven's desk.

". . . and then they ship the seed up to *North Vietnam,* where it becomes the foundation for *their* agricultural revolution, and *Time* magazine tells the world about it. *Our* miracle rice that we brought to South Vietnam has been planted in the rice fields of *North Vietnam!* They're gonna have a record crop this year! *Jesus!*"

"Jesus so what?" Captain Haven said implacably.

"Jesus," Guy said, exasperated, "if the *North* Vietnamese can grow this stuff on their own, what do the South Vietnamese farmers need *me* for?"

Captain Haven put his hands behind his head and tipped back in his chair.

"I don't ever want to have a combat command," he said after a while. "This kind of job is fine with me. I don't ever want to send kids like you down some jungle trail or up some hill to look for people to shoot at. But I guess that's kind of off the subject, isn't it?"

"Somewhat," Guy replied.

"I don't see the big military picture," Captain Haven said, "I don't understand tactics and strategy. But after being here awhile, I think I understand the basics of rice. Do you understand the basics of rice, Specialist Lopaca?"

"Like, in what way?" Guy asked, not particularly thrilled with the direction the conversation was taking.

"The most elemental way possible," Captain Haven said. "Tell me the basics of rice, according to the best information in your possession, drawing on the full extent of your experience as a member of the 5th Platoon's agricultural mission."

Guy thought a few seconds and then told the commanding officer everything he, Guy Lopaca, knew about rice.

"You plant it, you grow it, you cook it, then you eat it," Guy said.

"Exactly," Captain Haven said. "That's all there is to it. And the Vietnamese already know that. So your usefulness here is, as you suggest, rather limited."

"I was hoping for a little more encouragement," Guy said, "if you don't mind me saying that."

"I don't mind," Captain Haven said.

Lopaca blinked. He waited for the encouragement.

"Try to see the big picture about rice," Captain Haven finally said. He got up and walked to the large paper map that was taped and pinned and stapled and nailed to his wall. It was knocked down two or three times a month, as people in a hurry passed it by.

"Here is North Vietnam," he said, "and here is South Vietnam." He pointed to each. "And here is Vietnam." He ran his hand around the combined perimeter.

"You think that the likelihood of the country staying divided after we're gone is pretty frigging remote," Captain Haven said. Then he sat down again.

"There's no need to discuss what I think," he said, "except to say that I am happy to send you out there to bring the miracle rice to hungry Vietnamese, *wherever* the reporter from *Time* magazine finds them eating it. Do you understand me?"

"You don't care who gets the rice seed?" Guy asked. "I mean, actually, to tell you the truth, I don't care so much either . . . But it's kind of surprising to hear *you* say it . . ."

"I care most of all that the seed gets planted and the harvest gets eaten," Captain Haven said. "It's that simple. If you don't come back from a trip to the boondocks someday, I want to believe that bringing miracle rice to Vietnam was *an absolutely good thing,* wherever it went after leaving your hands. Do you see that now? I want to believe that you were doing some good, and that you weren't a fool to do it. Do you get the point?"

"Why don't we just ship the damn seed from Burma straight to Hanoi?" Guy asked. "There's no question I'd get your point if we did that. I promise you I would."

"That would be too easy," Captain Haven said. "Congress would never let us do something that crazy. No, I think you'll just keep hauling the seed out to the villages, and let the North Vietnamese keep hauling the seed to Hanoi on their return trips up the Ho Chi Minh Trail. Even when it comes to rice seed, we have to respect the pretense of animosity."

●   ●   ●

They had set up a plain table with two bowls of rice. The bowls were unmarked. The rice in the bowls was steaming hot, fresh from the water, perfectly prepared in separate pots, without seasoning, by the old man's personal kitchen staff.

The old man was escorted into the room, and one of his aides held the chair as the old man sat down. Beside each bowl was a set of chopsticks.

Ho Chi Minh took a big dollop of rice from one bowl, chewed it, and rolled it around in his mouth. He took a drink of water then, using clean chopsticks, he sampled the rice from the second bowl. He stood up.

"The first bowl was the usual rice, was it not?" he asked. His aides smiled and nodded and assured him that it was.

"And the rice from the second bowl was the new rice, the super rice," he asked, "that the people dislike so much?"

They smiled and said, yes, it was true. It grew like weeds, but it tasted terrible. The traditional rice was much better, although the yield was meager in comparison to the new rice.

Ho smiled.

"The new rice tastes wonderful," he said conclusively. "Tell the people it tastes like victory."

It Don't Mean Nothing

Arthur Grissom was hanging around the basketball court, watching some men playing four-on-four, when one of them dropped out and Pete Steptoe, the scholarship player from Drexel University, took pity on Arthur and asked him to fill in.

"Just play tough defense, and pass, don't dribble," Pete counseled him. "Don't be afraid to foul. The other guy has to call the foul." Pete squinted at him. "Foul a lot," he said.

Arthur's team fell behind early, and stayed that way nearly the whole game, but Pete Steptoe kept the team close. With the game almost out of reach, Steptoe went on a terrific tear and hit four shots in a row, stealing a lead at 20 to 19, one point short of the win. During the frenzied scramble that erupted in the next minute of the game, someone on Arthur's team lost his senses and threw the basketball to Arthur.

The ball hit Arthur in his hands, and stuck. Arthur looked down at the ball, not knowing how it got there, then he sort of bounced it, and twisted a little then . . .

Upsa-daisy!

I'll be damned. It went in. How'd that happen? Wasn't someone guarding me?

Pete was laughing and hooting and doing chin-ups on the rim.

Arthur blushed and shrugged as Pete Steptoe boasted and bellowed. Sweet times all right. Arthur had never experienced a moment like that.

Later, at the Enlisted Men's Club, Arthur had a drink with a few players including Pete and a GI who had been on the losing side of Arthur's miracle. Arthur was still plenty charged; he felt like a high-voltage battery, eager to explode again.

When the top sergeant came through the door, Arthur tossed him a hearty hi-how-ya-doing-nice-to-see-ya kind of wave.

"You seen Riggins anywhere?" the first sergeant asked Arthur.

"No, I haven't seen him," Arthur replied. Then he felt his high spirits crash in flames. He knew exactly where Riggins had gone. Riggins and some other men had gone to the beach, where hired ladies would join them in a frolicsome surf-and-screw. To enable this, Arthur had promised *to take the place of old Riggins* at the office that afternoon.

"Son of a bitch had Charge of Quarters," the first sergeant muttered. "Gonna fry his ass when I catch up with him."

"It's my fault, Top," Arthur confessed. "I screwed up. Riggins asked me to swap shifts with him. I forgot. I'm the one who missed CQ, not Riggins."

"And you forgot to clear it with me," the first sergeant said. He scowled. "It was up to Riggins to clear it with me, but seein' as you're the chief clerk he probably thought clearin' it with you was enough." He gnashed his teeth for a while, deliberating the punishment.

"I think you're gonna need some time to think about what you did," the first sergeant said. "You'll have all the time you need if you take weekend CQ for the rest of the month." That's not so bad, Top thought. It's really only three extra shifts.

"Goddamn it!" Arthur yelled, surprising even himself. Without giving Arthur any notice at all, his uncontrollable body smashed an empty soda can on the tabletop, and threw the can against a wall. It hit

hard, bounced off at an angle, struck an intersecting wall near the corner, and caromed off to fall—*Swish!*—into a trash barrel.

"My man!" Pete shouted. "Hell of a *shot,* my brother. You're on *fire* today."

"He's a jerk," Pete's buddy sitting next to him said. "I got twenty dollars says he can't do it again."

The first sergeant, who was about to tongue-lash his insubordinate chief clerk, put a clamp on that and directed all his anger at the stranger who had uttered disrespectful words to someone in the top sergeant's own command.

"Twenty dollars?" Top asked the man.

"Twenty dollars says he can't make that shot again," Pete's buddy said, "with or without hitting the walls. Twenty dollars says no way he sinks it again from here. If he's got the balls to try it."

The first sergeant took a folded packet of bills from his pocket and put two tens on the table.

"I'll cover that," he said. He walked to the trash barrel, pulled out the crumpled soda can, and came back to the table, where he slowly deposited the can in front of Arthur, and looked into his chief clerk's eyes.

"Here's how this goes, son," Top said. "You don't have to try the shot, in which case you get to do that extra CQ I was discussing with you before this asshole butted in. Or, you can take the shot and make it, in which case you skate on the CQ duty and we split twenty dollars of this asshole's money. Or, you can take the shot and miss it, in which case I lose twenty dollars, but you don't—listen now—you *don't* have to do the extra shifts. That's how this thing works. All you have to do is try, and the CQ deal is off. What do you say, son?"

Arthur pushed the soda can with one finger, looked over at the trash barrel—which seemed to have moved about thirty feet while his attention was diverted—and considered all the factors that made the shot impossible.

The soda can was irregularly flat and out of balance and couldn't possibly fly predictably straight. The ceiling was too low for a soft underhanded toss, and a reliable carom off the wall couldn't possibly be planned. The angle of incidence equals the angle of reflection only in theoretical plane geometry, where there's no friction or gravity, and there are no first sergeants putting their pride and twenty dollars on the table.

Top squinted his eyes at him, the way Arthur's own father had squinted once, a long time ago.

"It's what us remfs do for excitement," the first sergeant said. "It don't mean nothing."

But, of course, Arthur knew it did mean something. It meant something to the first sergeant, who clearly wanted it to mean something to Arthur, his champion. And so it did. It meant something. Exactly *what*, Arthur wasn't sure.

Arthur picked up the soda can. He listened closely and heard God breaking the glass slippers, turning the horses to mice and the carriages to pumpkins, making Arthur Grissom a klutz again, as he had always been a klutz before.

He hefted the crumpled soda can, considered the impossible shot, *and smiled.*

"Make it forty dollars and I'll do it," Arthur said.

So I'm a klutz, Arthur thought. *It's worth twenty dollars to show them I don't care.* It's worth twenty dollars to make that asshole worry that I might *not* be a klutz. For sixty seconds, that guy has to worry about what I do. *For sixty seconds, I'll be dangerous.* That's worth twenty dollars any day. If Top can spend twenty dollars giving me a boost, so can I.

Arthur began to reach for the soda can.

"Make it a hundred bucks, tough guy," Pete's friend said, grinning a hangman's grin, "and you get two chances."

Arthur watched in despair as God appeared, put a hand on the man's shoulder, and whispered in his ear: "Let him have *three* shots. Trust me, it won't matter."

"I'll let you have *three* shots," the man said, sneering at Arthur.

Arthur froze, paralyzed by doubt and indecision. A hundred dollars? Who would risk *a hundred dollars* throwing a piece of garbage into a trash barrel? Who was that crazy? Well, obviously *this* asshole was that crazy, but who *else* could be that crazy? He looked at Pete, then at the first sergeant. Well, obviously *they* were that crazy, too, but who *else* could be that crazy? Do they expect *me* to be that crazy?

After a few seconds, the first sergeant leaned over and retrieved his twenty dollars from the table. "That's enough," Top said, "no bet."

He patted Arthur on the shoulder. "CQ duty," he said, "first thing tomorrow morning."

Arthur watched Top leave. He had watched his father walk away like that, with that same sag in his shoulders, a long time ago.

Passing Time

Virgin Mary sat down and asked for Guy's advice. She had just come from a table where two GIs were getting sloppy homesick. "I'm gonna go with one of them," she said, "but I can't decide which one. You've got to help me."

"I'll try," Guy said, "but I may not be qualified. I'm a stranger to the marketplace."

"One of them's a runner and the other one's a drinker," Mary said. "They both love their wives and can't wait to be home. The runner runs three miles a day. He says he's got two hundred forty more miles to run and then he'll be home again. The other guy says he's got about fifty more gallons of beer to drink and then he'll be home again. So which one should I cheat on his wife with?"

Guy leaned over, so the men could not possibly hear. "Go ask each of them, privately, who you remind him of most, compared to all the other women he knows."

She went back to the table and had a confidential whispered chat with each of the men, then returned. "One says I remind him of his mother, which is sick," she said, grimacing, "and the other says I remind him of his younger sister, which is . . ." She cocked her head.

"Interesting?" Guy said.

"*Also* sick," she said, "but I can live with it."

She took a swig from his glass of soda. "I have a trick about time myself. I pass the time by planning my house," she said. "I read stateside newspapers and check the real estate sections, and imagine a house that's not too big or too small and that I won't need a mortgage for." She laughed a little. "I thought I had saved all that I needed and was ready to go home months ago," she said, "and then I started thinking about a swimming pool, and a bigger garage. So I extended my tour. What do you do?"

"It wasn't my idea originally, but it goes like this," Guy said. "I'll be in the Army a total of twenty-four months. I treat every month as if it were one hour on a clock. I pretend that I was drafted at midnight, and I will get out of the Army at midnight one day later. When I finished two months of basic training it was two A.M. By the time I finished language school, took a leave, and came here it was already noon. Every month that goes by is worth another hour. Every day two minutes goes by. It works for me."

"Your way's better than their way," Mary said. "It's constant, there's nothing you can do about it. One of those guys"—she jerked her head sideways—"will run himself into the ground some day trying to knock more miles off, as if that could make the time go faster."

"You can't control time," Guy said, "you can only try to cope with it. Some people run laps, I turn the hands on an imaginary clock. That's my trick. Tyler DeMudge says spending time here is good training for us, in case we ever have to live through a war in Vietnam again."

"They say time's money," Mary responded. "It's an extra bedroom or a better neighborhood."

"I don't try to figure out what it is," Guy said. "I know when I wish it went faster, and I know when I wish it passed more slowly. That's about all I know about it."

Mary slid his soda glass back and forth in its slippery patch of condensation.

"I wish parts like this would pass slower," she said, "there aren't enough of those parts." She got up. "Duty calls," she said. "How's the girl back home?"

"She's still back home," Guy said.

"How does she pass the time?" Mary asked.

"Without me," Guy replied. "The girl back home passes the time without me."

"See now," Virgin Mary said as she walked away, "that's a trick I haven't had to learn yet."

Father Dominigo's Farm

Their latest agricultural client was a little Vietnamese priest who wanted to get back into farming. He once had a nice orange grove and fields full of watermelon and vegetables. Then the nearby forests became a popular place for hiding soldiers, which led inevitably to the forests being targeted for defoliation.

As the contamination began to kill the priest's farm, he tried very hard to understand the military logic. He could understand that it would be easier to see and kill people in a forest if the trees were all dead and had no leaves, but he could not understand why those people would stay in the forest long enough to be seen and killed. By the time the trees were naked enough to see through them, wouldn't the people have left? How was he wrong in this analysis? It troubled him to misunderstand the logic, as he watched his parish die.

The destruction of the priest's farm was an especially painful loss, because many Montagnard tribesmen had been relocated to his region— probably because there was so much defoliation and collateral damage. The Montagnards would never be relocated to truly worthwhile land.

The priest spoke excellent French, meager English, and Vietnamese at an absurdly rapid rate. It didn't take Guy long to understand that what this wiry little man of God needed most of all was not insecticide or seed, but large-diameter rubber hose. The priest was a big fan of rubber hose and wanted as much as he could possibly get.

The priest gave Guy a tour of the farm, where dozens of Montagnards were pulling weeds and hacking at the concrete earth with sticks. The priest took Guy for a walk to the edge of a river from which water could be drawn for irrigation. The priest showed Guy an enormous, immaculate pump that was set up under a metal roof close by the river. A Vietnamese even older and smaller than the priest sat on a chair with a dirty rag in one hand, the other hand holding on to the pump, as if it would run away if the man let go.

The priest yelled at the man, who jumped up and manipulated several mechanical things, none of which Guy recognized, except for the last: a red button, which the old man wiped clean with his rag. Then the priest stepped forward, pressed the button, and unleashed the voice of God. An engine, easily loud enough to shout down a helicopter, cleared its throat and roared.

Guy jumped back. The priest stepped forward and patted the bellowing pump, and smiled proudly. He took Guy by the hand and led him to the back of the pump, showing him a large inlet hose which led down a gently sloping bank into the river. With his hands the priest described how he would use this great machine to move water from that river, up that hill, then over the crest onto his farm, where the soil would be cleansed, cured, and made bountiful again.

He said something to the old mechanic, who opened a valve. Immediately, the heavy inlet hose buckled inward, squeezed flat by a tremendous sudden vacuum. The hose swelled again as it filled. The big pump shuddered, then a fat and angry jet of water shot 100 feet through the air to . . . nowhere. As the pump grumbled, thousands of gallons of water made a fierce parabolic arc that ended in the woods, where the ground was mashed into molten mud, out of which a dirty stream began to rush downhill, back to the river.

The priest had no way to get the water to his farm. He needed rubber hose. Many hose. Much length. The Americans had rubber hoses.

He knew they had rubber hoses. They have everything. If they could just give him some hose. No matter that their poison had killed his farm. No matter that the Montagnards had been driven from their homes. Those were of no consequence. All that mattered now was the hose. Nothing mattered but the hose.

● ● ●

Between the dead farmland and the river was a wounded building, a combination church and rectory, where the old priest had lived and worked contentedly before men began fighting over the forests that were now naked and peaceful. The building was pocked from battle, its windows shot out, large holes in its roof. Inside the building, Guy met with the priest to consider his problem.

The old priest offered Guy a seat and, eventually, some sliced banana to eat and a glass of African wine to make it seem like a feast. Guy had not experienced either a Vietnamese banana or any wine from Africa, and in the dank rubble of this home, where every bite and sip was probably precious, the meal seemed lavish enough to make Guy feel lucky to share it.

The old priest was called Father Dominigo, which was probably Spanish, Guy thought, but who could be sure where such a name came from, when it was attached to a stringy little Vietnamese, a strip of beef jerky with sunken eyes, in a worn black dress and a wide-brimmed black hat.

Before he left the old priest, Guy made a promise that he would try to find as much rubber hose as he could, as quickly as he could. At The Villa, he reported the request to Captain Haven; but he also put a note in each man's mail slot asking for help in tracking down rubber hose. For the next few weeks, Guy would ask Captain Haven every few days about the hose, and each time Captain Haven would send another message upstream, asking for help.

Guy's Civil Affairs platoon handed out rice seed and fertilizer, drugs for inoculating livestock, sometimes cement and other building materials. But heavy-gauge rubber hose? Whose job was that? The request was just enough out of phase, sufficiently out of the ordinary, to be within no one's jurisdiction and therefore impossible.

In a perfect world, the military would find a way to shift from dropping bombs to delivering rubber hose. In that world, the Catholic priest would find a way to shift from delivering sacraments to installing irrigation systems. And in that world, the Montagnards would find a way to harvest from a poisoned earth just enough food to survive without provoking the Vietnamese to reclaim their homeland.

But the world was not perfect, Guy feared, and it was not very likely that the priest's problem would ever find its way to someone whose job it was to solve it.

War in the Pacific

At noon the 101st Airborne Division declared war on the Pacific Ocean.

First thing that morning, Gianelli requisitioned Guy for a planning meeting at the site of Paul's next concrete-block dispensary. The meeting never took place because it had never been scheduled. Gianelli brought Guy instead to the Screaming Eagle beach where battle-weary GIs took some rest, and where short-timers spent their final days before the trip back home. The beach was full of men playing volleyball, tossing footballs, eating meat off the grill—everything but swimming. About half the men were strung out along the wet margin of the beach, standing or sitting in the foam, staring at the sea and muttering to one another.

"Sharks," one of the lifeguards told Paul and Guy, "we've been spotting them all morning. Nobody can go in until they leave."

"Are you sure they're sharks?" Gianelli asked.

"Well," the lifeguard said, "every once in a while you can see one of them slapping at the surface. They're fish, and they're really big, and they have fins. That's all I know. If you want to swim out and check their ID, it's OK by me."

Guy stared at the water as long as he could—which wasn't long in the midday glare—but he couldn't see any dorsal fins or tails. The moderate surf looked pretty nice, though. He saw himself bodysurfing down the rolling slope of a wave, a big shark chewing on his heels.

An airborne major came kicking through the sand. "How much longer we gonna keep these boys on the beach?" he asked the lifeguard.

"I'm not sure," the lifeguard said. "Until the sharks go away, I guess."

"Son, let's us assume that they are actually sharks out there," the major said. "Exactly how are we gonna know when they're gone away? How we gonna know they not hiding underwater waiting for us, like gooks in the bushes?"

"I'm not sure, sir," the lifeguard said. "You'll have to ask someone at the control shed."

The major kicked sand down the beach to a red-roofed shed that had about twenty men milling around it. He disappeared in the crowd. After a minute or two, Guy began to hear some shouting. At first it was just a loud babble, unintelligible. Then it turned into a chant: "Airborne! Airborne!"

The crowd broke up and the men started running around the beach delivering the news: *We ain't gonna take no shit from no sharks!*

A detail of about a dozen soldiers eventually appeared carrying M-79 grenade launchers and bandoliers of ammunition. They took up a skirmish line, spaced about fifty meters apart. The major was positioned at the middle of the line, binoculars to eyes, searching the Pacific Ocean for signs of sharks. He didn't see one of them. Shit, what did he expect? When did he ever see the enemy alive in this godforsaken country?

He shouted something, and the firing squad began to shoot high-explosive grenade rounds into the sea. *Whump! Whump! Plop! Whump!* The rounds arced into the air and then fell into the water, most of them exploding, but some just splashing like a golf ball or a rock, then disappearing, out of sight, out of mind, perhaps to corrode into oblivion, perhaps to cause some future mischief—who knew? who cared? It was the heat of battle and the warriors on shore shouted and cheered and the malevolent ocean swallowed up all the explosions and the lovely waves kept crashing on the beach until finally the men ran out of ammunition and their major put down his binoculars and pronounced this part of the Pacific Ocean safe again for swimming.

After they had been for a long swim, Guy and Gianelli lay on a couple of borrowed Screaming Eagle blankets in the tingling sun.

"I was rooting for the sharks," Gianelli said, "but apparently they lost."

"Don't be too sure," Guy said. "There was no body count."

"You ought to know better," Gianelli said. "In Vietnam, there's always a body count."

"No," Guy said. "Sometimes there isn't a body count or any other kind of count. Sometimes a nice swim in the ocean is all there is. Look around. The war won't last forever. Someday it might be like this all the time."

Gianelli sat up and looked around. It was a beautiful beach all right. The water was lovely, the surf was fun and forgiving, the sky was a gorgeous deep blue and the clouds were puffy, white, and enormous. Lopaca was right. Someday it might be like this all the time. The sharks would never attack and the unexploded shells on the bottom of the bay would never go off. Wouldn't that be nice?

You Got a Skill

It was time to requalify as soldiers. Guy's Civil Affairs platoon and troopers in every other unit at The Hotel had to be "refamiliarized" with small arms. All over the world, from time to time, cooks and clerks and radio geeks had to hold a gun and fire a few rounds so the trigger-pulling part—at least that part—wouldn't come as a complete surprise to them if, someday, they were improbably thrust into battle.

A lifer captain named Nickle was happy to have the assignment. His first little caravan of jeeps and trucks drove a few miles from town to a makeshift firing range: some flat, dry ground lying directly off the main road. A couple of hundred yards from the road's edge the flatland met a small, steep hill that formed a natural berm—a backstop for the shooting. The only improvement to the land—the only thing that turned it from wasteland into a valuable military training facility—was a set of wooden stakes pounded into the ground just short of the berm. Each stake had a square of plywood nailed to the top.

"We use the targets as something for you to point at," Captain Nickle explained. "When you get your weapon, there are only two things you can point it at, whether it's empty or it's loaded. You can point it at the sky, or you can point it at those targets. If I see one of you point a weapon at anything else, you will be the sorriest GI who ever lived."

It's basic training all over again, Guy thought. The Army will not tolerate reckless kids doing stupid things with guns, *while on a target range.* Five teenagers killed on a reconnaissance patrol to the wrong damn hill is all in a day's work; but one kid shot in the toe on a firing range is a freaking congressional investigation.

Captain Nickle stood by and glared into each soldier's eyes as the rifles were distributed. He marched back and forth along the firing line as two privates stapled paper targets to the plywood squares. When they were finished, Captain Nickle handed out the ammunition personally. Each man got four loaded magazines. "Don't shoot until I give the order," he told each man.

When conditions were right, Captain Nickle began to pronounce the ritual:

"Ready on the left?" he asked loudly.

"Ready on the left!" one of his assistants shouted.

"Ready on the right?" he asked.

"Ready on the right!" the other private shouted.

"Ready on the firing line?" Captain Nickle asked.

"Ready on the firing line!" the two privates shouted back.

After a magnificent pause, during which each of the men should have been considering—as Captain Nickle was—his small but vital contribution to the hallowed tradition of military arms, the order was given: "Commence firing!"

On the line, twenty-four men pulled their triggers. In three seconds, a horizontal hailstorm of M-16 bullets blew from the line to the berm, causing a ribbon of dust suddenly to appear. Some of the hundreds of bullets passed through a target or two on their journey to the berm. The men hooted and cheered.

●   ●   ●

Meanwhile, at the far left end of the firing line, Guy Lopaca was disassembling his rifle's fabric sling. He unfastened the hooks from the front and rear of the rifle's stock, then rerouted the sling through the adjustment clamp a different way. In less than a minute, he had converted the utilitarian shoulder sling into a position-marksman's competition sling.

Guy angled his body forty-five degrees to the right of his target, then kneeled down on his right leg. He assumed a solid three-point kneeling position in the International Free Rifle Competition mode. With the reconfigured sling hooked on his left biceps, the rifle was locked between his left hand and right shoulder. Even before he started to aim it, the rifle pointed naturally and steadily toward the target. Guy had done this a thousand times before, on his college rifle team, and it was a joy to be doing it again.

As the other men on the line cheered and joked about the formidable ribbon of dust they had made, Guy raised his right hand to the rifle's pistol grip. Guy took a breath, let half of it out, and then let the front sight settle comfortably on the black circle across the field. The front sight rose and fell in time with the beating of Guy's heart. He squeezed the trigger . . . tighter . . . gradually tighter . . . until the mechanism released, and a round burst with excitement.

Across the field, Guy could see his target tremble slightly then go still. Guy took a few breaths, and repeated the process.

He let off five deliberate shots before he realized that the firing line had gone silent. He looked to the right and saw that all the men were staring at him.

"Shee-it!" Captain Nickle muttered from behind him.

Guy twisted around—it was not easy to look to the rear while maintaining a three-point kneeling position—and saw Captain Nickle looking through OD green binoculars.

"How am I doing?" Guy asked.

"Not bad for a dead man," Captain Nickle replied. "Where'd you learn to shoot that way?"

"In college," Guy said. "Our rifle team was run through the ROTC department, and the Army came around and gave us some basic instruction."

"Clear your rifles!" Captain Nickle yelled at the rest of the men. "Lay your weapons carefully on the ground, pointing downrange, and make a semicircle around Specialist Lopaca here. I want you to learn something."

While the men gathered around, Guy twitched. His muscles were starting to cramp. It had been a long time since he had maintained a rock-solid three-point kneeling position.

"Specialist Lopaca here has just fired five rounds at that target," Captain Nickle said, pointing down range, "and he has put all five rounds in the black. And I mean in the *middle* of the black. That is a remarkable thing, since Specialist Lopaca has never fired that weapon before and has never had a chance to zero it in." Some of the men nodded, impressed.

"And if the purpose of our military effort here in Vietnam was to poke holes in pieces of paper that hold still while you shoot them," Captain Nickle continued, "then Lopaca here would be the man to show us how."

Guy's muscles were shifting into full-cramp-agony now, at the same time he realized how long this afternoon was going to be, now that he had volunteered to be a bad example.

"Lopaca," hissed Captain Nickle, "while you are kneeling there contemplating your second shot into that NVA target you just killed with your first shot, what do think the other twenty-four NVA targets are going to be doing?"

"I don't know, sir," Guy said stupidly.

"Guess," Captain Nickle hissed.

"Shooting back?" Guy guessed.

"Good guess, Specialist Lopaca," Captain Nickle said. "The other twenty-four NVA targets will be shooting back, but you know what else? I'll tell you what else. At the same time they are shooting back they will also be *hiding*. They will be taking cover so deep and remote that you will never see them again. Their whole patrol will be taking cover. Their base camp in Cambodia will be taking cover. Their wives and kids and grannies in Hanoi will be taking cover."

Captain Nickle looked from man to man, staring each one down, until the whole group was fidgeting, ashamed to be wearing the same uniform as that miserable wretch in the rock-solid (but now very painful) three-point kneeling position.

"Lopaca," snarled Captain Nickle, "I want to suggest a small modification to your shooting technique. Wait here."

He left the line, went to the equipment truck, and came back carrying an M-60 machine gun. He set it up on its bipod, opened an ammunition canister, fed the belt and leading round into place, then locked the weapon ready.

"Are you watching, Lopaca?" he said.

Guy was watching.

Captain Nickle pulled the trigger and the gun came alive. At the other end of the range, the berm behind the targets was a percolating horizontal band of dust clouds, dirt clumps, and rocks that were blasted in all directions. The targets in front of the berm were coming apart. As Captain Nickle panned the barrel from side to side, the plywood squares and lumber stakes suddenly splintered, shattered, shredded, and tore.

Captain Nickle ran through the whole belt. When the firing stopped, the men were silent. They stared at the smoking barrel, which seemed impossibly hot for such a brief employment. They stared at the target line, a shambles. Captain Nickle had turned it into a haphazard scatter of wooden splinters and paper flecks.

The men looked at debris. But what the men actually *saw,* including Guy Lopaca, was a clutter of assorted American body parts—*young arms and legs and shattered hopes*—that would be sent home in disarray, to be buried helter-skelter, largely erroneously, in eternally mixed-up graves . . . if American soldiers approached riflery the way Guy Lopaca did.

"How'd I do?" Captain Nickle asked Guy.

"You did fine," Guy replied. "You got them all."

"Nah," said Captain Nickle. "Maybe I would have gotten two or three before they hunkered down." He spat on the barrel so the men could hear it sizzle.

Guy expected the lecture to go on forever, but it stopped right there. Captain Nickle packed up the M-60 and brought it back to the truck. He stayed away for ten minutes, while Guy released himself from his three-point kneeling position and tried to reinsert himself into the general society of men who had witnessed his quite-well-deserved humiliation.

It was too soon for Guy to expect forgiveness. After all, Guy had just exhibited a capacity to manage the business of war in a way that would endanger all their lives. Like a mature, skilled marksman, he had been shooting at targets. Like lion cubs at play, they had been learning how to kill.

They were clerks and cooks and radio geeks who would never have to empty their weapons in a horizontal hailstorm designed to kill other men. But on this afternoon they had experienced at least the sound and the smell of doing so, and were that little bit more *likely* to do it someday if they had to.

Back in the office or kitchen or radio room these men would sometimes remember the feel of their weapon, the look of the berm erupting into dust and ricocheting pebbles. They had been given just that small, peephole look at combat; but it was more than they had been given before. Some of the metal-jacketed bullets in the soil of Vietnam were their bullets now. By that small increment, the war had become just a little bit more their war.

• • •

Guy rode back in a jeep, mostly in silence. It was as if Captain Nickle had issued a warning: watch out for Guy Lopaca; he's a flake; he will get you killed. And there was some truth in the warning. He had been showing off, and that was a dangerous thing to do in a place like this.

The jeep driver finally tried to cheer him up.

"Hey, man," he said, "that captain was too tough on you. You got to flush that shit away, you know? Don't let it get to you. You got a skill. You should be proud of it. Don't the gooks have snipers? The Army has snipers, too. You could be one of those."

Oh, right, Guy thought. That makes me feel a lot better. Me and an enemy sniper, facing each other across an open field. Like sportsmen, in our three-point kneeling positions. That'll be the day.

Pork Noodle Soup

As Guy and Paul Gianelli were driving at their usual slow pace over the main bridge in Hue, they were attacked by a Vietnamese cowboy in black pajama pants and a yellow Hawaiian shirt.

"Gianelli!" the man screamed. "Give me one cigarette! Give me one Lucky Strike!" He started fumbling at Gianelli's flak vest.

"Lucky Strikes? Who the hell smokes Lucky Strikes?" Gianelli shouted, recoiling. "Who the hell smokes at all? You know where the PX is. Take some of that American money you steal from us and buy your own cigarettes."

Sergeant Dong climbed onto the backseat of the jeep.

"My wife is angry with me for not spending enough time at home," Sergeant Dong said sadly. "And my mistress is angry because I break so often my appointments with her."

"That's what you get for trying to act like a Frenchman," Gianelli said.

"It's the war," Sergeant Dong said. "That is what I tell them. I tell them to blame the war. Sadly, they do not always believe me. I blame the war for their distrust."

"Where are you headed?" Gianelli asked as the jeep moved an inch or two.

"I was hoping to have some lunch," Sergeant Dong said, "but now I am wondering if it will be dinner."

He stood up on the seat and fired two shots from his pistol into the air. The pace of traffic became more brisk. He sat down again.

"We will eat now," Sergeant Dong said, smiling and nodding. "Turn left at the end of the bridge, and I will show you the way to my favorite restaurant." He smiled. "You will be my special guests."

After a couple of miles of twists and turns, he waved them to a stop in front of a roadside restaurant. There was a central cooking area, surrounded by some benches and stools, covered by a tenuous metal roof held up by an assortment of crooked poles. About half the stools were occupied by Vietnamese men babbling and slurping—and deciding which of them would strip from Guy's corpse its pistol, boots, watch, wallet, and scalp.

Sergeant Dong grabbed Paul and Guy by an arm each, and marched them into the restaurant, to an empty bench, where he took up position on a stool between them. Dong babbled loudly to the cooks, who swore at him. He laughed back, and they swore at him some more.

"We will have some pork noodle soup," Sergeant Dong said. "They make a memorable pork noodle soup. You will enjoy it so much."

Before Guy could assemble enough Vietnamese to say to the waiter, "I'm not hungry," a bowl of soup and a spoon had been placed on the bench in front of him. Sergeant Dong was nodding and smiling and pointing at the bowl, and spitting through his rotten teeth that Guy should eat-eat-hah-hah-hah.

They use spoons to eat soup, Guy thought numbly, *not chopsticks.* He picked up the dirty spoon, discreetly wiped it on his dusty fatigue pants, grinned appreciatively at Sergeant Dong, and tried to work out a plan of attack. Well, some of the thin oily broth was going to get inside him whatever else he ate, so he might as well try that first. And the vegetables can't be so bad. The soup was boiled, after all. But the pork . . .

He dipped the tip of the spoon into the soup and took up a few drops of broth, which he deposited on his tongue gradually, as if testing it for acid. Hmm. Actually, although he was no great lover of soup, this seemed to be pretty good soup. He took a couple of spoonfuls, and decided to try some onion. Hmm. Cooked all the way through, nice and soft . . . So far so good. Next he tried some noodle. Familiar. Overcooked and soggy. No surprises there.

"Good soup?" Sergeant Dong asked.

"Yes, very good," Guy said, "better than Campbell's."

"I have not met him yet," Sergeant Dong said. "Does he work in your mess hall?"

"No, sorry," Guy said, "I was referring to an American soup company. Campbell's soup company. Everyone in America drinks their soup. It comes in cans."

"One does not find soup like this in cans." Sergeant Dong frowned. "This is most special soup, you should believe me. It is very much special. The people here take great pride in their soup."

Guy looked around for someone who looked proud, but all he could see were people slurping sullenly and other people sweating miserably over the cooking stoves while cursing at one another.

"I am enjoying it very much," Guy said. He picked up a spoonful of broth, and slurped magnificently. *Sluuuuuuurp.* Sergeant Dong smiled and slurped back.

Then Guy picked up a piece of pork. . . . He viewed the pork in his spoon from up close. . . . It was Vietnamese *pork,* for chrissake! Guy had been in Vietnam, working with hog farmers, long enough to know what that could mean for his chances of a healthy survival.

He looked to Paul for help but Paul was mostly out of sight behind Dong; and anyway Paul's nose seemed to be immersed in a soup bowl. He must have built up some kind of immunity during his long tours in-country. Maybe he had found a vaccine.

Guy thought about the menacing pork some more, and looked helplessly at Sergeant Dong, who was nodding and smiling like a drunk at a bachelor party, urging the groom to dance with the stripper. Go ahead, Sergeant Dong seemed to say. Don't be afraid. It's only a little woman you will never see again. It's only a little piece of pork. Loosen up. Be reckless. Enjoy.

Guy looked back down at the pork . . .

It was a big lump of greasy pork fat, to which a few little shards of meat were clinging, like tiny Sherpas on a pork-fat mountain. If I eat this, Guy thought, what happens next? Does my liver burst in a month, or do my muscles turn to stone? What is trichinosis anyway? Is that the stuff that corrodes your brain?

Guy squinted at the fat lump and tried to estimate the threat. Zillions of invisible trichinella worms waved back at Guy. They leaped and frolicked, shouting and singing: *"Hooray! He's going to eat us! We're going to America!"*

As Guy was trying to decide whether to eat the pork or run away, he felt something tug at his uniform, around the ankle. When he looked down he saw a dog with Guy's pant leg in its mouth, looking up at him through milky eyes.

The dog released the fabric and, with some effort, began slowly to wag its tail. The dog's fur was matted and muddy wherever there was fur, which was not nearly everywhere. The dog was pretty bald, as a matter of fact. It was hard to tell whether this was a furry dog with extensive blotches of bare skin, or a rare breed of bald terrier with occasional blotches of shaggy hair.

Even with all the babbling and slurping from the men at their soup, Guy believed he could hear the dog wheeze. Guy had never heard a dog wheeze before. Can dogs get asthma? Is this the pollen season, and is the air full of dog-inflammation spores?

Do dogs get *tuberculosis*?

The dog blinked its milky eyes—*was it blind, too?*—and feebly knocked Guy's shin twice with its snout, out of which thick ooze was dripping from both nostrils. *And did it have a cold? The flu?*

The dog was trying to say something to him. The dog was struggling to get the words out. What was the dog trying to say to him? Was it "feed me"? Yes, certainly, it must be that at least . . . but was it more? Was the dog also trying to *warn* him?

Look at me, the dog was saying, *I eat here every day! Do you want to end up like me? If you do, then go ahead and eat that pork!*

Guy tipped the spoon and the glob of pork fat slipped off. The dog missed catching it by three inches, then wearily nibbled it out of the dirt.

The dog looked up again, sadly, through its translucent, tired eyes, and told Guy to jettison anything Guy didn't want.

I'll eat it, the dog said. *Whatever you don't eat, I will. I'll eat all of it. I always do. I'm a dog. It's my lot in life to eat that stuff, whatever the consequences.*

Guy was sorry the dog was such a mess, but happy that the dog was there to warn him, and to gobble all the pork that Guy dropped when Sergeant Dong wasn't looking.

After lunch Paul and Guy thanked Sergeant Dong for his generosity, and Guy told Sergeant Dong that the noodle soup was very tasty.

"Yes, it is my favorite restaurant in all of Hue for pork noodle soup," Dong replied. "They grow their own onions, very special kind of onions. That makes a very special flavor for the soup. That and, of course, some dog meat."

Officer Tennis

It was Sunday morning and Arthur had Charge of Quarters duty again. At noon he could knock off for the day, but then he would be alone. Everyone who was going to Nha Trang's lovely beach had left on the bus already.

Arthur stood by the door and watched the wall clock as the second hand approached true vertical at noon. The next CQ was going to be late, but for once Arthur didn't care. Let him cover his own butt for a change. As the clock ticked its first tick of the afternoon, Arthur stepped into half a day off with nothing to do but whatever there was.

He wasn't hungry enough for lunch, so he visited the tennis court where some officers were playing officer tennis—the only kind they played—in a manner that made Arthur ill. Although they never played with enlisted men, it wasn't their exclusivity Arthur resented. He simply disliked the way most of these officers mistreated the game.

Arthur especially disliked Captain Bloat, who was six feet tall, weighed at least 270 pounds, and appeared to be trying for more. Captain Bloat would lumber onto the tennis court as if it were a driveway or a parking lot, with no sense of reverence at all. Despite having enough power in his body to drive a tennis ball all the way through a tank, the captain played what is known in tennis circles as a "dink" game. He would let the ball bounce limply off the strings of his upturned racket, applying just enough energy to send the ball on a high, weak arc, like an upside-down U. A dink shot is a good surprise shot for a strong player to use maybe twice a year. Captain Bloat used his embarrassing dink shot almost every time he hit the ball. And he often giggled like a schoolgirl when he hit it.

Arthur didn't know what made the Army tolerate men like Captain Bloat. He was a supply officer. As military postings go, it was no more hazardous than a plumbing warehouse in Topeka, Kansas. Bloat must have connections. He must be the nephew of a congressman or something, for a big sissy like him to get a cushy job in a safe place like Nha Trang, with a captain's bars no less.

Captain Bloat didn't have sense enough to be inconspicuous. No, he had to be loud and chatty and incomparably obese, just the opposite of the ideal wartime officer. And there he was, dripping gallons of ignorant pig sweat on a tennis court for which Captain Bloat obviously had no respectful appreciation. In the meantime, Arthur Grissom, who had some regard for the game, had to stand off and watch, as Captain Bloat and his gelatin belly heaved and swayed from one bad shot to the next, chuckling and giggling.

Unlike his disgust for Captain Bloat, Arthur felt genuine admiration for Major Hill, a tall, solid man who played a sound and respectful game of tennis.

Although they had never said a word to each other, Arthur felt a close, conspiratorial affinity with Major Hill, because only the two of them appreciated the intricate game the major played, surreptitiously. There was a secret to Hill's game, and Arthur knew it.

Major Hill would never hit a passing shot the first three times he struck the ball. Those first three shots he would just punch the ball back into play, within easy reach of the opposition every time. But if Major Hill ever got a fourth shot, he would use all of his skill and power to put it away.

From observation, Arthur knew—*only Arthur knew*—that during the first three volleys Major Hill's opponents were playing with the functional equivalent of a ball machine or a brick wall. Major Hill played real tennis only on those rare occasions when his opponents lasted long enough to give him a fourth shot.

It must have been painful for him to suppress and disguise his excellence. Only Arthur could imagine the depth of Major Hill's disappointment, having to play so far below his level so that the others could play with him at all. He never let on what he was doing. He never seemed to be toying with an opponent, during those first few shots.

But if Hill ever did get a fourth shot, he owned it. He put everything he had into it, and that was a lot. The fourth shot always belonged to Major Hill.

●   ●   ●

As Arthur watched Major Hill play out his charade, someone on the other side of the net hit a looping but makable shot above Major Hill's partner, Captain Bloat. The big man took a wild swing at the ball, and completely missed it. *"Jeez!"* Captain Bloat squeaked.

Major Hill started running even before his partner fanned at the ball. The ball bounced high and began floating toward the far corner of the court, heading for the fence. Hill's two opponents casually waited for the point to be over. Arthur held his breath, because he appreciated what they did not: *This was the fourth shot.* This was the shot Major Hill would take seriously, and would never give up on.

As the ball passed through the top of its arc and started to fall, Major Hill streaked toward the corner of the fence, at the same time bringing his right hand behind his left hip, preparing for a backhand shot. When the ball was only a foot off the ground and not far from the fence, Major Hill swept his racquet up into the ball—almost hitting the ground with his racquet—swatting the ball into a flat return loop, with topspin. The two officers on the other side of the net watched helplessly as the ball arced just out of reach over their heads, came down safely inside the baseline behind them, and spun flat into the fence, propelled by the heavy topspin of a perfect topspin lob.

Arthur clapped his hands. He couldn't help it. What he had just seen was extraordinary, the perfect blending of physical talent, acquired skill, and raw determination. It was the stuff that made ancient Greeks throw the discus and sculptors freeze their effort in eternal stone.

Arthur's applause was intended as a salute, but Major Hill spun around and glared at Arthur, not with appreciation, but with anger.

"This is a private game," Major Hill snapped. "Why don't you move along."

Arthur flushed, and his heart sank. The connection he felt with Major Hill was broken.

Major Hill quickly approached the flummoxed Captain Bloat, tousled the fat man's sweat-soaked hair, and told him: "It's only tennis. All that matters is having fun. Anyway, we won."

"You guys buy the beer!" Captain Bloat squealed. Across the net, two officers Arthur had never seen before were glowering angrily not at the victorious Bloat and Hill, but at Arthur Grissom, who had butted in where he didn't belong. Arthur turned and walked away alone, into the silence of his empty afternoon.

* * *

After a quick beer at the Officers' Club, Captain Bloat and the rest of the doubles game agreed to shower and meet later for a gentlemanly dinner.

Captain Bloat sat on the edge of his bed and attacked the exhausting project of taking off his tennis shoes and socks, which he could barely reach under his massive bulging belly. He managed his left foot and sighed, put his hands on his knees, and took a rest before starting on the right foot. It wasn't always like this, he remembered sadly. He didn't always have this sloppy gut, the swollen legs, and beefy arms of a man without pride.

And he didn't always have to be protected. There was a time in his life when he could take care of himself. There was something hurtful and demeaning in the way Major Hill had come to his defense after he muffed that last shot. The way Hill had taken after that kid Grissom. It was only a tennis ball, for chrissake, so what if Bloat had missed it? So what if the kid made a ruckus? Bloat was not ashamed. It was only a game. *Jeez.* It didn't mean a thing.

He had only a few weeks to go. In a few weeks, he would rotate back to the States and take his retirement. It was all fixed. He would be promoted to major, then retire on partial disability at the higher rank and pay. It was fair all around. He had given the Army all he could give. The Army had taken it, and not without appreciation. Sometimes the Army did things that made sense from any angle. Maybe not often, but sometimes.

Captain Bloat stripped off his shirt and stood in front of the mirror. He chuckled, because he still had one tennis shoe on his right foot, and that made him tip left. Getting that shoe off would be another tough project, sure. He grabbed his gut with both hands and shook it up and down. Then he let the belly flop and looked at it.

Like a map of the interstate highway system, his torso was covered by erratic, intersecting lines: a complicated network of welts and scars. He held up his arms and crossed them over his head. There were multiple scars on the undersides of his arms. *Jeez,* what a freak I am, he thought.

*   *   *

On a trip with his battlefield commander during his first week in Vietnam, two years before, their helicopter had gone down and only Lieutenant Bloat survived what happened next. He remembered very little. There was a sudden skirmish as they tried to get out of the chopper. He remembered shooting his pistol. He remembered the look on a young Asian face as one of the bullets struck home. And Lieutenant Bloat remembered something floating through the air, tumbling slowly, before he crossed his arms over his face and experienced a sound as loud as the birth-roar of the universe.

Soon after that, a squadron of Rangers happened by, in time to shoo away the Vietcong and pick up the American bodies. They were all dead—except this fellow Bloat, who had suffered massive bloody wounds, but who had somehow survived. Although he was full of shrapnel from the grenade, it turned out that none of the wounds was serious. He lost some blood, and it took hours to remove the metal fragments; but nothing had penetrated deeply, and no vital organs had been hit. The grenade was no dud; it was merely punk, underpowered, the result of sloppy manufacture or some kind of chemical deterioration.

Lieutenant Bloat was out of the field hospital in no time at all, and was sent to Saigon for follow-up care. That was over soon as well. When he left, they presented him with a handwritten citation: *"To the most extensively wounded* healthy *man in the Army."* He and his network of sutures went briefly to a mainland hospital and then on leave back home, where relatives and friends put their arms around him, toasted his good luck, and asked to take a look. He was a newly promoted captain, a medal winner . . . and a curiosity.

He felt no pride in his adventure. Before he was wounded, he had spent only seven days in Vietnam, six of them consumed by orientation and in-country transit. He had spent less than four hours with his assigned unit in the war. He had met none of the men he would have commanded. The chopper in which he crashed wasn't even on a combat mission: Bloat's battalion commander was picking up some lobster tails for the big monthly barbecue.

Four hours. Captain Bloat couldn't get it out of his mind. *Four hours!* On a mission to bring back lobster tails. *Lobster tails!* What did your daddy do in the war, Sonny? *He killed the bad man who was trying to take his lobster tails.*

As the days passed, Captain Bloat began to recoil from conversations about his battle and his medals and his tremendously entertaining network of scars. It became clear that people asking him to tell the story had already heard it from someone else. He could imagine how: "Yeah, Billy Bloat. Got himself shot his first day, looking for lobster tails. In Vietnam. Can you believe it?"

All his life he had respected the sacrifice of common soldiers and believed that the privilege of sacred battle was earned by the deprivation that preceded it. In Captain Bloat's heart he carried images of soldiers freezing in muddy foxholes, hacking their ways through steaming jungles infested with insects and snakes, watching their friends fall along the way.

Bloat's admiration was fixed on the fatigue and hardship that fighting men bore as they plodded toward their final confrontation. Every step the soldier advanced toward battle was an act of quiet courage, every blister and mosquito bite was a badge of honor. It was in the days of quiet determination, between the battles, that their bravery burned the brightest.

To Bloat, the men who would make such a sacrifice were honorable men, all of them, they were the very best of men in the worst of circumstances. William Bloat believed there could be no better hope in life than to be one of them and to be with them and to lead them through their tribulations.

When he arrived at his unit in Vietnam, and shook the hand of his commanding officer, Billy Bloat was overcome with a sense of accomplishment, anticipation, and . . . He searched for the correct, manly term, but all he could think of was *love.* He wanted so desperately to love the soldiers he would command, and earn their affection and respect. But he never met them. Not one.

He began to think: I have been wounded in Vietnam, but I have never really served there. I have never done anything but survive for— what?—*four hours!*

Jeez, Captain Bloat admitted to himself one night while chewing through a box of fried chicken, I wasn't there long enough even to be scared, much less heroic.

At this point he also admitted that he had been eating a lot of fried chicken lately. Fried chicken and a lot of other stuff. Ever since he got out of the hospital, he had been hungry and no amount of eating ever made him feel that he had eaten enough. He found a new appreciation for all the foods he had ever loved; only this time he appreciated them in massive quantities. He had a pint of ice cream instead of a scoop. He had three hamburgers instead of one or two. He melted half a stick of butter on a bowl of popcorn, and followed it up with a quart of Coca-Cola. He ate spaghetti with meatballs and sausage and veal. He bought two Boston cream pies at a time, so he wouldn't run out.

During his first leave at home, he put on thirty pounds. During the next twelve months in his stateside Army posting, he put on another fifty pounds. He didn't know why he was eating so much. Or why he started crying so much. He would erupt in tears at night, not knowing why he did, and unable to stop.

He became nervous and jittery and unsure of himself. He became shy around his friends and relatives. At home on leave he stopped talking about his wartime experience and walked away from anyone who brought it up. At his new posting, in a training detachment, all the men knew the story, the great joke, and passed it around as a comic legend: "Purple heart, silver star . . . *that man must love his lobster tails!*"

Bloat became compulsively needy of the approval of other men. He would join every poker game, every game of football or basketball. He was terrified of being left out. Once let in, however, things got worse for him. At poker he ate too much and drank too much. At sports the formidable belly he carried made him slow, ungainly, ridiculous. In the gym one night, instead of catching a pass, he crossed his arms over his face and cried out, sharp and shrill. Later, after he endured the display of his scars in the shower, some officers asked him to join them for dinner. Was he in the mood for *seafood*?

He watched himself turning into an adolescent schoolgirl. Terrified of losing his place in the world, Captain Bloat reacted by pushing himself deeper into the cloister of the other men, making sure that he drank their drinks, cursed their curses, even screwed their whores if that's what it took to remain a member of their pack. Except eventually, in the company of other men, he ended up behaving like a clown or a fool, intemperate and loutish. At night he often got drunk, and two of the men would have to help him back to his quarters, while he sagged heavily in their arms and weepily thanked them for their trouble . . . and told them he loved them.

Finally, desperately, he longed for another tour in Vietnam. Captain Bloat felt he needed to put some months of military service alongside the wounding and the killing he had already achieved. I had the action, he thought to himself crazily, but the other guys have endured all those days and months of sacrifice. I missed that. I need that.

Unfortunately, Bloat requested a transfer to Vietnam just when the Army was planning to give him a disability discharge, because he was going nuts.

Captain Bloat's family tree was dripping with officer brass. Men in his clan had served in every war since the Revolution. When he saw that his hope for a return to Vietnam might be in danger, Captain Bloat pleaded for help from well-connected cousins, uncles, and—finally, with terrific embarrassment—from the heaviest artillery of all, his grandfather, the old general, Buster Bloat.

By now everyone in his family knew exactly what a mess he had become. They all knew that the killer with the silver star was something . . . different.

The best posting they could arrange for him was supply officer in a sleepy, static, relatively safe base where there was no action. He would not get a full tour, just a few months. He would undergo a monthly medical checkup. And after he returned, he would have to retire. At the rank of major, with a nice pension, which he truly deserved even if he was not yet convinced that he deserved it.

Without deliberation, Bloat jumped at the chance to return to the war zone, regardless of the lousy circumstances.

As soon as he woke up on his first full day in his new posting in Nha Trang, Captain Bloat sat up in his bed and sagged in sorrow. He was in the war zone again, all right. But other men were taking the real risk, and someone else was doing the job he was meant to do, commanding men at arms, out there in the wilderness that he had never seen and never would see.

After his first trip to Vietnam, he had returned to his legendary family, however quickly, with medals and scars earned in a battlefield assignment. This second time he would return as a noncombatant, a weak sister, a *remf*. Maybe it was a horrible mistake that he had come back to Vietnam. Maybe he would get nothing from it except more humiliation.

● ● ●

Captain Bloat expected his tour in Nha Trang to be unendurable. To his surprise, he fell into his assignment and found it fit him perfectly. He had no hard decisions to make, no man's fate to decide, no lives to weigh in the balance of mission value. Sometimes he could hear the rumble of battle beyond the horizon, and while it pained him to know he was not with the men under fire, it helped him to know he was in their vicinity.

That cushy job in Nha Trang was, after all, what Captain Bloat needed to begin healing the worst of his wounds. In fact, as the weeks passed, he became less ashamed of his visible wounds. Almost proud of them. Forgot almost. He *was* proud of them, a little.

Ultimately, what counted was not that a humiliating supply posting was the best assignment Billy Bloat could get, but that he proved to himself—the one who counted most—that he was willing to do *any-thing* to be part of it all. If they wanted him to sleep in a freezing muddy hole, he would do it. If they wanted him to take a hill or a pillbox, he would do it. If they wanted him to put boots on shelves according to foot size, he would do that, too. He would do whatever they wanted him to do, however dangerous or safe, however indispensable or insignificant. There was no limit to his willingness to serve.

Eventually, for Billy Bloat, it was his willingness to sacrifice even his manly pride that would finally give him peace. He didn't care what people said about him, what jokes they told behind his back or to his face. If he was a rear-echelon motherfucker—a *remf*—so be it. If he was a clown, so be it. He was proud to be a remf or a clown in Vietnam. He was proud to be anything the men he loved needed him to be in Vietnam.

Before meeting his tennis partners for dinner, Captain Bloat ran his fingers across his copious belly with its road map of scars, and sighed. Then he sat down and attacked the difficult project of taking off his remaining tennis shoe.

* * *

After dinner, Major Hill let the other three officers say good night before he sat at the bar and ordered his whiskey. He needed an efficient light buzz to take the edge off his melancholy. He was only an occasional drinker of hard liquor. At dinner that night he had drunk only one glass of white wine; and most days he drank nothing at all. But tonight he was feeling lonely again; something had gotten to him, and he knew it was probably that kid at the tennis court. That could be it. Who was he kidding; he knew it was.

* * *

Major Ben Hill's older brother Tommy Hill was the kind of athlete every girl fell for and every boy wanted to be. He had charm, talent, and

a competitive fire that seemed to come from heaven or hell, depending
on whether he played beside you or across the net.

When Ben was just a little boy his brother Tom was winning junior
tournaments, often playing above his age. He played with flair and won
with grace, and managed to make even tennis brats admit that it wasn't
bad calls and leg cramps when Tom came out on top. When Ben was
ready to hold a racquet, Tommy taught him how. And then, over time,
Tommy taught Ben how to play the game. Not just any game: Tommy's
game.

"Some guys want to win quick, with big shots that blow the other
guy away," Tommy counseled Ben at the start, "but not many guys can
do that against a smart player. When I play, I don't care when I win a
point, as long as I don't lose it early. I never want to lose a point on the
serve or on any of my first three shots. I play those shots as if my life
depended on it. What happens after that, I don't care so much. Then
I'll take chances, go for drop shots or tough angles. For those first
three shots, though, I make them all count; I hit what I know how to hit
best, and I let the other guy go for broke."

"It must wear the other player down," Ben said.

"It does if I'm good enough to stretch him for those first three shots,
set after set," Tom replied. "If I fade because the other guy is stronger,
he deserves to win. But the way I play, there aren't many guys who keep
up with me. The weak ones fade and the flashy ones get frustrated."

When they started Ben's lessons, Tom would hit soft ones down the
middle and Ben would hit them back wherever he could manage. On the
fourth shot, Tommy would blast a line drive at Ben's head or crotch; or
shoot it into the corner two steps out of reach. Tommy got Ben accustomed to hitting many balls soundly; but on those fourth shots Tom also
gave Ben a constant taste of power tennis and intelligent placement. As
the boys got older and bigger, the pattern continued but the level of play
picked up. For the first three shots Ben could concentrate on developing
his own power, crispness, and position. On the fourth shot, he learned to
volley Tommy's murderous crotch shot, or rush the net to intercept the
angle Tom would try.

Ben got better, but Tommy always won. Even in practice, when it
seemed he was playing Tommy even up, Ben rarely won enough fourth

shots to matter. "The first three shots are for you," Tommy would say, "but the fourth shot is for me, because I have to practice, too."

Tom was nationally ranked in high school and could have gone to a college anywhere he wanted, but he went to West Point instead. "I don't know why," he told Ben, "and I don't want you to ask me."

Ben moved through junior tournaments himself, but not nearly as decisively as his older brother. He accepted a partial tennis scholarship at a California university just before Tommy graduated from West Point. Later, Ben followed Tommy into the Army and went to Officer Candidate School. They kept in touch, sometimes took their leaves together. Neither married. They played their last game while Tom was on leave before shipping out for Vietnam.

Tom had not kept up his tennis nearly so well at West Point, and in the Army he played only once or twice a week; but in their last match he beat Ben anyway. The match seemed to go on endlessly, wonderfully, filling a summer afternoon with physical exertion and mutual respect.

When it was over, they showered and had a few whiskeys at the bar. And that was that. Tommy left for Vietnam and never came back.

Their parents and the rest of the family learned only that Tom was missing in action but certainly dead. As a fellow officer, Ben had access to back channels and was able to learn more. Tommy's men had found his genitalia wrapped in a plastic bag nailed to a tree, with his dog tags draped over them, along with a note. It said: "Your officer was alive when we took these."

Tommy's soldiers would not permit his meager remains to be sent back to the family for a pitiful, half-comic burial that would have caused them unbearable anguish. So the lingering fragments of Tommy Hill were disposed of by some other means. Ben did not know how.

After Ben discovered the truth about Tommy's death, he went on a two-month bender, doing things that should have gotten him court-martialed but did not. At night he drank too much whiskey and bellowed at the moon. *Tommy! Tommy! You beautiful boy. You should have stayed home and played tennis with me. Did you think they played your game in Vietnam?*

Ben Hill eventually settled down. The Army waited patiently for him to do it. He was a good officer; he was smart and had class and he could build a solid administrative career if he wanted to. But he would never get a combat command, and didn't want one.

Major Hill's request to serve in Vietnam was eventually granted. While in Nha Trang, he was surprised to find a tennis court and a few officers who could help him fill an hour or two. Most of them were incompetent, especially Captain Bloat. Strangely, it was to Bloat that Ben Hill became attached. It was with Bloat that he usually teamed up to play doubles. They were both exiles from their destiny, derailed from the tracks they expected to follow in their lives. For different reasons, each had lost his capacity to be a battlefield commander. Was that it? Was that their connection? Major Hill wondered.

That kid Grissom sure had rattled him today, Major Hill remembered. What an asshole. To applaud a shot is OK; but not after my partner had muffed it. That was not OK. That was insensitive. Bloat deserved better. Bloat had earned better.

Ben Hill could see the terrible vulnerability that had transformed Captain Bloat. He knew that the war had diminished the man, and felt sorry for him. Sometimes Major Hill would wonder: Do I put up with this fat, timid guy because he seems so much like a eunuch? Do I take care of this sissy because he acts like his balls have been cut off, as Tommy's were? Major Hill didn't know. He hoped not.

●   ●   ●

He told the bartender to pour four shots of whiskey. Major Hill set them in a row. He looked around The Club, which was almost empty. He didn't want to talk with anyone anyway. The person he wanted to talk to was dead and gone. He drank three of the whiskeys quickly.

"I'll be right back with the glass," he told the lifer sergeant who tended bar. The sergeant nodded and Major Hill stepped outside. The tears started flowing as he walked across the compound, past the tennis court, to a small flower garden near the gate.

As he had done half a dozen times before, Major Hill spilled a glass of whiskey on the soil of Vietnam, where his brother had spilled his blood. For as long as Ben Hill lived, the fourth shot would always belong to Tommy.

Youth Affairs

Tyler DeMudge was sent to Saigon on some Youth Services business. He stayed at a hotel because the Army's nearest transient barracks was too far from where he had to be in the morning. As soon as DeMudge stepped into his room an ugly Vietnamese whore walked through the door, put her arms around him, and tried to upend him onto the bed. In pidgin English she proposed an evening together: Saigon tea in the bar before retiring back to the room where she would take care of DeMudge number one all night long.

DeMudge figured he could get along fine on his own, without this whore and her diseases. It took only twenty minutes to shove her out the door. Then he went to find some dinner alone. He was planning on having a nice solitary night on the town. He was actually in a good mood. Even before finding a nice bar where a single gentleman could stay single, he was singing.

The most beautiful girl in the world
Isn't Brit-ish

Not a bit-ish
Slightly Yid-dish
The most beautiful girl in the woooorld . . .

When he returned to the hotel, sick in the guts from USO chili, he told the desk clerk that he just wanted to sleep. No broads. No girl-friends. No visitors of any kind.

At 10 P.M. the girl came back. There was a knock on the door, and when he opened it she scooted in and jumped onto the bed. She laughed and smiled and began taking her clothes off. It took Tyler a half hour to get her out of the room again, the last fifteen minutes of which con-tained not a single smile or laugh. She yelled, she spat, she punched him on the chest when he tried to push her out the door, and she punched him on the back when he tried to run away from her. Finally he wrapped her in a blanket and dragged her out of the room and told her nicely, in Vietnamese, to go away. Then he went inside the room and locked the door.

For the next hour, DeMudge was under siege. She kept pressing the buzzer until he muffled it with toilet paper. She hammered on the door and shouted and kicked. Sometimes she would step back, get a running start, and throw herself at the door.

Eventually she went away. DeMudge realized, at some point, that this room he had paid for was actually *her* room, her place of business, and by sleeping alone in his bed DeMudge was cheating her out of something she thought of as her natural vested right.

DeMudge was thinking that perhaps he should pay her to leave him alone. That would be good insurance, and he really wanted a good night's sleep. Just when he was thinking that he might go out and look for her, there was an explosion of shouting and banging, which seemed to be coming from the room next door. Through the separating wall DeMudge could hear a man's voice bellowing, and from out in the hall DeMudge could hear some women wailing, snarling, banging, and scratching.

When DeMudge found enough courage to take a peek, he cracked his own door a little. Two Vietnamese whores were pummeling the door to the next room, while squatting silently on the floor was a thin old man working on the lock with a screwdriver and chisel.

DeMudge closed his door, locked it, and wondered what else he must do to survive the persistent attention of the local ladies. The bed was crude, all metal, and it seemed pretty heavy, so DeMudge moved it in front of the door, with the foot of the bed frame pressed tight against the door. DeMudge went to bed fully clothed, including his boots, which at this point had become implements of self-defense.

● ● ●

When he woke in the morning, Tyler didn't bother to take a shower or shave. He was afraid to be nakedly vulnerable in the room alone. He went to the meeting rumpled, drowsy, and unhappy. The other men at the meeting all complimented him on the terrific time he must have had the night before. "Looks like you've been engaging in some Youth Services of your own," an officer chuckled while winking and jabbing him in the ribs.

"I've heard some of the Vietnamese whores hide razor blades in their private parts to ruin American soldiers," Tyler replied. "Why would they need to do that?"

A Real Connection

Guy borrowed a desk and one of the typewriters at The Villa to write a letter to his parents. The typewriter was old, gray, and battleship-heavy. Two adhesive labels were affixed. The top one, a black label with raised white letters, bore the name "Miss Ni Vo Thi." The bottom one, a red label with raised white letters, bore the name "Miss Vo Thi Ni."

Guy was more than intrigued. Were these the same person? Was one of the labels an error? If so, which one? Could it be that two different Vietnamese misses with such strikingly similar names had been assigned to this same machine?

He leaned back in his chair and stared at the two labels for a while. We don't even get their nomenclature right, he thought. I've had nine months of language training and months of practical experience, and I have no idea which of these two names is correct. Which one is true and therefore important? When we make a list, which one should we use?

He didn't know. He was hypnotized by questions. When Miss Vo or Miss Thi or Miss Ni sat at her desk each day, did she never see the labels and want to do something about them? Was she afraid to remove the incorrect label; afraid even to point out the error? Or did she treasure their appearance in her life, as a ridiculous but tangible reminder of Western fallibility?

In Vietnam, names counted. Families counted. The young woman who had once used this typewriter would have maintained a reverential link to her ancestors, the much-adored clan Ni . . . or Thi . . . or Vo. Misuse of her name was an insult that would have been levied retroactively on her honored dead.

Guy multiplied his own state of confusion by the number of ignorant Americans responsible for monitoring the native population. It was a formidable opportunity for error. Guy shuddered to think of it. If the American mind could accommodate two different names for the same typist, think how elastically Americans would relate to a payroll roster of phantom soldiers or—Guy winced—a list of assassination targets.

We don't know who these people are, Guy thought. *They remain strangers. We are building in Vietnam a great Tomb of the Unknown Ally. When we finish dying for each other, America will walk away without ever having made a real connection.*

●   ●   ●

Across the water, the former typist—now a housewife and mother of two—asked a divorce judge for permission to resume use of her Vietnamese name, Ni Vo Thi.

"So easier than Krschewski," she said. What about the children, the judge asked.

"They must use the father's name," the young woman said.

The judge granted her request, made a note in his file, announced the terms of his decree—in keeping with the settlement agreement the lawyers had negotiated—and then told the court reporter to go off the record.

"Where were you based?" the judge asked, fixing a sympathetic gaze on the red-eyed ironworker slumped at the defense table. The man stopped thinking about the next seventeen years of child support, and roused a little.

"Different places," the ironworker said. "I was at Khe Sanh for a while."

"I was in Cam Ranh Bay the whole time," the judge said.

It was the last case of the day. The only people sitting in the pews "behind the rail" were friends and relatives of the two divorcing spouses. On one side, behind the ruined Mr. Krschewski, were his parents, the mother crying and the father maintaining a rigid, proud defiance. Behind the wife's table were a dozen Vietnamese, neatly dressed, attentive and content.

"I'm sorry things haven't worked out for you," the judge said. "You got through Vietnam; you'll get through this if you try."

Krschewski pushed back his chair and stood up. Incredibly, he found himself saluting the judge. "Thank you, sir," he said.

"Sergeant Krschewski, lose the salute," the judge said. "You outranked me."

The judge smiled, and Krschewski smiled back, and sealed into his heart the judge's gift of one redeeming moment in an otherwise calamitous day. The judge nodded to his bailiff, who called, "All rise!" Krschewski's exhausted parents stayed seated with their arms around each other. The Vietnamese all rose and stood in respectful silence. An old woman bowed slightly from the hips.

Once in his chambers, the judge sagged into his padded leather chair, leaned back, the springs squeaking slightly, and thought about how different life can be for a man who actually marries the refugee mother of his bastard child.

All the Easy, Clever Laughs

You know who should run this war?" Guy Lopaca asked Mary one evening. "Paul Gianelli. He may not have the tactical training, or know anything about logistics, but he has a good sense of humor. The Army needs someone like him, who can scrounge something funny out of the bombing and burning. But you know how the Army feels about military humor."

"Yes, I know exactly what you mean," Mary said. "The Army just doesn't ever get the point. That General Frostmire, for example . . ."

"I'd like to stick a light up the end of his tunnel," Guy broke in.

"Yes, well, as I was saying, that General Frostmire doesn't ever seem to laugh. Have you noticed that? Ho Chi Minh looks like he's laughing all the time. Not Frostmire. You would think someone who expected to win wouldn't look so much grimmer than the little man he expected to beat."

"Frostmire doesn't know how to laugh," Guy said. "He thinks this is a crusade. They don't let you laugh on a crusade."

"That's his biggest problem," Mary said. "It's his war and he doesn't know a thing about it. He is absolutely in the wrong business if he can't take a joke."

"When was the last time you saw a grunt who couldn't laugh?" Guy said.

"They laugh all the time," Mary said. "They have an excellent sense of the ridiculous."

"When the war is over they should erect a big statue in Washington," Guy said. "A huge bronze grunt, laughing, covered with mud, holding a gun in one hand and a nice fat marijuana joint in the other. The plaque should read: *It don't mean nothin'.*"

"Frostmire would rather be on a bronze horse," Mary said, "pointing his saber to the horizon, with a serious look in his eyes, wearing a really, really brilliant haircut."

"Not even the horse will be smiling," Guy said. "That will be some solemn bronze horse old Frostmire will be riding on forever. The mantle of posterity will hang heavy on them both."

"Maybe they could surround Frostmire with respectful bronze grunts," Mary said.

"Not laughing grunts, though," Guy said.

"No, of course not," Mary said. "We're talking posterity here. The bronze grunts shouldn't even smile. They should all gaze with admiration at their solemn general on the snarling bronze horse."

"If he's holding a saber in one hand," Guy said, "can he still hold a flagstick in the other? A big bronze billowing flag would look nice."

"Absolutely," Mary said. "There's no reason not to include everything that matters."

"Then there should be some bronze girls from the Steam and Cream in there with the grunts," Guy said. "And some bronze cowboys on scooters with little bronze bags of heroin."

"If only Frostmire could laugh at the same things the grunts laugh at," Mary said. "How can he manage the war they're fighting if he can't understand what they laugh at?"

"Do you know what the grunts laugh at?" Guy asked.

"No," Mary said. "I was afraid you were going to ask me that. Do you know?"

"Hell no," Guy said. "I don't know what the grunts laugh at. They keep that secret to themselves. The rest of us get to laugh at Frostmire. We get all the easy laughs. We get all the clever laughs. That's another thing the grunts do for us. They give us the easy, clever laughs, that don't cost so much."

"You think they do that much for us," Mary said, "even when the war is a bad war. You admire them that much."

"It's easy to see the good in us when it's a good war," Guy said. "The grunts see the good in us even when we're throwing their lives away. I don't know how to keep pace with them. Tell me how to keep pace with them."

"Let's hope being so spectacularly jealous is enough," Mary said angrily, and Guy finally shut up about it.

When You're Horny
in Vietnam

Arthur Grissom was feeling moderately horny and decided to have a nice, quiet, anonymous jerkoff. So he walked a few hundred yards across the big Nha Trang installation to one of the latrines that no one in the vicinity of his own hootch would ever use. Arthur knew the way because he had been there before. He had scouted half a dozen latrines and this one was remote enough and usually clean enough for his purpose.

In his right shirt pocket Arthur carried a rolled-up page from a recent issue of *Playboy* magazine. Arthur could have folded the page and tucked it in his pocket completely out of sight, but then the folds might have caused creases to appear in unfortunate places, anatomically speaking, and what you wanted when you're jerking off in a crummy Army latrine was a set of nice, clean, *crease-free* chubby American nudes.

He was getting harder and stiffer the more he thought about them. Especially that cute brunette with the hair that fell in heavy luscious curls over her shoulders. Arthur would rather die than put a crease anywhere on her.

Holding his towel and toothbrush and toothpaste in one hand, with the other hand Arthur opened the screen door to his favorite jack-off latrine and walked inside. It was two o'clock in the morning; he would almost certainly be alone for a nice leisurely . . . *What the hell?* There was someone else in there already. Some kid standing over there next to a sink, the last sink in line before the toilet stalls. Some kid standing there, looking wide-eyed at Arthur. Some kid with a toothbrush and toothpaste . . . Damn!

The kid turned quickly to the sink and began to put paste on his brush. He looked sideways at Arthur then faced front, stared at himself in the mirror, and furiously whipped the inside of his mouth into an anxious froth of foamy paste.

It was two frigging A.M., and here's another guy brushing his teeth, Arthur thought. Who's he kidding? How pathetic. Look at him; he didn't even bring a towel. At least Arthur had thought of that. I can wait this guy out, Arthur thought. Must be a new guy, an amateur. Jeez, Arthur thought, was I ever as young as that?

Arthur casually squeezed a fat blob of toothpaste onto his toothbrush, and brought the brush to his lips as the other young man watched out of the corner of an eye. Then, just before touching his teeth with the paste, Arthur feigned a look of mild surprise, put the toothbrush down, and began to fiddle with an imaginary pimple on his left cheek—the cheek the other man couldn't see.

The kid continued to brush his teeth. Brush brush brush . . . switch sides . . . brush brush brush . . . open jaw . . . brush brush brush . . .

That fellow is doing a world-class job brushing his teeth, Arthur thought, *but how does he expect to prevail over me when I have not even started brushing yet?* It's pathetic. That's what it is, pathetic.

Arthur smiled down at his shower clogs. They were store-bought, sent from home, not the local rigs made out of cut-up black rubber tires. Arthur's clogs had bright white tops and bright blue bottoms, and on the wide toe strap of each clog he had printed in thick black marker the name *Mike,* so anyone checking his feet while he was in the stall wouldn't know it was him.

After a while he stopped primping his imaginary pimple and redirected his attention to brushing his teeth . . . slowly. The young man turned to look at Arthur. The young man's mouth was full of foam, and some of it was drizzling down his chin. He looked pretty sad, Arthur thought. He must be almost done.

A few seconds later the young man spat, dried his face with his sleeve—he would think of the towel next time, for sure—and shuffled dejectedly out of the latrine. Arthur smiled. *He'll learn,* Arthur thought. *Everyone has to learn how to jack off discreetly when you're horny in Vietnam.*

A few seconds later, three men came into the latrine carrying copies of *Playboy* magazine. They all wore MP helmets, had MP patches on their sleeves, and wore flak vests and .45 caliber pistols. They began to hang their helmets, vests, and gun belts on the wooden hooks.

"You need to use a shitter real soon?" one of the men asked Arthur.

"Uh, no, I don't think so," Arthur replied.

"Great," the man said. "You in a big hurry to get anywheres?" the man asked.

"Uh, no, not really," Arthur replied.

"Terrific," the man said. "Do us a favor. Hold this for us. It's the stake. And watch our guns."

He handed Arthur three twenty-dollar bills.

"It's a race," the man said. "First man comes out of the stall with jism, he wins."

"Jism?" Arthur asked.

"You know, cum . . . spunk . . . whatever," the man said. "Whoever comes out first with a load in his fist or in a wad of toilet paper, whatever, he wins."

Arthur gave him a look of dull confusion.

"OK, all right . . ." the man said, exasperated, "listen, um . . ." He looked at Arthur's clogs. "Listen, Mike, you just hold the money and we'll figure it out later." He turned to his friends. "Ready . . . set . . . *go!*" he shouted, and they scrambled and elbowed their ways to the three toilet stalls, *Playboy* pages fluttering.

"Jesus Christ!" one of them shouted. "There must've been an elephant used this one and didn't flush! I want a restart!"

"No restarts!" another man shouted.

"Shut the hell up so I can concentrate!" the third man shouted, as all

three toilet stalls shuddered and shook with the fury of their simultane-
ous manly masturbation.

Arthur stood numbly in the main part of the latrine, paste spittle on
his chin, sixty dollars in his hand, and three automatic pistols hanging
on their wooden hooks, like world-class penises in green canvas jock-
straps.

I need some more testosterone, Arthur thought. *The world is apparently so full of it. I should be able to get my share. Is that too much to
ask?*

Methods of Agricultural Improvement

Between Hue and Da Nang was the Hai Van Pass, in global terms the unimportant rupture of an insignificant ripple in the Southeast Asia continental crust. However, if you were driving an open truck into the bosom of the Hai Van Pass, it was a wonder and delight.

The mountains were lovely in their own right, and today they soared into an upside-down lake of pure white clouds. You could measure to the inch where the clouds began. As he and Captain Haven moved into the cloud line, Guy Lopaca could feel the mist embrace him, cool and delicious.

After a while they made the peak and started down again. Below them was the beautiful harbor—and the sprawling ugly mess they called Da Nang.

Billions of American dollars, spent on hundreds of ad hoc plans, had created a mongrel community that was big, busy, powerful, and disposable. You don't pay attention to posterity when you're building a warehouse or a barracks for a no-account war you intend to win quickly. You build shoddy, inelegant things you will abandon as soon as you can.

To the American military, Da Nang was a city that aspired to be junk some day.

. . .

Guy and Captain Haven had to spend time in a Da Nang office with a dozen other men in Civil Affairs, getting briefed on a new plan to "Vietnamize" the Army's agricultural mission.

Some whiz kid back home had written a cogent, well-documented report arguing that the Vietnamese should gradually assume responsibility for the miracle-rice campaign, and the various other land-use and animal husbandry initiatives the Army had undertaken. The logic was explained so well in a newly published book, *Methods of Agricultural Improvement,* by Professor Ông Ba Tên.

Their meeting host read from the whiz kid's amazing study: "There has to be a more cost-effective program than taking young Americans into the Army, training them as soldiers, training them as agriculture specialists, and then sending them to Asia to teach Asians to grow rice and peanuts, requiring that even more American soldiers be trained to act as interpreters in the process."

"He really wrote that?" Guy whispered to Captain Haven. "That's what I've been telling you all along."

"Shut up and listen," Captain Haven whispered back. "This is the Army."

There had to be a better way, all right, and the whiz kid had found it.

Guy Lopaca screamed out loud when he heard that active-duty Vietnamese soldiers with high test scores had been transferred to a two-year program at Louisiana State University, where they were learning English, and being trained as agricultural advisors by Professor Ông Ba Tên.

. . .

Leaving Da Nang later that day, in a seething mutineering funk, Guy drove the jeep past a bustling military facility. A dozen huge, roaring pumps were set in a line, their sucking intake hoses trailing down a slope into a river.

Army vehicles of all kinds circled the station like buffalo at a watering hole, waiting their turn. A truck would pull up and stagger under the shock of a heavy water blast. After a few minutes the truck would grumble on its way back to its unit, where officers who appreciated clean trucks and brightly polished boots never thought a whit about some skinny Catholic priest and his hungry Montagnards and their thirsty patch of poisoned farm.

When he arrived at The Villa, Guy tracked down Buddy Brier and sat him at a desk with a telephone.

"I'm tired of wasting my time!" Lopaca shouted. "I'm tired of being ineffective. You're going to help me actually do something worthwhile." Brier was speechless.

"I need to get some rubber hose for a big water pump," Guy barked. "They have miles of it in Da Nang. I need about two thousand feet of rubber hose. You're going to help me get it. Right now." Buddy blinked. "We're not leaving this office until you and I have spoken to someone who knows where we can get some rubber hose," Guy said.

"Is there a reason why I should spend my time scrounging for some stupid rubber hose?" Brier asked innocently.

"Yes there is," Guy said. "I already know an old priest who needs the rubber hose real bad." He paused. "And I think I can find at least one officer in Da Nang who would like to have a clean new jeep to call his own."

You Guys Are
So Arrogant

It was a wonderful day for a holiday. The sun was bright but not too hot; the sky was unusually blue; and the clouds were the kind you would point out to your children, if you lived long enough to have children.

The government in Saigon called the new holiday "Land Reformation Day." The whole country was celebrating agriculture, farming, the revolution in land use that was taking place despite the ravages of war. It was a very big deal. President Thanh himself was coming to Huong Tra to give away Kubota tractors.

The men of the 5th Platoon were not invited to the celebration. In fact, they had been *disinvited*.

Just two days before the celebration, Captain Haven had been called into the office of Mr. Lich, the district agriculture chief, who complained loudly—through his extremely soft-spoken interpreter—that the Americans had been making too many *demands* upon his underfunded staff, that many *promises* had not been kept, and that American *insults* could no longer be tolerated.

For these reasons and others, Mr. Lich had instructed all the agriculture workers in his district to have nothing to do with the Americans "in the future." All projects currently under way would be halted, or if continued they would do so without American involvement.

On Land Reformation Day, the men of the 5th Platoon were restricted to base along with all the other residents of The Hotel.

Captain Haven and his lieutenants fretted the loss of the 5th Platoon's most important mission responsibility. By lunchtime they had reached an officer in Da Nang with enough sense to calm their fears. *Back off, and sit tight,* he advised. *The festival won't last forever. You'll be back on the job soon enough.*

So while Land Reformation Day filled downtown Hue with noisy festivity, Guy Lopaca lay on a plastic mat improving his tan, while Tyler DeMudge sipped his chilly martinis, and Paul Gianelli left The Hotel (against orders) to check on the surf at the Screaming Eagle beach.

That night, Tyler reminded everyone that he, personally, played no part in the unit's agriculture mission and could not be held responsible for whatever the Americans had done to aggravate Mr. Lich. He patted Guy Lopaca on the back.

"I know you guys do your best," Tyler said. "You go out to those messy little places and it's really wonderful how hard you work and the risks you take to do it. You ought to be proud, really," he commiserated.

"But you guys are so arrogant," Tyler said. "You're always trying to take credit for everything. It's just bad luck that the Vietnamese finally lost patience with your arrogance just before they decided to celebrate all the success they had achieved, despite being weighed down by you."

"Tyler," Guy said, "they're eating our rice seed instead of planting it. They're selling our rice seed to North Vietnam."

"See," Tyler said, "there you go, claiming it's still your rice seed even after you gave it away."

Like Being at Home

Lieutenant Rossi stared up from his bed at the roof. It was an outrage that he could see the roof. The roof was made from sheets of corrugated steel that let in rusty rain when it rained. The roof turned the officers' barracks into an oven when the sun was shining. It could never be a satisfactory roof as long as Rossi could see it.

The enlisted men couldn't see the metal roof of their hootch, because their hootch had a ceiling. Nothing fancy. Just a layer of plywood that acted as an insulating attic, trapping the hot air and water leaks.

Lieutenant Rossi didn't know why enlisted men should have a ceiling if officers did not. True, the ceiling had been put in the EM Hootch by enterprising enlisted men who had scrounged wood from shipping crates and had nailed it up themselves. But Lieutenant Rossi was not too proud to do some scrounging and nailing, if it would give him a ceiling.

"We're going to look for some wood," he told Guy one day. "Saddle up."

"Is this for one of our projects?" Guy asked.

"It's for one of our most important projects," Lieutenant Rossi said. "Getting me some sleep at night." He explained his predicament as Guy drove to the supply depot at Phu Bai, where Lieutenant Rossi intended to grab all the wood he needed from incoming packing crates. "It's not just the heat," Lieutenant Rossi said. "When the rain hits, the noise is crazy loud. You guys don't know how lucky you are to have a ceiling."

Guy nodded and agreed that the enlisted men were really very lucky to have the ceiling that they were lucky enough to have built with their own hands from wood they had been lucky enough to scrounge on their own time, without help from any of the officers.

When they got to the supply depot Lieutenant Rossi tracked down the specialist fourth class who was "the guy in charge" that day. Instead of greasing the wheels, Lieutenant Rossi stood stiffly in front of the young man and frowned, foolishly compelling a respectful if somewhat reluctant salute.

"I need some plywood from packing crates to build a ceiling in the officers' hootch at our base in Hue," Lieutenant Rossi said, telling the man in the fewest possible seconds exactly everything the man deserved to know.

"Yes, sir, I understand completely, sir," the SP/4 said. "We get that request all the time. Here's the situation now," the young man said. "Could I offer you a nice can of soda or some juice, by the way? Would you like one of those?"

"Just the wood, thanks," Lieutenant Rossi said.

"Yes, sir," the SP/4 said. "Well, as I said, there's a situation now. We used to break the crates apart and give the wood to folks for ceilings and what have you. But . . ." He paused. "We have ice for the soda, or the juice if you prefer . . ."

"But what?" Lieutenant Rossi said.

"But, well," the young man said, "the Vietnamese contractors who operate the garbage concession started to complain. See, we pay them to provide the drivers and the trucks that take away all the trash, and they started to complain that the prices they bid reflected the value of the trash they took away. Like, I guess they would charge us more if the trash didn't include the scrap wood. So, anyway . . ." The SP/4 paused once more.

"If you ask me about juice again I'm going to make you do push-ups," Lieutenant Rossi growled.

"Yes, sir . . . sorry," the SP/4 said. "Anyway, now we have orders that we can't give away any more wood from the packing crates. We have to leave the wooden trash to be picked up by the Vietnamese contractors along with all the rest of the trash."

"But the wood isn't trash," Lieutenant Rossi said. "I have a use for it. I need it."

"I don't make the rules, sir," the SP/4 said.

"Listen, that's American wood we're talking about," Lieutenant Rossi reasoned. "I'm an American taxpayer. I paid to have that wood shipped here. It can't be considered trash if I need it to fulfill my military duties, and I do. So you're going to have to let me have some."

"If it were up to me, sir," the SP/4 said, "you could have all the wood you wanted. Really, you could take all the boxes and crates and build a whole goddamn—sorry, sir—a whole city out of packing crates, that would be fine with me. But, you know, this kind of deal is set down by people at the higher echelons, higher than you and me, and all I know is"—he paused again—"if you take a piece of wood bigger than a toothpick I have to call the MPs and report you."

Lieutenant Rossi was turning purple again. His hands were clenched and most of the blood in his body had shot up to his head, where it threatened to explode through his eye sockets if not released by the sheer joy of killing this goddamn SP/4 as soon as Rossi could hold his gun steady enough to aim and pull the trigger . . .

Guy Lopaca took Lieutenant Rossi by the arm and gently suggested they step outside and view the beautiful scenery in the supply depot, and talk things over just a bit, and wouldn't he like a nice cold can of fruit juice after all?

Lieutenant Rossi let himself be led out to the supply yard, where the scenery consisted mostly of wooden packing crates of many sizes and shapes, some of them bigger than the room he slept in.

"Do you think you could wait here for a few minutes?" Guy asked Lieutenant Rossi, "while I have a little talk with this supply clerk?"

"Sure," Lieutenant Rossi said. "Tell him if he hasn't written a will yet, he should think about it."

"I'm hoping to work something out with him," Lopaca said. "Something less than homicide, involving some wood if possible."

Guy went into the warehouse and tracked down the SP/4, and asked for two cans of the best cold pineapple juice they had on hand, and wondered, by the way, if the SP/4 had enough rum to mix with the pineapple juice, and dope to make it taste so good. The SP/4 smiled graciously, and reminded Guy that the SP/4 worked in *supply,* and therefore had plenty of almost everything there was to have in Vietnam. Except, of course, money, which was always appreciated.

Fifteen minutes later Guy returned and collected his lieutenant. They went back to Hue, and that night Lieutenant Rossi made the rounds of the 5th Platoon officers, taking contributions for their new wooden ceiling.

· · ·

The next day, a small convoy from Phu Bai arrived at The Hotel, bearing big wooden boxes full of truck transmissions. All the men from the 5th Platoon were there to accept delivery. They unpacked the transmissions, took the wooden crates, and left the transmissions on the trucks. When the transmissions made it back to Phu Bai, the supply clerk noted their return into inventory.

"I hate the Army," Lieutenant Rossi said that night, after the ceiling party had done its work. The officers and enlisted men were getting drunk together for the first and only time they would ever congregate in the officers' hootch. "Don't be surprised if some morning you come in to work and I tell you to spend the rest of your tour at Eagle Beach."

Guy clinked the glass the lieutenant offered for the clinking. "Don't feel so bad," Guy said. "What we did today is one of those things that makes the Army really interesting."

Lieutenant Rossi looked confused.

"American money, American wood, American transmissions, American ceilings," Guy said. "American idiots, American thieves, and even American booze we're drinking. For twenty-four hours we have been nothing but American. You and I haven't interacted with a Vietnamese person or plant or pig since the day before yesterday. All the lying and cheating and stealing was entirely between friends. It was like being at home."

"No," Lieutenant Rossi said, "it was like being in Chicago."

Points A and B

Warfare is a point-A-to-point-B exercise. They may say it's about taking land, or counting bodies, but most of warfare is actually about logistics: getting things and people from one place to another: America to Vietnam; airport to base; base to target; target back to base again, with luck. Supplies here, troops there. WHAM! Junk over here, bodies this way, survivors that way. A to B, A to B, A to B.

Civilian Guy Lopaca to Fort Dix, New Jersey. Private Lopaca from New Jersey to Texas. Texas to California. America to Asia. Enlisted Men's Hootch to The Villa. Villa to boondocks. A to B, A to B, A to B.

As Lopaca stood in his newest point A (Captain Haven's office) waiting for orders, the nagging question was—as always—where the hell would point B be this morning?

According to Captain Haven, Guy Lopaca and Tyler DeMudge were to meet Sergeant Dong at the Vietnamese Youth Services office inside The Citadel, and do what Dong told them to do. A Youth Sports Festival was involved, some kind of antidrug campaign.

But point B for Sergeant Dong this morning must have been somewhere else. The two Americans waited at The Citadel for an hour. Tyler
began to fidget. Then he began to sing from *My Fair Lady,* and that was
worse:

> *I have often walked down this street before*
> *But the pavement never blew off both my feet before . . .*

After a while, Guy borrowed a phone to call Captain Haven. He was
out, so Guy and Tyler waited for Sergeant Dong some more, nesting
their little jeep in a delicious patch of shade, eager to let one-eighth of
one percent of their Vietnam tour slip by before they went back to The
Hotel for lunch.

It was late in the morning when one of the Vietnamese office workers sought them out with a request. The nice fellow standing silently beside the office worker was the new assistant director of Youth Services
(said the office worker in brittle English) and he had to relocate some
chairs from point A (gesturing at a French provincial relic with a shady
veranda) to point B (gesturing at the western surface of the planet
Earth).

It would be a half-hour trip one way, the office worker said. Could
Guy and Tyler provide a vehicle to move the chairs? They would need
a larger vehicle than the jeep they were sitting in. They would need a
truck. A truck like that one. He gestured toward a sparkling ARVN truck
parked right next to the building from which the chairs had to be moved.

Guy and Tyler looked at each other, then Tyler checked his watch.
Neither man asked, "Why us? Why our truck?" Neither man bothered to
ask why the Vietnamese Youth Services chairs could not be moved
using that ARVN truck parked right there in plain sight.

"Lunch first," DeMudge said to Guy, "then back here for the chairs
about two o'clock. That would do it for the day."

"A full day gone," Guy agreed happily.

"One-quarter of a percent of tour would be totally used up,"
DeMudge said.

"Sounds good to me," Guy said. So he told the office worker they
would be back at two o'clock, and the office worker passed the message

in Vietnamese to the Youth Services Assistant Director, who smiled and bowed and thanked them with a flourish: *"Bong bong bong ga bong bong."*

When Tyler and Guy got back at two o'clock (driving a truck), the Youth Services assistant director was standing on the veranda, in the cool shade, atop a wide flight of wooden stairs. As they approached, the assistant director smiled and waved. At first Tyler stopped the truck at the foot of the stairs, facing forward. Then, to make loading easier, DeMudge decided to back the truck up to the stairs. He made a magnificent reverse three-point turn (all the way left, reverse gear, gas, stop, all the way right, forward gear, gas, stop, all the way left, reverse gear, gas, stop) and backed the truck slowly until its tail was almost touching the stairs.

The Youth Services assistant director smiled and waved, obviously impressed with Tyler's skillful maneuver. Guy and Tyler got out of the truck, let the tailgate down, then folded the troop seat and secured it flat against the side of the truck bed to make room for the chairs. Then they climbed up the stairs and shook hands with the Vietnamese Youth Services assistant director, who told them in unexpectedly excellent English that the chairs had already been delivered by some Vietnamese using the same ARVN truck they had all seen that morning, thank you very much, nice to see you again.

Guy and Tyler looked at each other for a second—just that long— then Tyler shrugged and pushed Lopaca down the stairs. There was no use asking why the assistant director of Youth Services didn't step out of his chilly shade and tell the Americans they were no longer needed *before* they made that magnificent reverse three-point turn, then let down the gate, then secured the troop seat, then climbed up the stairs. The assistant director's steadfast, inconsiderate silence would remain a cross-cultural mystery, not worth solving, not worth remembering for the rest of their lives—although they surely would remember it for the rest of their lives, worth remembering or not.

Guy and Tyler resecured the tailgate and headed back to the platoon's parking lot, point A early this morning but point B for them right now.

"Point A to point B," Tyler said. "We went where they told us to go and did everything they told us to do, or not do. All in all, a good day's work."

"A quarter of a percent of tour used up," Guy agreed.

Still, the assistant director's small act of indifference bothered them. For some young American that day, the last point B he would ever know was a land mine, or an intersecting segment of the flat arc of a bullet. For all of the young Americans, their lives would be interrupted by months of training and then a year of departures and arrivals—points A then B—in a country that presented nothing of interest to them except its casualty rates.

"At least he didn't ask us to assault Hill 217," Guy said after a while.

"I hear there are a lot of shady verandas near Hill 217," Tyler replied. "The French built shady verandas near every strategic hill."

The truck nosed into The Villa parking lot and Tyler found another shady spot under a tree. He shut off the engine, and wiped the dust from his eyes with a handkerchief.

"Would you willingly risk your life for a fellow like that?" Tyler asked after a while.

"I just did," Lopaca said. "I made an unprotected two-way trip in a war zone in a truck that doesn't even have a canvas roof anymore because someone stole it. I seem to remember you were sitting beside me."

DeMudge smiled and sighed a little.

"Getting short," Tyler said.

"Shorter every day," Lopaca said.

They stepped out of the truck at The Villa and their newest point A was their familiar parking lot again. All the points B that were left in their tours would start right now, with their progression from Villa to Hotel to Hootch to shower to club to bar to table and after that . . . It was a complicated journey designed haphazardly by others, that led to muddy death or home, a connect-the-dots itinerary whose infinitely separate legs would be arranged by the trigonometry of chance, and sometimes—as it was today—by unfathomable contempt, as it seemed to them it always had been.

Wedding Arrangements

Mr. Hoa, the resident overseer of the Montagnard farm, had a serious problem only the Americans could solve.

"He wants us to give him five thousand piastres," Guy told Lieutenant Rossi, "so he can marry his girlfriend."

An unusually lean Montagnard about a head shorter than Guy, Mr. Hoa was proud to introduce his bride-to-be, who was a head shorter still, and quite the package. She looked like two or three dusty turnips bound together by a sarong of earth-toned tapestry, held up by the legs of a midget sumo wrestler.

In the Miss Montagnard Universe competition, Guy thought, *there is no swimsuit event. They pull stumps.*

"How old is she?" Lieutenant Rossi asked.

"Bong bong bong ga bong bong?" Guy asked Mr. Hoa.

"Bock bock bock ga bock bock," Mr. Hoa replied proudly.

"He says she's fifteen years old," Guy told Lieutenant Rossi, "but I think he's lying."

Mr. Hoa whispered something to his sweetheart, who moved forward half a step. She had the face of a Teamster on strike, or a Mafia button on a contract. She removed a pipe from the corner of her mouth, nodded once, put the pipe back, and watched sourly as her honey worked the suckers over.

"Ask him why we should give him five thousand piastres," Lieutenant Rossi said.

"He had a wife and son," Guy replied a moment later. "The wife got killed somehow and now he has only the son. He needs another wife."

"But that doesn't tell me why we should pay him five thousand piastres to get married," Lieutenant Rossi said. "We didn't hire him to get married. It's none of our business. I mean, if they think we're going to pay all the Montagnards before they marry each other, their race is going to die out long before the checks arrive."

"He says working on the agriculture projects has made him an important man in the village," Guy reported after a long back-and-forth, *bong-and-bock,* with Mr. Hoa. "He says now he has to throw a wedding party to maintain his position. He says it's his responsibility. That's what he gets for working with us."

Captain Haven had been entirely correct: you would never take Lieutenant Rossi for Italian. He had fair skin that turned strawberry red in too much sun. His face was smooth and boyish, his hair fine and almost whitely blond, and the sunburned blushes on his cheeks made him look like an angel, a happy cherub—a Protestant cherub, possibly even a Scandinavian cherub, if there are such things.

But when Gunnar Rossi got angry, as he did now, there was always that rush of purple Sicilian blood to his face.

"No!" he shouted. "We're not gonna do it!"

He turned and stormed away a few steps, realized the jeep was in the opposite direction, clenched his fists and came back again.

"Tell him it's not our job to pay for frigging wedding parties," Lieutenant Rossi stammered angrily. "Tell him we don't care if he gets married or he doesn't. Tell him we don't care who they screw or how they do it or when they do it or why they do it. We're here because of the peanuts and the corn and . . . *and that's it!* Nothing else. If they don't want that, fine, we won't come anymore. But tell him they're gonna have to figure out how to get married without me . . . without us. Tell him if they can't do that without us, they aren't worth saving. You tell him that."

"Bong bong bong ga bong bong," Guy told Mr. Hoa. "We help you cannot do."

The bride's eyes turned to machine-gun portals. She took out her pipe and spat some juice onto the sun-baked dirt.

"Bock bock bock ga bock bock," Mr. Hoa replied, without betraying the least disappointment.

"He says he understands," Guy told Lieutenant Rossi.

On the road back to Hue, Lieutenant Rossi apologized.

"My wife wanted a big wedding, like her sisters had," Lieutenant Rossi explained. "We planned to get married after I got back from Vietnam. But just before I left she changed her mind. She wanted to get married right away. I told her that was crazy, there wasn't enough time, but she made me do it. We had to put the whole thing together in a week. Practically no one was there. It was pitiful."

He took off his hat and let the wind ruffle his hair. He was silent for a while, remembering parts of the story he didn't want to tell.

"She said . . ."

There was a catch in his throat, and he paused.

"She said that when two people get married they become one, and this way we would never be apart."

"She sounds like the kind you want to marry," Guy said, "if you get the chance."

"Yeah," Lieutenant Rossi said. "Mr. Hoa should be so lucky."

• • •

"I told you they would say no," Mr. Hoa reminded his fiancée after the Americans had left.

"So you will sell some seed," she said, "and one or two of the spray cans. You will manage according to the opportunities you have. If this is impossible for you to do alone, tell me and I will help you."

"It is not impossible," Mr. Hoa replied sadly, "it is just that they trust me."

"Yes, I understand," his fiancée said, "their trust is what presents the opportunities. But I trust you as well. They can find more spray cans. I will have only one wedding."

"I did not understand my first wife," Mr. Hoa lamented, "and I don't understand you. I understand seed and spray cans. I don't understand women at all."

"Well," his fiancée said, refilling her pipe, "perhaps if you marry me you will know me better, and you will understand."

"You said if I marry you and not when," Mr. Hoa pointed out.

"The world is an uncertain place," his fiancée said.

She has an old mind for a girl of fourteen years, Mr. Hoa thought. That Lieutenant Rossi was surely angry today. How could he, Mr. Hoa, have been induced to provoke such anger in his business associates? Could it be that he, Mr. Hoa, had cause to be angry as well?

"The world is indeed an uncertain place," Mr. Hoa agreed. "It is not certain that our crops will thrive without the chemicals that come out of the spray cans. It is not certain that we will get new spray cans if I sell some of them to pay for your wedding. It is not certain that the people will continue to respect me if the crops should fail."

His lady's face screwed into a knot of anger.

"A wedding worth having is worth waiting for," Mr. Hoa said with the heavy voice of an important man. "I think I should see if the farm will thrive, before taking on the responsibility of marriage. Have your father bring you to see me in a few weeks, after we have begun to harvest something from the ground. Then if you are still interested, and you have not found someone who has better opportunities, we may talk again."

She left in a rage, her bowlegged feet pumping like pistons, kicking up dust. She would have to find a way to mend this breach and bring this important man to marriage. She was already sixteen years old. She would not be attractive forever.

We Pretend So Well Together

How come I'm never in any of your letters?" Virgin Mary asked after proofreading his most recent effort. "Everybody else gets in. The girl back home probably knows more about Gianelli than she does about her next-door neighbor. She knows about the old Catholic priest and Rossi's ceiling and you even told her about Danny's crying pregnant lady. But you never mention me. Why is that?"

"Why do you think?" Guy replied.

"No, you don't get to wiggle out that way," Mary said. "Just go ahead and tell me. That's all you get to do. Tell me why you never mention me in your letters to the girl back home."

"It isn't enough that I let you read what I write?" Guy said. "Now I have to give you reasons for leaving things out?"

"Yes, that's exactly it," Mary said. "You have to tell me the reason why you are leaving me out of your letters to the girl back home."

"Maybe I'm not leaving you out," Guy said. "Maybe there are other letters that I don't show you, and you're in those."

"Are there other letters that you don't show me, that you put me in?"

"No."

"Well that was a useful path to take me down," Mary said. "You have avoided the issue for at least ten, maybe fifteen seconds."

"Possibly twenty," Guy said.

"Make it thirty and I'll leave and never come back," Mary said.

"Well," Guy conceded, "if I mentioned you in a letter, I would either have to write it in a way that pleased you, or I would have to conceal the letter from you, and in either case it would not be the natural thing for me to do."

"You mean that anything you said about me to the girl back home would displease me?"

"No, I mean you would experience that part of the letter in a different way than you experience the other parts," Guy said. "That would affect how I had to write it."

"I think you're afraid to tell her about me," Mary said. "You're afraid to tell the girl back home that one of your friends is an American girl who does tricks for money with American soldiers."

"If I told the girl back home exactly that, word for word," Guy said, "how would you react when you read it?"

"I see what you mean," Mary said.

"You may see what I mean," Guy said, "but now you're the one who isn't answering the question. Are you only a friend? Are you more than a friend? Will the girl back home know what I mean when I say you're a friend? Should I use one word with you and another with her? When I write to her, should I tell her some of the things you've said to me in private, just as I tell her about things that Gianelli says to me?"

"I see what you mean," Mary said.

"No you don't," Guy said. He flipped his pad to a blank sheet of paper. "PS," he said out loud, writing at the same time, "I am sitting here having a drink with Mary Crocker. Mary is . . ."

Guy stopped, his pen poised above the unfinished line. "Go ahead," he said, "complete that for me. Tell the girl back home who you are. Tell the girl back home who I think you are. Tell her and tell me at the same time. Trust me: the girl back home is definitely interested in the topic. And so am I."

"It's better to avoid the subject altogether," Mary said.

"I thought so," Guy replied.

"I kept looking for some mention of me," Mary said.

"You were never going to find it," Guy said.

"But you're not ashamed of me," Mary said.

"Of course not," Guy said.

"And we are friends," Mary said.

"Yes we are," Guy said.

"And when you use the word *friend* . . ."

"I mean exactly what you mean," Guy said.

"You might be wrong about that," Mary said.

"Then let's pretend we mean the same thing," Guy said. "We pretend so well together."

"We're good at pretending," Mary said.

"We're world-class doubles at pretending," Guy said.

"I'd like to go to Europe someday," Mary said, "especially Spain."

"Should we pretend about going to Europe for a while?" Guy asked. "Is that the next topic that will help us pretend our way out of this hole we've just dug for ourselves?"

"What hole?" Mary said.

• NHA TRANG •

Beautiful and True

Arthur Grissom spent some time playing cards in Tessitore's room, then took a walk around parts of the base, then stumbled back to his own cell, which was empty and dark. He flopped on his bunk and closed his eyes and wished he had someone he cherished to whom he could write a love letter.

He had assembled all the ingredients for the making of a very fine love letter.

He was young and smart and sensitive. He was in a fascinating war zone, far from home. His education had been sound, and his powers of observation were strong and precise. He had good taste. And, most of all, he had a natural desire to connect with another loving soul over the broad abyss of time and space.

With his eyes tightly shut, Arthur considered how painful it was to have no young woman at home to fret about him, and to pray for his safe return. How sweet it might be, to recall the face and voice and figure of that one young woman about whom he could worry, and to whom he could send beautiful words of comfort, assurance, regret, and adoration.

He rose from the bed, turned on the light, and began to write a love letter to the girl back home.

It was a long letter, in which he thanked her for her love, explored her many virtues, and pledged his own fidelity and survival against all temptations, risks, and hazards. He recalled the unique, wonderful times they had spent together; and he laid out his plans for a rich, ennobling future.

Arthur was such a devoted, chivalrous lover. He began to write to her about how badly he felt, having to leave her back there alone and unprotected.

> The trouble is, I can't put you under my puny wing. I can't reach that far. It's like you're drifting around in a fog, and there's all these shoals and sharks and icebergs, and you're all alone and I know it, and I can't get anywhere near you.
>
> If there was a rope around your waist right now, I believe I could pull you through ten thousand miles of icebergs, oceans, shoals, and sharks, just to bring us together. Which only shows, I suppose, how incredibly selfish I can be.
>
> If there is a rope around your waist, untie it quickly before you feel my tug . . .

Arthur stopped writing. *What dreadful, ponderous shit this was!* It was verbose, cumbersome, overstuffed, and pretentious. Christ, he sounded nearly *British*.

The situation was as pitiful as it could get.

There's no one back there, Arthur thought. *I'm writing this crummy letter to myself.*

Why did he always feel so alone? Why did so many soldiers here ignore him? Why did the men in the office dislike him? He didn't ask to be chief clerk, he just tried to do his job; and all he got for the title was longer hours and more responsibility. Why did they envy him? Why was he always so alone at home? Why was it so hard to make acquaintance with interesting young women who would exhibit any interest in him?

Arthur reread some of the drivel he had just written. God it was awful. Maybe that was his problem.

Do real young women, the kind I want, see me as the kind of juvenile, insipid guy who would write letters like this, Arthur thought, *and do they stay away from me because of it?*

He would have to be more manly, more *vigorous*.

Arthur picked up a clean sheet of paper and began to write.

> I may not wait until we get home. I may throw you down on the airport floor and bang your brains out right there. I might screw you on the sidewalk, and in the backseat of your car, and chew on your breasts while you drive me home . . .

Arthur wondered if he should try to be *that* kind of man, the kind who leaves young women gasping, sweating, *ruined* for other men. But he was so poorly equipped, physically as well as emotionally, for so much exercise. And to whom could he write such a letter?

He picked up a clean sheet of paper and began to write again.

> Dear Arthur: You probably don't remember me. You probably never even noticed me. I just felt compelled to write to you and let you know how much I have admired you for a long time, and how I wish we had a chance to get to know each other before you left for Vietnam.
>
> If I tell you something about myself, and why I like you, maybe you will want to write back to me . . . and who knows where that might lead?

In this way, Arthur began to construct the imaginary object of his heart's desire.

On odd-numbered days I will be her, writing to me, Arthur decided. *On even-numbered days I will be me, writing to her.*

It's sick, he thought, but I don't care. I will write from the heart, and everything I write will be beautiful and true. When I stop writing someday, I will have the memory of something fine. The others will have only the stains on their blankets where they screwed their whores.

And so, at night, he would draft his love letters, craft his girlfriend's rapturous replies: a lonely young man playing lover's chess with him-self.

The writing made him yearn even more for a real young woman, but the pain of having no one was tempered by the pride of wanting some-one who had the qualities of his imaginary girl, who was so worthy of being loved.

I am a good lover, Arthur thought, *even if I am presently alone.*

Lug Nuts

The truck had a leaky tire so naturally a Vietnamese linguist was needed to repair the inner tube.

"Myself?" Guy asked Captain Haven. "You want me to fix it myself?"

"It's only one wheel," Captain Haven replied.

"Sure," Guy said, "but there's the jacking and the tire has to come off the rim, and if the truck falls on me with no one there . . ."

"All right," Captain Haven said, "take DeMudge with you."

Two linguists to change one tire. That was much better. Guy found DeMudge and gave him the bad news.

"Why me?" DeMudge wailed. "Why does he need two people to change one tire?"

"Some kind of safety thing," Guy replied. "If you think you can talk Captain Haven out of it, it's OK with me."

"Screw it," DeMudge said, "let's get it done quick and get lost for the rest of the day."

They collected their tools and materials and set to work. Both of them had changed tires before, and they knew you start by loosening the lug nuts *before* jacking up the truck, because while the wheel is still on the ground the wheel won't rotate as you begin to turn the sticky lug nuts. Even privileged young Americans with degrees from good colleges and great Army test scores knew *that*.

Guy put the lug wrench on the first lug nut and pulled hard. Nothing. He repositioned the lug wrench so it was parallel to the ground, and used all the strength in his back and thighs to turn it. Nothing. Tyler tried. Nothing. They both tried together. Double nothing. Tyler held on to the side of the truck, and jumped up and down on the end of the lug wrench. At first there were some noises. *Creek. Crack. Urk.* And then the noises stopped. Tyler continued to jump, but nothing happened. Nothing, bounce, nothing, bounce, nothing.

They tried all five of the lug nuts, and the same thing happened, which is to say that nothing happened in exactly the same way. They spent half an hour straining at the nuts, and all they did was soak their clothes with sweat and turn their hands to grimy claws.

"Bong bong bong ga bong bong," Guy swore in Vietnamese.

"You got that right," Tyler replied. "And his sister, too."

Tyler sat under a tree and sulked for a while as Guy went to find some leverage. He came back with a four-foot length of iron pipe.

Guy stuck the end of the lug wrench into one end of the pipe, then he and Tyler both grabbed the other end of the pipe and pulled upward. Two healthy young Americans straining at a lever four feet long. The goddamn nut had no choice but to move.

Creek, crick, the lug nut gasped. There was a tiny little jerk, then a spasm. The nut barely nudged. Tyler and Guy strained harder, harder. The nut emitted a faint cry of agony, and ticked just a wee small bit.

Guy got an idea and began pouring gasoline from a jerry can over the nut, to lubricate the frozen threads. "I should have thought of this an hour ago," he said. "This will do the trick."

A few minutes later Tyler was screaming at the implacable nut and hitting the end of the iron pipe with a sledgehammer while Guy jumped on it with both feet.

"OK, this has got to work," Guy said. He positioned the jack under the end of the four-foot-long iron pipe and began to pump the jack skyward. "Can you imagine the amount of torque this is going to generate?" he said. "Thousands of foot-pounds."

"Foot-pounds are good," Tyler said wearily. "Give it a lot of foot-pounds."

Inevitably, the lug nut began to turn. Soon Guy didn't need the jack. He could even turn the lug nut without the four-foot iron pipe. He could turn the lug nut easily with just the lug wrench. Turn, turn, turn. Round and round the lug nut turned, like a bright new lug nut in a tub of butter. Look how easy it was turning. A child could turn it. The lug nut stayed just exactly where it had always been, *attached to the truck,* but turning turning turning without any resistance whatsoever.

"The threads are stripped," Guy said finally.

"Bong bong bong ga bong bong," DeMudge replied.

• • •

Eventually they had to report the problem to Captain Haven. All five lug nuts were now stripped, they told him. They had spent hours trying them all, and not a single one of them would come out. The lug nuts must have been frozen in there since the invasion of Normandy, DeMudge said. Maybe it was the salt water that did it. The two men held out no hope. They had tried their best, their very best.

Captain Haven asked for verification. He needed to be absolutely clear on one point.

Not just *one* frozen lug nut, but all *five* lug nuts had been stripped? Was that the situation now? They had stripped the threads of *all five* lug nuts, one after the other, *in exactly the same way?*

Lopaca and DeMudge looked at each other, like privileged young Americans with degrees from good colleges and great Army test scores, but not a lick of common sense. Did they really do that? How did that happen? When they had finished stripping the first, second, third, and fourth lug nuts, did they really go on and try *another?* Why would they do *that?* Only stupid people would try the same thing, over and over, failing each time. If they had gotten the fifth nut off, how would that have helped them, with the other four lug nuts still stuck on the truck?

What were they thinking? How could they be that dumb? It was a mystery, a profound mystery, that left Tyler and Guy utterly dazed and bewildered.

"Do you mean the truck is sidelined indefinitely because of one leaky tire?" Captain Haven asked.

"We can send it to the motor pool," DeMudge suggested.

"Sure, I've sent vehicles to the motor pool before," Captain Haven said, "and if they ever finish changing the tire they can send me a postcard to my home address in the States, where I will be when my tour is over. Shit, why do you think I ordered a linguist to change the tire in the first place?"

"You ordered *two* linguists to do it," DeMudge reminded him. Guy held his breath.

"Track down Buddy Brier," Captain Haven said after a while. "He knows people in every motor pool in I Corps. I should have thought of him first. He'll find someone to fix the truck and get it back to me. I want that truck back on line."

Guy and Tyler stood there, sagging and moping. They had committed an act of unprecedented stupidity. All five nuts stripped. Not one, not two. All five. They had lost their senses. They could not have been more stupid.

●　●　●

Lieutenant Prout had been sitting in a chair all the while, witnessing their shame, and finally spoke up.

"Say, Specialist Lopaca," Prout said, "what side of the truck is that wheel on?"

"It's the left front wheel," Guy said.

"The left front?" Prout asked.

"Yeah," Guy said, "left front wheel."

"The left side. Oh," Lieutenant Prout said. "You did know that on Chrysler products all the lug nuts on the left side have reverse threads. You did know that, didn't you?"

Guy and Tyler looked at Lieutenant Prout but were too afraid to look at Captain Haven.

Reverse threads, Guy thought numbly. How about that. Never

thought about turning the wrench the other way. Imagine me being that stupid. Who would have thought someone like me could be that stupid? My being that stupid is coming as quite a surprise to me.

A voice behind him broke through the fog of self-loathing.

"Do you have anything to say, anything at all," Captain Haven sputtered, "to explain away the utter imbecility of what you guys have done today? Can you tell me anything to excuse it? Is there anything that will make me want to wring your miserable frigging necks less than I want to wring them right now?"

Tyler hitched himself up straight and turned to face Captain Haven.

"All I can say, sir, is that General Frostmire wants the president to send more troops to Vietnam." Lieutenant Prout guffawed a mouthful of coffee on the floor. DeMudge didn't flinch.

"To me it's kind of the same thing," he said, "at least so far as both situations seem to involve a lack of imagination and some nuts."

Lieutenant Prout laughed, and eventually so did Captain Haven. It took Lopaca a while longer to catch up with them. Captain Haven broke out chilled gin and tonic from his little refrigerator, which helped a lot. What helped Guy most of all was finally remembering why he had sworn, before he joined the Army, that he would never, never permit himself to become an officer.

What's Good
for Him to Have

Buddy Brier had the knack all right. All the phoning and the haggling and the deal-making had paid off. Maybe pulling some heartstrings had also helped, who knows? At any rate, after a month of nearly constant work, Buddy had been able to do what Guy Lopaca had feared might be impossible: find a source for at least two thousand feet of large-diameter rubber hose for Father Dominigo.

Buddy had called or visited every supply sarge and officer he knew. He had spoken to Army and Navy engineers. He had spread the word that he was interested, and let it be known how helpful he could be in return. It was the Navy Construction Battalion—SeaBees—that finally came through.

And now he and Guy Lopaca were taking a ride out to the old priest's place, in Buddy's handmade jeep, to give Father Dominigo the good news and get a better estimate of the length of the hose the priest would need. And there were connectors to think about, and maybe valves and that sort of thing.

When they got to the rectory, Guy leaned over and beeped the horn a couple of times, and soon enough the priest appeared at the front door with a smile on his face, and his arms spread wide in greeting.

So nice to see you again, he told Guy. So nice to meet you, he told Buddy Brier. Buddy thought Dominigo was small enough to fit in your back pocket, but as a parish priest you could tell he would be first rate.

Guy explained to the old priest how heroically Buddy had worked to get the hose for him, and what a miracle had finally occurred when the source of the hose came to light. You must have been praying awfully hard, Guy told Father Dominigo.

Father Dominigo told Guy that he had indeed been praying hard.

It had been so hard for him, he said with difficulty, to know that the pump was down there by the river, just out of reach, but for the matter of the hose, which, once located, would change their lives forever. As he explained how hard it had been, he took Guy by the hand and led the two men at a slow pace down the familiar path.

"Everybody we know has been trying to get the hose for you," Guy assured him. "You are well known and well loved all over the region."

"I agree that I am well known," Father Dominigo said, as he led Guy and Buddy down the path to the empty pad on which the big pump used to sit.

"I am the old priest who selfishly kept to himself a valuable pump for which he had no reasonable use, since he had no hose to carry the water," Father Dominigo said. "So some men relieved me of my foolish burden."

The place where the pump had been was quiet as a grotto. The old mechanic was gone. His rag was tied to the slender limb of a tree. Father Dominigo stood on the concrete pad, held his hands out wide and smiled sadly, perfectly resigned to the fact that God's plan for him did not currently involve moving water up the hill.

Guy tried to find the words to . . . *what?* Apologize? Commiserate?

No, no, Father Dominigo protested, don't fret. Don't worry. It was only after the pump had gone that Father Dominigo realized how foolish his quest had been. If Guy and Buddy had obtained the hose for him, what then? Who would have protected the hose and the pump? Would the people have to stand guard? Would force be used to take it from them? Was there ever a reason to believe that they could raise water from the river, bring the farm back to life, and keep it?

It will happen in time, he said, come back to see us in ten or twenty years.

"That's a real strong guy," Buddy said as they drove back to Hue. "He has the patience of a saint."

"Sure," Guy replied. "Patience is a good thing for people like him to have. It's the kind of thing other people will let him keep."

A Separate Peace

What exactly do you do, anyway?" Guy asked from the backseat of a jeep that was hitting nearly every pothole in Hue.

"Oh, I have a flexible brief, like Gianelli," Sergeant Dong said. "I help with various activities. I am a liaison."

"That doesn't tell me much," Guy said.

"I agree," Sergeant Dong said. "So now I must ask you, are you trustworthy? Is he trustworthy, Gianelli?"

"Sure," Gianelli said, aiming for the deepest pothole in his path. "You can trust Lopaca the way you trust me."

"Well, in that case," Sergeant Dong told Guy, "I cannot tell you so much."

"I bet you sell drugs," Guy joked. "I bet you control all the drugs in Hue."

"Oh, no," Sergeant Dong said, "I don't control the drugs. I am, as I have already told you, a liaison. I only provide assistance to those who control the drugs, such as your Sergeant Nesbitt. He is making a big fortune, I think, selling heroin."

Guy flinched. Look at Dong's face! He wasn't joking!

"Nesbitt is our guy with the Vietnamese police," Guy whimpered. He punched Gianelli in the back. "And he deals heroin? Did you know that?"

"I told you all the cops were crooks," Gianelli said. "Didn't I tell you that? You should listen to me more."

Sergeant Dong laughed. Gianelli looked hard at Guy—the traffic was slow enough to do it—and spoke deliberately. "Do you remember your first day in Hue? Do you remember the 'Why We Are Here' lecture? Do you remember Captain Haven saying that I turned down Nesbitt's job because the cops are all crooks? Do you remember that Nesbitt was sitting there in the room when the captain said it?"

Guy nodded. He didn't really remember, but he nodded anyway.

"The cops are all crooks," Gianelli said. "We told you that, everyone in Vietnam knows that, so what's the problem that only you can't seem to understand it?"

Gianelli turned to Sergeant Dong.

"Hey, Dong," Gianelli said, "maybe if you could say 'the cops are all crooks' in both Vietnamese and French, my boy here will understand it. Could you do that for me please?"

"Ah, I think he can understand if he wants," Sergeant Dong said. "I think he resists understanding only that his American sergeant is also a crook along with the rest of us Vietnamese crooks."

"That would be Lopaca, all right," Gianelli said. "Is that it, Lopaca?"

"Probably," Lopaca replied. "That's probably it." He faced Sergeant Dong again.

"A lot of guys are getting messed up on heroin," Lopaca said. "Really messed up. Don't you think you should stop?"

"Of course not," Sergeant Dong replied.

"And neither does Sergeant Nesbitt," Gianelli interjected.

"And neither does your friend Buddy Brier," Sergeant Dong told Gianelli.

"Jesus, him, too?" Gianelli screamed. "Little Buddy Brier's a crook?"

"Well, you know, Sergeant Nesbitt doesn't speak Vietnamese so well," Sergeant Dong said. "Your Buddy Brier speaks it very well. And he is so resourceful. I thought you might know."

"Nope," said Gianelli, "I was one crook short. Brier's been holding out on me. I don't mind that he's a crook. I mind that he kept it a secret. I can't trust a crook who won't tell me he is one."

"He is a good boy. You can trust him," Sergeant Dong said, "the way that you trust me."

"Well, in that case," Gianelli replied, "maybe I cannot trust him so much."

"You will hurt my feelings," Sergeant Dong said.

"What's it worth if I say I'm sorry for the insult?" Gianelli asked.

"Are we selling remorse now, too?" Guy asked. "Is every goddamn thing in Vietnam for sale?"

"Of course," Sergeant Dong replied. "All you must do is ask. Your soldiers are guests in my country, and as respectful hosts we must provide for them. Think of Vietnam as a large hotel, with very good service.

"And anyway," he said, "when it comes to your refreshments we don't keep things on so many different shelves the way you Americans do. On this shelf the heroin, on that shelf the whiskey." He patted Guy on the shoulder.

"On which shelf, the good one or the bad one," Dong said, "should we keep the marijuana that you smoke from the ceiling in your hootch? Was I a crook when I provided that to Gianelli? Or was I a good host?"

Paul laughed heartily. "He's a crook all right," Gianelli said, "but he's *our* crook."

• • •

Later that night, long after the three men had finished lamenting America's stupid drug laws, and had lamented with equal passion the tragedy of all the GI drug addicts, and had lamented with even greater passion the sorry fact that drug-equivalent piles of money could not be earned in *honest* professions that the three men liked and were suited for, Paul finally gave up all the stupid lamenting, which was giving him a headache, and went back to the hootch for a good book and some nice marijuana to make the reading so much better.

Guy and Sergeant Dong were left alone together, to unravel the awesome mystery of why Sergeant Dong would want to spend so much time in an American Enlisted Men's Club, when he had two women angrily counting each of the minutes that he was away.

Guy ran his finger around the rim of a soda can, then tapped the rim a couple of times, and then looked up at his friend. Sergeant Dong's smile was broad and his eyes were glistening as always. Guy looked into his sparkly eyes, smiled back, and finally asked him, "You're VC, aren't you?"

Dong's smile twitched just slightly at the corners, then brightened even more. "Yes, Lopaca, I think you are correct." He paused. "Your people would call me VC. Some of my people call me too much American." He chuckled.

"When I am here, I am very much American. See me now." He took a long sip from a glass full of Coke. "This is very good soda. I like it too much." He put it down. "In other places, I drink tea. Too much tea. I like soda, but I drink more tea."

Guy just watched him talk. It appeared that Sergeant Dong wanted to talk. Dong's voice was bright with delight, as if he were discussing vacation plans, or a favorite restaurant or whorehouse. No one at the surrounding tables would have suspected how dangerous the conversation had become.

"When I am here"—he made a sweeping gesture—"When I am with Americans you can say I am very much American." He leaned forward. "Why would I deny that? Who in this country would not want to live like an American?" Then he leaned back. "But when I am with my people, I am Vietnamese. And I am with my people more than I am with you."

He stopped smiling. "You see how it is? I am one or the other, depending on my situation." He took another sip. "If I want Coca-Cola, I will sit in here and be an American with you. But if I want to drink tea after you leave my country, then in most other places I will be what you call VC. If not, I will be nothing when you are gone."

Lopaca felt suddenly sad. He regretted having started the discussion. He began to wonder what he was going to do. What was he going to do with this man, his friend, who might well become the deadly enemy of some American kid, someday, somewhere?

"Specialist Lopaca," Sergeant Dong went on, "why didn't you stay home and drink your Coca-Cola?"

"I came because I was told to come," Lopaca said. "You also do what you are told to do. Am I right?"

"Oh, sure." Dong laughed. "Politics. But you see, you came to me. Here we were, drinking our tea, killing each other a little, a private matter. And then there is some politics, and you come down on us with your helicopters."

"Well," Lopaca said, "America has that stuff. It has the helicopters and the bombs and the planes. We're not going to fight a war without them. Your people would use the helicopters and the planes if you had them. Am I right?"

Dong shook his head impatiently. He paused before speaking, as if he had to summon strength for the effort. "You are right," he said. "We would use them. My people would use all of them. But your people didn't have to use them. To win this war? Do you think you need bombs to win this war, Lopaca?" He paused again, and when there was no answer, he went on.

"You will not lose this war, my friend. America can't lose this war. Impossible. Take away the helicopters, take away the planes, take away even all the soldiers"—sweeping the room with a finger—"you don't need them. You need only this."

He held up the glass of Coca-Cola. He shook it. The ice clinked. Lopaca could see the heavy beads of moisture, humid air condensing on the frigid glass.

"How much did America pay to have this soda sent so far?" Dong asked. "How much work to send the ice machines? That nice sergeant there"—he pointed to the lifer behind the bar—"how much to send him here, to pay him, to feed him, to feed his family in America, so he can count these cans, and protect them from harm, and so he can sell them to you for ten cents each can, the ice and glass for free?

"It is a very wonderful thing America does for you, sending you all this soda and all this ice," Dong said. "My people cannot defeat a country that can do such wonderful things. Not really. We can kill you. We can drive you away. But we can't defeat you. We don't know how to do it.

"Lopaca, you know we steal your soda. Or we buy it from sergeants like that one, Army thieves. You know we sell it everywhere." Guy nodded. Every village had its stacks of soda cans; every city had dozens of streetside vendors, squatting behind pyramids of soda cans. "But have you ever seen it with ice?" Dong asked. "Have you ever seen a Vietnamese sell a can of soda with ice? Served in a glass with ice, as much ice as you want? Have you ever seen that?"

"No, Sergeant Dong," Guy replied. "I have never seen that."

"Lopaca," Dong said, "we Vietnamese like to drink cold soda, too. If we kill every American boy who gets off the planes at Tan Son Nhut, we will still want to drink their cold soda, with ice, just like this one. Don't you see?" He shook the glass, and the cubes tinkled even louder. To Guy, it was loud as fireworks.

"When you come to Vietnam," Dong said, "you bring your whole life with you." He pointed to the door. "Outside, there is your PX. You go in there, and you come out, and what do you have? Everything. Potato chips. Cans of pineapples from Hawaii. You have radios and tape players from Japan. Your soldiers fill the night playing loud American music from machines made in Japan.

"Our soldiers are lucky if they can get a letter sometime," Dong said. "They are lucky if sometime they can get a few pieces of paper to remind them there is a wife and children. They sit in the dark, afraid to make a sound in their own country, afraid to make a light because of your airplanes and your helicopters. And everywhere is your music. All day, all night, your music, so loud, so unafraid. It's too much.

"The batteries!" Dong said fervently, but quietly, looking around to see if attention had been called. "So many batteries. Where do you get them all? Your men have more batteries than our men have bullets. I know there is a great river of batteries, from Hollywood to Vietnam, because Americans don't fight wars without their batteries, to run their radios from Japan that they buy in their PX next door to their club where they drink their soda in glasses with ice while they listen to their music as loud as they want it. In my country, where wounded soldiers have no drugs and are afraid to cry at night, because the noise might give you the idea to bomb them."

Guy knew he was not capable of understanding all this. He was, in fact, numb. He realized that he was getting a reckless lecture—was it economics, or something else?—from a ridiculously exposed and out-numbered unarmed enemy collaborator, in the middle of an extremely well armed Army compound in the middle of a war zone in the middle of a shooting war. And yet Guy felt as if he were on the defensive side of the dangerous line that he himself had just drawn, but that Sergeant Dong had courageously crossed.

Let's face it, Guy thought, I'm helpless here. This guy knows I'm not going to turn him in. I know I'm not going to turn him in. I know we are going to finish our Cokes, and maybe have another one or two. What I don't know is if I am smart enough to begin to understand this stuff he's spouting before he leaves.

Dong took a long, slow sip from his glass. He wiped a finger down the side, then dabbed some of the cold condensation on the back of his neck.

"You didn't have to bring the airplanes and the helicopters," Dong said after a while. "All you need is the soda and the ice and the batter-ies. Your potato chips. Your hamburgers.

"Eventually you will get tired of this war and go home. We will continue killing each other for a while—we have always killed each other—but someday we will stop and later we will remember the ice, you know?"

He smiled. "We will remember the ice in the soda, and we will want to be like Americans again, like I am now."

Guy considered this a long time. Well, for a minute or two, which seemed like a long time now that he knew that the man sitting across the table from him was VC, whatever that meant. Sergeant Dong was wait-ing for a response. Guy badly wanted to prove that he understood what his friend had been saying, that it had penetrated the thick fog of privi-lege that enshrouded American soldiers like him. When Guy had con-sidered it long enough, he finally reached across the table, put his hand on Sergeant Dong's own hand, and said:

"Sergeant Dong, that's a big load of water-buffalo crap."

Dong arched his eyebrows, sighed, and replied, "Yes, I know it is buffalo crap, but is it not good how I said it?"

"Yes," Guy assured him, "it was very well said. Your English is very good, I really do admire your English. But let's face it, if all you want is our ice and our batteries, you could stop killing us and just ask for some."

"Oh, well, you see," said Sergeant Dong, "not all of my people understand these things. Since you are here, the first thing on their minds is to kill you all or chase you home. Later, when you are gone, they will think more about the ice. They will remember the ice . . . and the batteries . . . and the hamburgers. And they will want what you brought with you when you came. And so that is how you will win the war, some day. You won't defeat us, but someday you will recognize us. You will look across the ocean, and see all of us drinking soda with ice. That is my idea. It is not such a big idea."

"No," said Guy, "it is a very small idea. We should both be very sad someday, after all of this, if it turned out that your small idea was big enough."

"Yes," Dong said, "it would be sad."

"You know," Guy said, "when I first came to Hue I thought that my platoon's stupid little Army farming projects didn't make any sense. They were ridiculous. They were completely out of character with all the shooting and the bombing. You know what I mean?" Dong nodded. "But sometimes I think I have it backwards," Guy continued. "Maybe the shooting and the bombing are out of character with the rice and peanuts and pigs. Maybe we should have stuck to beans and watermelon and left it at that. Am I making any sense?"

"Yes, it's possible," said Dong. "I have also been looking at those soldiers there in the corner. Do you see them?" Dong nodded toward a group of three transient grunts, still grimy from a hot trip through the boondocks. "America is arrogant," Dong said, "and will send her soldiers off to die in silly wars. But America will work so hard to supply their soldiers with soda and ice. Everyone in your army can get the ice. Not just some, everyone. We will remember that. Even after my friends have killed enough of you to make you leave, we will remember that."

"Before you kill me and all my friends," Guy said, "do we have time for another soda?"

"Sure, yes, we will have another soda," Dong said, "and I won't kill you or any of your friends. I am not that kind of man.

"I am like you, Lopaca," Dong said. "I don't shoot, I talk. I talk to you, I talk to your friends, I talk to my friends in the government, in the army, in the police; and then I go for a ride in my jeep and I talk to my other friends. I just talk. I talk, and let others do their shooting."

When he stopped talking, the irregular chatter that had always been there in the background—the distant, muffled chatter of automatic weapons, other Americans squaring off against other Vietnamese in other places—became more prominent. The gap across the table, between Sergeant Dong and Guy Lopaca, seemed to grow wider—but still not unbridgeable—with the sound of their friends killing one another in the night.

Bean Counter

The former carmaker's accountant—who ran the Pentagon now—
had communed with his numbers. He had fondled them, stroked
them, wheedled them, and inveigled them, and their response to his attention was always the same: "insufficient data." He reluctantly decided
that with progress being so slow, and with new ideas for ending the war
being in such short supply, he would go along with General Frostmire's
request to send more units to Vietnam.

"One thing we learn in Detroit," the bean counter said at his press
conference to announce the troop increase, *"there is no substitute for
cubic inches."*

"Does this represent another escalation of the war?" asked one of
the senior reporters on the coveted Pentagon beat.

"Certainly not, Millie," said the Secretary of Defense. "It is *a temporary redeployment of forces* that will enable an orderly *transition* to
the safe execution of our troop *withdrawal* plan. Yes, Stuart, you're
next."

"Are you saying that these troops are being sent simply to protect the other troops while they withdraw?" Stuart asked, scrambling the air with his glasses for emphasis, as his world-famous voice filled the room. "Or are these troops intended to engage in offensive operations as well?"

"Well, Stuart, you know we don't send in the Army to rescue the Army," the Secretary laughed. Stuart smiled knowingly for the second camera that the network always sent along for his reaction shots.

"No," the Secretary said, "the situation on the ground in a conflict like this one is more *dynamic* than the standard engagement where battle lines are *clearly drawn*. Any troop withdrawal, especially a staged withdrawal such as ours, might present to a *cynical* enemy the false appearance that there are opportunities for them to obtain an unfair advantage by the *escalation* of the conflict on their part during our withdrawal process. Our current *redeployment* is intended to nip in the bud any such *aggressive* notions that the communists might have."

Jesus, I'm good! McNaught beamed.

"Could you explain what you mean by that cubic horsepower thing?" one of the newer reporters shouted, nearly jumping out of his shoes to be next.

"Well," McNaught said patiently, "in Detroit carmakers know, and professional car-racers agree, that there's absolutely no substitute for cubic inches. It's power that wins races and the size of your engine is the best measure of its power. So we're going to give the Joint Chiefs what they need, and put more cubic inches on the battlefield."

"And by cubic inches," the reporter followed up, establishing a bold new direction for war reportage, "do you mean thousands of nineteen-year-old American boys?"

"Well, sure," the Secretary of Defense shot back, "if that's the way *you* need to think about it."

●　●　●

Tyler DeMudge turned off the radio.

"What a country," he said. "They give us B-52 bombers, B-rations, and B-spectacled idiots like McNaught, but no one can find me a nice tangerine when I need one."

"You could go look for one at the mess hall," Gianelli suggested.

"Too far," DeMudge responded. "I think I'll just wait here for our cubic inches to arrive and ask one of them to get me a tangerine. How many cubic inches do you think they'll send us?"

"I don't know," Gianelli said, "although I think two hundred eighty-nine cubic inches would be pretty good. I drove in a Mustang once, and that had two hundred eighty-nine cubic inches. Let me tell you, it could scoot."

"I think this cubic-inch thing could actually turn the war," DeMudge said. "We could parachute thousands of Mustangs in to soft landings all over the country. We could give all the communists Mustang convertibles. Then they'll need roads and gasoline and replacement parts, and those cardboard pine trees that smell nice that hang from the rearview mirrors. That's when we'll have them by the balls."

●   ●   ●

McNaught was angry all right. He called his press secretary into the office, closed the door, and ran his right hand twice through his hair that was so thick with grease no one had seen a strand out of place since he graduated high school.

"Since when do we allow follow-up questions like that one?" he shouted at his news flak.

"I'm sorry," the press secretary said, "it caught me by surprise. I'll talk to his boss."

"You'll do more than that," McNaught said. "I mean to take *control* of these press conferences, and I mean to do it *right now.* Do you *understand*? Good. First thing you'll do is call the asshole's boss and tell him that reporter is not welcome on this beat. *Period.* Then you'll draft a statement of policy that clearly expresses our guidelines. Send it out to every managing editor, and every network, and have a copy ready for every reporter who steps into the briefing room at the next press conference. They sign off, or they don't get in. You got that? Have I made myself *clear*?"

"Yes, sir," the press secretary whispered.

"Good, I'm glad to hear it," McNaught fumed. Then his brow furrowed, and his nose twitched, and his eyelids came together in a contemplative squint. "Submit a draft before sending it out," he said sternly. "And send a copy of the draft over to the Joint Chiefs for their comments. I'm not going to let these press guys kick me around. I've handled tougher bunches of creeps than they'll ever be. I've handled stockholders for chrissake. Now get the hell out of here."

"Sorry, sir," the press secretary said as he slinked to the door.

"Hold on!" McNaught said. "Come to think of it, you better send a copy of that draft over to State, too. Better let State look at it. Better get input from State. . . . Make me a list of anybody else who should see the draft. Can't be too careful. Who do you think should look at it?"

"I think the president's chief of staff might want to see it," the cowering press secretary suggested. "The Pentagon press guys are just going to compare our new policy with the White House policy, and you know where that can lead."

"Yeah, right," said McNaught, "the bastards will make a story out of that, too. So here's what you do. You draft the new policy, let me look at it, and you schedule a meeting here sometime next week, midweek, breakfast kind of thing, and have the White House and State and the Joint Chiefs and, oh, I don't know, one or two others send someone over here to work out the details of the new briefing policy. I'll chair the meeting. Not a big heavy breakfast. Something light. Light snack. Coffee. Muffins. Bagels. Cream cheese, but no salmon. Hate salmon. Juice. Could you make sure there are some bran muffins in there? Spoons for the coffee. Knives for the cheese. No forks. And butter."

"Yes, sir," the press secretary said.

"Yeah, well, OK," said the Secretary of Defense, "you get on that now. I need to think."

The door closed and McNaught stood at his desk knocking his knuckles on the shiny empty desktop, where no messy piles of paper lay because nothing bogged down on *his* desk, because *that's just how frigging good he was*! And he fumed and he fumed and he simmered like a fine Irish stew . . .

Nineteen-year-old kids. Nineteen-year-old kids. Well, of course, by cubic inches I mean troop strength, which means soldiers, and by soldiers I necessarily refer to boys who are young enough and fit enough to do the work. What kind of frigging namby-pamby question was that for a member of the Pentagon press corps to ask the Secretary of Defense? Of course power means troop strength. Of course troop strength means lots of young men, and yes, that means thousands of them. Does that idiot think I send them over one at a time?

Methods of
Melon Farming

The watermelon plants at Nam Hoa were burning to death. Lieutenant Rossi could see that. He had pushed and prodded and thrashed the Montagnards to nurture a plot of land that could only be described, now, as a weed farm.

From neat rows of perfectly furrowed soil, there sprouted a geometrically exquisite arrangement of ragged, weary weeds. They would never mature into watermelon, never be promoted to the rank of food. Those plants, which Rossi had somehow killed, would surely droop and desiccate a few more days, shrivel into dusty particles, then blow away.

Rossi had got the chemicals wrong. He felt the brittle leaves, smelled the soil, and took samples for testing, but he knew the fault for this calamity was his. He muttered about using too much nitrogen; he muttered about a lot of things.

He searched for answers in his copy of *Methods of Melon Farming*, by Professor Ông Ba Tên, but there were no answers to be found there or anywhere else.

He muttered and moped, and wondered what he could say to Guy

Lopaca that could be translated clearly to Mr. Hoa, and then conveyed to this village in such a way that Rossi could shoulder the blame himself—*all of it himself*—so the villagers wouldn't lose hope in the other important projects they had under way.

Lieutenant Rossi could think of only one thing that might save the melon plants: *water.* The villagers would have to put a lot more water into the irrigation ditches, or spray and drizzle the plants individually by hand. The Montagnards would have to fetch and carry lots of water double-time, triple-time, and it would have to start right away.

He and Lopaca would have to scrounge for buckets and empty cans. They would have to pester the cooks for those big metal cans in which fruit and beans and other stuff were shipped in bulk. They would have to get wire or string, so the cans could be tied to the ends of saplings or bamboo poles, so dozens of Montagnards could carry water from the river, much more quickly than they had been fetching it before.

The project would take manpower of the most menial sort, with tools of the most rudimentary kind—and it would be harder to arrange than an air strike by a squadron of jets. Hell, an air strike would be easy.

In an hour or two Lieutenant Rossi could probably reduce the Montagnard village at Nam Hoa to a collection of large bomb craters, at the bottom of which—the holes would be so very deep—there would be tons of casual water. But let Lieutenant Rossi try to put some water up on the surface of the land, where the watermelons needed it? That was too hard, too hard. Impossible.

Guy translated for Mr. Hoa what the village would have to do. The little man took it well, and said his people would start soaking the soil around the plants as best they could, which wouldn't be nearly well enough with the few makeshift water buckets they had available. Guy and Lieutenant Rossi would return the next afternoon with whatever materials they could gather before then.

•   •   •

Early the next morning, it began to rain. It was raining when Guy woke up. It was raining heavily when he went to breakfast. It was a torrent by the time he got to The Villa to meet Lieutenant Rossi. All the streets were flooded; in fact it seemed that all of Hue was flooded. It was raining like the countdown to the launching of an ark.

At The Villa parking lot, Gianelli and DeMudge were trying to catch fish. The flood must have overrun little ponds and streams and . . . who knows? Maybe underground nests that the fish go to sleep in. Wherever the fish had come from, there they were: small silver fish jumping and splashing all over the parking lot.

This is too weird, Lopaca thought. Fish in the parking lot? *Here, boy, park my jeep between the catfish and the carp.* Too weird. It had the feel of a European art film, impossible things happening in such an interesting way. Tyler DeMudge was bounding around like a little kid, trying to scoop up fish with his hat. Paul Gianelli was waving an open umbrella, kicking his feet and dancing: *"I'm siiiinging with the fish, just siiiinging with the fish . . ."*

Lieutenant Rossi was a wreck.

"This rain might save us," he told Lopaca when they met inside, where a pot of hot coffee was waiting. "It might save the melon crop, maybe." His hands were shaking.

"Lucky break," Guy said.

They sipped their coffee for a while.

"Last night I prayed for rain," Lieutenant Rossi said in a low voice that wouldn't be heard by anyone but Guy. "Can you believe that?"

"I can believe it," Guy said. "I can believe you prayed for rain. That doesn't mean there's a connection between the praying and the raining."

"Well, all I know for sure is this," Lieutenant Rossi said, "I prayed for rain, and we got rain. But I forgot to pray for a miraculous visitation of water cans in Nam Hoa. So let's get our asses in gear. I promised them water cans and I'm damn well going to deliver some, even if they're not going to need them much today. Get the key and unchain the truck. I already told the mess hall we're on our way." His hands were still shaking as he put down his cup. "We're also getting some clean fifty-five-gallon drums from the ARVN motor pool inside The Citadel. Mr. Hoa can use those as cisterns to warehouse the water. It's better than just fetching and dumping."

In a couple of hours they had a nice load of junk containers that, simply by not being thrown away somewhere else, would help salvage the future of their Montagnard tribe in Nam Hoa. Lopaca and Rossi were trying to feel optimistic as they made the slow drive over muddy roads in the hammering rain.

"I don't remember the last time I prayed for something," Lieutenant Rossi said. "When I prayed last night I had no other option, it was a knee-jerk reaction." He grimaced. "I don't know if I gave in to a silly superstition, and got coincidentally lucky, or if maybe I actually caught the ear of God. Can you believe that?" He fell silent. His enormous burden had not yet been unloaded. After all, the heavy rain did not guarantee that the melon farm would succeed. The poisoned plants might be past saving already.

"The Montagnards believe in you," Guy said after a while. "Right now they have no one else who can help them. Maybe you brought them the rain. Maybe you didn't. Does it matter? It looks like it will work out OK for everybody, regardless of who takes credit for the lucky breaks."

Lieutenant Rossi nodded and then turned his head so Lopaca couldn't see him tremble under the weight he was carrying.

* * *

When they got to the village Mr. Hoa ran to meet them, and shook their hands heartily, and waved his hat at the sky, and shouted *Rain!* in four languages. The people turned out in a happy, sodden crowd, all of them clean and shiny because the miraculous shower had washed away the dust and grime. They took delivery of the big oil drums and the multitude of empty cans, the coils of wire and rope, even some slender wood and metal poles they could use to carry the water cans, balancing the shafts on their shoulders.

Some of the men hefted the oil drums to the corners of the demonstration plots, where they would be kept full for use in the days to come. Mr. Hoa showed the Americans how he had arranged to siphon off today's rainwater from the irrigation channels, so the plants would not be washed away. They had hastily dug a containment basin, to catch as much of the water as they could before the downpour ended.

Some kids pulled Guy and Lieutenant Rossi to a muddy patch where the kids were sliding, and holding mud-wrestling matches. The village was having a carnival.

"What a difference a day makes," Guy said.

"We're not out of the woods yet," Lieutenant Rossi replied, "but I feel a lot better."

Lieutenant Rossi felt better than better. He felt nearly adored. After a bad spell of fear and depression, his confidence had begun to soar again. The villagers laughed their hope and confidence back into him. The children grabbed his hands and pulled on his uniform, giggling and laughing loudly. He didn't know whether they were ignorant of his error with the watermelons, or forgave him for it. Either way, it was clear that he was still a part of their community. Rossi felt as if he were at the center of a choir during high mass on Easter.

* * *

After the two Americans began to drive back to Hue, Mr. Hoa called the village together for a meeting.

"We should not rejoice too heartily, or appear to be unconcerned about our future," Mr. Hoa cautioned them. "This is only one rainstorm, only one day. We have crops to grow and to harvest and many things may yet happen that will turn our happiness to tears. We have to make the farm succeed, this year and the next and the year after that.

"You know how hard that will be," Mr. Hoa said gravely. "If the farm succeeds, then we will have to protect our share of the harvest from those who will come to take it. Our struggle may never again seem as easy as it seems today.

"It seems easy today only because we feel the grace of God," Mr. Hoa began to preach. "Because our prayers have been answered. We have the rain and we have the materials to carry the water. We thank God for that. Tomorrow is another day. There will be many hard days to come, and many prayers. We must accept God's blessing that we receive today with humble gratitude and fear, lest we never get another."

"And that Rossi," one of the men shouted, "shall we pray again that they send us some new officer to replace that fool?"

"Why not?" Mr. Hoa responded optimistically. "Perhaps our luck will persist." He held both arms wide as wings, palms and face raised to the ears of heaven.

"Oh God," Mr. Hoa said with a deep and hearty voice, "please give Lieutenant Rossi to the Vietnamese."

Staying Thirsty
All Day Long

Virgin Mary was happy all right. She had bagged a bird colonel yesterday afternoon, and an Air Force general the night before. "The conversation sucked," she told Guy, "but the hourly rate was fantastic."

They sat in the shade of a bunker, sipping the Cokes she had brought, thinking of home. It wouldn't be long now, for either of them. A couple of weeks for Mary—she had not started talking in terms of days—and less than three months longer than that for Guy.

"Except I might try to re-up," Mary said. "The money is so attractive to me right now. And the work . . ." she paused. "You know, over here being a nurse is something special. The way the guys look at me . . ."

Guy almost said something, about her part-time job, and why the men might look at her the way they do, but he caught himself in time.

"I'm not *just* a whore," she said, sensing criticism. "I've never neglected my job. I've screwed a lot of soldiers over here, and none of them got as close to me as the boy I gave an enema to this morning."

"I never used that word with you," Guy said.

"Yeah, but when you think about me you use it in your head," she said. She pouted. "You think I'm a slut."

"No more than I think I am," he said. "You know, everybody's a slut compared to the image he has of that other wonderful person he would be, back home."

She pulled out a silver flask and dripped an ounce into her Coke. Guy shook his head when she offered some, then changed his mind and took it.

"I'm glad I never screwed you," she said after a while.

"I'm glad we didn't have to," Guy replied.

"This is better," she said, making an aimless little sweep with her rum-and-Coke, taking in the tranquil solitude of the bunker, the conversation, and the intimacy they had found a way to share. "I hope your girl back home knows what she has to look forward to."

"The girl back home isn't the girl back home anymore," Guy said.

Mary sat up and looked him square in the eyes. "What the hell are you talking about?" she demanded.

Guy sighed slightly. He might as well go ahead.

"The girl back home hasn't been the girl back home for months. She moved on long ago. You know the drill. I got the letter, and that was that. No big deal."

"No big deal?" Mary spat. "*No big deal?* You told me you were going to marry her. You told me you couldn't cheat on her."

"All true when I said it," Guy replied. "But that was long ago."

"Well, when it changed why didn't you *tell* me?" she said, her eyes blazing.

"Because by then you and I had developed this," Guy said, making a little sweep with his rum-and-Coke, taking in the conversation and the intimacy they had found a way to share.

Mary flopped back, dispirited. "All this time you never wanted me," she said.

"All this time I had you," Guy said, "more than any of the others. More than all the others put together. They had parts of a part of you. I had all the rest."

"You are such a selfish, phony asshole, Lopaca," Mary said. "You pretended to be something you are not."

"No," Lopaca replied, "I have stayed exactly the same, and by ignoring the irrelevant fact that my former girlfriend had changed, you
and I have managed to stay exactly the same together."

"We have never been together," Mary said.

"We have been together, and you know it," Guy said.

There was a long pause, during which Guy remained impassive,
and Mary's face exhibited dramatic changes in expression, like tectonic
shifts. It was a long time before she spoke again.

"But you kept writing letters," Mary said. "You kept writing letters
to the girl back home. I read some of them."

"You read all of them," Guy said. "After a while, you were the girl
back home. It was nice to watch you read them."

She picked up a pebble and threw it at him.

"It doesn't seem fair," Mary said. "You knew and I didn't."

"It wouldn't have worked if you knew," Guy said. "Nothing would
have worked the way it did."

"Would you screw me now if I asked you to?" she said.

"No," Guy replied, "not even for free."

"Would you kiss me if I asked you to?" she said.

"No," Guy said, "not even that."

"You don't want me at all that way, do you?" she said.

"I don't want you that way yet," Guy said, "not here, not now."

Mary turned to look at him more closely, confusion in her eyes.

"Lopaca," she said, "if you have this idea that we're going to have
some kind of amazingly spiritual romantic relationship, and that it
doesn't ever have to involve messy physical things like sex, you're
crazy."

"I'm not crazy," Guy said. "I'm just patient. Right now I don't have
any sex, and you have quite a lot of it. We average out. At some point I
hope to bring my average up and yours down."

"Jesus God almighty," Mary groaned. "*We average out?* You guys
and your goddamn sports. Like I bat five hundred, and you go zero for
the season, but as a team we bat two-fifty? Is that supposed to mean
something to me?"

"It was a stupid comment," Guy said, "whose only purpose was to
give me time to figure out why I just told you that the girl back home

had gone away. I probably should not have told you that. Look how things have changed. Already. So soon. So much."

"They haven't changed that much," Mary said after a while. She snuggled back against the clammy-cool wall of the bunker. "They haven't changed at all." She said it not as a matter of fact, but as a command. She started to say something, but stopped.

"You know," she said after a long silence, "if I did re-up and the war suddenly ended, I don't know where they would send me."

"That's true," Guy said.

"That could be a problem," Mary said. "They could put me on a base in the States. In the real world. Thousands of round-eyed girls with good legs in miniskirts, and there would be me in bad Army clothes."

"Not a pretty picture," Guy said.

"I better not re-up," she decided. "I better go home and look for a house and a job in a hospital. Where are you going when your tour is up?" she asked.

"Well, I was thinking of making a short visit to Louisiana State University," Guy said, "to meet a professor they have there named Ông Ba Tên." Mary looked at him with a whole lot of *why?* in her eyes.

"He has a nose I need to punch a few times," Guy said.

"Oh," Mary said, completely satisfied. "And where are you going after assaulting this Professor Whatshisname?"

"Somewhere I have never been before," Guy said. "I was thinking of New Mexico."

"I hear that's a nice place," Mary said.

"I'm hoping it is," Guy replied. "Possibly Arizona. Someplace warm. Where are you going?"

"Oh, home to visit the folks first, and then I was thinking maybe Arizona," Mary said, "or possibly New Mexico. Some place really warm."

"When you get there, you should write me a letter," Guy said.

"I intend to," Mary said. "Do you think we'll bump into each other someday soon?"

"I have every intention of bumping into you," Guy said. "Frequently."

"Why not here?" Mary asked. "Why give up the chance?"

"This is not a good time or place for certain kinds of things," Guy said. "Some things don't flourish here."

"You're completely nuts," she said. "Do you realize how nuts you are?"

"No, I just second-guess myself a lot," he said, rubbing the narrow bridge of his nose between his eyes, thinking really hard. "I'm afraid to make any permanent decisions here. This isn't a good place for making decisions that have to last. Too many things have caught me by surprise."

"Like what?" she asked.

"Besides you?"

"Yeah, besides me. What else did you find here that you didn't expect?"

"Well," he replied, "I came here pretty full of contempt, and I don't have much of that anymore. I didn't expect to find so many people I admire. People who are true to something worth being true to. It's hard to believe that you could find even one of them in a place like this, but actually you find them everywhere you look. It hurts when I think of the waste. They do all the right things for all the right reasons. They know that their sacrifice is wasted in a bad war. They do it anyway. I admire them."

"I admire you," Mary said. "Do you admire me?"

"Yes I do," Guy said.

"So why can't we admire each other together," she said. "What's wrong with that?"

"Did you ever have a Vietnam Soda Thirst?" Guy asked.

"Here we go again," Mary said. "What's that?"

"You start in the morning of a really hot day," Guy said. "You drink as little as you can all day long, getting more and more thirsty every minute, and at the end of the day, when you can't stand it anymore, you take a sip of soda on ice and it's the best drink of any kind you ever had."

"This is a quiz, isn't it?" Mary said. "I'm supposed to guess what you're talking about."

"There are parts of life that I won't touch in a place like this," Guy said. "I want to, but I won't. I'm going to hold on and stay thirsty until this long, hot Vietnam day is over."

"You have to kiss me once before I leave," Mary said. "There has to be some part of you that I can hold on to."

"All right," Guy said. "That will be nice. I will kiss you once before you leave. Only once. That will make it special. You pick the time and place."

"See, that's the difference between you and me," Mary said. "You think you know the value of that forever stuff. I know the value of right now."

The Things You
Bring Home

As usual, Arthur was the first of the day shift to arrive at the orderly room. Reardon, whose shift on night duty was just ending, sat outside the front door, smoking a cigarette. He should have been inside. As Arthur approached, Reardon nodded toward the door and said, "Top's waiting for you."

Top was in his office, sitting at his desk. It looked pretty clean, as if he had been working all night long. His face had that look as well: puffy and ready for some sleep.

The first sergeant asked Arthur to sit awhile. "Close the door first," Top said. "If the phone rings, don't bother to answer it."

Arthur sat down. This sounded serious. Did Top know how often Arthur messed around in everybody's desks? Or maybe he found out about Arthur's monkeying with the Army regulations. Arthur wondered how much money he would lose each month if he got busted.

"I'm going to be leaving soon," the first sergeant said. "I don't think I'll be back for a while. I may not be back at all."

He fiddled with his stapler.

"They gave me an emergency leave so I can go home with my son," Top said. "He's dead. I'm flying back in the same plane with him. I'm waiting for a radio hookup inside the fence to call my wife. She doesn't know yet. Her sister is on the way to be there when she gets the news."

Arthur didn't know what to say. He didn't know Top had a son.

"You're a good kid," the first sergeant said. "You do your job well. You're the best clerk I ever worked with. I've been lucky to have you. The Army would be lucky if it could keep kids like you. But I know it can't."

He wiped his eyes with his fingers.

"You remind me of my son. The first day you walked in here, I looked at you, and said 'It's Mark.' I mean, not that you look exactly like him; just close enough to trigger memories. Take a look."

He spun a snapshot across the desk. A group of combat soldiers, covered in mud and dust, were bunched together in front of the open bay of a helicopter. It was a posed shot. Four of the men were squatting in front, three were standing in the rear, all of them tightly packed against each other. They all wore flak vests and helmets. The men on the end of the back row held their rifles in the air, defiant, and a couple of the men had their mouths open as if they were issuing a battle cry.

The boy in the middle of the back row must have been Mark. He cradled his rifle to his chest, hugging it as a child might hug his favorite teddy bear. On his face was a bashful smile exactly half as exuberant as the others.

The two men in the back row, the two warriors brandishing their guns, had their inner arms around Mark's shoulders, hugging him from both sides.

He's their mascot, Arthur thought. *He's with them, and they love him, but he's not one of them. And they know it.*

There was some superficial resemblance between Arthur and the boy in the picture. Similar sandy hair. Similar pale mustache. But no one would mistake them for twins. At first Arthur was ready to be insulted by Top's comparison with this bashful boy. But then Arthur saw the contentment on Mark's face. He had been accepted into the company of soldiers, who clearly treated him with tenderness.

There are worse stations in life, Arthur thought, *than to be a mascot for men like these.*

"I'm sorry, Top," he said at last. "He seems like a nice guy."

"He was," the first sergeant said. "He was a good son."

Top was crying now. It had been building up since before Arthur entered the room. It was a controlled cry. Top apparently had some emotional spigot, which he could open to relieve the pressure, but not so much he would lose control.

"In a week or two," Top said, "if I'm not coming back they'll send someone to take my place. I'm leaving him a letter, telling him not to get in your way too much. The office is running pretty well, and the next guy shouldn't want to screw it up because that will only cause him grief in the long run. He'll probably change a policy or two, just to plant his flag. He might even find some reason to chew you out, to test you. But give him time and it'll be all right."

"Thanks, Top," Arthur said. He couldn't think of much more to say. He was still holding the photo of the dead boy, who was now somewhere in a plastic bag, waiting for his father to take him home in a dismal cargo plane full of plastic bags in metal boxes.

"I want you to do me a favor," Top said after a while. "I want you to take this envelope"—he tossed it across the desk—"It's got my home address on it. When your tour is over, when you get home, I want you to write me a letter. All you have to say is that you made it. You don't have to write your whole life story. Just tell me you made it home."

Arthur could see that the first sergeant was having trouble with his spigot; he was fighting the tears as they spilled down his cheeks.

"I'll do it, Top," Arthur promised, picking up the envelope. He started to hand back the photograph, but the first sergeant waved it away.

"You keep it," Top said. "Keep it with the things you bring home that are worth having. There may not be much, you may not think so right now. When you look back you'll see them better.

"You would have liked my son," Top said. "You two would have got along real good. He was a college kid. Smart. Polite. Worked hard. Not afraid of work." The first sergeant paused.

"He hated the war, just like you do." The first sergeant looked out the window. "I could have kept him out. When he got his notice, I was going to talk to someone for him, but he wouldn't let me. Said if I got in the way, he would enlist, and that meant he'd be in for a longer hitch. Said we had to let him go. He was the son of a military man. Said he wouldn't lie on a beach while his old man shouldered the load.

"What they do with you kids . . ." Top said, his voice trailing off. And then, "I never fired an angry shot my whole career. No one ever shot at me. I'm an office worker. My son is dead because I work in this goddamn office.

"You get home," he said at last, and tenderly. "You write to me and let me know you're all right. I need to know that."

"I'll do it," Arthur said.

"Mark was going to be an ornithologist," Top said. "He loved birds. All through high school, he studied birds on his own. Had photographs and pictures from magazines all over his bedroom walls. Even had a bird skeleton hanging from the ceiling light. They took him into the 101st Airborne. Screaming Eagles. Can you imagine? Mark said that was lucky. He was up near Hue when . . . when he died."

"I'll send you the letter, Top," Arthur said.

"I know you will," the first sergeant said. "When you get back home, be proud of what you did here. Whatever anybody says, you remember to be proud. You had a good attitude. You did what your country asked you to do. You be proud of that. It wasn't your fault they put you in an office instead of a combat unit. There's no need for"—he paused—"for you to be ashamed."

"I'll remember," Arthur said.

"Good," Top said. "Now take the morning off. It will take a couple of hours for me to clean up around here. It'll be better if you come back after noon."

"Good-bye, First Sergeant," Arthur said.

"Good-bye, son," the first sergeant said.

That Kind of Soldier

Dear Mary:

This is the first real letter I've written to an actual "girl back home" in a long time. At least now you know I'm writing it to you. It won't be the same here, not being able to see you read it.

I guess it's up to me to pick the topic. I can't think of anything very cheerful right now. Sorry. I'm just going to write what I think and we'll see how it goes.

• • •

There was a big party last night at The Hotel. Some Army hotshots were there, and some civilian visitors of the American, Australian, and British persuasion. The booze was free, the food was free, and important men rubbed elbows or bellies with one another and with young Vietnamese girls hired on as hostesses.

I think there are more hostesses in Vietnam than there are Vietnamese women. I think they import hostesses from the Philippines. Without enough hostesses, war as we know it could not be conducted.

That's an aside. You have to watch out for those.

Someone had put up a big banner shouting "Welcome to Peacemakers of Thua Thien." In the Army, they still think peace has to be "made." As silence has to be "made" to put an occasional stop to perpetual noise.

Another aside again. Sorry.

Although I was not invited to the party because of my bad case of enlisted man's disease, I decided I should go anyway, pretend to be a civilian advisor, get drunk for free and watch all those frustrated peckers score on the little Asian girls. I dressed in my civilian khaki pants and my civilian madras shirt, borrowed Buddy Brier's pipe and some fine Hawaiian tobacco, and went to the party to make a pest of myself. These big guys would have the little girls cornered, angling to be good friends in an hour and lovers in two. When the guys noticed me I'd stare right into their eyes and blow smoke rings. *Poof! Poof! Poof!* Then I'd walk up and say a few words to the little girls in Vietnamese. You should have seen them smile. You should have seen the look in their eyes when I asked about their families.

After a minute or two I would leave them, and watch the couple work through their reunion. Suddenly the guys didn't know how to talk to the girls. Suddenly the girls didn't understand the guys, didn't laugh at their jokes, and looked at the floor a lot. By speaking to the girls in their own language, I had demolished the pretense. They were left with nothing but the power of the men on one side and the need of the girls on the other side, with no pretense in between to sweeten it. The guys hated me. I loved it. They were oafs, creeps, jerks. I was showing them all right. What a blow I was striking for integrity and truth and mutual respect.

I know what you're thinking. You're thinking that I wasn't there striking any blows an hour later when the little girls were getting into bed with their new best friends. If I made a guy seem coarse and insignificant, imagine what I did to the little girl who would agree to be his toy.

What kind of person would do that? I threw my skills around and ended up hurting little Vietnamese girls who are weaker than I am. Have I become that kind of American soldier after all?

You may pause to take a breath here. An intermission . . .

Wherever I go now in this country, I find guilt waiting for me. I have survivor's guilt because I'm still alive and unhurt and the grunts are taking all the risk. I have guilt from being a rich American in a ruined country. I have guilt from knowing that when the war ends the people I met here might be killed or devastated just because they knew me. And I feel guilty because I know that if given the choice I would take my pathetic turn in this crummy war all over again, feeling the same ridiculous compulsion, unable to resist it, too stupid to see any other way.

Oh well. This is the point where you would pick a new topic.

I have a few more weeks to go and then I'll be there for a nice long visit. I'm at that point in my tour when I have a short-timer's fear of the ordinary day, and I just want to hang in, hang on, grip the edge of the ledge with my fingernails, and count the seconds until it's over. I'm also at that point where I'm more comfortable with my job and I wander through the country with less nervous bristling of the little hairs on the back of my neck (where the bullet will hit), and less anxious gnashing of my private parts (under which the land mine will burst).

•   •   •

We should take it easy when I get to Santa Fe. I suggest a nice dinner and a movie. My treat.

We won't entirely recognize each other. I'm predicting it will feel like a blind date. We should play it that way.

I'll be the guy that you never met, that your cousin, the United States Army, fixed you up with because you're in a strange town and don't know any single guys, and I have such a nice personality.

Or is it the blind-date girl who is supposed to have the nice personality? I get confused. All I know is that one is supposed to have a nice personality, and the other one is supposed to be fun to be with. . . . Don't ask me which is which.

Love, GUY

PS: I'm no artist but I started doodling one day and the result is enclosed. I wanted to remember where I spent my war, and the Army maps are too big. This is the route to the Montagnard village. It's not to scale.

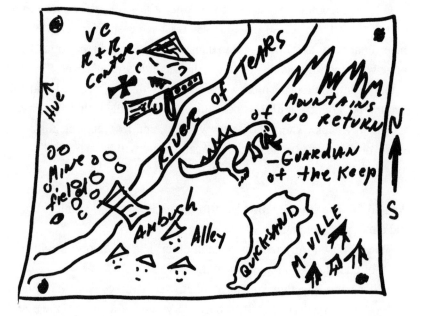

Martian Eyes

Arthur could hear the sound of chattering—loud chattering, a duet of angry chattering—as he neared his barracks. He rounded a corner and saw the two people who were causing the ruckus. The Vietnamese foreman—the one everyone called Harry—was screaming at the latrine girl, who stood as still as a wooden post, taking it. Harry was short, but he was half a head taller than the girl, and he had moved close to her. As he shouted and spat, he waved his arms violently. She stood stiff, not moving at all, her two arms rigid by her sides, her hands balled defiantly, her head bowed down so Harry had nothing to yell at but her scalp.

After a few seconds of yelling, when Harry took a breath, the latrine girl spat something back at him, short and implacable, and Harry rose up on his feet and yelled even louder. And louder still. And when she didn't move, not even a small bend or a sway, Harry made his right hand into a fist and shook it in her downturned face.

That did it.

She flinched—she couldn't help it—she flinched at the sight of the fist, and Harry laughed triumphantly, yelled some more and then, *unclenching* his hand out of some sense of decency, he slapped her hard with his open hand, very hard, slapped her upper head and ear, causing her whole body to shudder, stagger from the shock of the physical impact, and from the surprise that made her mouth open and her face lift up sideways, wide eyes full of fear.

"Hey," Arthur yelled, "hey, stop that!"

As the latrine girl tried to right herself, regain her balance, Harry turned to see who had spoken. Harry saw Arthur, and smiled, and said something pleasant in Vietnamese.

"Don't hit her," Arthur said, wondering if any of this was translating at all.

Harry smiled again, and bowed slightly, and smiled yet again. Then he turned to the latrine girl and, without saying anything, he balled his fist and punched her as hard as he could in the face, up high against the cheekbone, snapping her head back and throwing her against the wall of the latrine, down which she slid until she was squatting on the ground, with her head in her hands, no longer a sturdy wooden post, but just a beat-up little thing.

Harry turned back to Arthur, smiled again, and bowed again—only lower and more formally this time—and then walked away laughing, kicking the latrine girl's bucket as he passed, tumbling it down the sidewalk. Arthur watched the bucket tumble. Some foamy water splashed out, and a sponge and a scrub brush, a sodden rag, and a bottle of cleaning fluid. Arthur tried to read the label. Suddenly Arthur wanted to know if the cleaning fluid had been imported from America for the war effort, as he had been. Arthur kept looking at the bucket and its scattered contents as long as he could, because he didn't want to look at the latrine girl very soon. He needed to compose himself before doing that.

When he finally did look at her, he could see that her shoulders were quivering. She squatted with her back to the latrine wall, her knees drawn up and her arms enveloping them, so in her two thin hands her forehead touched her knees and she made of her body the smallest possible bundle—and it was really extraordinarily small by now—that was partially hidden from the world by a curtain of straight black hair.

Arthur could have turned right and walked on, but his feet tricked him and pulled him left. In a couple of seconds Arthur was standing next to her, looking down at her, yet the distance between them seemed vast.

"Are you all right?" he asked, thinking: *Screw the language. She'll understand.*

The latrine girl shook her head, and held out one hand, the palm and fingers flat, and flapped her hand up and down. Arthur believed that the gesture meant "come here," or "go away," or—and this was the unfortunate truth—something else entirely.

The girl obviously needed someone to help her now. What she needed was another woman, one of her own kind, who could bring her solace. Someone who understood sorrow and despair, but also understood and could maneuver inside the alien, intricate social structure within which the Vietnamese—in general—lived their complicated lives and within which this foreman and this latrine girl—in particular—played their mysterious parts.

And so, knowing that this latrine girl needed someone—an *appropriate* someone—Arthur foolishly looked around, half hoping that her sister or her aunt would happen by, flutter in, and take control. But that was not the way the world was working today. The world, today, had left Arthur standing over the sobbing latrine girl, the two of them alone.

Instead of walking away, Arthur found himself—*this was strange*—kneeling down beside her.

"Are you all right?" he repeated.

Her hands parted and she turned her face to him, and she seemed so small . . . and so miserably alone . . . that his right hand reached out to gently pat her hair . . . and . . .

At the same time Arthur, surprised, stopped his hand in midair, the latrine girl, surprised, pulled back her head. And they froze in that position, the hand and the head frozen in space, as their two sets of eyes met in mutual astonishment.

After a short flicker of time, Arthur's hand reached an inch closer to her, and paused. After a short flicker of time, the latrine girl's head bent toward the hand. Arthur's hand was cupped, and the curve of her head settled into the curve of his hand, and it was amazing how small she was and how her head seemed to fill up his hand, every part of it. Her black hair was a universe of fine strands, that seemed to settle into the very loops and whorls of his fingertips.

Through the smooth insulation of her hair, Arthur could feel her trembling, and wondered if it was all from the beating she had just taken or if it might be from something else now, as well.

• • •

Arthur looked into her eyes, strange eyes, eyes such as he had never seen before, eyes from another culture or another species or perhaps another galaxy—he didn't know—and all he did know was that for the first time in his life he saw in those Martian eyes the same kind of longing, desperate longing, that he himself had been feeling for so long, in such solitude, that he thought he would never be able to quench the longing, or share it.

The latrine girl pressed her head against his cupped palm slightly, and twisted her head slightly, to make a better fit. She blinked and tried to smile a little.

So this is it, Arthur thought, amazed. *This is how it is.*

• H U E •

Souvenir

The road back from Phu Bai seemed longer than usual. Time seemed to be hitting the brakes, dragging its feet.

Guy's tour was winding down, and for some of his friends their time in Vietnam was finished or soon would be. During World War II, a soldier could spend two or three years in peril without knowing when or whether it would ever end. Here in Vietnam, a man could spend eight months and feel like a used-up veteran. While a year here was inconsequentially short compared to the achingly indefinite tours of World War II, in Vietnam your whole rotation was spent watching other men go home. It was always someone else's turn to go home. You were always left behind.

Mary was already in Santa Fe now, an American Blonde in a country full of them. Tyler DeMudge would be leaving in a couple of weeks, and Paul Gianelli would end his third superextended tour a week after that. Guy could imagine a Vietnam without helicopters, but not without Paul Gianelli. Guy could imagine himself in Vietnam, but not without Paul and Tyler and Mary.

Guy was on a road that was straight and bordered closely on both sides by rice paddies. The rice seed had taken hold, the roots grasped lightly into the mud below, and the densely packed tips of many thousands of rice shoots had just started to pierce the glassy surface of the water. The shoots were slender, pointed, and impossibly green. The glaring energy of a maximum midday sun was soaked up by the roots and converted to a rice-shoot carpet of iridescent golden green unlike any color Guy had ever seen.

He pulled the jeep off the road, shut off the engine, and sat there for a few minutes just looking at the paddies. He knew that the golden green wouldn't last long. The shoots would get older, fatter, stronger, and darker. The farmers would eventually uproot them and replant them over a wider area, and as the plants matured their color would become cooler, quieter, at one with the surroundings. For only a little while, as the rice shoots broke through the crystal water and stretched into the air above, they would shine with this evanescent, incandescent, transitory golden green.

It was one of the things Guy would miss about Vietnam.

He got out of the jeep and walked close to the sharply sloping bank of the paddy. He took off his sunglasses to capture the pure brilliance of the color. Lopaca was no nature lover. At home he didn't go on hikes or sightseeing tours or long drives in the country. Guy hated farming, to tell the truth. He hated the dust and the mud and the smell of manure and fertilizer and chemical spray. He hated the sweaty labor and the terrible hours. There was nothing in farming that attracted him.

But this seemed so different. The difference between farming and these golden green paddies was like the difference between the labor of childbirth and the glow of a baby's smile. Also, he confessed to himself, he felt something like a rice-shoot daddy.

He wondered whose rice seed had been planted here. Was it the native seed, or was it some of the TN-8 or TN-20 that he and others like him had brought to Vietnam? He had no way of knowing. He hoped it made no difference, so far as the color was concerned. He hoped that the color he saw would always return, for a few days each season, no matter whose rice was planted, no matter who planted it. Wouldn't it be nice, Guy thought, if I could remember this color when I am home? Why, Guy thought, am I suddenly so obsessed with this color? Is it because Mary is gone and the others are going, and I'm just getting generally soft and weepy?

He looked up and down the road, and turned in a full circle to see if anyone else was around. Spotting no one at all, the country desolate and silent, Guy stepped down from the bank into the paddy, sinking partway into the peripheral mud and soaking his boots and trousers. He stretched out his right arm and passed his open hand in a delicate caress over the tips of the tender rice shoots.

• • •

Across the emerald quilt of paddy land, a young Vietnamese sniper monitored Guy's movements through the targeting scope of a bolt-action rifle. His older comrade watched Guy through binoculars.

"Is there anyone else around?" the young man said.

"No one," the older man said.

"He sure is asking for it," the young man said.

"He's making it easy," the older man said. "Even you could hit him."

The young man flipped off the safety lever and snuggled more comfortably against the ground.

Guy made another sweep with his hand above the delicate stubble of the rice shoots.

"Have you ever seen one of them do that?" the older man asked.

"Nope, not ever," the young man said.

"He's not an officer," the older man said. "I wish he were an officer."

"He is what he is," the young man said.

"But the officers usually come from better families," the older man said. "The politics is better when an officer dies. I think more trouble is generally made."

"You old farts and your politics," the young man said.

"I am just pointing out the propaganda value of officers," the older man huffed. "I am not discussing any other politics."

"With you it's always politics," the young man replied brusquely.

"After you shoot him, are you going to cook him for supper?" the older man snapped disapprovingly. "If you are not going to eat him, you must have some other reason for killing him. The reason is politics."

"Could we postpone the cooking lecture a moment," the young man sneered, "until I have pulled this trigger a little?"

"The death of your friends has made it easier for you to pull the trigger," the older man said. "That man's death will also have consequences. Someone will be more willing to do something to hurt us. If considering things like that is politics, so be it. I hope the headache you get from thinking about it won't be too painful to bear."

"Let's just get this over," the young man said. "Today this is the target we get. We get that crazy fellow over there. We take them as they come, one at a time. Maybe he is some senator's imbecile son. Who cares? Let's just drop him, fill a bag, and send him home. I can drop him easy. Even you could drop him." The marksman laughed.

"Isn't he one of those fools who deliver the rice seed?" the older man said. "The ones who deliver rice and medicine for the hogs, and dig holes for fish?"

"He could be," the young man said. "So what? Does it make any difference?"

"We generally stay away from them," the older man said. "They don't bother us, and the stuff they haul around is worth more to us than the body count."

"But I could use the points," the young man whined.

•　•　•

Guy felt a small, refreshing breeze against his sweaty face, and was happy that he had finally made peace with the country's climate. He tried to shift his weight, and felt the paddy bottom suck at his feet. The mud was like a vat of contact cement. It seemed that the mud would never let go of him, now that he was planted in it.

My boots are going to be a muddy mess, he thought, then smiled.

"Look at him," the older man said. "Look at the way he touches the plants."

"So?" the young man said.

"It's too strange," the older man said. "I don't feel right about it. It would be like shooting an idiot. Why don't we let him go."

"He will go home either way," the young man said.

"I don't feel right shooting someone so strange," the older man said. "And killing him doesn't help us. He's harmless. Look at him. Did you ever see anything more foolish than that?"

"It seems you have fallen in love with him," the young man said.

"Pull down your pants and I will show you who I love," the older man said. "And remember, I have a little rank over you."

"I am blinded by your rank," the young man said.

• • •

Sergeant Dong sighed. Lopaca had presented another of life's innumerable complications. Lopaca was an enemy, to be sure, and also a friend, however casual. Up close, he was something of a friend. From this far away, he was a green enemy target of opportunity, however discretionary. What to do? How to do it?

Sergeant Dong's companion had his finger on a trigger that duty required the boy to pull, when Dong was not around to interfere. Should Dong interfere? Should he explain himself while doing so?

Why was life so complicated? Dong's life was full of these complications. Sometimes he wished the war would end, but the Americans would stay to keep him company. He had no one else to talk to. He had a wife and mistress, but if he said a word to one the other would become furiously jealous. Why did he take on these entanglements? Blame it on the French. It was always the French who were to blame . . . Oh, he better hurry up and think of something before the kid moved his finger a centimeter and started bragging about his miraculous shot.

"Don't you think a man with your skill deserves a better target?" Dong asked. "This fool can't be the best shot you will see today. You should wait for a real soldier to come along."

"I don't like him," the young man said. "In a minute he will tear off one of our rice shoots and take it home as a trophy."

"I don't think so," Dong replied, seeing his gambit at last.

"I think he will," the young man said.

"Let's make a bet," Dong said. "If he tears off just one piece from one plant, you shoot him. If not, we let him go. If the wager doesn't interest you, then go ahead and shoot him now."

The young man thought about it. The American's strange show of affection for the rice shoots would make a good story tonight whether the American was killed or not. But it would be an even better story with the wager. For an old man, that Dong had an interesting mind. The odd American would decide his own fate. He would live or die, according to what he did in that paddy. That would be a story worth telling.

•   •   •

Guy finished tickling his palm with rice shoots and stood with both hands on his hips. *This is silly,* he thought. *Well, not so silly,* he reconsidered. *Isn't this what it was all about, really?*

The war was being fought over the right to control the land, especially farming land like this. Guy was in the country to serve the land and to help it blossom as it was blossoming today. If he made any difference at all, it would benefit whoever won the war. It would also benefit whoever lost the war. If he deserved to be proud of anything he ever did in his life, this might be it.

He bent to touch the leaves again. He could almost feel them touching back.

I should probably take one home with me, Guy thought. *I don't ever want to forget the way I feel today.*

Nice to See You Again

It was his last full day in Nha Trang, and Captain William Bloat was almost done with his packing. He was poking through his books, choosing a couple to bring with him. The rest he would drop off at the base library.

Major Hill got the credit for motivating Captain Bloat to start packing so early. "Everything you take you have to carry," Hill counseled him. "Love it or leave it. Carry it around the world, or leave it where it sits."

Hill started prodding Bloat four days ago, and checked back yesterday morning, and came in last night as well, just before Bloat tucked himself into bed. Now it was early in the morning of his last full day, Captain Bloat was all packed, practically, and—*Jeez!*—here comes Hill again, as if he had nothing else to do.

"You busy?" Major Hill asked, after tapping politely on the frame of Captain Bloat's half-open door.

"Nah," Bloat said. "The guy replacing me came in yesterday. I think he's over there now swapping the A racks with the Z racks. You know how it is. The guy who's leaving is always crap, and the hotshot who takes over is a god-almighty genius."

"Look," Major Hill said, "I don't get off the base much, and I know you didn't either. I have to go a few miles into the boonies this morning, to meet some people who came in from Saigon. I thought you might want to come along. We'll be back this afternoon. You might like to take in some scenery before you leave. If you don't mind riding in a chopper . . ."

"Shit, I'm not worried about that," Captain Bloat said. "Choppers don't bother me."

Still, he thought about saying no. Not much sense going on a joyride his last day on the job. What was he going to see in only an hour or two? He thought about that. Well, what was he going to see if he stayed on the base? These four walls and the dining hall and the bar, he thought. And jealous soldiers saying good-bye.

"Sure, I'll go," he said.

•   •   •

Major Hill told him to be at the nearest chopper pad at eleven o'clock. At 10:40, Captain Bloat put down the book he was reading and, over the next few minutes, with difficulty, put on his boots. Then he opened his locker, took a deep breath, and put his meaty hand inside. It came back out holding a .45 caliber pistol. It had been in his locker since the day he arrived in Nha Trang. He had never fired this weapon, never even loaded it, and didn't want to do so now . . . but he remembered where he was, and who he was supposed to be, so he strapped it around his waist and hoped Major Hill wouldn't mention it.

The chopper was already fired up with Major Hill inside when Captain Bloat arrived at the landing zone. The enlisted man who was riding crew that day snapped a salute and introduced himself before helping Bloat aboard.

The chopper took off and for a while, down below, the base at Nha Trang looked a lot bigger than it seemed while he was living within it. Big and complicated, and powerful. All those buildings, all those vehicles, all those busy men. As the helicopter climbed and sped away, the camp began to look compact and fragile, and the land around it seemed to swallow it, as a large fish does a smaller one. Within minutes, Captain Bloat could no longer see the camp within the porridge of sea and hills and plains, the geography into which the camp had disappeared, as if digested.

As they sped along, Major Hill leaned over and yelled: "Does any of this remind you of your first tour?" Captain Bloat shook his head. None of it reminded him of his first tour. There was not much first tour to be reminded of.

They furrowed the sky for mile after unfamiliar mile, until finally the pilot said the military base Major Hill was aiming for was just ahead. Captain Bloat could see it, a mountain of green whose top had been scraped brown, so that the breeze stirred up dust like a snowstorm in the Alps. As they got closer he could see the tents and bunkers, the perimeter lines of wire and gun emplacements, the roads and helicopter pads. A few men walked from here to there within the perimeter. At one end of the camp was a big open area, either a landing zone or a parade ground, on which many men were standing in a thick line waiting for a meal. Smoke rose from a few sliced-in-half oil drums that were used as charcoal barbecue pits all over the world where the American Army planted its flag.

The men along the chow line watched as the helicopter set down a few dozen yards away. "Looks like we're in time for lunch," Major Hill said, as the crewman opened the door and debarked ahead of them. Major Hill climbed out next, followed by Captain Bloat.

"I hope they have hot dogs," Captain Bloat said, "and brown mustard."

They began to walk toward the chow line. Captain Bloat scanned the tables near the barbecue drums. They had piles of raw steak, he was sure of that, and—yes!—lots of hot dogs, and something else, stacked like corn, tubular and fat like corn, but not yellow like corn, more green, maybe corn still in its husks, or maybe . . .

Jeez Louise!

Captain Bloat stopped and his heart began to race. They were *lobster tails*. Stack after stack, platter after platter of unshelled, uncooked lobster tails.

Major Hill pushed him. "Come on, Captain," he said, "eyes front. Move your feet."

As Billy Bloat stumbled forward the men in the chow line came into focus. There were hundreds of GIs he had never seen before. But standing in front of them were two men he had seen before. One of them was his cousin Bobby Bloat, and the other—*Oh Jeez!*—was the Old Man: his grandfather, General Buster Bloat. Billy froze in place. This wasn't possible. Bobby was in civilian clothes—he had left the army three years ago—and Buster was in his Fourth-of-July-parade-watching uniform.

The two Bloat men slowly walked toward him. It was especially slow going for Buster, who had an artificial leg. When they got close enough, they stopped. Buster drew himself up tall—which was his natural posture anyway—and fixed a frigid stare on his grandson, who helplessly blinked back.

"I'll take a salute any time you got to spare one," Buster hissed at Billy. "There's men watching us, and as I remember the stuff on this uniform outranks the stuff on yours."

Billy numbly saluted, and wondered where this nightmare was heading.

Buster's part of the nightmare was heading right at him. The old man limped a couple of steps closer, grabbed Billy by the hand, and said, more gently than was normal for him, "Hey, Billy, nice to see you again. You're looking real good."

"What are you doing here?" Billy asked.

"I take it Major Hill has not divulged any part of this thing," Buster said. "I take it you are as empty-headed about this deal as you are about most other things." He chuckled.

"Walk with me a little," Buster said. "Give me your arm if you don't mind."

Billy and Buster began moving slowly toward the soldiers, and as they did so Bobby took up a flanking position on Billy's empty side. They got about twenty yards from the line of GIs, and then Buster started to speak in his Old Man you-better-listen-'cause-I'm-only-gonna-say-this-once official voice, which was not more than a stage whisper but could carry, it seemed, for miles and years and maybe generations.

"Some of you men heard the story 'cause I told it to you earlier today," Buster began, "but I'm gonna tell parts of it again, because some of you over there and some of us over here are newcomers to the party."

He let go of Billy's arm, and put his own arm around Billy's copious shoulders.

"This is my grandson, Billy Bloat. He's a captain in the United States Army. He's just come from Nha Trang, and he's about to go back home with us tomorrow, 'cause his tour of duty in this damn war is over. This wasn't his first tour. A coupla years ago he came to Vietnam a young lieutenant. He was gonna be a platoon leader, an LT like some of you. Like Bobby here was before him, and like I was before Bobby." Bobby seemed to grow an inch taller as Buster spoke.

"Billy wanted to be one of us," Buster continued. "He wanted to be one of you. He was going to lead a platoon in this battalion. It was based somewhere else, and maybe most of you weren't with the battalion back then, but it was this battalion nonetheless.

"Things didn't work out for him," Buster said. "He got kind of blown up the first day, and never had a chance to do what he set out to do. When he came back home, I think some of us in the family weren't too nice to Billy. We're a rugged bunch of Yankee bastards, and we got a rugged sense of humor. We heard Billy got himself blown up chasing after a load of lobster tails, and some of us—I'm not naming any names, Bobby—some of us kinda went hard on him, and I think things got out of hand. We're here now because we got some explaining to do, to everybody.

"First," the old man said, "I want to explain to this battalion about those lobster tails. It took me a while to get interested. It took a push from Major Hill here, who had started asking around just a while ago, and then I did some checking myself with folks I know. Here's what we found out. A coupla years ago you guys—not all you guys but the guys that were in the battalion back then—you had yourself a damn fine battalion commander. He must have loved his men, because he took some of his own money and arranged to have a load of lobster tails dry-iced and brought over here for a treat. Don't ask me why lobster tails instead of Hawaiian wahines"—the men laughed—"but the point is that he wanted you to have something special that you would write home about, and remember, and"—he paused—"know it came from his heart."

The men were really quiet now.

"I know how he felt," the general continued. "I've felt like that about the men I served with. About the line officers, and the grunts, and the cooks and the clerks and even the guys who stack shirts and boots on shelves so they'll be there when we need 'em.

"The commanding officer of this battalion died on a mission to bring you lobster tails," the old man said. "My grandson was wounded on that mission. That mission was never completed. Today it will be. The Bloat boys from Chicopee, Massachusetts, all chipped in for the tails you're gonna eat today. We're gonna cook and eat them tails, get roaring drunk, and then me and Bobby are gonna take Billy home with us where he belongs, mission accomplished, while the rest of you go on and win this goddamn war. And that's all I got to say."

●   ●   ●

The men all cheered as the Bloat boys hugged one another and punched one another on the arm and hugged some more. Major Hill stood apart, wishing Tommy could be here to see it. The enemy spotters in the trees across the valley heard the shouting from the battalion and huddled together anxiously, wondered what was happening, wondered if an attack was in the works, and how many of their friends would have to die. A lonely kid from Mississippi hunkered down in a sandbagged bunker on the other side of the base, terrified in his first shift on perimeter defense, convinced that a targeting rock was a helmet that was inching slowly toward him. A clerk finished typing a letter to his girlfriend. A private at the motor pool rewashed a jeep that he hadn't washed well enough the first time. An electrician wired a generator. A communications geek tape-recorded incomprehensible enemy radio traffic: *"Bong bong bong ga bong bong."* Guy Lopaca looked through photographs he had taken at the Buddhist Temple—unaware that more than thirty Vietcong lived in tunnels underneath it—and put an extra set of the pictures in an envelope for Mary in Santa Fe. Arthur Grissom sat under a half-dead tree with his arm around an Asian waif who had no idea what he was saying to her. Sergeant Dong had an argument with his mistress before returning to his wife, who wasn't there. Paul Gianelli put down a university catalog, and thought about extending his tour yet again. Someone huddled over a map and drew lines that changed a hundred thousand lives. An old woman finished cleaning the Enlisted Men's Hootch and smoked a stolen cigarette before starting the long walk home.

* * *

Home. Billy Bloat was going home all right. The Bloat clan had opened its arms and was taking him in for sure this time. Not for getting himself blown up; any fool can get himself blown up. As can any hero. He wasn't one of the Bloat boys because he was a hero. He was one of them because he came to Vietnam, and that was all it took, really.

It didn't even take that. The most important thing happened long before Billy Bloat stepped on the dangerous soil of Vietnam. It started in Billy with the feeling that he couldn't stay home.

The Bloat boys—like so many big-hearted American boys—had been fabulous suckers for two hundred years, and were proud of it. Leaders or followers, fierce or timid, smart or dumb, they had one trait in common: *If you wanted them to go, they couldn't stay home.*

But now his tour was over, and Billy was truly going home, an American Bloat boy like the rest of them, magnificent and mundane, unique and common in his own particular war-participating way. He had gone where you asked him to go, he had done what you asked him to do, and he had become what you asked him to become. He was a Vietcong-killing, Purple-Heart-wearing, dink-ball-hitting, lobster-tail-delivering, inventory-taking, new-boot-dispensing, sissified warrior remf.

Afterword

You can't portray Vietnam without helicopters and cynicism. The powerful *whap-whap-whap* of the rotors still shakes my bones thirty-five years after I left the country. And I still harbor a baby-boomer's bitter disappointment because a fabulously gallant generation stood by and watched its children waste their lives living up to standards of duty and honor that their elders had set.

It seems the gallant generation spent all of its awesome strength and courage on the Depression and Adolf Hitler and the Cold War, and there was no strength or courage left to spend in defense of its own kids. Those who fought that brave fight in the 1940s had sacrificed so much, and so many of them had died, to give their kids a better world. But many of their kids got an Asian meat grinder instead. And, lest we forget, so did the Asians.

My generation let it happen to us. We were citizens of a great democracy, and when it veered in the wrong direction, we went along. Sure, we smoked dope, grew our hair long, talked loud, and did shocking, psychedelic things. But we kept faith with the generations that came before us, and most of us surrendered our personal interests when the country told us it was our turn to do so.

The memory of a young soldier dying on a Normandy beach on D-Day—it appears in Chapter Two—is as real to me now as it was when I was a GI-hero-worshiping ten-year-old boy, and later a young remf on my way to Vietnam. But I lived through the Sixties, and like Guy Lopaca, I was there too long to be naïve. I can't help but wonder: if that unlucky young D-Day soldier I think of so often had managed to survive his war, would he too have turned his back on us?

You can taste the disappointment, can't you? So much went so wrong during the Vietnam years. So much disappointment. So much anger.

It took me thirty-five years to turn down the heat and tell the story I really wanted to tell.

* * *

Vietnam was the Great Event of my generation. We deserved a better Great Event. We did the best we could with the one they gave us.

I found in Vietnam a group of young men and women who were brave, honest, and decent. Some of them were also smart as hell. And funny? You have no idea. Neither my memory nor my writing does them justice.

I started to write this book in 1971 but quickly put it aside. I was too frustrated back then. The war lingered on, the living kept dying. I lost touch with my memories. Over the next three decades, other authors wrote works that vivified the war's destruction and despair. I didn't often challenge the conventional assessment that nothing could be found in Vietnam but bad examples.

Eventually I grew weary of a memory with so much rage in it. I spent less time brooding about self-obsessed apologists such as McNaught and General Frostmire. I spent more time remembering my brief but impressionable comradeship with people who became blended into Paul Gianelli and Tyler DeMudge and even Danny Maniac. I remembered the gleam in the eye and the constant laugh of a young Vietnamese woman who served as our clerk, who never made it into the book because writing about her and her abandoned kind proved too painful for me to bear.

When the first draft of the book was complete, I began chopping out of it big chunks of harsh material, that represented the darkest tides of my lingering pessimism. Writing some of those sections was good therapy for me; but they belonged in someone else's book, not this one.

I didn't want to take you where you've been before. I wanted to take you to a quieter place, where despite all we know about that misbegotten war, there is room—in my memory, and perhaps now in yours as well—for a smile, a chuckle, even a laugh or two. And yes, there ought to be room in our tortured memory of Vietnam for love. It took me more than half my lifetime to recognize it. I finally had to write the book, and then read it myself, to see it.

At its gentle heart, behind the clown's paint, this book is about longing and a sense of duty. We gave in to the terrible force of duty, which we owed to others because they felt the same obligation to us. We longed desperately to believe that even in a bad war we could find something—*anything*—to be proud of. And we longed to be home, hoping we would be welcome when we got there.

The gallant generation that spawned us is waning now, and my own generation is beginning to dribble away as well. After so many years, I thought it was time to put my sorrow into temporary storage, and try to recapture the feeling I had in Vietnam, when my equilibrium was ruined but my sense of wonder took its place. It was so sad, knowing it was all such a waste. But it was so wonderful, that we kept one another's heads up and our faith alive while we soldiered through it.

Three million Americans served in the Vietnam War. You would have been proud to know most of us. Had it been a better war, you would have loved us.

ABOUT THE AUTHOR

RICHARD GALLI was a draftee in basic training, on a target range, when he learned that graduate-student deferments had been reinstated, and he could have been pursuing his master's degree and teaching freshman English after all, if he had put up just a little more foot-dragging resistance for a month or two.

He was a member of GIs for Peace, learning Vietnamese at the Defense Language Institute in El Paso, Texas, when the brand-new draft lottery assigned the call-up number "330" to his birthday. This lucky draw would have required his entry into the Armed Forces only if the North Vietnamese had established a beachhead in California.

Once in Vietnam, he was assigned to temporary office duty as a clerk, while waiting for a higher security clearance to come through. One of his temporary duties was to prepare applications—including his own—for security background investigations. He put his own application in the bottom left drawer of his desk, where it stayed until he was kicked out of the unit for being some sort of security risk.

He was tossed from that boring office posting into the best job the Army offered in Vietnam: interpreter for a Civil Affairs platoon based in Hue. He has sworn to his wife in the clearest and most emphatic terms that while some of the characters in this book might seem familiar from his letters, at no time did he ever have orange soda with anyone like Virgin Mary Crocker.

Since 1976 Richard has been a litigation lawyer in Providence, Rhode Island. In 1999, he closed his law office so he could spend more time at home helping to care for his son, who had become paralyzed in a swimming accident on the Fourth of July, 1998. Richard's first book, *Rescuing Jeffrey,* is an unconventional memoir about the first ten days following the accident.

To learn more:
www.ofriceandmen.com
www.richardgalli.com